THE QUIET EDGE OF MEMORY

A NOVEL

THERESE VERCELLONE

To my daughters. You are the sunshine in my life.
And to all the South Korean adoptees who inspired me to write this
story.

1

MATERNITY

YOUR VOICE IS my favorite sound. I want to hear you talk about gentle things like gardens and homemade soup or the tide. I want you to tell me stories about the first time you held me or how much you love me. I know. Love is complicated. You fell in love hard and fast. You realized how quickly and easily you can get hurt and hurt him.

Now your love for me is like sand; it's coarse, grainy. It shifts. That's not entirely your fault. I'm sorry you suffered and were pressed into a mold that didn't fit your body and mind. But your mistakes and hasty decisions fell on me. I can't carry the weight anymore. Can you help me?

I wish you could. You've retreated into shame and regret. Come out and hold me. I will never let go of you, because I'm your child. Can we talk about that? It's such a primal and stark truth, but life scuffed our relationship.

I have friends, and there's family. I'm not alone, but I'm lonely. I can write a five-paragraph essay, drive, and cook dinner, but I still need you. You're here but not really here. I ache for you so much.

It's a hot sore in my chest, so I can never touch it to mend it. You didn't have to go. You could have left your comforts and tried harder. Did you ever love fiercely? I want to ask you a pile of questions but can't. That would break me, and the feelings I'm hiding would run down my skin.

I unlock myself. I love the definition of maternal, but I hate the word.

The damage widens. You're a shadow.

I break inside. What would it feel like to fall in love and be a parent? I'm scared that I'll be like you. Love will be disposable. I'll press my children against me, and they will hear the thuds of chaos.

I'm so sorry.

Maybe you tried or you're trying, but what I have isn't enough. I'm still fighting to earn a place inside you, when the sacred bond between us should have done everything.

2

MARTHA

I DON'T BELONG in room 320. It's crammed with too many desks, and its gray cinder-block walls make it look like a prison. Next to the whiteboard is a bulletin board with an image of a tree, a POE'TREE, drawn with purple marker. There are no windows, and the light in the back left corner of the ceiling keeps flickering.

Someone's boasting about how her short story made it into a literary magazine. The guy to her right is telling a girl about a poetry slam that's next Thursday. A couple is talking about how horrible their creative writing class was in high school, and they hope this one is better.

I was supposed to do an independent study with my favorite women's studies professor, Jacklyn Solden, on women's health. Too bad she was fired last week. I heard she filled in her summer course surveys with high scores for herself and forged her students' names on them.

This crushed me. Jacklyn knew I'm a women's studies major. She knew an independent study would shine on my application to Montclair State. And she knew I spent all of August working on my project proposal for the pregnancy care center I hope to run someday.

All that effort, and I was left scrambling to find another class. Creative writing fits into my schedule.

Pain pounds on the right side of my head. I dig for the Excedrin in the front pocket of my backpack and swallow two pills with some water. Migraines love to hold my brain hostage when I'm under a lot of stress. It's the first day of my last semester of community college, and I'm starting my first job this weekend at a crafts store.

Professor Guerra is Emily Dickinson in a school uniform. She's wearing a black skirt with a white polo shirt. Her pale oval face is flawless, and her dark hair is pulled into a bun at the nape of her neck.

My phone vibrates in my purse while she's taking attendance. I lift it out of my bag just enough to read the text from Kaylin. Earlier, I asked her if she survived biology class. She's stuck with a professor who has a low rating on RateMyProfessor.com.

> **Kay**
> He's a decent guy but explains things like we're all bio majors. Heard his tests are brutal. Anyway, I know what day it is. Are you OK?

We've stood by each other through everything since first grade. She's the only one I can talk to about my grandparents, because mentioning them to Mom and Dad will turn my house into a battleground.

The backlight on my phone makes my eyes throb as I type.

> You got this! I still have my bio flash cards. You can have them. Re: me—I'm surviving.

"Martha Lane?" Professor Guerra calls out.

I jam my phone into my bag and raise my hand.

When Professor Guerra finishes taking attendance, she says, "You'll be writing fiction, creative nonfiction, and poetry. At the end of the semester, you'll compile your best writings into a portfolio."

This class is going to slash my 3.83 GPA. I don't have a creative skin cell on my body.

"Let's do a freewrite to get you pumped up," Professor Guerra chirps. "I've cut out some phrases from newspapers." She places her hand on the wooden table in front of her. "Take one without looking and write whatever comes to mind. This will help you get rid of the chatter in your head and find the juicy ideas hidden underneath."

My classmates hurry to the front as if they'd waited all summer for this moment. I'm the last one to grab a clipping, which reads *STUDENT CHALLENGES*.

Everyone bows their heads like they're praying in church. Their pens gallop across their notebooks while mine crawls down the first line. *Student challenges what you're expected to feel when a family member dies,* I write.

The memories spill onto the page. Grandma died eleven years ago today from a heart attack. I'm pulled back to the funeral home. Mom sat to Dad's left with her head slightly bent and her hands in her lap. Suzanna fixed her eyes on the coffin as if she feared Grandma would sit up and start screaming at us. I kept rubbing some of my dress between my pointer finger and thumb. Dad gently smacked my hand and told me to stop. Grandma's friends were the only ones crying; they thought they had lost a godly woman. The only things that were true in Uncle Tim's eulogy were that Grandma had been active in her church and a fabulous cook.

Grandma's friend Lorraine said she was praying for us. She was wasting her energy. We didn't need prayers. No one in my family missed her. Prayers do nothing anyway because God does nothing. He didn't care about all the abuse Mom and Uncle Tim suffered growing up or what my grandparents did to me.

I write, *Someone said at the repast that Grandpa looked like a lost boy without Grandma.* I cross this out so hard with my pen, its point cuts into the page.

"Time's up," Professor Guerra announces. She scrawls *Protagonist* on the board with a blue marker that's drying out. "This is the hero in your story. Readers feel the most empathy for this person because he or she is going to suffer the most." She presses the marker harder against the board, but the ink isn't any darker. Where is all the tuition money going? "For homework, read the first two chapters in your book on character development, and think about who your protagonist will be for your story. Make him or her someone you're not. See what your imagination gives you. Let this person talk to you so he or she can tell the story, not you."

I press my palm to my forehead. Creative writing is useless. I'm a transcriber for my character, and my grade is based on how much I let her snack on my ear.

SUZANNA'S red jeep sits in the driveway when I get home. She's been married for five years, but it feels as if she never left. She comes over when she isn't waiting tables at Lombardi's (not the best Italian food in our suburb of New York City, but the crème brûlée is passable), or if her husband, Carl, is working late on a renovation job. But she never stops by at lunchtime, like she's doing today.

Suzanna is standing next to Mom at the kitchen island when I walk in. She opens a bag of potato chips and dumps a handful on her plate.

"Here for the day?" I ask.

Suzanna shakes her head without looking at me. Her cherry-brown hair is twisted in a French braid.

"She needs some time away from Carl," Mom says.

I snatch a grape from the bowl next to a jar of pickles. "We went to his parents' house for Labor Day. You two were fine."

"We *looked* fine."

The edge in her voice makes me flinch. "What happened?"

Suzanna doesn't respond and stays focused on her sandwich.

Mom shoves a plate in my hands to steer my attention elsewhere. "Do you feel all right? You look pale."

"I have a migraine. I'm stressing about work."

"You're starting in five days. Relax."

"Can't," I say before swallowing another grape. Must. Avoid. The chips.

"Ham or turkey, Marty?" Mom slathers mayonnaise on a slice of rye bread.

I wedge myself between Mom and Suzanna and drop some turkey on two pieces of bread that are already covered with cheese. I slap my sandwich together and start for the stairs. Mom knows what's up with Suzanna's marriage, but neither of them will tell me. That's no surprise. They're tight, like friends.

"Good thing you cleaned out your room," Mom calls after me. "We don't know how long Suzanna's going to be here. I washed the sheets on your trundle bed."

I stop chewing on my sandwich. Last month she thought I was imbalanced for going on a purging rampage after I took an eco-feminism class over the summer. I felt guilty about overconsumption and workers being exploited in factories in the developing world.

I didn't understand why Mom was so against my massive declutter. She and Dad sold our home in Neptune (I was born in

New Jersey, not on the eighth planet.) and downsized to a two-bed, two-bath townhouse after Suzanna got married. The Lane family rule is that once you move out, you don't come back. (I'm supposed to be out after I earn my BA, so I'd better land a good job in grad school.) Suzanna must be in bad shape for them to make allowances.

When I open the door to my room, remnants of my migraine prick my skull. Boxes and bags stuffed with Suzanna's clothes and accessories cover the floor except for a narrow pathway she created to the closet.

I get Suzanna wants a break, but I didn't think she'd be moving all her stuff here.

I sweep several cosmetic bags off my bed. They land on a box overflowing with books. A journal titled *Catch the Little Things* topples to the floor. I take off my backpack and sit on the cleared space to finish my lunch.

A trumpet sounds from under a photo album. I scoot to the edge of the bed and unearth Suzanna's phone from its hiding place. Carl texted her.

I hear Suzanna's light, rapid footsteps coming down the hall. I hold her phone out to her when she appears in the doorframe. "It's Carl."

She gives me a blank stare.

"You want me to read it for you?"

"No, give me." She sighs as she drags herself across the room. She reads the screen, then looks at me. Tears glimmer in her charcoal-gray eyes.

"What's wrong?" I ask.

She hurls a sneaker across the room. It knocks my floral nesting doll off my desk hutch. The doll hits the corner of my bookshelf and rolls onto the floor.

I gasp and step around some boxes to pick it up. I rub my

Books are a tourniquet for the abandonment wound she inflicted on me fourteen years ago.

"You can live here so you won't need campus housing. After all your father's done for you ..." She doesn't finish.

Mom left Dad and me when I was five to live in Connecticut with her former boyfriend, Nathan Shepard, a Yale graduate and defense attorney. She never crossed the New Jersey border again. I don't see what he has over Dad, other than more money. She left us, even though my paternal grandma, my halmoni, prayed with me when she and Grandpa babysat me. She pressed my hands together, and we asked God to help my parents find happiness and heal from losing their firstborn, Caleb. Our prayers didn't help, but Halmoni said I should still love God. It's hard to feel that sometimes.

It's hard, because that wasn't the first time a mother left me. My omma put me up for adoption right after I was born in a clinic in Seoul. Thirteen months later, I left my foster mother, Mrs. Shin, and an escort from the adoption agency brought me to the States and handed me to my new family.

"Mom, really. You and Nathan don't have to do this."

"Don't make hasty decisions, Ian. More education never hurts."

I stifle a laugh. "It always hurts. I'm only getting an associate's because Dad wanted me to do something besides work after high school."

"You've only been there for a year. A lot of people who hated public school say college is better."

My mouth waters as I slide my pancake onto a plate. "I would have known by now if I loved school enough to continue."

"If you want to move up in retail, a business degree would help."

"I'm getting my associate's in business, and I got promoted."

She sighs. "Honey, do you want to spend your life watching people shop? How's that making the world a better place? Gemma's thirteen, and her ambitions are higher than yours."

I drop the pan into the sink with too much force, making it clatter against a glass bowl. Gemma wants to be a teacher for the blind. She has retinopathy of prematurity and lost sight in her left eye from a detached retina. She can still read print, but Mom pushed her to learn braille because her other eye is at risk too. Gemma fell in love with those dots and wants to combat the low literacy rate in the blind community.

On the other hand, Mom thinks I'm lazy. She jokes about how much I dislike school, given that my last name is Berkley, minus the second *e*.

"I don't *love* selling craft items. Liz was the only one who hired me after the farmer's market closed. Any retail experience is valuable on my resume. I'll apply to a bookstore again when I have more time in the summer." I bite into my lunch. Kimchi juice trickles onto my tongue.

Mom says nothing.

"Can you respect my decision?"

"I respect it. Doesn't mean I like it."

I flinch. I send a short prayer to God for thicker skin. Mom's attitude is really getting to me.

"You were fine with my plans a few days ago."

"You're smart, Ian. You do a fantastic job when you apply yourself. You got a 1960 on the SATs."

"Mom, I need to go. I have work at three," I say before I shove more pancake into my mouth.

"Don't forget Caleb's birthday. He would have been twenty-two this month."

Both of Mom's pregnancies were tough. She had complications due to preeclampsia when she carried Gemma, and Caleb died from a cranial hemorrhage when Mom was thirty weeks along. She and Dad tried having another baby, but that never happened. Dad suggested they adopt from Korea, where Halmoni was from. He thought this would make Mom feel better and fix their marriage. Adopting me didn't fix anything.

"I know. I never forget. We'll talk soon. Love you, Mom."

I puff out some air and return Dad's phone to the table. Our reverse schedules make life pretty lonely, but I let Dad do his job and don't complain.

I finish lunch and double-check that I have the store's key on my lanyard. It's my first day as a supervisor at Needle, Yarn, and Crafts Corner, and I'll be closing tonight. On my way there, I get stuck behind a woman driving under the speed limit. Then, as I head to the stockroom, a man starts arguing with me about our coupon policy. I'm almost to the time clock when a girl approaches me and asks for a shopping basket.

Finally, I punch in at 3:03.

"Two more minutes and you would have been late," Liz says when I enter her office.

I sit in the chair in front of her desk. "I got behind a slow driver, and I had to deal with customers when I came in."

"I appreciate you putting them first, but if you get bombarded walking in, ask an associate to take over." She slides my new name tag across her desk. "Congratulations on being my newest supervisor."

I swap it with the old one on my light-blue polo shirt.

Liz holds out a clipboard. "Anthony's the only one who hasn't signed the updated policy on ladder safety."

"Okay."

"And you're training our new associate on Sunday."

I lift an eyebrow. "Wait, what?"

Liz adjusts her glasses on her nose. "Is this a problem?"

"No. I thought Evan was going to do it while I job-shadowed."

"Not anymore. This will save time, and I know you can train her."

"Okay." In a dubious tone I add, "I'm not sure she'll take me seriously."

"Why wouldn't she?"

"People still ask me what grade I'm in."

With humor in her eyes she says, "Just do your job and do it smart."

Rule 1 here is you let Liz Falcone do what she wants. She's bony and always looks tired, but the craftiest shoplifter can't sneak past her eyes, and she has no problem working a twelve-hour shift during the holidays. She's seventy-six and still the big boss of the company she started thirty-eight years ago in Asbury Park with no plans to retire soon.

Liz pushes her slate-gray hair behind her. "She has no work experience, but she taught herself how to knit a few months ago. I saw pictures of her projects. She's pretty good, so I hired her. It's about time someone here knew how to knit." Liz throws a name tag toward me like a Frisbee. The sticker reads MARTHA. "Show me what you're made of."

I shove Martha's name tag in my pocket and head to customer service. After I count Alicia's drawer, I call Anthony over to sign the form on ladder safety.

He glances down at me as he scribbles his initials. "Aren't you the only one who has to sign this?"

"Liz isn't guilty of size discrimination."

I'm the shortest person in my family at five foot three. Five foot two and three-quarters, according to Gemma. She measured me last year to prove she passed me by half an inch.

I start my first shift as a supervisor with a woman who tries to use a counterfeit one-hundred-dollar bill she swears the bank gave her, and then a couple wants to return a picture frame they bought seven years ago.

As I fix these piddly issues, Mom's words hit me—that my job isn't making the world a better place. But she didn't try to improve my world when I was younger. If the adoption agency's home study specialist knew what Mom had in store for me, he would have never let her be my mother.

4

MARTHA

FREEHOLD, NJ—Martha Lane is reported safe after sharing her room with Suzanna Alexander for twenty-one hours. There have been no incidents of her sister throwing or damaging items, and the piles of clutter on the floor no longer exceed the height of four feet.

That's because, thanks to whatever deity actually cares about me, I return to my room after a shower to find Suzanna going through her boxes. She hugs an empty mosaic picture frame, and her fingers are wrapped around two champagne glasses that are crisscrossed at their stems. She sets the items inside a box labeled *DONATE*. The fuchsia-and-silver *Bride to Be* sash from her bachelorette party is draped over one of the box's flaps.

"You're donating your wedding mementos?"

Suzanna throws her hands up. "I'm donating almost everything."

"Lovely," I chirp as I secure my hair in a loose ponytail. "My room won't be a fire hazard anymore."

Suzanna plops down on a bag of clothes and cradles her forehead in her hand. "I don't know what I'm doing. I love him. I hate him. I miss him. I want divorce papers." She folds a pair of black pants on her lap and offers them to me. "They're dressy enough for work. A size ten."

I snatch the pants from her and drop them into a box. "I'm supposed to wear beige, and they're too small."

"Just thought you'd want them for the future."

I put on my backpack. If Suzanna thinks I need to shed more pounds after I went on that strict diet three years ago, she needs an eye exam.

When I get to school, I head into the science building for Russian class. I dart into the room and choose a desk in the third row.

My instructor, Aleksey Federov, is lanky with squinty powder-blue eyes and strawberry-blond hair that's cut short at the sides and is longer at the top. We can call him by his Russian diminutive, Alyosha.

As he goes through the roster, he tells us the Russian equivalents of our names. If you don't have one, you can reinvent yourself with a name from a list in the back of the textbook. Judging from the names he's calling, a majority of the students are of Russian descent. They have names like Yulya Brodsky, Dmitry Katin, and Hellen Treece-Serov. He calls me Marfa. I cover the grin stretching across my face. Babka used to call me that.

He drops the roster on his desk. "Let's be honest. How many of you already speak Russian?"

Everyone, except for me and four other students, raise their hands.

"The course description says fluent speakers aren't allowed to register, but your advisors can't make judgments based on your names or see all that Russian in your heads."

That's a good thing, because if native speakers didn't sign up, this class would have been canceled too, and I'd be sitting in something more useless than creative writing, like theater appreciation.

Sweeping his arm in front of him, Alyosha asks, "How many of you can read and write it?"

A few hands go down.

He scoops a pile of packets off his desk and hands a few to each person in the front row. "I don't care how much Russian you know or don't know. Everyone's learning the same material at the same pace." His face hardens. "This class is for those with little to no knowledge of Russian, so I'm starting from the beginning. If you find this boring, you have until this Friday to change your schedule."

Soft whispers float across the room.

He jerks his head up. "I fought for this class. The language department apparently thinks my job is useless because so many native speakers sign up. If you feel the same way, you can tell me why in front of everyone."

No one speaks. The guy in front of me passes back a packet. I flip through the pages. It was xeroxed from a handwriting book. Arrows surround each letter, telling me where to begin and end the strokes I make with my pencil. I already know all this. I was so excited about Russian, I taught myself the Cyrillic script over the summer.

Alyosha walks up to the board and grabs a marker. "Now, let's learn some Russian."

We get through the first five letters of the alphabet, then he says, "You can write your first Russian word already: *da*." He writes this on the board. "It means yes."

I'm ahead of everyone, tracing Л. Alyosha glances at me. I flip back to the first page in my packet. I hope he doesn't think I'm fluent and lied to him.

At the end of class, my packet is decorated with my Cyrillic letters and some basic words. *Nyet* is no. *Malchik* is boy. *Rabota* is work. I'm writing in Babka's language. I squeeze my hands together in my lap to keep myself still. I want to grab my textbook and swallow all the lessons.

"Alphabet quiz on Friday," Alyosha says as everyone packs up to leave. *"Do svidaniya."* I'm about to head out the door when he calls, "Hey, Marfa?"

This is it. He thinks I'm a liar.

"You were on fire with the alphabet. Keep it up."

Now my face is on fire. "Oh. Thanks. I studied Cyrillic over the summer."

"Glad you want to be here." He reaches for my shoulder, but I back away. His arm drops to his side. "Sometimes I wonder if I'm supposed to be bagging groceries."

I scoot out of the classroom. Friday can't arrive soon enough. Alyosha is in the right place. I think I am too.

———

AT DINNER, the first thing Dad says is, "I have some news. The library's hours have been shortened, and it's closed on Sundays because of budget cuts."

It's only the second day of the semester. Suzanna moves in. Dad's income shrinks. What next?

Mom dives into a panic. "Which means you're not full-time anymore. We'll lose our benefits."

"Everything will be fine," he assures her.

She fingers the end of her braid. "I can get a job."

"It's okay, Jenn." Dad drops his napkin in his almost-empty bowl of pot roast. "We'll make a budget."

Mom sinks against her chair like a deflated balloon. She's

gorgeous, like Suzanna. When she wears her butterscotch hair loose, it bounces on her shoulders like you see in shampoo commercials. Mom and Suzanna are tall with broad shoulders and tiny waists, and they share clothes like sisters. They were spared the weight problems that used to plague my apple-shaped body. I don't have their heart-shaped faces or slightly upturned noses either. Mom compliments Suzanna on how good she looks in her designer clothes, but I don't recall the last time Mom told me I was beautiful.

Suzanna scrapes pieces of meat and potato off the sides of her bowl with her spoon and gets up to leave. "We can start extreme couponing."

"Work somewhere else, David." Mom suggests. "I'm sure other places need a reference librarian."

Dad runs a hand through his auburn hair. He does this whenever he's stressed. Suzanna and I used to giggle at the idea of him going bald, but his hair is thick, and he has a lot of it.

"I'd hate to leave after being there for twenty years, but supporting all of you comes first."

"The girls can chip in some of their paychecks."

I throw Dad a panicked look, but he doesn't notice. Any money I save is for grad school.

"That won't be necessary." I'm surprised to see him touch Mom's hand. I thought their affection reached its expiration date years ago. "I know what I'm doing."

When I was little, Dad used to sit at the kitchen table with me in his lap while Mom cooked dinner. They had happy-couple conversations. If he said something silly, Mom came over and ruffled his short, choppy bangs. I'd reach up and try to do the same. He would squeeze me hard and laugh. "Not you too, Marty!"

As Suzanna and I grew up, my parents grew out of love. They don't talk to each other as much or go on dates anymore. Dad doesn't give Mom's hand an occasional squeeze as he drives. Duty and respect anchor their relationship now. She married Dad right after high school out of necessity. My grandparents hated Dad for getting Mom pregnant before marriage and threw her out.

The dryer buzzes. Mom stands up and wrenches her hand out of Dad's. He grabs her fingers, but she pulls away and heads to the laundry room.

"I hope your day was better than mine," he says to me.

"I really like Russian class."

"Oh, yeah?"

"There's an alphabet quiz on Friday, but I'm already writing vocabulary on flash cards. I'm spending my day off tomorrow in my textbook."

Dad's face finally lights up. "Attagirl. What days are you working?"

I tick off the days on my fingers. "I'm on for Tuesdays, Thursdays, Fridays, and Sundays."

"I want you to work as hard at the store as you do in school, but if it gets to be too much, say something. It's important to build up your resume, but school comes first."

Mom was disappointed when Suzanna abandoned college after she got married, but Dad was livid. He prizes education and wants the best for his daughters.

He doesn't have to worry about me; I always loved learning. Schoolwork drowned out the voices of my peers taunting my body and curbed the depression I kept secret.

I get up and stack the dirty dishes. Dad collects the silverware and follows me to the sink.

"I wish my mother had taught me Russian," he says. "It might have given me more job opportunities."

"This is probably temporary. You'll get your hours back."

"We're not immune from financial hardship, Marty," he warns

as he closes the dishwasher. "We've had it good, but everyone gets hit with something. You either crash or fight, and I'll fight."

"I know." I want to hug him good night and say I love him, even though we're not a cuddly family. "Dad?"

He stands between the kitchen and the living room. "Marty, go somewhere."

I climb the stairs to my room. His words hurt, but I can't tell him that. My family doesn't talk about pain and feelings, so I numb myself. I've done this for fourteen years. But we should talk more, especially after what my grandparents put Mom and Dad through. And me.

5

IAN

MY EX-GIRLFRIEND, Hana, holds the sides of a canvas tote bag that says *READ, EAT, SLEEP, REPEAT* in black typewriter font and upends it. A slew of books spills onto the cream-colored rug that lies in the center of the room. We just spent two hours browsing a new-and-used bookstore, and now we're back at her dorm at Montclair State University.

"Okay, Ian. Pick one."

I sit next to her and take Katherine Min's *Secondhand World*. We're continuing a tradition we made up when we dated in high school. Every time one of us adds books to our library, the other person picks a random title to read.

Hana gives me a wry smile. "I knew you'd pick that one."

"I want to read a story that could have been mine."

Her frosted brown hair falls around her shoulders like a shawl as she sits on the floor to shelve her books. "Write *your* story. Contribute to the cannon and write about Korean adoption."

"I'd blow a crater in the cannon." This comes out harder than I intended.

Her brow creases.

Hana and I have talked about my adoption, but I never told her I'm angry at Korea for ostracizing single mothers like Omma and fatherless kids like me, or that I'm not as thankful as I'm expected to be for the life I have.

I could try telling her now.

"Adoptees are supposed to be thankful. I don't feel that way about what my mom put me through." I want to say more, but no more words come.

"At least your dad's always been there."

Sometimes *at least* isn't enough.

Hana touches my leg. I stiffen. We haven't had a lot of physical contact since we started hanging out again in mid-August. "Stay for a bit. I'll heat up chicken pot pies in the microwave, and we can watch a movie. Jess went home this weekend."

I rub the back of my neck. "I don't think I should."

"You always say that."

"Because it's not a good idea."

Hana holds a book called *A Northern Light*. "I remember the boundaries."

"I know, but I have schoolwork to finish. There's church in the morning, and then I have work. I'm training someone for the first time."

"Church. Right." She motions toward me. "Because of church, you can't spend a lot of time here." She's not bitter; she sounds sad.

She doesn't get that I can't stay here for long because of church *and* Jesus. Being alone leaves room for sin. A kiss that's too deep or a touch somewhere too intimate might tempt us to do something we'd regret later.

I lean closer to her and gently ask, "Hana, what's wrong? Talk to me."

She looks at the *Little Women* poster hanging over her bed.

"Come on. Let's go talk somewhere."

Hana gets up to grab her sweater from her desk chair. I touch her back as we walk out the door, but she inches away.

I miss touching her. She's fine-boned and small with creamy tan skin. I've known her for five years, but taking in her dark eyes, full lips, and the gentle curves of her body I should have never touched makes me feel like I'm back in ninth-grade English, crushing on her from a distance.

On our way to Café Diem, I link my arm through Hana's and squeeze it in the crook of my elbow. She doesn't resist.

"I wish you weren't so legalistic," she says once we're there.

"I don't want us to be alone in your dorm. You know that, Hana."

"We used to hang out on our own at each other's houses. We made some mistakes, and you put up all these safeguards. Do you trust me at all?"

"I do, but even if those things didn't happen, I'd still be like this."

We stop at a table outside the café. "Like this," she echoes with exasperation as she yanks a chair out from under the table. "It wasn't until after prom when you told me *I* needed to be like *you*."

I sit across from her. "Hana ..."

"You know, my family and I go to church every weekend too. My pastor said we should respect other religions; they all believe in God."

"Not all religions lead to the God in the Bible."

Hana's eyes narrow. "The God in the Bible sends people to hell."

"He doesn't send people there. Their decision to reject Jesus does."

A man at the table to our left stares at me. I stare back, which makes him look away.

Hana touches my arm. "I want things to be like they used to."

I look up at the gray sky. I want the clouds to form into letters and spell the answer that can make us both happy.

"You can't ... give him up?" she carefully asks.

"No, I can't." She lets go of me. I grip the armrests of my chair and try to hold down my frustration.

It's Christian common sense that this conversation is a doorway to bring Hana to faith, but I wish she hadn't mentioned it so soon. I wanted more time for us to catch up and just be together.

"You think I'm going to hell," Hana accuses.

The guy next to us springs up from his seat and briskly walks off.

Hana's right, and that is the hardest truth to tell your loved ones who don't know Jesus.

I lean forward and rest my arms on my knees. "You're still here, so you can change that."

She smacks her hands down on her lap in frustration. "It's always me, Ian. I'm always the one who needs to change to make this work."

"Let's not go there." I hold her hand. It's limp in mine. "You want things to be like they used to? Let's have that, because I want that too."

Hana looks at our hands, then at me. She relaxes and squeezes my fingers. "You still want me to change."

I nod. "But can we try to work things out?"

She starts pulling her hand away. I squeeze it before letting go.

When Hana asked me if we could hang out, I said yes and ignored everything that tore us apart last year. I'd prayed for her to come back, and she did, so I won't push her this time. I'll love her with Christ's love and hope she'll want to know him too.

"We can try." She moves her chair back and stands to go.

I take her wrist. "Wait, can I get you something? An everything bagel?"

She smiles. "You can get me an everything bagel."

We walk into Café Diem. While we stand in line, Hana hugs my waist and briefly leans her head on my shoulder. I buy her a bagel and order a smoked turkey panini sandwich. We spend an hour chatting about school and what we've been reading. It feels like old times.

Before we part ways, I close Hana in a tight hug. "Same time, different place next week?"

"Of course." We share a light kiss on the lips before she hides her face in my shoulder. Sounding muffled, she adds, "Then your cousin's wedding the week after."

I cup the back of her head in my hand. "I can't wait."

———

I MET Hana Baek in English class in ninth grade. Our teacher, Ms. Malinowski, arranged everyone's seats in alphabetical order, which put Hana in front of me. When I was supposed to be writing down the vocabulary words for the week or listening to Ms. Malinowski give background information on Harper Lee, I thought about Hana. She must have felt me staring at her, because two weeks after school started she placed a crumpled note on my desk before scooting out of class.

Stop looking at me so much. I have a phone.

Below her message was her number.

I walked around the house with my phone for twenty minutes

before I called her. I had nothing to worry about. Talking to Hana was as easy as talking to my best friend, Chris.

Hana read as much as I did. She didn't think it was weird that Patti Kim's *A Cab Called Reliable* was my favorite book, and we were both awful at math. When she said she was from Inchon, I told her I was from Seoul. I was hesitant to say I was adopted, though. I'd heard stories of Korean adoptees dating Koreans, and their boyfriend or girlfriend's parents weren't thrilled.

"Can you speak Korean?"

"I was adopted," I blurted out. Then, steadily, I started sharing the little information I have about my birth parents into the phone.

When I finished talking, Hana said, "Ian, it's okay."

"My adoptive family has baggage too. My dad's dad met my halmoni when he served in Korea after the war. Her parents disapproved of the relationship because he wasn't Korean. They told her it was either my grandfather or them. She chose Grandpa and was cut off from her family."

"Wait, so your adoptive dad is half Korean like you?"

"Yeah. This confuses a lot of people. His twin sisters were born in Korea in 1954, then he came along seven years later."

"Ian, your grandparents' story isn't uncommon. It's part of our history. And I have some half-Korean friends."

I pressed on my stomach, which hurt from anxiety. And what I wanted to ask Hana would make it worse. "Can *we* be friends?"

"Ian, do you like Korean food?" I heard the smile in her voice.

"I can talk about that forever."

"Then let's be friends, because I want to talk about it forever."

I moved my hand off my stomach and fell back on my bed. That was when I knew I wanted Hana to be my girlfriend.

We called each other a few times a week after we finished our homework and talked for hours. She invited me to join the editing team for the school's literary magazine, and we started exchanging books.

I finally had the guts to ask Hana out during spring break. We ate dinner at the mall, shared an ice cream sundae for dessert, and walked around until closing. A month later, we had our first kiss. It was during the summer when we started going to each other's houses. I loved hearing Hana talk in Korean with her parents and younger brothers. Their voices rose and fell in a singsong rhythm, a trademark of the Korean language. I strained my ears to catch anything I could understand from the little Korean I'd learned from Halmoni.

When I went to Hana's house, we cooked Korean food and shared recipes. I stuffed my hotteok—Korean pancakes—with kimchi and meat, but Hana was more creative and filled hers with peanut butter or chocolate. I topped my steamed eggs with red pepper flakes, and she liked to add fish sauce to hers as they cooked in her earthenware pot. We ate dinner with her family and visited for hours. These times almost made me believe life could be perfect. I thought Hana and I would always be connected because it would take more than a lifetime to read all the stories that were ever written and try every recipe that was ever created. Stupid logic, but I was too infatuated to understand the depth of a relationship.

I also didn't know God's love is what really holds a man and woman together.

I found that love in twelfth grade. Dad asked me to come back to church after sitting out for five years. He said being a nice guy wasn't going to get me into heaven but following Jesus would. I'd ditched church when I was twelve. I thought God was boring, and I didn't get why Dad loved someone who had taken his firstborn and let Mom walk away. And if God loved the little children of the world, he wouldn't have let Korean adoption thrive for decades after the war and given me another mom who did what she did to me.

But it felt as if Jesus was always in the background, asking, Are you going to see me?

It took me a month to see him. I went to church, and I read Dad's KJV Bible in two weeks. On December 29, I became a Christian. I had eternal life. I was going to heaven, and I wanted this for Hana too.

She was happy for me but wasn't interested in my conversion. I didn't want to lose her, so I prayed for her and didn't push her to believe what I did.

Then prom night happened. Hana and I went back to my place instead of sticking with our friends, like we had planned. After that, I couldn't keep my faith out of our relationship anymore. Things were never the same. We exchanged awkward hellos and small talk in the hallways. Our phone calls became a chore to stay in touch. Once in a while we'd go out and talk about books and starting college. Hana would ask me if I changed my mind about God, I would get defensive, and we would fight.

A week after graduation, we ended things for good. We were exhausted and two very different people.

We didn't talk for over a year. I missed Hana so much and blamed myself for our breakup; I had pushed my beliefs too hard on her. I didn't mean to hurt her, but I did.

I owe her now. I'll give her all the time she wants.

6

MARTHA

I'M LEAVING for work on Sunday, when Mom stops me in the kitchen. "We need you to chip in some money. Dad's going to be part-time indefinitely. We'll reimburse you when things get better."

Panic springs inside me. "Is Suzanna helping?"

Mom kneads some bread dough. "People keep leaving her chintzy tips. If she and Carl split up, she's going to need every cent."

I nodded to her on my way out. We were never drowning in cash, but we always had it good, and now my parents need my help. It's hard to digest that.

It takes me a little over twenty minutes to drive to NYC Corner. When I come in, Billy Preston's "Nothing from Nothing" is on the radio. The store smells like candy and potpourri. As I walk to the office, I make mental notes of where things are. Seasonal is by the entrance. Then comes paper crafts, kids' aisle, discount bins, paint —oh, the yarn!

"Martha?" Liz calls from a few aisles away. "Come for the grand tour."

I follow her to the office. She shows me how to slip my card into the time clock before taking me past the framing counter and through a set of double doors.

Liz pushes the one open with a sign that reads *EMPLOYEES ONLY*. "This is the stockroom."

It's cold in here, and the concrete floor is scuffed and corroded in several spots. We maneuver around piles of boxes and stop at a set of red lockers.

Liz points to the top locker farthest from the left and hands me a slip of paper. "Here's your combination. Put your things away and hop on register two. Ian will be up there in a few minutes to train you."

I try my combination three times before the shackle comes loose. I stuff my purse and Coke in my locker and head to the front. A Black woman with a braid down her back is counting change at the register next to mine. Her name tag reads *Alicia*.

She hands the customer a small bag and says, "Have a good day."

Liz comes to her side. "I'll count your drawer. Ian's getting Martha's packet."

I rest my elbow on the counter and cradle my chin in my hand as Liz counts the money in the cash drawer. She rips a small piece of paper from the receipt printer for Alicia to sign and says, "Perfect," before walking away.

Suddenly, I hear a man's voice. "Come on, Martha, stand up straight. You're working, and people are watching you."

Heat floods my cheeks as I fix my posture. I read his name tag. It's Ian.

If Liz didn't tell me he's a supervisor, I would think he needed working papers to be here; he looks so young. He's my height at five foot three. His olive skin, hazel eyes, and boyish face framed by his matted black hair grab me for a second. He looks as if he might be part Asian or Mediterranean.

He looks good.

Ian comes around the counter. I lift my hand for him to shake, but he passes me and drops a packet down in front of me. "Fill out the top and memorize your employee number. You'll need it to sign in to your register." He hands me my name tag.

I weave the needle through the cotton material of my shirt.

He's attractive, but his personality needs a facelift.

Ian hits a few buttons on the register's screen and steps back. "Ready?"

I try to sign in to my register, but I type my password incorrectly three times. The system locks me out, so I need a new password. I keep forgetting to hit TOTAL to add the tax after I ring up items. I can't remember how to add a gift card to a transaction even though Ian helps me with the process twice, so he writes the steps down and tapes them to my register. I accidentally clock out for my fifteen-minute break, so I pop into the office to ask the assistant manager, Evan Kinley, to adjust my time card, but my combination on the keypad isn't working.

Evan casts me an I'm-going-to-kill-you look. He's tall with a long face and a fuzzy ash-brown beard and mustache. He looks like my boring eighth-grade English teacher who despised his job.

Ian's at my register after my break. He rakes his fingers through his side-swept fringed bangs and sighs. If I give him a nickel for every time he's sighed while training me, Liz won't owe him a paystub on Friday. "We finished all the prompts in the packet. Are you ready to ring up customers, or do you want more practice?"

"I'm ready."

Ian regards me. "Martha, you're shaking."

I wrap my arms around my middle. "I'm nervous about handling cash."

He gathers the receipts from my dummy transactions and staples them to my paperwork. His cologne smells like peppermint and cinnamon. He has an attitude, but he knows how to smell nice without damaging your sinuses.

"Count twice if you need to. And if you tell customers you're new, they'll probably understand."

"Okay."

Ian points to a nearby endcap. A bumpy scar starts halfway up the inside of his arm and veers toward his elbow. What did he go through to be left with that? "I'm going to hang up some pegs. Yell if you need me."

I'm still trembling, so I hug myself tighter. I feel like I've been thrown off a ship without a raft now that Ian's gone. I'm responsible for customers' *and* NYC Corner's money. I wish I'd gotten that warehouse cleaning job with the toy company near Kaylin's house.

A woman holding a little boy's hand comes toward me. "Hi, how are you?" I sound like I'm really excited to see her.

"Hello." She puts some sheets of felt on the counter.

I'm still shaking as I ring her up and bag her items. I count her change twice, like Ian suggested.

"Are you new?" she asks.

"Yes."

She puts her wallet away and hangs her purse on her shoulder. "Good luck with the job."

My anxiety melts after three transactions. Only one customer puts her things down and leaves when I refuse to let her use two coupons.

Business slows around four o'clock. According to Ian, there are pockets of time when there's nothing to do except stand at your register and wait for a customer. So that's what I do for forty-five minutes. Finally, a middle-aged woman with her dark hair in a pixie cut comes over with a cart full of merchandise.

"Hi, how are you today?" I pipe up.

"I'm in a hurry," she snaps as she starts to unload her cart.

My gut fills with panic as I scan her items. Two packages of stitch markers, four skeins of blue yarn, five sheets of stickers …

"Did you get all the yarn?"

I grab a skein of pink yarn and scan it to show her I'm not done.

"Put the quantity in and ring up one of them. They're the same price and brand."

"Each color has a different code." I turn in Ian's direction. A portable phone is nestled between his shoulder and the side of his face.

"Can you get a move-on?" the woman demands.

I finish ringing up her yarn. Before I can lift the bag off the metal rack, she grabs it and tosses it into her cart.

"Did you ring up the crayons?"

I ignore her and rub the sides of a new bag between my fingers to separate them.

"Give me the bag; give me the bag!" she shrieks and rips it from my hand. She can't open it either, so she throws it behind the counter and starts tossing the photo albums into her cart. Geez. She has a bad case of what Kailyn and I call the Jersey Rush. It's usually found in New Jerseyans who go through life as if there's a firecracker under their butt.

I snatch an album off the counter before she can take it. "I didn't scan those."

Her eyes darken with anger. "I'll tell you how many I have."

"I need to count them."

She dumps the albums on the counter. "You don't know what you're doing!"

I lean forward and get in her face. "My supervisor's finishing your order because I'm done with your attitude."

"Hang on," Ian interjects from behind me.

I move aside. He throws me a disgusted look before he drags his finger down my screen to see which photo albums I've scanned. Heat runs up the back of my neck and spreads over my face. He leaves what needs to be rung up on the counter and steps back. "Finish up."

When I'm done and hand the woman her change, she says, "Some people shouldn't be cashiers," in a sarcastic, pleasant tone.

I slam my drawer closed.

"She's in training." Ian places her bags on the counter. "Have a good—"

She snatches the receipt out of my hand and abruptly turns toward the exit and leaves.

"What happened?" Ian demands.

"She was harassing me."

"It doesn't matter. You have to watch what you say up here. Even if the customer's wrong, Liz wants us to put up a good front. We get people like her every day."

I cross my arms. "We shouldn't take customers' abuse."

"It comes with retail. You'll learn how to brush it off."

A woman approaches me with a basket filled with drawing supplies.

I force a smile. "Hi."

"Can you be done in two minutes? I gotta go pick up my daughter."

———

LIZ AND EVAN leave at five, so I have to close the store with Ian. We haven't said a word to each other since the drama with the rude customer.

When eight o'clock rolls around, Ian comes over and says, "Time to count your drawer."

Butterfly wings tickle the inside of my stomach. "What if there's a difference?"

"It's okay if you're off by a few cents, but if it's more than five dollars, you get written up." Ian gathers the pennies and begins to drop them one at a time back into their compartment. "Did things calm down after that lady left?"

"Yeah."

"Retail gives you thick skin. Your first rude customer is like an initiation. After that, you're broken in."

"Consider me in," I remark. "We should have recorded that lady and put a speaker by the door that would go off every time someone walks in. Some people shouldn't be cashiers!" I cackle. "It would be perfect for Halloween."

Ian stops counting the dimes and lets out a hearty laugh. A dimple appears on his left cheek. "I'm not a fan of Halloween, but that's hilarious."

"You're not?"

"No. It's against my beliefs."

I lean on the counter. "Why?"

He's about to enter the number of singles he just counted but stops to look at me. "I'm a Christian. I'm not celebrating a so-called holiday that glorifies death and evil."

"A lot of Christians celebrate Halloween."

"Now you know one who doesn't." He finishes counting the money and closes my drawer. He reads my variance on the piece of register tape. His eyes widen with horror. "Martha," he gasps. "It's seven under."

My stomach clenches with fear. "Seven dollars?"

Ian's serious face breaks into a grin.

I grab the paper from him. "You made me panic over seven cents? You're not funny."

Ian hands me a pen. "Sign this, then you count me."

I press the pen into the paper as I write my initials. "What next?"

"We put the money in the safe, you vacuum the vestibule and straighten up the store, and I clean the bathrooms."

After we clock out, Ian checks my purse to make sure I didn't shoplift. "You did good today."

"If that's good, then what's bad?" I don't give him time to answer because I head toward my car.

He locks the store and calls after me, "I'm sorry I joked about your drawer. You had a rough first day."

"I still think you're a jerk," I shoot back without facing him, "and if you're a Christian, your attitude needs work." I turn and add, "People are watching you."

We stare at each other, then we head in opposite directions.

I don't regret what I said.

7

IAN

I HIT the bookstore in the student center after my American literature class Monday morning. I always buy the books I need for a class after the first session. That eases the shock of having $400 wiped from my account after buying everything I need for three courses.

I weave through the register lines that stretch to the back of the store and find the humanities section. I spot the anthology for English 245, early to modern American literature, and open it. I put my nose against the page. I love the smell of ink and fresh paper.

"The first thing he says is, 'Come on, Martha, stand up straight. You're working, and people are watching you.'"

My head snaps up. I grab *Glengarry Glen Ross, Death of a Salesman, Fences,* a collection of early American poetry, and *The Coquette* and sneak around the bookshelf. Martha's back is to me. Her copper-brown hair is tied in a low ponytail like it was yesterday. She has on jeans and a light-pink flannel shirt.

I cringe. Your insults always sound worse coming from

someone else. She shouldn't have been standing at her register looking bored, but I should have respected her.

Martha is with a friend who's smaller than her and has dark-blond curly hair piled on top of her head. "Customers don't care about that." Martha's friend types something on her phone. "They want bargains and coupons."

I pretend to browse the other titles on the shelf.

"Then I get *Maleficent* for a customer and tell her I'm not dealing with her attitude." Martha adjusts her backpack on her shoulder and flips through another textbook. "Ian looks at me like I've committed a deadly sin."

"You said he's really short. You can't blame him for trying to look tough."

She's right. When I was a freshman, a senior on my bus named Steve Clementi bullied anyone he considered below him: the heavyset kids, the girl with crutches, or the kid with the second-hand clothes. He came up behind me after we got off the bus and threw me into Mrs. Glazer's trash can. Afterward, I reeked of fish and dog food.

I promised myself then and there that I'd speak up to let people know I'm older and stronger than I look. What I say and do matters. How I feel matters. But I didn't have to be an insolent ambassador for Liz's store.

"If you want to keep your job, you have to deal with him, even if his ego's bigger than he is," Martha's friend continues.

"This copy has too many markings and highlights," she mumbles.

She tugs Martha's sleeve. "You never buy used books."

"I need to, Kaylin," she says softly. "You know why." She checks out another copy with bent edges and clicks her tongue. "I don't like notes in the margins. They might influence how I interpret what I'm reading."

Kaylin skims through a copy with a bent cover. "This is for creative writing? You have that class *tomorrow*. You never procrastinate either."

Martha closes the book and turns to leave. "It's hard."

Kaylin's mouth hangs open. "Why? It's a one-hundred-level course. That independent study you were supposed to do was Humanities 305."

"Kaylin," Martha says, her voice edgy, "I didn't fall off the nerdy wagon. I'm doing the best I can and steering toward Montclair State."

They head for the registers. The lines are half the length they were when I came in. I'm not sure if I should follow Martha or let some people go between us.

"So, going back to Ian," I hear her say. "He tricked me into thinking my drawer was seven dollars off when it was only seven cents. I almost hyperventilated."

I rush to get behind them, but a couple beats me to it.

"If it bugs you this much, talk to the manager. She might slap Ian on the wrist. That'll knock him over."

I hug my books tightly. Another jab at my height.

Martha shakes her head and scoffs. "Lay off his height, okay? The thing about him is he's a Christian. I made some crack about Halloween. He said he doesn't celebrate because it's against his beliefs."

Kaylin touches Martha's shoulder. "I hope he's not like your grandparents."

I catch her words like a kid trapping a lightning bug in a net.

"Who knows? He didn't even introduce himself. I offered him my hand to shake, and he tossed my packet at me. He was testy during most of my shift." Martha adds in a quieter voice, "That really offended me."

My face floods with heat.

She deserves an apology. I was so anxious about training her and looking authoritative, my social etiquette left my common sense.

"I forgot highlighters," the woman in front of me tells the guy she's with and drags him out of the line.

I step forward. My mouth is dry.

If I apologize, Martha will know I was eavesdropping, but the remorse is ganging up on me. I'll be dragging this around until I see her at work tomorrow.

"Hi, Martha," I say.

Martha whirls around. "Ian!" Her face is as red as the pimple on her left cheek. Kaylin stares at me.

I play with a corner of my anthology's cover. "I'm sorry for how I treated you yesterday."

"It's nothing. Don't worry about it."

She and Kaylin face forward again. Martha blows out a heavy sigh. They say nothing to each other for the rest of the time they wait in line. The space between us is stuffed with awkwardness. A cashier calls them up. Kaylin whispers something to Martha, who looks back at me and shakes her head. When Martha leaves the store, she presses her textbook against her chest like a shield.

8

MARTHA

I'M NOT LISTENING to Dr. Sloan reviewing the syllabus for Women and Art. The women's studies classes here are like English courses. You read a ton, write essays, do one big project, and participation is key. I'm focused on what Kaylin had the nerve to say before we left the bookstore.

He apologized. Your grandparents never did that. And he's cute.

Accepting Ian's apology doesn't mean I'm going to revamp my impression of Christians. Kaylin's agnostic. She knows Grandpa loved alcohol more than God, and Grandma felt more joy abusing her family than praying. She knows what happened on that Christmas. She knows I hate thinking about them because that activates flashbacks. She knows I hate *them*.

Besides, I thought a decade would pass before Kaylin would compliment a guy after her boyfriend, Phil, of four years dumped her last fall. He wanted to date other girls to see if there was someone better out there, and, if not, they could get back together. She told him that was fine because he obviously wasn't her best option.

Dr. Sloan picks up a piece of chalk. Everyone opens their note-books. She decorates the board with descriptions of the different kinds of feminism: liberal, radical, postmodern, and social. Then she dives into the different waves of the feminist movement.

My hand is starting to cramp, but I keep writing. Kaylin removes her glasses and drops her pen. She slips her hand inside her purse for a nacho chip and lets it dissolve on her tongue. She always has food with her and somehow maintains a size-four waist.

Dr. Sloan finally stops writing. "Someone define feminism for me."

Her body bounces with every sentence as if women's studies terms zap her with excitement. She's rotund with sleek carrot-red hair that curls under her chin, and her cheeks are low and pink. Pearl earrings dangle from her ears, and she's wearing black tights and a floral tunic.

In my peripheral vision, Kaylin's right cheek is bloated with a nacho chip.

"Anyone want to try?" Dr. Sloan suddenly turns to Kaylin as if her eyes are contraband magnets. "No eating."

Kaylin snaps her purse closed.

"It's the fight for women's equality," someone calls out.

"It's about social change." That's Josh Wesley. He's the only guy here among the fourteen of us. He was in my sociology class last semester.

"Redefining assumptions about women."

"Is anyone in this room a feminist?" Dr. Sloan asks.

My hand shoots up. Besides Kaylin and me, only two other students raise their hand.

"Wow," Dr. Sloan deadpans, "are we really in 2010?"

I'm not afraid to say I'm a feminist. When guidance coun-selors and teachers nagged everyone to chart their futures in eleventh grade, I wanted to help expectant women in trouble, and women's studies would get me there. So, I pored over the literature by writers like bell hooks, Maya Angelou, Margaret Atwood, and Charlotte Perkins-Gilman. That's when I found my people.

"I'm not a feminist, but I support feministic causes," the woman in front of me chimes in.

Dr. Sloan rolls her eyes. "*Feministic* isn't a word!"

The student who just spoke jumps in her seat.

"Feminist is a noun *and* an adjective," Dr. Sloan explains. "And I was hoping to see everyone raise their hands. I was hoping that, even if this course is an elective for your degree, you care about ending the oppression against women." Her hazel eyes bulge a little.

Someone a few rows behind me says, "I don't attend rallies and hate men."

Dr. Sloan looks frustrated. "Those of you who raised your hands—ever been to rallies?"

We all shake our heads.

"Do you hate men?"

"No," we say together.

Dr. Sloan crosses her arms. "I had a small sample, but I made my point."

I cautiously raise my hand.

She looks over and points to me. "Don't be afraid. Change can't happen with fear."

Kaylin's lips twitch.

"You can't push everyone into feminism," I protest. "This might be some people's first women's studies class. The feminist movement is huge. Everyone needs to decide what they want to stand for."

Dr. Sloan leans against her desk. "Someone here knows how to think critically. Now, can we discuss feminist theory, or will some of you think this is Physics 101?"

Feministic gets up and leaves. Josh snorts from the back of the room.

Without raising my hand, I say, "You're judging everyone's intelligence based on what one person said. Women have been misjudged for centuries. If we do that here, we can't make any progress."

Kaylin's blue-green eyes look like they'll pop out of their sockets. I shoot her a look.

"What's your name?" Dr. Sloan asks.

"Martha."

She strokes her chin. "Martha," she muses. "You said in your introductory email that you're a women's studies major. Correct?"

"Yes."

She walks up to the chalkboard and writes, *What does a feminist look like?* She pauses, then adds *Martha.* She opens a box of chalk and drops the pieces on the board's ledge. "Anyone want to participate?"

Everyone rises from their chairs and ambles to the blackboard.

Mother. Doctor. Sojourner Truth. People of all colors. Josh writes *men.* Kaylin writes her name. I draw an arrow toward mine.

———

"DON'T BE MAD AT ME," Kaylin says once we step out of class. "I thought what you said to Dr. Sloan was really cool."

"That's not it. Some instructors love to say stupid things to stir up"—I make air quotes—"lively discussions."

"Then what's bugging you?"

"Why were you in Ian's corner? You know why I'm uncomfortable with Christianity."

Kaylin pulls me aside to let a group of students pass. "Look, I hate religion too, but it hurts me to see you have so many trust issues. I thought what Ian did was commendable."

"It ... was."

"And does he look like someone who'd do what your grandparents did?"

I remember Ian's eyes pleading with me to accept his apology. Grandma and Grandpa should have looked like that after they brought me home that Christmas morning.

"No, Ian's ... okay."

"Are *you* okay?" she asks.

I lower my eyes and rub the end of my backpack strap between my fingers, a habit I've had since fifth grade. "I'm trying to be okay."

"Do you want to talk about it?"

I shake my head. "Please humor me."

"Come on. Let's devour an extra-large cheese fry."

I reach into my bag for my old biology flash cards and offer them to her. "You have a different teacher, but I hope these help."

"Thanks so much." Kaylin sticks them in her bag and hangs her arm around my shoulders. "Tell your mom you're not crazy for your big purge. You remembered me."

We head for the stairs. "My vault of old schoolwork is always at your service."

9

———

IAN

MARTHA IS on her way to the break room when a line starts to form at my register. She dashes over to her post and calls out, "I can take someone on register two!"

She's in full retail mode. She straightened up the shopping carts by the entrance and shelved returned items without being asked. She persuaded a woman to buy some expensive merino wool yarn for a baby blanket she wants to knit. Then, a few minutes ago, someone gave her an attitude about our coupon policy. Martha told her she needed to follow the rules, even though the woman complained the entire time Martha rang up her order.

Now, it's almost closing. I'm cleaning up the jewelry aisle and see a young guy with blond hair and a sturdy build come to Martha's register with a skein of green yarn.

"Two dollars and eighty-eight cents," Martha says after she scans the barcode.

I hear the magnetic head on the counterfeit detector beep, which means he gave her a fifty- or one-hundred-dollar bill, and, thankfully, it's real. She opens a drawer to get the counterfeit pen to double-check.

"I'm getting this yarn for my wife," the man says. "If I got her the wrong kind, what's your return policy?"

"You have sixty days to bring it back. If you don't have a receipt, we'll give you store credit. There's ninety dollars ... a five ... two singles ..." Martha drops some coins in his hand. "And twelve cents."

"While I'm here, I thought I'd ask you about knitting needles. My wife has an aluminum set but wants to try bamboo. Do you have those?"

"Yeah, they're two aisles over from the yarn."

He pats the skein of yarn. "And do you have this brand in blue?"

I spot a package of charms someone threw in with the bracelets and slip it back on its peg. Something's weird about this guy. Liz warned us about change artists. They pay for something cheap with a large bill and distract the cashier. Then they want to use a smaller amount of money. If he's trying this on Martha and she isn't paying attention, she might give him the one hundred dollars back without asking for the ninety-seven dollars and twelve cents first.

I creep to the end of the aisle. Martha's back is to me.

"Excuse me," a woman says with a Brooklyn accent. "Do you have bungee cords?"

"You're in the right aisle," I answer.

"All the colors in this line of yarn have the same barcode." Martha taps some buttons on the screen and scans the yarn. "We're out, but truck day is on Wednesday."

"Can you hold two skeins for me?" he asks.

Martha writes down the yarn's code. "I need your name and number."

"My name's Scott," he says, and he recites his number. He gave his information, but he might be throwing a red herring at her to build her trust.

"We'll call you next week."

Scott fishes his wallet out of his pocket. "I have a five here. Can I have my hundred back?"

I'm itching to bolt across the store and yell to Martha that Scott needs to return the ninety-seven dollars and twelve cents before she can return his one hundred, but I don't move. She needs to handle this on her own.

Martha's drawer is open. She pulls the one hundred dollars out of its compartment.

Don't be fooled, I silently plead.

She scratches the side of her neck. "I need the change I gave you. Then I'll return your money. My supervisor can void the transaction, and we'll start over."

Scott takes the bag off the counter. He's ready to leave. "Cash handling can be confusing. I used to work in retail."

Martha doesn't buy his empathy. She closes her drawer.

"I already gave you the money," Scott insists.

Martha proved herself, so I step in. "I'll tell you if you did," I say to him as I march to the front.

I log into Martha's register and count her drawer. Its variance is zero.

"You have two options," I tell Scott. "We can leave things as they are, or you give me the yarn and the change, and I'll let you use the five dollars."

"There's something wrong with your system. I gave her the money."

I put a hand on my hip. "I watched you. You never did that. Make your decision so we can close."

The vein in Scott's neck bulges as he scowls at me. "I'll make sure you won't have a job tomorrow!"

"Okay. Have a nice night."

He leans forward and spits at me, leaving a glob of saliva on my hairline. "Go back to China!"

Scott's hate pushes me back. I watch him rush out the door, swinging the bag of yarn at his side.

This isn't about one hundred dollars anymore; it's about power. Scott thinks I don't belong here because of the golden undertone in my skin and the shape of my eyelids. He thinks he can harass me because I'm Asian.

Martha shoves a paper towel in my hand. "Are you going to do anything about it?"

"No." I wipe the spit off my forehead. "What *could* I do?"

"He assaulted you."

"The police have bigger things to worry about, and he didn't steal from your drawer."

I'm used to this kind of aggression. Fourth grade: Trevor Hart threw worms in my face during recess and asked if they tasted like Lo Mein. I slugged him, and we both got detention. Seventh grade: Maria Sorensen threw an empty Chinese takeout carton at me during lunch. Ninth grade: a guy I didn't even know said if North Korea attacked the US, he'd insult me to my face every day until we graduated.

The woman who asked me about bungee cords is ready to check out. "I caught the whole incident on my phone if you need it for anything."

"I'll let it go, but thanks. Just keep it off Facebook."

After she leaves, I lock the store, then hurry over to Martha, who's counting my drawer. I get this unexpected urge to be near her. We had a bumpy start, but our differences didn't matter tonight. We had each other's backs.

"I'm proud of you," I tell her. "Change artists are quick to confuse people."

"Thanks." She counts the nickels and punches the quantity into the calculator on the screen. "I bet his name isn't Scott and he's not married."

"If he is, his wife has to keep those aluminum needles."

Martha stops counting and cracks up. Our humor makes us lock eyes, then Martha goes back to counting tens.

"I'll tell Liz what happened. She'll look at the camera footage so she can identify him if he comes back." I fiddle with a bent corner on a small display of tea lights on the counter. "Not everyone who hands you a large bill for a small purchase is a change artist; sometimes it's the only thing they have, but be alert when that happens."

Martha's done counting the money. "You're twenty cents under."

"Okay." I place the cash drawers in a shopping cart, and we go to the office.

"Do you get attacked like that a lot, like what Scott did?" she asks.

"I used to, in school."

Martha studies my face. "If you don't mind me asking, what's your ethnic background?"

"You mean what country am I from?" I joke in a low voice. "I actually am from another country. I was adopted from Korea. I'm biracial. What about you?"

"My mom's German, and my dad's Russian, Swedish, and English." As I unlock the office, she adds, "I'm sorry your birth parents couldn't raise you."

I'm about to put the cash drawers in the safe, but I stop. What made her say that? Martha isn't fond of Christianity, but she isn't heartless. Remorse shone in her eyes the other day in the bookstore. It softened her features. She almost looked pretty.

She's also the first person to ever apologize for my adoption. When people learn that I'm adopted, they say the usual: "You're one of the lucky ones" or "That's so nice your birth mother wanted you to have a better life." For too long, social workers and adoptive parents have written adoptees' stories and assigned us our feelings. I was spared the oppression Korea would have dumped on me if Omma had kept me. Her friends and family might have cut her off for having a child out of wedlock, and I'd be ostracized for being fatherless and mixed.

But Omma and I lost each other the day I was born. I'm not grateful for that.

"Did you ever try to find them?" Martha asks.

"I did a search through the adoption agency this past summer for my birth mother. The police in Korea couldn't find her."

"That's really sad."

I lock the safe.

"Ian, I'm sorry about what I said in the bookstore."

"I'm sorry for snapping at you after we met." I open the door for Martha, and she pushes the shopping cart out of the office.

"I didn't know retail is so dramatic."

I stick out my hand. "Welcome aboard."

Martha shakes it and gives me a weak smile.

10

MARTHA

I'M three weeks into this semester, and I haven't had a meltdown juggling school and work. I have an hour-and-fifteen-minute gap between classes and work on Tuesdays and Fridays, so I wear my uniform to school. I spend that time eating lunch and reading for women's studies and creative writing, or I study my Russian flash cards. Once I get home, I go straight for my desk and work until all my assignments are done. I take short breaks to work on the spiral scarf I'm knitting for Kaylin for Christmas. Sometimes I'm up until one or two a.m. Phew!

Dad's job hunting. He's even applying to lower full-time positions to get benefits. Mom keeps offering to go to work, but she might have a hard time finding something; she's forty-four with no employment history.

I return home from work after a shift that felt too long. The constant beeping of barcode scanners sounded extra irritating, and customers complained too much about coupons and long lines. I'm ready to open my textbooks and unwind in silence. Suzanna has work soon, so the room is all mine.

Or not.

She's in bed, wrapped in the blankets like a burrito. Her shift at Lombardi's starts in forty-five minutes.

I pull at the covers. "You're going to be late."

She fights me and snaps, "Get lost."

"Lose your attitude."

"I said go! I'll call out."

"Are you sick? Do you need anything?"

Suzanna rolls onto her back. "Yeah, privacy. Leave!"

"You *really* should get your own place," I retort as I grab my creative writing notebook, "because I want my privacy back."

I slam the door and head downstairs. The garage door opens. Mom comes in, dragging green tote bags stuffed with food. The store is giving customers five cents back for every reusable bag they use in lieu of plastic, and those meager savings matter to her.

In her efforts to save more money, Mom has embraced the earth. We used to go out for dinner every Saturday, but restaurants are now forbidden territory. The grocery store's weekly ads are her Bible. She's buying cleaning products in bulk, and Suzanna and I are rubbing coconut oil in the ends of our hair instead of leave-in conditioner after we shower. We're only allowed to shower, run the dishwasher, and do laundry during off-peak hours. A stack of microfiber cloths has replaced paper towels under the sink, and a window stays open in every room, weather permitting, to keep the air conditioning off. I feel honored Mom discarded the sponge at the sink and is using the dishcloths I knit her over the summer. I felt like a child giving her a pointless gift that would take up space and get thrown away in a few weeks, but she thought they were useful enough to keep.

Dad rolled his eyes at these lifestyle changes. He jokes Mom will be churning butter or plucking feathers from a chicken next.

An apocalypse would happen before he acknowledges she's making a difference in their bank account.

"Suzanna's still in bed," I inform her.

Mom clicks her tongue and goes upstairs. "I'm going to kill Carl."

A few nights ago, Suzanna finally told me she and Carl are having trouble starting a family, and it's her body that's the problem. She suffers from anovulation. Fertility drugs failed to help after so many cycles. She was hoping to prove her OB/GYN wrong and conceive, but Carl doesn't want to hope with her anymore.

Suzanna met Carl in eleventh-grade math class. "He's the sweetest thing. He's big but so quiet and shy," she'd told me. "And his eyes are a gorgeous fiery blue." Her grin was so wide, I thought the corners of her lips would stretch past her face. "One day we'll get married, and you'll be my maid of honor."

Suzanna couldn't wait to show him off. Dad hated how Carl wanted to do renovation work with his dad after high school, and Mom thought he wasn't anyone special, but Suzanna told me she felt proud to love him.

I want to love someone that way. But no divorce, please.

They got married after Suzanna's third semester of college, and she never looked back. They were only twenty years old. All she wanted was a brood of children and a happily ever after with Carl.

Now they won't have any of that.

Mom and Suzanna talk in muffled tones. Suzanna chokes out a sob and moans a *no*.

"Don't sleep your life away," Mom says, irritated. "Get up and go to work." She closes the door and comes back downstairs.

"Am I allowed to know?"

"I'll explain after she leaves."

I hold my pencil between my thumb and pointer finger and

flick its ends against my notebook so it looks like a wild seesaw. My story is due in five days, but I have nothing to show.

"I have writer's block."

Mom puts a container of sour cream in the fridge. "You need new experiences."

"Can't. No time. Name someone I'm not." I rest my arms on the counter. "Name the first person who pops into your head."

"It makes more sense to write about yourself."

"I'll leave that for creative nonfiction."

"What's that?"

"It's memoir writing. This needs to be fiction."

Suzanna rushes downstairs and cuts through the kitchen. She snags her lunch bag out of the fridge. There's a tiny stain on the left sleeve of her work shirt, and she's not wearing makeup.

"Work will keep your mind off everything for a while," Mom says.

Suzanna gives Mom dagger eyes and slams the door to the garage with so much force that the floor vibrates.

Mom sits next to me at the island. "Carl wants a divorce."

"Are you serious?" I lean back, as if the news hit me in the chest. "So much for 'in sickness and in health,'" I mutter.

Dad's parents thought they'd never have a baby until Babka got pregnant at forty-two. They were married for nineteen years already and would have stayed married regardless of what their reproductive systems were capable of doing.

Mom nods with a frown. "Suzanna mentioned domestic adoption, but they can't afford that, and Carl's not interested."

Adoption makes me think of Ian. When I apologized to him the other week about his adoption, he looked surprised. I didn't ask why. It's a sensitive topic. I know about the mixed-race children who were adopted after the Korean War. Children are still being shuttled out of the country for a better life. There was a

Korean adoptee in my tenth-grade biology class. Nichole Sutherland was a month old when she was abandoned at a police station in Daegu. She knew nothing about her birth parents. When we had to draw Punnett squares for a trait in our families, our teacher told her to do her best. I'll never forget the sadness I caught in Nichole's eyes.

Mom fingers the corner of my notebook. "You know what? Reach into yourself and rip out the worst Christmas no kid should ever have."

I blink rapidly at the blank page. I'll never untangle myself from what Grandma and Grandpa did to me. No matter how much I'm consumed in school or work, images from that Christmas still invade my mind. I shove them back, hoping they'll tumble into a pit. But they always spring out at me, like a creepy jack-in-the-box that taunts me for thinking I could outsmart the memories from paying me another visit.

"Mom, I can't."

"You don't need to share everything," she points out, "because it—"

I slip off the stool and reach for my notebook. "No."

She pulls me toward her by the arm. "Let me finish. Don't share everything, because—remember—it's fiction."

Well, Professor Guerra said the protagonist usually suffers the most.

11

IAN

"DID you tell Liz about the change artist?" is the first thing Martha asks me when she starts her shift on Friday.

"She looked at the surveillance footage and said we can scratch his hold on the yarn." I tear a sheet out of the holds/special orders binder and crumple it. "He's not allowed in here anymore." She also called Scott a bunch of choice words when I explained what he did to me.

"I think you should have done something," Martha insists. "He knows where you work."

"Yeah." I throw the balled paper toward the trash. Score! "I should have punched him in the throat."

Martha looks shocked, but she doesn't know about the anger that's been eating me up since my childhood. It likes to show its face once in a while.

I shrug. "I'm not a choirboy."

I head for the scrapbook aisle. Liz left us a lengthy to-do list. There are boxes from yesterday's shipment that still need to be unpacked. It looks as if a hurricane ripped through the jewelry aisle. The dollar bins have to be moved closer to the registers to push impulse buying on customers as they wait in line, and the shelves under the registers are dusty. Business is slow tonight, so Martha and I cross everything off the list an hour before it's time to go.

After I check Martha's bag, I lock the store and head outside. I take out my phone and see that Mom left me a voicemail around four fifteen.

"Hi, Ian. I'm calling because Gemma might have a detached retina in her other eye."

Panic races up my spine. Gemma's been seeing a retinal specialist every six months ever since her first retina detached. Dr. Rick always says everything looks good, but symptoms of a retinal detachment can pop up when they want to. When that happens, Gemma has to get checked out ASAP to find out if she needs emergency surgery.

Mom continues. "We're hoping it's a retinal tear. Everything's going to be fine. Gemma recognized the flashes and floaters right away, so things should turn out better than they did the first time this happened."

I sit on the curb. The first time this happened, Gemma was losing vision in her left eye for two weeks but never complained about it. Mom eventually noticed her eye was red and took her to the ophthalmologist. Gemma had surgery the next day. Her retina was reattached, but she only has light perception in that eye.

Martha approaches in her white Ford Taurus and rolls down her window. "What's going on?"

"I got a voicemail from my mom. My sister's having eye problems." I realize she's probably wondering why I'm not in my car.

"Oh. Are you waiting for someone?"

"I'll call a cab."

"Where's your car?"

"My dad's using it. His is in the shop."

Martha reaches across the passenger seat and opens the door. "Need a ride?"

"No, I'm good."

"I obviously passed my background check when Liz hired me. I won't kidnap and murder you."

I stand and walk around the car. The passenger seat is littered with a Russian textbook, a stainless-steel water bottle, papers, and a knitting bag. She tosses everything in the backseat. I get in and give her my address.

Martha drives out of the empty parking lot too quickly. "Did you grow up in Manasquan?"

"We lived in Manalapan, then my dad sold our house last year. We never looked back."

"Why?"

"Bad memories. School was hard." I tighten my seat belt. "Martha, you're supposed to turn here."

She veers sharply to the left. Gemma needs prayer, and I might need some as well, to get home alive.

"My sister used to hang out with a lot of Manalapan girls." Martha flips the subject and asks, "How old is your sister?"

"Gemma's thirteen. We're almost six years apart."

"So, you're nineteen?"

"Correct. What about you?"

"I'm twenty." Her voice drops a notch with worry. "What's wrong with her eyes?"

"She has retinopathy of prematurity. She's nearsighted and had a detached retina when she was eight. Now her better eye might have the same problem."

"Dang. Can her doctor save her vision?"

I wish Martha would stop talking. I'd like to spend this time praying for Gemma. "I hope so."

"Will your little god give you that hope?"

My gut lurches. "Huh?" She's using Gemma's pain to debate about religion.

"I want to know." Martha squeezes the steering wheel. Her knuckles whiten. "Why do you believe in a god that might not give you what you want?"

I don't want to have this conversation, but I answer her anyway. "Whatever happens is his will."

"So why bother praying?"

"Why are you so upset all of a sudden?"

"Can you answer my question?" She sounds like a demanding teacher.

"Prayer isn't just asking God for what you want. You're talking to him or praising him. If he doesn't respond the way you want, he's still faithful."

"I don't see how." She comes to a stop sign. "Which way?"

"Make a left, then your second right."

"You still love him even when he doesn't grant your wishes?" she challenges, returning to our debate.

"He's not a genie. I don't know why he allowed this to happen, but Gemma's going to pull through."

"That's right!" Martha erupts. "He *allows* people to suffer and watches from his fluffy cloud in heaven!"

I make a disgusted face. "Are you okay?"

Obviously she's not.

"Then he expects them to figure out *why* they suffered so they can give inspirational testimonies in front of hordes of lost souls and brainwash them!"

"No!"

"Do you like how he *allowed* your sister to have eye problems?" Martha's brows scrunch, and her forehead creases. "Do you like that he *allowed* your adoption to happen?"

"You're going too far," I tell her in a low voice. "None of that's your business."

This makes her quiet.

Martha pulls into my apartment complex and unlocks the car.

I take out the six bucks in my wallet and offer them to her.

She keeps her eyes forward. "I don't want your money."

"Please take it."

"I said no."

I stuff the bills in my pocket and leave. Martha holds the sides of her head and shudders.

"Did something happen to you?"

She drops her hands to her lap. "We're not talking about this anymore."

I close the door and walk to my apartment. I step inside and linger in the living room. I'm pretty sure God allowed something awful to happen to Martha, and now she thinks he's a sadistic beast.

Her car's still running in the parking lot. I think about checking to see if she's okay, but then I hear her drive off.

Do you like that he allowed *your adoption to happen?*

I press my forehead to the door. "No, I don't." Then I pray for Martha. "God, comfort her in whatever's hurting her, and I hope that one day she learns to trust you."

12

MARTHA

I DRIVE HOME AS QUICKLY as I can without getting a ticket. I know Ian's not a creepy stalker, but I need to get away. I need to be with Mom and Dad.

The thing is, Ian knows something's wrong. He's sensible, confident. That terrifies me. He's trying to twist me open like a nesting doll so he can pull my layers apart and see what's at the core.

But if he thinks he can earn exclusive access to me, he's nuts. My parents, Suzanna, and Kaylin don't even know the whole story.

I sit in my car for several minutes before I go inside. My jaw is clenched, and I breathe heavily through my nose.

Blot out the images and tune out the noise. Switch off my memory. Get out and climb the stairs. Survive.

When I walk through the door, I almost clobber Dad in the head.

"Marty, I was going to drive to your work." He's irritated. "I texted and called you, then I called the store twice and no one answered. Mom and I thought something happened there, or you got in a car accident."

I scoot past him into the kitchen and grab a lemonade from the fridge before sitting at the table. The smell of Mom's home-made pizza suddenly seems like the most beautiful aroma.

"What's the matter?" Dad asks.

"Just a bad day."

He steps back. "Okay."

"I drove a coworker home. I forgot to turn my phone on."

"Who needed a ride?" Mom asks as she slides two slices of pizza in front of me.

"Ian, the guy who trained me. His dad's borrowing his car."

Ian's name feels clunky in my mouth. I owe him an apology. I probably said the number one thing you should never tell an adoptee, and, on top of that, I was harsh about his sister when he just discovered she has a medical issue.

"I'm glad you're ... socializing more," she says hesitantly.

I pause, holding my pizza in midair. Yeah, hurrah. The formerly bullied Martha is expanding her social life. And to guys!

"The HOA sent an assessment for the clubhouse renovations. It's due on New Year's Eve," Mom reminds Dad as she puts pizza ingredients back in the fridge.

Dad sits across from me and glides his finger over the touchpad on his laptop. "I know."

"It's two thousand dollars."

Mom needs to stop counting pennies. Dad takes pride in supporting us, but he'd never pretend things are okay if he can't pay the utility bills anymore.

"Have some confidence in me, Jenn!"

She slides the container of Parmesan cheese onto a shelf and slams the fridge closed. "You're applying to all these jobs. No one's calling you. If I work, I won't worry about money anymore."

I put my pizza down and watch Dad close his laptop and give it to Mom. They share it, which is kind of cute.

"Use it for as long as you want," he says.

Mom pauses. If she's afraid to work, I don't blame her. Her parents didn't care if she finished high school. She only had a short-term babysitting job while she lived with Dad and his parents after she got pregnant.

"Really," Dad says. "I was only checking my email."

"Thanks." Mom takes their laptop and heads into the living room.

Dad rubs his eyes. "I have a master's and have been at the same job for almost two decades. The recession hits, and I'm staring at the checking account every night."

"I don't have to transfer to Montclair. I'll stay home and work."

"No. Get your degree." His voice is raspy with exhaustion. "You'll need it for your pregnancy care center. You promise me you'll do that."

I cut eye contact with him. "I promise."

The pressure pushes on my chest. My ambition always grabbed my parents' hearts. When Mom was pregnant with Suzanna, Grandma told her it was either an abortion (not very Christian, huh?) or adoption, so she moved in with Dad and his parents to keep her baby. The thought of my sister being absent from my life is nauseating, and I love the idea of keeping a child with its parents. But sometimes I wish I was the only one holding my career goal.

"Did you request your transcript for Montclair?" Dad asks.

"Yeah, and I filled out my graduation form." I chew on some pizza crust. "Do you know anything about detached retinas?"

"They're common in people who are nearsighted." He jokes, "Are you wanting to be a retinal specialist too?"

"No. Ian's sister might have one."

Dad's expression falls. "That's too bad." He takes my plate to the sink and wipes the counter with a cloth. "How old is she? Retinal problems usually hit people who are older."

"She's thirteen. Ian said she's already blind in her other eye."

"Poor kid. I hope she makes it through okay."

I run my hands over the sides of my face to mask the embarrassment burning my cheeks. I was so out of line with Ian in the car.

I wonder, is Gemma in surgery now? Was she also adopted? I imagine Ian sitting with his parents in the waiting room. A TV blaring the latest crimes and weather reports keeps them company. His mom and dad sit next to each other, tightly holding hands. The three of them pray to a God they believe could break through the statistics and chances and exceed the work of doctors. They love a God who allowed this medical emergency to attack Gemma's eyes.

But if your daughter or sister might be going blind, you grab on to anything that gives you hope, even if it's a being above the clouds who doesn't really care about your needs and pain. You take hope from whatever makes you feel good, even if it doesn't make sense.

I did that the morning Grandma and Grandpa took me from my parents' house fourteen years ago. God didn't listen to me, so I never spoke to him again.

Dad opens the pantry and scans the shelves. "I'd better go food shopping. We can't snack on pasta, oatmeal, flour, and chicken broth."

I pull the hem of my shirt. "My clothes are getting tight. I eat snacks on campus. Can't bring the contraband home."

"You look the same to me."

I drink some lemonade. "You don't understand body image."

He closes the pantry. "How's work?"

"Okay. Sort of. Ian and I don't always get along."

Dad returns to the table and sits sideways in his chair. "Why?"

A Korean woman materializes in my mind. She holds her newborn son and nuzzles her face against his before she hands him to a social worker. Her steps stretch the space between them. Feet become miles and expand into continents and oceans. Nineteen years pass. Ian's mother hasn't seen him in nineteen years.

I insulted him about the most drastic moment in his life, and he cares about why I'm so angry at God.

I slide back in my seat. "Forget I said anything," I tell Dad.

"You're at work to get things done. Not everyone's going to like each other."

"I know."

His eyes cut into me. He knows there's more going on. He can always read me better than Mom. She and Suzanna are tight, and Dad and I branched off into our own team. He was the first one to hold me after I was born. He's the one who rescued me that Christmas. That horrible day that Ian's Christianity is looping my memory back to. I wish I could cut the circuit and be free.

"Dad, I'm remembering the things Grandma and Grandpa did," I blurt out.

The corners of his mouth dip, and he scratches the back of his neck. "Um, okay ..." He sighs. "It's good you're telling me this."

I sink back in my chair and rub my eyes as if I can wipe out the memories. I want to tell Dad these memories made me harass Ian. That maybe something is wrong with me.

He leans over the table. "Marty, baby, you need some help to cope with this. Mom and I've mentioned therapy—"

"Stop!" I jump out of my seat and dart out of the kitchen, passing Mom on the way to the stairs.

She clicks her tongue. "Marty, what's wrong?"

"I won't ... I can't," I push out of my throat.

I'm trembling. Mom gives a sympathetic "Mmm" and touches my arm, but I jerk away and flee to my room. I lock the door and pound it with my fist.

Mom and Dad talk quietly in the kitchen about that Christmas. I hate when they do this. They always end up fighting. Dad will say I need therapy. Mom will tell him I'm an adult, so they can't force me to go. Dad's afraid I'll have a conniption, but Mom tells him I'm stronger than that. This time, their conversation doesn't escalate past hushed whispers.

I think about Ian. He's been decent, normal, caring. Not like Grandma and Grandpa.

I flick on my lamp. My creative writing notebook is on my nightstand. I glare at it as if it has feelings. My story is due in four days, and I haven't penned a word.

Mom's suggestion comes back to me. *If you don't have any ideas, write about what happened to you.*

I take a pencil from the front pocket of my backpack and grab my notebook. I turn to a clean page and draw a line, a letter, a word.

The old man presses me

Christmas morning crashes into my head. I throw my notebook across the room and curse. It falls like a bird that's been shot and killed and lands facedown with the pages curled underneath its covers.

Tomorrow, I'm withdrawing from creative writing.

13

IAN

I WAKE up at 4:29 and stare at the ceiling fan for too long before I realize I'm not going back to sleep. I grab *Secondhand World*, which is lying next to my pillow, and start reading.

Reading Korean American novels feels as if I'm splitting the characters' homes open like a dollhouse and seeing what it's like to have Korean parents. Or one.

A Step from Heaven lets me imagine what it would have been like to immigrate to the States with my birth parents. *A Cab Called Reliable* reminded me how much it hurts to have a mother abruptly leave you. And *Secondhand World* is letting me know a lot of Asian kids in America get harassed for being Asian, adopted or not. Like Isa, I was on the school bus when I first realized I wasn't like most of the other kids. And, like Isa, I felt so alone. That was the first time I hated someone. His name was Justin Massey.

I get a text.

Hana
I'm up writing a paper. Can you hang out on
your way up to CT?

I call her. "I'd rather hear your voice than read your texts," I say when she answers.

"What are you doing up?"

"I couldn't sleep, so I was reading *Secondhand World*."

"How is it?"

I roll onto my side and prop myself up on one elbow. "If I could drive to my mom's and read at the same time, I would."

"I looked up an excerpt. The first page says her parents die in a fire. I hate when beginnings ruin the ending." I hear a smile behind her exasperation.

"Sometimes the end isn't important; it's how the characters get there that matters."

"I miss hearing you talk about books," she says. "I miss *you*."

Her words wake me a little. They make me believe we can sort through our past and create that happy ending we believed in back in high school. I get out of bed and switch off my alarm.

"So, can we hang out today?" she asks.

"I wish, but I told my mom I'd be there by lunchtime."

"Next week then?" The eagerness in her voice is adorable.

"Next week."

After we hang up, I read two more chapters in *Secondhand World* and take a shower.

When I'm done getting ready, a text rolls in from Dad.

Dad
I'll be home late. Working overtime.
Heading to your mom's yet?

I wrinkle my forehead. I worry Dad's nursing job and long night hours at the Brighter Future Treatment Center are getting to be too much for him.

Was going to wait for you.

Dad
Don't wait. Not sure when I'll be home.
Love you.

My posture sags a little. Dad's graveyard shift leaves us barely any time to see each other.

I'm tempted to stick around, but I want to get to Mom's when I'd promised, so I put what I need for the weekend into my backpack and grab a bagel from the bag on the kitchen counter.

I called Mom back last night to get an update on Gemma. She had a retinal tear, so Dr. Rick did LASIK surgery. Gemma's astigmatism almost landed her in the operating room, but she managed to keep her eye still for the procedure to work. When I asked Mom if I could visit, she said, "Of course. You can come here whenever you want."

That surprised me. Our relationship could improve. She's never been eager to see me. When I was younger, Dad drove me to New Haven a few times a year to visit her. She loved on Gemma but barely paid attention to me. And I hated that Nathan was there. Then Mom stopped inviting me over. Dad got his job at the detox center and was, and still is, worn out. I learned to live without a mom.

It's tough, but I did it as a newborn.

When I reach Mom's, Nathan is outside grilling patties. Mom's mixing macaroni salad while Gemma pulls an extra place mat out of the closet, a reminder that my presence is an exception.

Gemma squeals, "You're here!" and her eyes round when she sees me. A clear plastic shield is taped over her right eye, and the pupil in her left one is off-center and a little red from the retinal detachment six years ago. She tosses the place mat on the table on her way over and gives me a death-grip hug.

"How've you been, Gem?" I ask.

She holds on to me for a few seconds longer before letting go. "Good. Just tired from yesterday."

Mom comes over, holding the salad, and pets my shoulder. "Hi, Ian."

I reach out to give her a side hug, but she turns away and walks to the table.

Mom doesn't show affection. I blame her parents for that. Her younger brother, John, was the golden boy, and Mom was as important as the light fixtures on the ceiling. Uncle John couldn't handle the problems and responsibilities that come with adulthood, so he turned to drugs and alcohol and went in and out of rehab. Instead of using tough love, my grandparents enabled him, which only pressed him deeper into his problems.

Nathan steps inside carrying a plate of burgers. "Hey, Ian!" he booms. If the guy ever has to give a speech in an auditorium, he won't need a microphone. "Thanks for visiting."

"Get in line!" Mom orders.

Gemma and I share a wink. Mom runs her kitchen like a cafeteria whether she's serving four or forty people.

Nathan shoves me forward. I hate when he touches me. "Guests first."

Mom gives him a look. "He's my son."

The way Mom treats me can be depicted with line graphs. She's either distant with me or gets in my corner when Nathan's doing something asinine to me.

Nathan grabs a plate and sighs. He's stout with blond hair brushed to one side and some stubble on his face. He and Gemma have the same deep-set brown eyes. He's mild-mannered and laid back, but in the courtroom he negotiates swiftly, and his mind catches the finest pinhole in the prosecutor's argument.

Too bad he doesn't understand God's laws. He stole Mom from Dad.

We have unspoken assigned seats. Gemma's on my right, Nathan's across from me, and Mom sits next to Nathan.

"How's the new job?" Nathan asks me.

I shoot the inside of a bun with ketchup. "It's good. I trained a new employee the other week."

Mom lifts a forkful of macaroni salad to her mouth. "That's ... nice."

Translation: I'm not impressed with your life.

She folds her arms on the table. "Ian, you're managing school and work just fine. Why is a four-year degree such a problem?"

"I don't love any subject enough to continue."

"I don't understand something." Frustration creeps into her voice. "You listened to your father when he made you choose between community college, trade school, or the military. Why are you against me?"

Frustration creeps up my gut. "Dad gave me options and respects my choice." It takes a lot of nerve to say that.

Mom opens her hands, palms facing upward. "I'm giving you choices. Pick any school in Connecticut. Your father raised you since we divorced, but I'm still your mother. I should also have a say in what you're doing."

I stop before biting into my burger. She barely co-parented me with Dad, and now she's swooping in to control my future. "Mom, I'm nineteen. I've made my decision. I'm not changing my mind."

She points at me with her fork. "You're settling for less because you're lazy and act like a martyr whenever you have to take some responsibility."

Okay. Our relationship veered off the better path. Why did I hope it was headed that way?

"Julie," Nathan cuts in, "he knows how to be responsible. He has a job."

Here goes Nathan, being fake to make himself look like a decent stepdad.

And why can't Mom just appreciate that I'm visiting? If she wants me to take her offer and live here, she's doing a terrible job mending our relationship. She's always been unpredictable though. When my parents were married, there were times when she'd dote on me, then she and Dad started fighting about something. Mom projected her anger on me and yelled at me for not cleaning up my blocks or getting spaghetti sauce on my pants she'd just washed. Then Dad would yell at her for yelling at me.

Nathan clears his throat. Gemma exhales a drawn-out sigh and cups the side of her head in her hand. The ends of her honey-blond hair hit the table. Mom lowers her head. Some of her bangs fall over her face as she dabs her mouth with her napkin.

A memory surfaces of Dad sweeping her hair out of her eyes. He looked at her like she had emerged from a fairy tale.

"What's wrong with my decision?" I challenge Mom.

"We're not talking about this anymore right now," she says dismissively and gets up, "but it's not over."

Mom's done because she's not getting her way. She left Dad because he wasn't dealing with Caleb's death her way. Her selfishness is her torch for burning relationships.

We finish eating. As I clear the table, Mom asks, "Can you pick up a prescription for Gemma?" and hands me some bills. "She's out of Timolol."

"No problem."

Nathan puts a hand on my shoulder. "Thanks, Ian."

I shrink away. Gemma watches me from the edge of the kitchen.

"Can I come?" she asks.

"You bet."

I'm relieved to have some alone time with Gemma.

We grab our sweaters from the coat closet and then leave through the front door and get into my car.

We ride in silence for a bit, then Gemma asks, "You really don't want to go to school here?"

I shake my head.

"Mom's never going to stop bugging you." Gemma crosses her ankles. "She thinks the only way to success is a ton of education. Grandpa forced her and Uncle John into it, so she's doing the same to us."

Uncle John got through a semester of college. My grandparents wanted him to be an engineer, but he squashed that dream with his substance abuse and settled on job hopping. Mom studied education at William Patterson, where she and Dad met. She taught kindergarten until they adopted me. She wanted to go back to work, but she couldn't put me in daycare. I suffered from separation anxiety until I was four and a half. Whether she was running errands or dropping me off at a birthday party, I cried my head off. I thought she'd suddenly vanish like Mrs. Shin did after I came to the States.

Then, one day, Mom did vanish.

When we get out of my car, I offer Gemma my arm, and she takes it.

"Don't let Mom depress you. You do what you want, and I'll be her overachiever."

"Sounds like a plan."

Gemma gets almost perfect grades and has already decided she wants to go to college for special education.

We walk to the pharmacy and wait in line. When it's Gemma's turn, the man behind the counter grins at her. "Shepard, right?"

"Yes," Gemma answers.

He looks through a drawer and withdraws a white paper bag. "Address?"

Gemma recites her address. She lifts the shield off her eye to read the text on the bag to make sure everything is correct.

After I pay, we wind through the store to the exit. "Need anything else here? Makeup? Junk food?"

"Definitely junk food!" she pipes up with a grin. "But not here. There's this new bakery a few blocks away. It's called Bake It Up. Their cookies are *huge*."

"I'm in. Let's go."

When we get there, Gemma orders a sugar cookie covered in buttercream. It's almost as big as her head. I pick a peanut butter and jelly muffin.

"I wish you weren't leaving so soon," Gemma says once we're back in my car. "I hate it when you go."

I chew on some muffin. "Are you okay? Are the kids in school bugging you?"

"I'm fine."

"Really?"

"Uh-huh. Walter's not in any of my classes this year, and Leo got expelled last May."

Last year, those two guys in her history class tormented her. They called her the blind girl and said things like if she got raped, Gemma wouldn't know who did it because she's blind, or, she won't be here in a few years because she'll get hit by a bus.

They only got suspensions for this. It wasn't until Leo stole his math teacher's keys and gave her a death threat for giving him an F on a test that he got thrown out of school.

He and Walter are lucky that assault is illegal. I wanted to send them to the ICU.

"Gemma, I know it's hard living apart."

"You hate my dad," she blurts out. "I see how you act around him. Is that why you don't want to live here?" Gemma's not aggressive; her voice is quiet and sad.

I stop chewing my muffin. I fold up inside but make myself answer her. "He took Mom from my dad, but that's not why I'm turning down Mom's offer. I really don't want to continue college."

"It's not all my dad's fault. Mom's guilty too."

"I know." I crumple my wrapper. "How about I spend Thanksgiving with you guys?"

"Really?" Gemma snuggles against me. "I don't love you to the moon and back."

"Neither do I, and I never will."

On my twelfth birthday, Gemma shouted into the phone, "Happy birthday, Ian! I miss you *so* much!" She made *so* sound a mile long and wanted to tell me a new saying she learned: "I love you to the moon and back."

"That's actually not a good thing."

"Why not?" she asked, surprised.

"We can measure the distance from the earth to the moon, but we can't measure how much we love each other, because it's a lot."

She thought about this. "Oh. Okay. I don't love you to the moon and back." She giggled. Since then, it's been our inside joke.

When we get home, I head for the guest room and take out my American lit anthology. I can't concentrate on John Smith's writings about New England; the conversation I had with Martha last night sticks with me. What did she go through to make her feel the things she does? That's too personal, and she'll never trust me with her story.

But I'm stuck on Martha. I shouldn't be. I don't like her, and she's not my idea of beautiful, but she's magnetic.

14

MARTHA

"WE'RE WORKSHOPPING TODAY!" Professor Guerra announces as soon as she enters the classroom. "Get into groups of three or four. Each person gets a copy of your work to mark up, so you'll have plenty of feedback." She pulls her glasses out of her wheelie bag. "I'll come around and check in on each group."

Some people get out of their seats to meet up with their critique partners. Kyle's on my right. He leans back in his seat and says to Francine, who's next to me, "How about you, me, and her?"

I'm relieved he reeled me into his group. Everyone else here clicks together. They either know someone from a previous class or their common interest in writing forms a kinship that I feel I'm not a part of.

Dad won't let me drop this class unless I'm failing. He said a withdrawal on my transcript during my last semester here would give Montclair the impression that I'm a quitter, and we wouldn't get any tuition money back. He also said leaving a class I don't like won't equip me for the real world.

Francine's story is about a woman who discovers that her older sister, who's fifteen years older than her, is really her mother. Kyle wrote a murder mystery set in Scotland. I only find grammatical errors in their stories. Their work is publishable. Their words flow beautifully, and their characters feel so real.

When it's my turn to read, my voice shakes, and the room suddenly feels too warm. I titled my story "Shattered at Six." I wrote about that Christmas, but I called myself by my middle name, Jene, a blend of Mom and Pop-Pop's names. The story begins when Grandpa carried me into the bathroom. My private pain isn't private anymore, which is terrifying. I try to decode Francine's and Kyle's faces as they read my work, but their expressions stay neutral.

"You grabbed me in the beginning," Francine says when I'm done reading. "'The elderly man presses me to him and says he loves me,'" she reads. "I thought a kidnapper was taking Jene, not her grandfather. But as the story goes on, I'm not feeling the suspense. You barely mention Jene's thoughts and feelings. Like, what is she thinking when she pees in the car? That's an intense moment, but you didn't build it up at all."

I want to be in Russian class. Alyosha tells us what to write about, what to say, and where to place our tongues in our mouths to make the right sounds. In Russian, there are right and wrong answers, but here, nothing I write is safe.

Professor Guerra is walking around to check in with each group. She stops behind Kyle with her hands clasped behind her back.

Francine continues. "I also wanted to know more about her family. Are her grandparents religious zealots? Do they have psychological problems? It's a list of events, not a story."

Her last comment stings. I shouldn't have procrastinated with this, but it was hard reliving what happened. While I typed, my hands fought against my sanity. I wanted to stop the images from coming back, but my fingers tap-danced over the keyboard and couldn't stop until the performance was finished.

"How's everything going?" Professor Guerra asks.

"It's good," Francine answers.

"Fine," Kyle says at the same time as he gives her a copy of his work. Francine and I do the same.

"Any questions?" Professor Guerra prompts.

"No," I answer.

She nods and walks over to another group.

"And, Martha? There's an error throughout your whole story." Kyle moves his pen in an arc over my writing. "You wrote in first person, present tense, but Jene sounds like an adult."

I nod. It feels as if a pile of rocks on my head is falling over. How did I miss that?

"You can rewrite the story in third person or change the word choice to make it sound like Jene's telling it," Francine suggests.

"And your story needs a lot more dialogue. I marked some spots where you could add some." Kyle slides my work toward me. "No one talks until page two. We learn things about characters from their actions *and* how they talk."

I avert my eyes from the lengthy comments he's dropped between the lines and in the margins.

Why did I take Mom's advice? This is fiction; I could have written anything. Jene wants to be a herpetologist. Jene triumphs over her weight loss goal and spirals into a shopping addiction for clothes and goes broke.

Francine hands me her copy of my story. Next to the sentence *Grandma's every move is a curse in my memory,* she wrote *Movements are NOT curses.* In other places, she scribbled things like *What?* or *Huh?* and even said, *I find it REALLY hard to believe Jene's grandma got away with mistreating her in church on Christmas. Christmas services are usually packed!*

My eyes sting. *Believe it, Francine, because it happened.*

I glance at the clock, which reads 1:41. Four more minutes of humiliation before I can drive to NYC Corner and hide in my car until my shift at three.

Work will be awkward with Ian there. He wasn't in on Sunday, probably because Gemma had surgery. I'd better apologize for what I said on Friday. I don't like what he believes, but I shouldn't have been so cruel to him.

"It looks like everyone's done workshopping," Professor Guerra observes over the sound of people zipping backpacks and shuffling papers. "Make sure I have a copy of your story. When I email you my critiques, I want to make an appointment with you during my office hours so we can chat about your writing."

She wants to chat about my writing. Let's add tea and scones. I'll tell her in my sophisticated voice that I feel honored she wants to see my face outside of class.

I'm the first one to leave the room. Dealing with rude customers is a mental health day compared to having your flesh and tears workshopped by complete strangers.

———

IAN IS COUNTING register two with Richard standing by when I walk up to the front after I clock in.

"You were supposed to wait for me before you do that," I remind him.

"Evan's orders," Richard explains. "He's rushing things today."

Ian counts the twenties and hits DONE on the screen. "Five cents over."

Richard signs the variance. "I made us some money."

"I guess you could look at it that way," Ian mumbles.

I want to ask him how Gemma's doing, but he slips the price

gun's strap across his body and says, "Page me if you need anything," before he heads to the paint aisle.

Twenty minutes into my shift, a thin woman with a dark-blond braid over her shoulder carries two floral arrangements to my register. "I'm paying for these separately. I have two coupons."

"I'm sorry. It's one coupon per day per customer."

"Look, I'm in here *all* the time. Make an exception, will you?"

"I can't do that."

She pushes the coupons toward me and takes out her credit card. "I don't have time to argue. Do your job and ring up my order the way I asked."

"I can't."

"I'm not moving until you let me use two coupons."

So much for having no time to argue.

"Can I speak to someone about this?"

I reach for the phone and page Ian to my register.

The woman doesn't even give him a chance to speak before she stomps her foot and whines, "Your name tag says you're a supervisor! I want a manager!"

"I'll get a manager," Ian says sternly and calls Evan on the portable.

"What's the problem?" Evan asks her in a kind voice I've never heard him use before.

"I want to use two coupons for these arrangements," she explains in a tone that's just as pleasant. "They're for someone who died, and she's refusing to accommodate me."

Evan glares at me, but Ian looks surprised.

"I didn't—"

"Martha, let her use two coupons," Evan orders.

"She didn't say they—"

"Do what I said," he demands over his shoulder.

I ring her items up in two transactions, and Ian bags her order for me.

"Have a good one," I say.

She yanks the receipt out of my hand so fast, it almost gives me a paper cut across my palm. "See how easy it is when you're nice?" She grunts and walks away.

Ian folds his arms. "Wow. The first time I see Evan show kindness to anyone, he rewards bad behavior."

"Yeah, and she didn't tell me those are for someone who died."

"I know. She manipulated the situation to make you feel guilty." He takes off the price gun. "Jamie forgot to take some of the old sale signs down. If I didn't notice, customers would have begged us for cheaper prices."

"You just added a day to my life," I joke.

"Let's hope for two or three more." The Greg Kihn Band's "The Break Up Song" is playing. Ian gets caught up in humming its refrain and tapping his fingers on the counter.

"Hey, I was wondering—"

I'm interrupted by a man coming to my register who is hugging a few tubes of paint against his stomach while holding a crying boy in his other arm. It's that tired, helpless wail you can't get mad at a kid for. My movements are swift as I ring up his order so he can get home and put his son down for a nap. A dark pink line bleeds down his receipt.

Ian hands me a new roll of paper. "What were you saying before?"

"How's Gemma doing?"

"She's all right. She had a retinal tear, so she needed LASIK surgery. She had some trouble keeping her eye still, but the doctor got things done."

I close the printer. "I was worried. You weren't here on Sunday."

"I took the day off to spend more time with her and my mom."

I take this in. "So your parents are—?"

"Divorced? Yes." Ian hangs some bags on the rack next to his register before he heads for the break room. "Gemma's from my mom's second marriage. They live in New Haven, and I'm with my dad."

There are no customers around, so I call out, "Ian, wait."

He stops and faces me.

I knot my fingers over my stomach. "I'm sorry about what I said on Friday. I don't know Gemma, and your adoption isn't my business."

Ian traces a fold in a tag hanging from a shelf that says PRICE DROP. "It was pretty low, Martha. One of the worst things anyone's said about my adoption."

I stare at the floor to avoid the hurt in his eyes.

"But I forgive you."

The heat runs to my face and slides down my neck. "It's that easy for you?"

"Not usually." He starts walking away. "Whatever's hurting you, I hope you feel better."

I almost thank him. His response is the nicest thing a Holy Roller has ever said to me.

15

IAN

MY EYES SNAP OPEN. It's 6:47. My shift starts at eight. I must have forgotten to set my alarm before I conked out at two this morning after cramming for tomorrow's German test.

It's September 29. Yesterday was my Adoption Day. Today is Caleb's birthday.

Dad's mixing waffle batter when I rush into the kitchen.

"I overslept."

"I thought you could use the extra rest, so I didn't wake you up," he explains.

I take the buttermilk out of the fridge. Dad always forgets this makes pancakes light and fluffy, not milk.

"I know how to make waffles."

I hold up the buttermilk.

Dad drops the whisk in the bowl of dry ingredients. "You win."

I usually get up at six to make breakfast before Dad gets back from the detox center. This has been our routine since the original nurse quit five months ago.

"How was work?" I ask.

"A patient tried to fight with me, a health technician stole a patient's cell phone when she was checking him in, and then a guy threw up in his wife's car on their way to the center." Dad scoffs before pouring his coffee. "She insisted we clean it up, and she got her way."

"Oof. Sorry, Dad."

The waffle maker beeps. Does Dad remember my Adoption Day? Mom hasn't mentioned it for years, but Dad never forgets. I didn't eat breakfast with him yesterday; he worked overtime, because his work is short-staffed. And we didn't eat dinner together; I had a closing shift. But he could have texted me. Hana did.

> **Hana**
> Isn't today the day you came to the US?
>
> Yeah. Having a lot of feelings about it.
>
> **Hana**
> I'm just glad you're here!

A lot of people are glad I'm here. What if my birth mother isn't?

"I'm sorry I didn't mention your Gotcha Day," Dad says.

I hold the ladle in midair as batter drips into the waffle plate.

"Ian, I didn't forget," he assures me and sits at the table.

"I thought you did."

"Did your mom call you?"

I shut the waffle maker. "No. She doesn't acknowledge my Adoption Day anymore."

"I was afraid of that." Dad presses his fingers against his eyes. "I'm going to call her today."

Dad and I used to eat at our favorite Korean restaurant on my Adoption Day. The tradition died when I was in middle school.

Dad got really quiet and tired around this time of year. I knew it was because of Caleb, and my parents losing their firstborn was more important than filling my stomach with bibimbap.

But I ache too, for different reasons.

"I'll call Gemma," I say. She's usually beside herself on Caleb's birthday. It bothers her that she never got to know her half-brother.

"Your mother and I should spread Caleb's ashes. I'm going to ask her again. It's time."

Mom took Caleb's ashes with her when she left, along with his stuffed bunny, blanket, and the pictures they took at the hospital. I remember his stuffed bunny. It was white and floppy. My parents used to let me hug it once a year on September 29.

I put breakfast on the table. "I think that will give everyone some closure."

Dad breaks his waffle into four pieces. "Every time I ask her to do this, I feel like I'm trying to make peace with North Korea."

"Dad?"

"Yeah, Ian?"

"Call it my Adoption Day, not my Gotcha Day."

He's about to drizzle syrup on his second waffle, but he sets the bottle down. "Is something bothering you?"

My parents went to an adoption information session in New York before they began the process. The social worker assured everyone that the moment the plane's wheels lifted off the runway in Korea, the birth parents couldn't reverse the adoptions. Eighteen years ago today, I was still on Korean soil. So, technically, Omma still had a few hours to get me back if she wanted to.

I tighten up inside. "Gotcha Day sounds like you and Mom beat Omma in the race of who can have me forever."

Dad looks lost. The first time I saw him wear this expression, he'd just found out Mom wanted to stay with Nathan. Before she left, she was reading *Little House on the Prairie* to me, so I call it the "lost in the prairie" look.

"I won't say Gotcha Day anymore if you're offended."

My muscles can't relax. Dad needs to know how the grief clobbered me last summer when the social worker said Detective Jeong in Korea couldn't find Omma. I expected the psychology major in Dad to nudge him to ask me if I was okay. I wasn't, and I couldn't tell him.

I finish my waffle, drink some orange juice, and rise to go into the bathroom. "I have to get ready. I'm opening the store."

In the bathroom, I press my toothbrush hard against my teeth, dig my fingertips into my skin when I wash my face, and turn the faucet all the way to the right to make the water ice cold when I rinse. It feels good to feel numb. I comb my hair. Walk out.

Dad's scrubbing the waffle plates at the sink. He heaves a sigh and takes a long pause before resuming.

Caleb's birthday month is always hard on Dad, harder than he'll ever admit.

I swipe my keys off the counter, which jolts Dad out of his thoughts.

"Dad, you okay?"

"I'm good." He gives me a faint smile. "Just spent from all this overtime. A new nurse is starting on Monday, thank God."

He always plays down his pain.

"All right. See you tonight. Love you."

"Love you too. I'm here to talk if you need someone to listen."

As I walk to my car, I consider going back, telling Dad I *do* need to talk, but I push this away. I reach work a few minutes early, so I stay in my car. I can't rip the truth out of me. That would mean admitting to Dad I'm glad he's my father and I'm grateful for my life here, but sometimes I wish I wasn't adopted.

16

MARTHA

ALYOSHA TOSSES five verbs on the board at the beginning of class and asks volunteers to come up and conjugate them. I stay seated. I'm afraid I'll make a mistake, and everyone will know it was me. But today he includes an irregular verb, *davat*, meaning "to give." That was in a dialogue we read last week.

No one's claimed it, so I saunter up to the board. I'm the last one to finish writing.

When Alyosha gets to my verb, he taps each line with his chalk as he reads. "*Horosho, Marfa*," he says when he finishes. "I put this up there as a challenge. Thanks for taking it."

That small victory is a ray of sunlight poking through storm clouds.

This morning was rough. Mom isn't getting any interviews for the slew of jobs she applied to and is afraid the bank account will dry up. Dad got angry at her for obsessing over finances. Suzanna yelled at them for fighting and said Carl hired a divorce attorney. Dad called Carl a bunch of foul names, and Suzanna yelled at him some more. Mom made a snide remark about Suzanna and Carl not having much money anyway, which made Suzanna burst into sobs, and Dad yelled at Mom.

I finished my oatmeal and drove to the grocery store for some snacks, then headed to school. I sat in the library, where I memorized fifty new vocabulary words and conjugated seventeen verbs before Russian class. An hour went by before Mom texted me to find out where I was. Does she have one or two daughters?

"Open your books to page thirty-three," Alyosha says. "We're reading a dialogue with vocabulary about languages and nationalities. Sasha, you be Tanya. Roman, read Oleg's lines."

I wish Babka were here. She passed away when I was seventeen, five months after Pop-Pop died. I wish I could show her my Russian quizzes with perfect scores and all the extra work I've done in my notebook. She would have been my conversation partner outside of class, and my speaking skills would have accelerated.

"Marfa, read Lyudmila's response to Oleg's question."

My eyes search the page.

"It's toward the end of the dialogue."

"Oh. 'Oleg, *ya tolka govoryu arabsky yazik choot-choot.*'"

"Translate, please."

"Oleg, I speak Arabic a little."

"*Otleechno,*" Alyosha says.

Roman continues reading Oleg's lines.

We spend the second half of the class taking a two-page quiz, filling in the blanks with verbs and adjectives.

After everyone hands in their work, Alyosha calls me over to his desk. "You're doing fantastic in the class. You have the highest average, and your handwriting is better than some native speakers'."

I blush. "*Spaseebo.*"

"I want you to participate more." He gathers the quizzes into a neat pile and tucks them into a manila folder. "It can really help your speaking."

"I'll do that," I promise eagerly.

"When are you graduating?"

"In December."

Alyosha bends forward, curling his fingers around the sides of his desk. "Have you thought about continuing Russian?"

"Not really. I applied to Montclair for women's studies."

"They have a Russian minor. You'd get to the advanced level. Think about it. Languages get you places."

I nod in agreement and fiddle with one of my backpack straps. "I'll definitely think about it."

More like *dream* about it. Continuing Russian requires money. I can't dish that out now unless I use what I'm saving for grad school.

Alyosha finishes packing up and hangs his messenger bag on his shoulder. "No pressure," he says with a grin, "but I think you're cut out for this."

We exit the classroom, bid each other *do svidaniya*, and go our separate ways.

I mull everything over as I walk to my car. A minor wouldn't equip me to dissect Anna Akhmatova's poetry with native speakers, but I'd go beyond talking about myself and the weather. And, if I really excel, a Russian minor might be enough to let me apply to a graduate program.

The excitement rising inside me quickens my pace. I remember something Babka told me when I was in seventh grade. I had to do a history project on a country, and I picked Russia. Babka laughed and said, "Russia has such a dark history, strong people, and a rich language. You can't fit that in a report."

I couldn't, but I'll squeeze as much as I can into this minor. I put my arms around myself as if Babka is squeezing me in those secure, tight hugs she used to give to everyone she loved.

Mom and Dad can't pay for additional credits. It's time to break into my savings account. This Russian minor is happening.

———

WHEN I GET to NYC Corner after class, I stay in my car and pull out my laptop to check my school email. The latest message is from Professor Guerra with the subject "Feedback on your short story."

It feels like a furnace is blasting inside me as I open the email.

```
Hi Martha,
My critique for "Shattered at Six" is in
the attachment. Please let me know when we
can meet during my office hours. I have
some flexibility on Wednesdays and Fridays
from 1 to 3 p.m. Thanks!
Prof. R.
```

I hit Reply and say I'm available at two o'clock on Wednesday. I click on the attachment at the bottom of the email and brace myself for her comments.

She put a long comment next to the first line of my story. I can't even write a decent beginning.

I think dialogue will bring the scene to life, Professor Riley wrote. *It seems unnatural for Jene's grandfather to say nothing to her when he wakes her up. What is Jene thinking and feeling at this point? Is this normal for him to do this? Do her grandparents stay at her house every Christmas Eve?*

What really happened when Grandpa shook me awake flashes

before me. I slam my laptop closed. I want to hurl it through the windshield to kill my story, but that won't destroy the memories branded on my mind.

My maternal grandparents were the worst people I've ever known. Growing up, Mom said Grandpa was always filling the recycle bin with beer bottles. He didn't come back some nights after his accounting job, but he made sure to be home Sunday mornings for church because he was an elder. Meanwhile, Grandma constantly beat Mom and Uncle Tim but ran a women's prayer group and coordinated the church's charity events. She slapped Mom across the face for thinking that Grandpa was with another woman those nights he didn't come home. She burned Uncle Tim's arm with a hot iron to get him out of bed for church one morning when he was ten.

Mom got her ears pierced on her eighteenth birthday. Grandma beat her and put her in a chokehold. Grandpa pried her off Mom. That was the nicest thing he ever did for her. Mom ran away to Dad's. Pop-Pop was on a business trip, and Babka was visiting a sick friend. Three weeks later, Mom discovered she was pregnant with Suzanna.

When I was six years old, my grandparents stayed overnight on Christmas Eve. Grandpa shook me awake while my parents and Suzanna were still sleeping.

The numbers on my clock read 5:58. "It's not eight yet." I pouted. That's when my parents said I could wake them up to open presents.

"Be quiet!" he whisper-shouted and pulled me out of bed. He carried me down the hall.

This is the opening I wrote in my story.

I eyed my parents' closed door. Suzanna was in there too, wrapped in her sleeping bag. Guests always used her room for its private bathroom. I extended my arm with my fingers spread out as if I could touch their door. It made no sense, but I was desperate.

Grandpa pushed me into Suzanna's bathroom. Grandma was there, holding a velvet evergreen dress.

"Isn't this pretty, Marty?" She was bent over a little and held the dress by its collar against her legs.

"Yeah," I answered in a monotone, rubbing my eyes.

Grandma knelt in front of me and gathered the dress at the neck.

I pulled off my pajamas. I remember Grandpa staring at us from where he sat on the bed, his frame big and shadowy.

"Grandma, I'm cold."

"Come, baby," she beckoned. She brushed my hair and pulled at a knot.

I grabbed the edge of the vanity to keep my balance. "Ow!" My eyelids felt like heavy shades that wanted to drop down and block the lights over the mirror. My excitement over what Santa left for me under the tree had kept me awake most of the night.

Grandma pulled at my hair again.

"I want to go back to sleep!"

"But we're going somewhere," Grandma said, twisting my hair into two braids.

"I want—!"

Her hand went to my mouth, and she put her face next to mine. "You're going to wake everyone up," she hissed. "If you're quiet, I'll give you cookies."

I saw her hand covering my mouth in the mirror. She held it there too long.

Grandma shot several mists of hairspray over my head. I pinched my nose to block out the overwhelming smell.

Grandma led me downstairs with Grandpa trailing close behind. She held my wrist so tightly I could barely move my fingers. The veins bulging underneath her skin looked like the lines on a map. When I tried to pull free, she applied more force.

"I'm cold," I told her again. "I want my jacket."

We stopped at the closet in the foyer and put on our coats. When we piled into the car, I noticed red lines on my wrist.

Grandma withdrew a stack of cookies from her bag and dangled them in my face as if she were trying to hypnotize me. "Here, because you're such a good girl."

I reached for the bag and stabbed the plastic with my finger. I didn't ask Grandma and Grandpa where we were going, nor did I think about Mom and Dad. I assumed they knew where I was. I cared about what made me happy, and it was food.

They took me to Seed of Faith Church. The parking lot was almost full, but Grandpa found a spot in the corner farthest from the building.

Grandma gripped my arm and squealed, "We found a spot. See, Marty? God wants you here."

I'd never gone to church before, so everything was unfamiliar and strange. When everyone bowed their heads to pray before the service, I asked Grandpa why they looked sad. I thought the song "O Come, O Come, Emmanuel" was sad too.

When I told Grandma I had to use the bathroom, she said, "Hold it in. You'll insult God if you leave." I didn't understand why this place was so special if all I was supposed to do was sit there and listen to things I didn't understand.

I lay down on the pew. I desperately wanted to sleep, but I couldn't with the noise around me and the pain in my bladder.

A man wore a black suit and stood at the front of the church, talking in a calm voice. He said, "Jesus loves you." I remember the words *God, son, perfect, gift,* and *die.* My six-year-old mind knew dying was terrible. I never forgot how Kaylin cried after leukemia took her aunt's life. But why was death a gift? Mom would later tell me Christians believe God sent Jesus, his son, to die on the cross for everyone's sins. You had to believe this to go to heaven. Mom thought her parents were cruel to think Jesus was the only one who could get you there. She said that wasn't love.

I slipped my fingers between my legs.

Grandpa turned and looked at me for a long moment before he leaned over and smacked my arm. "Sit up."

"I have to go to the bathroom," I whispered as I returned to a sitting position.

He ignored me and faced forward again.

When the service finally ended, I jumped off the pew to follow Grandma and Grandpa out. Grandpa leaned over and whispered something in Grandma's ear. She looked at me over her shoulder. Her eyes were narrow slits, and her mouth was a thin line. "We Three Kings" was flying out of the organ in the front of the church. That song always reminds me of the evil I saw on Grandma's face.

I ran ahead of them. I wanted to go home to Mom and Dad and open presents. And I *really* needed a toilet.

I stepped into the foyer and saw the blue sign on the wall with the stick figure wearing a dress. My fingertips grazed the doorknob, but Grandma's bony hand closed around my wrist.

"No, Marty. Public bathrooms are disgusting."

"I gotta go!"

"No!" she grunted, pulling me toward the exit.

When we got to the car, I scrambled behind the passenger seat. I had just buckled my seat belt when Grandma started screaming at me.

"Why would you touch yourself between your legs, especially in God's house!"

"I have to go to the bathroom!" I screamed as loud as I could. Then I pointed at Grandma. "*You* wouldn't let me go!"

Her jaw was set as she smacked my hand away. "We took you

to church so you'd learn some values, but you're just like your mother!" Grandma slapped my face. "Disobedient and immoral."

This was the first time anyone had hit me. The emotional and physical pain shocked my body. I held my cheek and started crying. "I want my mommy and daddy!"

"Jesus loves you," the man in the black suit said.

So, Jesus could have saved me, right?

Jesus? Do you see her hitting me?

Grandma screamed about my parents. I remember the word *harlot* and the name King Herod. I didn't know who she was referring to. They sounded like villains from a Disney movie. Her constant yelling shook me with terror, and I couldn't stop crying. Grandpa's voice occasionally cut through Grandma's rage. Maybe he was trying to calm her or defend me, but whatever he said did nothing to de-escalate the situation. I was so scared, I pulled the door handle even though the car was moving. I wanted to jump out and run home.

Then my bladder had had enough. I relieved myself.

Grandma's eyes went wild. "Look what you did, you wicked girl!" She smacked my cheek again.

"You hit me!" I shot back, holding the side of my face.

Grandma insulted my parents and me during the entire ride home. Never Suzanna, for some reason. I heard *swine* and *heathen*. Grandpa didn't say anything else as he drove. I sobbed, then whimpered until I lost all my energy and slumped over, like a cloth doll.

Grandma didn't stop her angry rampage until Grandpa turned in to our development. She sat up straight in her seat as if nothing had happened.

Seeing my house come into view was more exciting than gifts from Santa. When the garage door began to open, Dad ducked underneath it and ran toward the car. I smacked the window with my palm. "Daddy, get me out!"

Dad pulled the door handle. "Gabe, Eleanor, let her go!"

I stopped hitting the window and turned around. Grandpa didn't move. Grandma put her hands in her lap and looked at me. The corners of her lips lifted into a grin.

She and Grandpa were evil. And so was God.

"I'm going to break the window!" Dad shouted through the glass.

"Oh, David," Grandma chided. She reached over me to unlock the door. "You always overreact."

Dad lifted me out of the car. The bitter air made my teeth rattle, my legs were soaked with urine, and my tear-stained cheeks stung from Grandma's slaps. Dad's eyes moved in all directions as he looked me over. Years later, he told me he knew I had been hit. There were red handprints on my right cheek.

I slipped my arms around Dad's neck and threaded my fingers together. I knew Grandma couldn't tear me from his arms, but the fear wouldn't leave me.

I don't remember what he said to my grandparents, but he wanted answers.

Grandma told him they did the best thing for me and that I couldn't always get my way. She said my parents were doing the real harm, keeping me from God.

"No one in that church sees the demons inside you," Dad told her, "but we do."

Mom darted through the garage, holding a suitcase in each hand. She went around their car, opened the trunk, and threw their things inside.

"Jennette," Grandpa grumbled in a warning tone.

Mom rounded his side of the car and screamed at him, which made me cry again. Dad carried me inside. Mom screamed so loud, our neighbor Sydney panicked and rushed out of her home to console her. Mom screamed even after her parents' car sped down the street.

When Dad brought me upstairs to the bathroom, Suzanna poked her head out of her room. "What happened? Where'd they take Marty?"

"Not now," he said over his shoulder.

In the bath, I played with foam soap and an empty shampoo bottle. I pretended to make a magic potion that would turn my grandparents into worms.

I crept downstairs after my bath and stopped on the landing.

Mom was kneeling in front of the fireplace like it was an altar. She threw two black books inside and lit a match. Its flame kissed the pages' golden edges.

"Your parents are going to kill you," Dad said.

Mom gave him a solemn look. Behind her, the flame evolved into a dragon that slithered down one of the books' spines. "I'm not afraid of them anymore."

Babka and Pop-Pop came over around lunchtime. Babka had made me a doll, which I named after her.

Katya's eyes were brown buttons from one of Pop-Pop's old shirts, and her scarlet-red hair was made of yarn, which Suzanna wove into a braid for me. Babka also sewed a pale-blue dress that was dotted with pink roses for her.

Mom prompted me to thank Babka, but I only snuggled Katya against my chest.

I carried Katya around the house all day. Mom didn't even scold me for bringing her to the dinner table, and when I dropped a piece of prime rib on her dress, Mom rubbed the stain off with a sponge and placed her back in my arms.

Dad tucked me in that night. I grabbed Katya by the arm and burrowed under the blankets.

He pushed some hair behind my ear and asked, "Marty, sweetie, can you tell me what Grandma and Grandpa did?"

All I said was, "Grandma yelled a lot, and she hit me."

But I didn't tell Dad everything—not what happened when Grandpa woke me up. Grandpa warned me that if I did, God would tell him, and I'd be dumped into a very hot pit after I died called hell.

Dad sat with me for a while, then tucked the covers under my chin and left.

I hugged Katya and said, "Sorry I pulled you by the arm. I know it hurts."

17

IAN

"TWO VANILLA ICE CREAM CONES," the man behind the counter says as he holds them out to Hana and me.

We each take one and thank him. After we walk out of the creamery, Hana sits on a bench with her back against the table.

"Can I see the list?" she asks as I take a seat next to her.

I reach into my jeans pocket with my free hand and give her a folded piece of paper.

"'2010 Reading Challenge,'" she muses and turns it over. "You're going to finish this before New Year's?"

"Seventy-eight down, twenty-two to go. I made it up from all the classics book enthusiasts talk about."

"You read *The Bean Trees* for summer reading in ninth grade."

"Okay, I admit I skimmed through that one." I bite the side of my ice cream cone. "I really got into *American Born Chinese*."

"*The Bean Trees* has a sequel, *Pigs in Heaven*." Hana folds the list and hands it back to me. "And let me save you some time. *The Great Gatsby* isn't worth the hype."

"What do you recommend?"

Hana touches her chin. "*The Stepford Wives.* You'll really like the ending."

I nod.

"You should apply to a bookstore again, especially with the holidays coming up. You've been in retail for three years. And with all the record-keeping you do for pleasurable reading"— she points to her head—"you have a lot of book recommendations and discussions stored away."

I've been keeping reading notebooks since third grade. I record when I read a book and write something memorable about it or some kind of remark. My first entry was for *Harriet the Spy.* I wrote, *Harriet's parents taking her notebook away is like taking her brain.* I also write lists, like "The 5 Books I'd Take to a Deserted Island," which I update every year, or "The Book I'd Hide if *Fahrenheit 451* Were to Come True." I still haven't decided which book I would hide.

I eat some ice cream. "Actually, I want to stay where I am for a while."

Hana's eyes widen. "Why? I thought once you got promoted you were going to job hunt again. You said you hoped supervising would make your resume stand out."

I pocket my reading list. I suddenly feel boxed in, probably because this shadows the argument I've been having with Mom about college.

"Liz is a good manager. She's direct, knows her stuff. I'm learning a lot. Not just about returns and exchanges. I'm seeing what goes on behind the scenes of a business. And I have friends there."

Hana chews on what's left of her cone and turns this over in her head. "Do you want to keep that job for years or ...?" She moves her hand in a circular motion.

"What are you getting at?" I chuckle to lighten the mood. "You don't want to tell people your boyfriend sells knitting needles and kids' crafts?"

Her gaze sinks to her lap. "I don't think ... Ian, you're not ..." Hana squints at me. "Driven."

My stomach balls up, and I pull back a little. "What makes you say that?"

In the corner of my eye, I spot the couple at the next table staring at us. Apparently, Hana and I have become their live entertainment.

"I thought getting back together was going to be comfortable. I thought we had it good enough to make it this time. But I feel like we're going backward." Hana takes her napkin. She wipes her eyes and shudders. "It doesn't feel right."

No. God, please no. I'll keep trying. We'll keep trying.

My teeth shatter my cone. "Hang on. Can we back up?"

"Ian, you're the same person you were when we broke up." Hana flings her hands toward me in frustration. "Same kind of job, same salary." Her face crumbles. "Same religion."

My posture sags. I knew there was more to her picking me apart.

She's getting on my case like Mom does. Her love is shallow, and I'm not sure Hana's is much deeper.

"Do you want me to get a better job? We're only nineteen. We still have a lot of time to grow."

I stop there, even though I want to say more. Grow more before we plan a life together. Get engaged. Tie the knot. But it's not worth discussing any of this right now because it's not going to happen.

"I have my internship with a science magazine in the city. I'm graduating early. I'm going places—literally—and you're ... not."

I grab Hana's napkin from her and crumple it into a ball. "Come on. I'll take you back to Montclair."

"Don't be so defensive. I'm trying to help you." Hana stands and follows me to the trash can, her voice pleading. "I like your career goal. I just want you to do more—because I know you can do it."

I'm seething as I throw our garbage out, and we get into my car. The sun burns into the horizon. I'd love to melt with it.

I get behind the wheel. "You sound like my mom. You think I'm stuffing my life in a trinket box."

"You are." Hana frowns. The sadness in her eyes shows how disappointed she is in me.

"This is all you're getting." I point to myself. "I'm not enough?"

"You want to stand behind a register, and I'm becoming a marine biologist. I'm getting articles published."

"I like to read; you like to write. We're galaxies apart," I scoff. I'm shaking as I start the car.

We ride in an uncomfortable silence until Hana says, "We both know this can't work. You want me to follow Jesus, but you used your religion to hurt me. You use it to force me to be someone I'm not."

My hands tighten around the steering wheel. She touched the central pain point in our relationship. We must face it, try to heal it, or agree that it will sting forever.

"We can't do this anymore, Ian. We can't return to how things used to be. We want different things."

I wish I could close my eyes and let this settle in, because she's right. But I stay focused on the road.

"Remember senior year?" Hana goes on. "You said you'd offend God if we had sex, but you didn't think about how you hurt me."

"I did, Hana!"

"You went on about how we were sinning, how you wanted to respect your future wife, how I needed religion too. I would have been fine if you said you weren't ready, but you made me feel so *dirty*." She spits out her last word.

I'm at a stoplight, so I face her. "It's both our faults. I wanted it too."

Hana rests her arm on the door handle and rubs tears off her eyes. "You didn't bug me about your religion until then. No matter what you say, I'm always going to believe you thought I was worse than you for initiating sex." She breathes out the rest of her sentence. "And ... it hurts."

"Hana ..."

"I hoped you realized how much was at stake after you found God and you'd love me no matter what I believe." She squeezes her hands in her lap and sits up straight. "That's why I tried to reconnect with you. I thought you grew up. I was very wrong."

Hana's words are like an airbag slamming me in the face.

"You're going to spend your life thinking *your* religion is the only way," she continues. "That's not love, Ian. Love is accepting people for who they are."

"I love you. I *really* love you, but ..." My voice shakes. I want to pull over, be still and have some more time with her, but I keep driving. "I need to put God first, and I want to be with someone who can do that too. I understand this looks selfish, but it's ... Hana, it's the greatest kind of love."

She crosses her arms and looks out the window. "I'll never understand that, and we can't force each other to believe in things we don't want to."

When we arrive at her residence hall, I turn in my seat and ask her, "So, what do we do?"

She grabs her purse off the floor of the car and pushes some hair behind her ear. "I think we should make a clean break."

I lean back and draw out a breath. "I assume you don't want to come to Morgan and Zack's wedding."

"No," Hana croaks. "Ian, I'm sorry." She strokes my arm. This is probably the last time we will ever make physical contact. "We shouldn't pretend."

I reach in the backseat for my backpack and pull out *Second-hand World*. "Here. I have to give this back to you."

"Did you finish it?"

"Yeah. I want my own copy."

Hana takes the book and starts getting out of the car, then turns and says with a grin, "You want your own copy so you can mark it up."

I try to smile back. "You're right."

Before she leaves, she adds, "Take care, Ian."

"You too, Hana."

She shuts the passenger door. I watch her shuffle up the side-walk and disappear into her building.

I took Hana out for ice cream today as a throwback to our first date at the mall. Nostalgia is unreliable. It felt good, then I realized I can't revive old comforts. Hana and I could eat gallons of ice cream and cook until we smelled of oil and garlic, but the stability we once had is long gone. She wanted the old me back; I wanted her to change. We can't have a relationship with fantasy versions of each other. Love needs to be real. All of it.

———

TWO YEARS AGO, Hana and I lied to our parents so we could have some privacy to sin. We said we were hanging out with our friends, Steph and José, after prom. Dad was in Philadelphia, visiting Grandpa, who was recovering from heart surgery, and Halmoni needed help with some maintenance in their condo.

Dad texted me as Hana and I stepped inside my house.

"He's on his way home," I told her. I flung my suit jacket over a kitchen chair. "We don't have a lot of time."

Hana surveyed the house. Boxes were stacked in the center of the living room. Dad sold the dining room set and his piano, and the only things left on the kitchen counter were a utensil holder and a stand mixer.

"I'm surprised it took your dad this long to sell."

I shrugged. "This house reminds him of Caleb and my mom."

Hana thumbed toward the hallway leading to my bedroom. "Can I?"

"Yeah. I'm thirsty. You want something?"

Hana didn't answer and went to my room. I heard her kick off her shoes. Her bracelet jingled as she slipped it off her wrist.

I poured myself a glass of homemade iced tea. I was buying time. I could have said no and insisted we go to Steph's, but she wanted this, which made me want it too.

We kept this between us. Hana didn't want her friends black-mailing her for details, and I didn't want Chris reminding me of everything we learned about sexual purity at the youth retreat over spring break.

I knew premarital sex was wrong, but when Hana brought it up a few weeks before prom, intimate fantasies of us ran through my head. The more we talked about it, the more I convinced myself it was okay. I'd ask God for forgiveness and abstain from sex until I got married. Hana called herself a Christian, but faith was something she did on Sunday. For me, it was a relationship with Jesus, but putting God first would blow a chasm between me and Hana. I couldn't lose her.

When I entered my room, Hana rose from where she sat at the foot of the bed. She had already removed her hair clip.

My body temperature spiked when she embraced me and put her forehead against mine.

Hana kissed my nose, cheeks, and mouth. I pushed her against the bed. We fell on top of my comforter, holding each other tight. Our limbs were twisted together like vines.

This was rebellious, but being rebellious was thrilling.

My fingertips rested on her shoulder and crept around her neck to unzip the back of her dress. Her shoulders and collarbones were so defined. It was strange seeing her this close.

Hana started undoing my tie.

We had dated for over three years. We were going to marry after we finished college and found full-time work. We felt comfortable enough talking about money, kids, and spending our summers in Korea. This was fine. We were going to be *fine*.

Hana pulled my tie through my collar and threw it on the floor.

I looked at her sterling silver bracelet that lay on my nightstand. Next to that was a book. Its spine read *The Holy Bible*.

Hana's breath hit my face. Her arm lay across my waist, then her hand crept up my chest. She opened the first button on my shirt. "Ian, what are you thinking about?"

I stuffed the truth in my pocket for safekeeping and figured if I knew the gospel, I had a spot reserved for me in heaven. Meanwhile, I could sin as much as I wanted and repent later. After all, Jesus died for my sins, like the one I was about to commit.

But he was beaten and nailed to a cross because the religious leaders hated him and thought he was blaspheming for claiming he was God. In 2 Corinthians 5:21, it says Jesus became sin so we could have the righteousness of God through him. As a result, his Father turned away from him.

And here I was, trying to satisfy my lust and taking his sacrifice for granted.

I pushed Hana's hand off my shirt.

Salvation is more than a choice. It's a life. I was supposed to be loving God with all my heart and mind. I needed to be a light to the world so people saw Christ when they saw me.

Hana touched my belt buckle.

"Stop!" I pushed her hand back and rolled onto my side to sit on the edge of the bed.

She lifted the sleeve of her dress. A deep frown settled on her face, and pain flickered in her eyes. She wanted this so much, and I had destroyed it. I would never forget that look on her face.

Hana was still on my bed with her legs tucked to the side and supporting herself with one hand. "What's wrong?" she asked in a tender voice from behind. "Do you want to wait?"

"What if I got you pregnant? I'm not ready to be a dad."

She set her chin on my shoulder. "Ian, it's okay."

"We'd be setting a terrible example for Gemma. And if we didn't get married, would your parents shun you and our child because you'd be a single mom?"

"We're in America. They wouldn't be happy, but they wouldn't do that." Hana crawled around me and dangled her legs off the side of the bed. Her thigh pressed against mine. She moved over to leave some space between us. "I know you're upset, but you're overreacting. I said it's fine if you don't want to do this. Let's hang out until your dad gets home."

I got off my bed. I fixed the button she undid and picked my tie up off the floor. "Do you understand why I don't want it?"

"It's your religion," Hana answered in a tone that was just as soft.

I faced her. She looked like she was going to cry.

"Hana, we never really talked about it. You don't understand how I've changed. I don't just go to church and read the Bible. I want to be close to God. I want to be set apart. I need to be better than what the world expects. Premarital sex isn't a part of that."

"I didn't ask you to do this to pull you down," she said. "I want my first time to be with someone I really love."

The hurt in her voice made my face twist in pain. "I know. What I'm getting at is I love God so much, and I want to be with someone who loves him too."

Hana spread her fingers over her chest. "You want me to believe the same things?"

"Yes, you need him too. Everyone does."

She stood, looked straight at me, and held my shoulders. "Listen to yourself. This could tear us apart."

I pulled away from her and grabbed my keys off my night-stand. "Things can still work. They have to."

"Yeah." She sighed. "I should go home."

I nodded. "Okay. I think that's a good idea."

Hana slipped her shoes on and fastened her bracelet on her wrist. She sniffed and rubbed her nose as I zipped the back of her dress for her.

Looking back at that night now, I wish my future self could have warned me that my faith would tear Hana and me apart, twice. Christ warned believers that people would be offended by the gospel. The only comfort I have comes from knowing I did the right thing, putting God before Hana, even if it means losing her.

I'm back home after dropping Hana off at MSU. I walk into my room, sit on my bed, and grab my Bible. I hug it against me, as if it can hold in the joy and sorrow beating in my chest.

18

MARTHA

SOMETHING HEAVY LANDS on my stomach.

"Get up, honeypot!" Mom urges.

"What?" I ask groggily as I sit up. My hand glides over a big postmarked envelope. I gasp. "Is it from Montclair?"

Mom kneels beside the trundle bed. Her eyes dazzle with excitement. "Dad told me this morning that we have enough to cover your first two semesters."

Well, she's proven green living makes a difference.

I slit the envelope open and pull out a letter dated October fourth. Mom leans in to read it.

Dear Martha,

Congratulations! You have been accepted for admission to Montclair State University as a transfer student for the Spring 2011 semester. Your major is WOMEN'S STUDIES.

My heart's not doing a jig. I don't hear party horns going off in my head. I'm not relieved that I got accepted into the only college I applied to. I don't feel ... anything.

Mom kisses the side of my head. "We knew you'd get in! I'll text Dad the news."

"Okay."

"When you find out when orientation is, don't forget to tell your boss."

"I know."

The happiness melts on Mom's face once she notices my frown. "What's wrong?"

"I was up late studying for a Russian test." I was also wolfing down material Alyosha hadn't covered yet.

I've been obsessing about the Russian minor too. I need to talk to her about it. Now.

"I made bread pudding. Come and have some after you're done getting ready." Mom squeals, "We're so proud of you! I'll get my credit card for your deposit."

I hold my breath, then say, "Mom, can I ...?"

She pauses by the door.

"Can I minor in Russian?"

She blinks a few times.

I hug my legs. "I know I haven't been studying it for very long, but I love Russian class. A minor would get me up to the advanced level."

Mom's eyebrow twitches upward. "You really want this?"

"If it's too expensive, I'll pay for it."

"Look, we'll talk this over with Dad."

I leap off my bed and hug her waist. "Mom, you rock!"

She touches my back. "Make sure you really want this before making anything final."

I squeeze her and say, "I will."

"Let's pay that deposit and lock in your spot at Montclair. All right?"

I want to dance as I walk down the hall to the bathroom to shower. I can study more Russian. I won't reach fluency, but after I graduate, I'll keep studying it. Maybe move someplace with a high Russian population, like New York City. I can eat Russian food with Russian friends and read Russian literature in the original language.

A girl can dream. She will—and someday won't have to anymore.

When I return to my room, Mom's credit card is on my desk next to my laptop. She placed my acceptance letter on top of my Russian textbook.

I log into Montclair's web services and plug in Mom's credit card information. My heart is flying.

———

I'M the first one to finish the Russian test. Alyosha doesn't look surprised when I go up to his desk to hand it in. My appointment with Professor Guerra is in twenty minutes, so I head upstairs to the café and buy a croissant and text Kaylin about Montclair.

> **Kay**
> Yay! You put me to shame. I haven't started
> my application for Delaware. Could use
> some help with my essay.

> I'll have time on Sat.

> **Kay**
> Great, thanks!

At two o'clock, I take the elevator up to Professor Guerra's office. The door is ajar, and she's typing rapidly on a keyboard. I softly knock and push the door open.

Professor Guerra's hair isn't secured in a tight bun; it hangs loose down her back. And, for the first time, I see her wearing something other than a skirt. She has on black leggings and a loose cobalt chiffon shirt.

She looks up from her work. "I apologize, Martha! I was sucked into editing this article and lost track of time." She gathers the manila folders scattered across her desk and stuffs them into a file organizer. "Have a seat, dear."

I sit in the chair in front of her desk and take out the second draft of "Shattered at Six" that I've been working on.

"This is why Virginia Woolf told writers to have a room of their own." She wipes her palm over her desk. "I see you've been working on your story."

"I have a lot of questions about it."

Professor Guerra drinks some coffee and swallows loudly. "Before we discuss that, I want to get to know you. How far are you in your studies?"

"I'm graduating in December, and I got my acceptance letter from Montclair today."

She claps a little. "That's wonderful! Congratulations."

"Thanks. I'm majoring in women's studies and minoring in Russian." There. I said it.

Professor Guerra's pale-blue eyes light up. "I minored in women's studies. It's a fascinating subject. Women have suffered a lot, but we've carved our own discipline from it, and there's still so much work to be done. I'm glad you'll be a part of that."

I take in her words and think of Mom. Women are still suffering, and I'll be a catalyst to end some of their pain. I'm supposed to feel excited, but why does it feel like the emotion is repelling me? I'm too caught up in my craze for Russian. *Regain your footing, girl.*

"How's the class going for you, Martha?"

"It's going okay. I'm learning a lot."

"Only okay?" Professor Guerra asks with concern. "Is there anything I can do to make it better?"

I'm shocked that she has a gentle side. She's so flamboyant and loud in class.

"I didn't like workshopping. It was uncomfortable hearing Francine and Kyle criticize my work. And Francine's comments were kind of rude. I never took creative writing before, so this was all new to me."

"Mmm." Professor Guerra straightens her back and rests a hand on my story. "Critiques can be tough. When I workshopped in advanced fiction at Princeton, my instructor tore me to shreds. I went back to my dorm and cried. I needed to thicken my skin and accept that I wasn't always going to be right. Listening to what others had to say about my work was the only way I'd make it better."

"I wish I'd caught some of the mistakes I'd made before letting other people see it."

"You can never find them all. The errors disappear as we work on our drafts. We're too close to our writing. That's why objective readers are the healthiest thing for any project. Is this helping you understand workshopping better?"

I cross my legs and cup my hand around my knee. "It is."

"Now, your story ..." Professor Guerra holds my work in both hands. "This may be your first writing class, but you've already overcome something a lot of my students don't usually in the beginning of the semester. You were brave."

I lean forward. "What do you mean?"

"People usually don't write about such deep and painful things until they've gotten to know their classmates better." She makes a fist. "Your plot is gripping and upsetting."

My cheeks flame. I didn't think my story would stand out to her. I thought it was merely another paper she had to grade, another compilation of someone's imaginary thoughts she compared and contrasted to her own masterpieces.

"I get so many love stories, crime scenes, and, of course, family dramas, but this is something else."

Can I trust her and say that, except for Jene's name, the entire story is true? The words climb up my throat, but I shove them back with a swallow.

"Do you have questions about any of the comments I left or anything Francine and Kyle pointed out? Anything about the class in general?"

"I went back in my notes and reviewed what you taught us about writing strong endings, but I'm having trouble applying it to my story. I still want it to close with"—I almost say my parents—"Jene's parents telling her how to make it with her own strength instead of God's. I don't understand what you mean by ending it with a beat."

"A beat gives readers something to hang on to. In a chapter of a novel, it pushes them to read more or leaves them with some kind of impression of a character or situation. Your story needs to sound finished. Give it closure." Professor Guerra rubs her hands together and reads the last sentence of my work. "'Mommy and Daddy tell me to depend on my own strength when people do bad things to me because God can't help me. God doesn't care about little girls being taken from their homes without their parents knowing or about old people hurting children. God only cares about how many people flock to shiny buildings called churches.'"

I smile at the realization. "It *does* end abruptly."

"See? Reading your work aloud helps you catch some things your eyes can miss. We already know Jene's parents disapprove of what her grandparents did, so saying that they think God only cares about church attendance isn't necessary."

I nod in understanding. "How am I doing in the class? There were so many things wrong with my draft."

"I don't grade your drafts. I check them to make sure they don't look like something you slopped together right before class. Drafts and workshop are counted as participation."

I run my hand over the side of my head and push some hair behind my ear. "Oh." I must have whipped up something passable if Professor Guerra didn't detect my procrastination.

"If I graded drafts, I'd hate my job because I'd be giving everyone low marks. The creative process is about growth. That's why your portfolio is such a big part of your grade. I grade you based on how much you've improved as a writer, not on what you've gotten right and wrong in your drafts." She tilts her head with a smile tugging at her mouth. "What? You look surprised."

I point to myself. "You called me a writer."

Professor Guerra nods. "You've been a writer since you penned the first word on the first day of class. Writing is a profession *and* a craft. You don't need years of experience to be a painter or sculptor. The same goes for writing."

I nod. "Thanks for the encouragement."

"Anytime." She hands me my story and looks past me. "Martha, my next student's here. Email me if you have any other questions before our next class. Happy writing."

As I walk past the guy standing in the doorway, I think about myself as a writer. I don't believe everything happens for a life-altering reason, like my independent study being canceled made room for a new talent to flourish inside me. But using this time to write my way through my ugly past makes creative writing manageable, cathartic. Maybe even kind of worth it.

19

IAN

"THE HIGHEST GRADE someone got is a seventy-nine," Brigitte says at the start of German class. She removes the pile of last week's tests from her bag and plops them on her desk. "I know a lot of you are graduating, but don't get lazy. I do my part for you, so please do yours and *study*."

Murmurs trickle through the room as Brigitte returns the tests. A lot of people frown as they look at their scores.

Dread spreads through my body. I pray that I passed in the C-range. I studied plenty, rewriting vocabulary multiple times on scrap paper, like I used to do for spelling tests in grammar school. I practiced writing my About Me paragraph a dozen times. But during the test, my memory fogged on verb conjugations ...

"Ian," Brigitte says when she walks toward me, holding out my packet. *"Gut."*

Gut? I take it and stare at the seventy-nine on the page, my mouth agape. It's not a grade to rave about, but I got the highest score.

Maybe Mom's right. I can pull through okay when I apply myself.

———

WHEN I RETURN HOME from German class, I dig up everything I have in my closet that reminds me of Hana. I sit on the floor in my room, surrounded by pictures of her and me, birthday and Christmas cards she sent, and some of the notes she slipped in my locker throughout high school.

It's time to let go.

After Mom left us, Dad called her a few times to beg her to come home. She never answered the phone, so he stopped calling after two weeks. Right before Christmas, Mom told him she was pregnant. That's when Dad took his wedding ring off. He gave me the saddest look and said, "Mom's always going to be your mom, but she's not coming home." He hugged me and buried his face in my hair. "You know, maybe this hurt can help us. We can make things better for ourselves so we don't have to feel so much pain."

It took a while for the pain to subside. But, with Hana, the hurt *is* helping me. The feelings for her that I thought would linger are cooling. It's still hard, though, because I thought we could make things work this time.

I come across the poster Hana made for my sixteenth birthday of the Korean flag. She wrote my American name inside the red and blue yin-yang in the center. In place of the black trigrams in each corner, she wrote my Korean name, birthday, adoption case number—K91-917—and the day I came to the States. I tried to look happy when she gave this to me.

Hana thought she was celebrating my Korean-ness, but this reminded me that I was carted through the adoption system. It's been living in the back of my closet for three years, and for some reason Hana never asked about it. I fold the poster in half, and half again, and slide it inside the trash bag with the other mementos.

Dad's not surprised Hana dumped me again. He thinks she's selfish and figured this didn't bother me or that I'd see it eventually. I was too infatuated to face it.

My pulse pounds as I carry the bag outside. The hurt inside me is crushed with a sudden anger toward Hana. I throw the bag into the dumpster, purging everything that marks the first time I was in love.

I know Hana and I hurt each other in our breakups, but we could have gone to the wedding as friends so there wouldn't be an empty seat that Uncle Vinny and Aunt Naomi can't get refunded for. She could have also ended things without making me feel like a perpetual adolescent.

I read some of "The Coquette" to distract myself. I don't want to go to the wedding alone, but there's no one to ask.

Well, I can ask Martha.

I slap my hand over my forehead and laugh a little.

She and I are on better terms now, but we're not friends. Chances are she'll turn me down. Besides, I don't have her number, so the soonest I can ask her is tomorrow at work.

I sit back in my desk chair and text Chris what's been happening.

> Hana broke up with me and isn't going to the wedding. I might ask my coworker Martha.

We've only texted since the semester started. Chris is majoring in biblical studies at Belhaven University in Mississippi, alongside his girlfriend, Bethany. They plan to get married after they graduate and go on mission trips in Europe.

He replies instantly.

Chris
Sorry she did that. I know you were hoping
you guys would make it.

A pause, then he writes:

Chris
Is your coworker a Christian?

No.

Chris
You're walking into the same problems.

I'm not looking for a girlfriend.

No response. He loves being the righteous one.
A few minutes later, Mom texts me.

Mom
I know things were awkward when you
visited. Don't turn down school because
you don't like being there. Things get better
over time.

Sure they do.

I'll think about it.

I'm not going to do that.

I push my phone away. Sometimes I wish it was okay to hate people.

I'm asking Martha to the wedding. If she says no, then at least I tried. I can get my mind off my breakup with Hana and my mom's obsession with college, and it might be nice to get to know Martha. As long as we don't touch Christianity, I'm safe.

I'm also sick of being alone. I wouldn't mind if Martha kept me company.

AT WORK THE NEXT DAY, I'm putting my water bottle in the fridge when Martha comes in. We exchange a brief hello as she hangs up her sweater. It's twelve to three, and we can't clock in until five minutes before our shift.

Perfect. We're alone.

Liz bursts through the door. "Ian, Martha, clock in. Alicia's been at the register all day by herself, and the line's getting long."

I follow Martha to the registers. After I count her drawer, I say, "Show them what you're made of," and she gives me a thumbs-up.

I can't abruptly ask her to the wedding now. That would freak her out. Although, I think this invitation will freak her out no matter how I bring it up—because who asks someone to a wedding with a day's notice?

Every time I get ready to talk to Martha, something happens. I have two exchanges in a row. She goes on her break, but the phone rings. A woman tries to sneak a spool of ribbon into her purse when she thinks I'm not looking. A couple can't survive without their dog for the ten minutes they're in the store, and it pees on some merchandise in the vestibule.

Finally, it's eight o'clock. Martha and I check off the closing duties in less than twenty minutes and punch out. When we're walking to the break room, I say a prayer before I open my mouth.

"Hey, Martha?"

"Yeah?"

"Are you doing anything this Saturday?"

Martha lifts a brow, and I catch a smile pull at the corner of her lip. "Why? Are you inviting me to a revival service?"

I need an earthquake to open the floor and engulf me. "No. My cousin's getting married. I wanted you to come to the wedding." *Wanted.* Past tense. My request is irrelevant now.

Martha grabs her sweater off the coat rack and leaves the break room. "This Saturday? *Tomorrow*?"

I follow her out. "Yeah, but don't worry about it." My face heats up from embarrassment. "My girlfriend dumped me. I prefer not to go by myself. Okay, this is really awkward."

Martha folds her sweater over her arm. She looks like she just drank expired milk. I wish she would turn me down so we can be done with this. "So, you need a date? Ian, I barely know you."

"Then let's change that."

She stands with her back against the lockers. "How are we going to do that now?"

"Let's tell each other something we never told anyone else. It stays here. No judging or questions."

She rolls her eyes. "This is a game girls would play at sleepovers."

"I'm on limited time." I lean up against the lockers. Our shoulders almost touch.

"I'll play so I can get some secret information about you."

"Does that mean you're okay with going to the wedding?"

"Maybe."

I drag my hands through my hair and reach into my mind for something to say. "I wish I wasn't adopted."

Martha swears. I either surprised her or she's dreading her turn. She breathes in and says, "When my grandpa died, I wanted to ballroom dance over his grave."

My jaw drops a little. "Oh, man."

Martha shrugs.

"I stole a lighter and some cigarettes from my friend Luke's older brother when I was seventeen. He blamed Luke for it, and I never fessed up."

Martha tilts her head. "You're an icy stone like me."

Finally, Martha and I have stepped on common ground, so I feel comfortable enough saying, "We're scarred."

"Did you try a cigarette?"

"No questions. Remember?"

"Rules exist to be broken," she argues.

"I did try one." My face twists at the memory. "I felt so gross that, when I got home, I jumped in the shower with my clothes on."

"I stole something too. When I was fifteen, I took money from my parents' nest egg to buy a Dido CD." She pushes herself away from the lockers and opens hers to get her purse. "So, your girlfriend ditched you?"

"Pretty much."

"She couldn't spend a few more hours with you at this wedding?" There's a trace of sympathy in her voice.

"She didn't want us to take the friend route."

Martha throws her hands up at her sides. "Okay, if you want a date, I'll go with you."

"Thank you, Martha." I swing my locker open and stuff my wallet and phone into my pockets. "I really appreciate you going."

"There are a few conditions." She counts them on her fingers. "One: I'm not bringing a gift. Two: you're meeting my parents when you pick me up, because they're not going to trust you. And three: absolutely no dancing." She's suddenly charged up. "I'll sit next to you, and we can talk. Got it?"

The sudden change in her demeanor makes me go tense. "I have the gift covered, and I'll respect your boundaries."

"Okay. And where's the wedding going to be?"

"Freehold."

"I live in Freehold," Martha says.

"All right then. I'll pick you up at four thirty."

"That works. Let's exchange numbers and get out of here."

Once we're outside, I say, "I'm sorry if you feel like an afterthought."

"Ian, I don't care. I don't have any plans tomorrow night. We'll tolerate each other tomorrow, then we're coworkers again."

"You got it." I admit to myself that I'm disappointed we're going to pretend to be friends for a night.

20

MARTHA

FACT 1: Besides residing in New Jersey, attending the same school, and working at NYC Corner, Ian and I also harbor pain and have a short history of theft.

Fact 2: I agreed to attend a wedding with him that's in less than twenty-four hours.

Fact 3: I need to tell my parents my plans.

Fact 4: They're going to kill me.

Fact 5: If they kill me, Ian won't have a date for tomorrow.

I'm almost home as Fact 6 falls into my head: I really am sorry that Ian's girlfriend dumped him before this wedding. I mean, is he *that* bad?

Mom's scooping chili into bowls when I walk into the kitchen. Dad's flipping cornbread out of a cake pan onto a cutting board.

"You didn't have to wait for me to eat," I say. "It's almost nine o'clock."

Mom waves a dismissive hand. "That's what snacks are for. You're always the last one to eat on workdays. Let's eat together, for a change."

Mom's been in higher spirits lately. When she brought up my Russian minor to Dad yesterday at dinner, he said, "Why not? The elementary level of a language is the foundation. Keep building the house."

Mom suggested I pay for these credits, but Dad wants me to save my money. She didn't argue with him. Before I went to bed last night, I gave him a big hug and thanked him. He patted my back.

I wish he and Mom would hold me once in a while.

"How's work been?" Dad asks me.

"Richard's leaving, so everyone gets more hours until Liz hires someone else."

"Don't burn out, Marty," Dad warns before he eats some chili.

"I'm not required to take all the extra time Liz gives me. She knows I'm in school."

Dad's being cautious from experience. He worked two jobs and attended Rutgers when Mom was pregnant. He was so stressed, he had a breakdown. He doesn't talk about it. Suzanna and I only know it happened because Mom told us. Babka and Pop-Pop gave him and Mom a home and food to eat, but medical bills, gas, and half of Dad's tuition was on him. He still rolled out with a 4.0 GPA in both his undergrad and graduate studies.

Mom pipes up. "Let's go out for dinner tomorrow. I need a break from cooking."

"I have plans," I say before I bite into my cornbread.

"What plans?" Mom asks as she drops shredded cheese over her chili.

I could say I'm hanging out with Kaylin. But if I hide the wedding from them and they find out about it, like if Ian and I get in an accident, Mom and Dad will never trust me again.

"No, I ... I'm going to a wedding with Ian. You know, the guy who trained me."

Mom and Dad drop their silverware at the same time and stare at me.

"His cousin's getting married, and he needs a date. His girl-friend broke up with him."

"So, you're the last-minute choice," Dad remarks. "Why are you going if this is what he thinks of you? And I thought you didn't get along."

"It's not like that anymore."

"Stop analyzing everything," Mom chides Dad.

"Jenn, she's had this job for a month. I'm not letting some guy from there take her out, especially if this is how he asked her."

"Ian's not some guy." I mash some cornbread into my chili. "We work together three days a week."

"I don't care if you ended a war together." Dad bangs on the table, startling me and making the plates rattle. "You're not going."

"Dad, Ian's not inviting me to go hunting for the Jersey Devil in the Pine Barrens overnight. This is a *wedding*. It's right here in Freehold."

Mom cuts in with "And she's never gone out with—"

"A guy," I finish for her curtly. "I never went out with a guy because I was *fat*."

I'd shed that fat in eleventh grade and never gained it back. I couldn't let that happen after all the harassment I endured in school. I scored first place on Chloe MacGregor's list of people who would never have sex. Grace Schultz pretended to gag at me in the locker room when we changed for gym. My classmates could have written a series with all their "Martha's so fat" jokes.

"Ian and I aren't dating. He asked me to go as a friend." *Friend* is heavy on my tongue. "I'm going because I said I would."

Dad scrapes melted cheese off the side of his bowl. "All right, but be careful. Please."

"Ian's not going to do anything."

"If he does, I'll kill him."

"I set some boundaries. Ian said he'll respect them."

"Like how you set boundaries with Aaron?"

My stomach contracts at the mention of Aaron Oliviero, my lab partner from junior year. We worked well together in chemistry class. We studied at my house a few times. He asked me to prom. Then his friends started snickering about us. Aaron went from defending me to making comments about what I brought for lunch and talking down to me about my diet. Then he cut me off. He even asked our chem teacher for a new lab partner. He hated being seen with someone my size.

Mom shakes her head and runs her hand over her face. "David, stop. Aaron was three years ago."

"I'm afraid she's going to trust Ian, then—"

I dig my nails into my palms and pound my leg. "Dad, stop it!"

His eyes lock with mine. I drop my head and stare at my food.

Mom glances at Dad, then me. "David, why are you looking at her that way?"

My eyes flutter. The dam behind my eyes threatens to collapse.

"Marty, what's wrong?" Mom asks. She smacks Dad in the arm. "David, you shouldn't have brought up Aaron."

My left hand is still curled into a fist. I open it like a blooming rose. My nails have left a banner of half-moons across my palm.

If only Dad knew the why of what happened between Aaron and me.

"Marty." Dad snaps me back to the present. "I said I want Ian to come in and meet us when he picks you up."

Mom strokes my shoulder. "Just for a few minutes, because we don't know him."

"I already asked him to do that. He said he would. He'll be here at four thirty."

"Okay," Dad says hoarsely. "I appreciate that."

THE QUIET EDGE OF MEMORY

In my room, I call Kaylin to tell her my plans with Ian tomorrow night.

"Ooh, I'm so excited for you! You deserve a night out," she says when I'm done talking. "You work your butt off, and your house is a ticking time bomb. Go have some fun."

"I can help you with your Delaware essay beforehand, like after lunch."

I get a text notification.

"That works. So, what dress are you wearing?" she asks.

"The blue chiffon one."

"You'll look stunning, and Ian will know he asked the right girl to this wedding."

I pull the covers down on my bed and burrow under. "Thanks, Kay. I can always count on you for reality checks."

"I've got you. Always."

After I hang up, I see that Ian texted me.

Ian
Are your parents OK about tomorrow?

"You can't throw bad memories at Marty like that out of nowhere," Mom tells Dad in a raised voice as they ascend the stairs.

"They weren't from nowhere, Jenn," Dad counters. "She thought Aaron wasn't a concern, and look how he turned out."

My dad's worried because I haven't known you very long, but I'm still going.

Ian
If this is too much trouble, I understand if you can't come.

It's fine. See you at 4:30.

Kaylin's right. I should go out. Between Mom and Dad bickering and Suzanna's divorce, spending time with Ian will be a relief compared to staying home.

21

IAN

I GET to Martha's house a few minutes early and decide to ring the bell anyway.

Her father answers the door. I don't even come up to his shoulder. I see Martha in him with his close-set brown eyes, rounded nose, and diamond-shaped face.

I offer him my hand to shake, but he steps outside and closes the door behind him.

"Ian, I'm okay with you taking Marty out because you agreed not to touch her. I also want her home by ten."

I nod. "I know she doesn't want to be touched, and we'll be back on time."

Mr. Lane looks me up and down. "Good. Thank you. Come on in. Marty's almost ready."

When I step inside their home, a tall woman, whose brown hair is pulled back in a loose braid, comes through the foyer. She does a double take. Was she expecting me to look different? Did Martha tell her I'm biracial?

"Ian." She outstretches her hand. "I'm Marty's mom, Jenn." Her grip is light, and she struggles to make eye contact with me.

"Hi," I greet her.

Mrs. Lane lifts her face toward the stairs and exclaims, "Marty, Ian's here!"

"I'm trying to get my makeup just right!"

"She never fusses about makeup," Mrs. Lane muses under her breath.

I shove my hands in my pockets to give myself something to do.

Martha's dad rests his arm over the base of the stair railing. He doesn't look happy. I didn't expect Martha's parents to give me the warmest welcome, but I didn't think I'd get such a chilly vibe from them either.

Martha finally comes downstairs. I relax and look—gaze—at her. She's wearing a knee-length navy-blue dress with off-shoulder straps and a heart-shaped neckline. She looks great.

Martha pats the bun on the nape of her neck. "I worked *really* hard to keep this from falling out," she tells her mom. "Oh, and don't tell Suzanna I used her blush." She turns to me. Her brows go up. "Ian, I didn't recognize you in that suit."

I crack a smile. It *is* strange seeing her in something other than her uniform. "Ready to go?"

Martha nods. To her parents, she says, "Bye, Mom. Bye, Dad. I'll come home alive!"

"She's safe. Don't worry," I promise to her parents with a wave good-bye. Once we're outside I say to Martha, "You look nice."

She glances down at her dress and rests her fingertips on her collarbone. "Thanks. It's my go-to for formal events. The high waistline hides all the sins."

I open the passenger door, and she gets in.

"You don't need to hide any sins," I assure her. After I slide in behind the wheel, I ask, "Is there a particular station you like?"

"No. I've been listening to Russian pop these days."

I remember seeing the Russian textbook in her car. "Aren't you studying Russian?"

"Yeah. I had to fulfill a humanities requirement, but I *love* it."

"Nice."

"What music do you like?" Martha asks.

"Linkin Park, P.O.D., Evanescence."

We don't say much else during the ride there. When we get to the venue, I escort Martha to where the ceremony's going to be. Someone touches my back, and I jump.

"Come on," Dad says, "we're sitting with my sisters." He bends down a little and says to Martha, "I'm Ian's dad, Michael. Thanks for coming."

She nods. "Nice to meet you."

We sit near the back of the sea of chairs on the left side of the aisle. I'm between Dad and Martha. She puts her gray clutch next to her chair, crosses her legs, and puts her hands in her lap.

The officiant is Pastor Alex. He heads the church Aunt Naomi and Uncle Vinny have been going to for the past twenty-six years. Zach wears a tux and stands with his hands behind his back. He puts them at his side, then wrings them in front of him. Morgan comes down the aisle with Uncle Vinny. Her dress is so wide, Uncle Vinny is trying not to step on its hem.

"Vin's bottom lip is shaking," Aunt Addie whispers to Dad.

Uncle Vinny abruptly turns away when he reaches the gazebo with Morgan and sniffs. He's in such a hurry to sit, he forgets to shake Zach's hand.

Pastor Alex reads from Ephesians chapter 5, where God commands wives to submit to their husbands.

"This doesn't mean Zach can order Morgan to do whatever he

says," he explains. "We can't forget about verse 25, which says husbands must love their wives like Christ loved the church. Remember that Jesus died for the world's sins, so imagine the high standard God is putting on husbands regarding how they should treat their wives."

He reads Proverbs 31 and says, "This isn't in the Bible to make women feel like they must be perfect. God has a high standard for them too. They should have a purpose, work hard, raise godly children, and be forgiving."

Martha shifts uncomfortably in her chair. I'm not surprised she doesn't like what she's hearing.

After Morgan and Zach exchange their vows and are pronounced husband and wife, everyone heads inside for the cocktail hour. Martha leaps up from her seat and hurries toward the double doors.

"Where's the fire?" Dad remarks.

"She's flighty."

"I'll be sitting with my sisters and your grandpa. Bring Martha over at some point."

I catch up with Martha at the buffet. She piles some antipasto and fruit onto her plate. I take some scallops and shrimp and lead her over to a round table for two.

"Are you going to try any of the seafood?" I ask. "It's amazing."

"I don't like seafood," comes her curt reply.

I scan the room. Everyone's mingling in clusters. Half the people here are from Dad's side of the family, so I don't get why it feels like Martha and I are sitting at the isolation table at summer camp.

When it's time to enter the ballroom, I get our place cards. Martha and I are at table seven with Morgan's older sister, Rose, her husband, Dan, and their four-year-old twins, Lara and Georgie.

136

"Welcome to the kiddy table, Ian," Dan jokes when Martha and I sit.

I shed my suit jacket and hang it over the back of my chair. "One of these days someone will realize I'm not ten anymore."

The deejay introduces Morgan and Zach. The room fills with applause, and they dance to a Christian love song that I don't recognize. Uncle Vinny chose The Temptations' "My Girl" for him and Morgan, and then Zach and his mom step onto the dance floor as Lee Ann Womack's "I Hope You Dance" begins to play.

"Do you ever remember the songs from these dances?" I ask Martha over everyone's clapping when the song ends.

She shakes her head.

The commotion in the room dies down to soft music, people talking, and the sound of silverware and glasses clanking against plates.

Rose sips her water and turns in her seat to face Martha. "How did you and Ian meet?"

"We work together," she answers and returns her focus to her piece of bread.

"Oh. I thought Han—"

"So, Martha, are you graduating soon?" I cut in.

"Yeah, in December, then I'm going to Montclair."

"Congratulations. What's your major?"

We lean back in our seats as a waiter serves our chicken dinners.

"Women's studies, and there's my Russian minor," she answers.

I whistle under my breath. "Impressive."

"Speaking of Russian ..." She cuts into her chicken and says, "Secret number three: in seventh grade, I wanted to do a book report on *Notes from Underground*, but my teacher said no. I did it anyway. I loved that book."

"Nothing stops you, huh?"

"My teacher put a huge D on the first page. She requested that one of my parents sign it." Her lips are tight. "I forged my dad's signature."

I move closer to her, which causes my knee to touch hers. Martha shifts in her seat. "My number three: When I was ten, I was visiting my mom's when it was her and my stepdad's anniversary. I snuck into his office and ripped up the card he got her. I hid the pieces in my bag. My mom was mad he didn't include a card with his gift, and he kept insisting he had one."

Martha smirks. "Nervy. Did he suspect it was you?"

I snort. "Yup. When they were fighting, he looked over at me. I just shrugged and walked away."

Rose stands up to bring Georgie over to another table where a group of children are seated, and Lara pulls Dan out of his seat and begs him to dance. With longing eyes, Martha watches Dan scoop Lara up and carry her to the dance floor.

"You okay?" I ask her.

She nods and pokes some asparagus with her fork. "Where are you headed after graduating? I bet you have big plans."

I swallow some Pepsi. "Why do you think that?"

"You seem like the quiet nerd all the parents wanted their kids to be like."

I laugh. "I don't think anyone's parents were telling their kids to be like me unless they were talking about those reading logs in grade school."

"You read a lot?"

"Yes. A *lot*."

"Favorite book," Martha prompts.

"*A Cab Called Reliable*."

She bites into a dinner roll. "Sounds cool. What's it about?"

"It's a coming-of-age novel about a Korean American girl

whose mom abandons her and her dad. The mom takes her son with her, though."

"Oh." Martha tips her head. "Does that resonate with you at all?"

"Yeah," I say slowly. "When my parents' marriage fell apart, my mom was the one who wanted to walk away."

"I'm sorry, Ian."

"Thanks. But, hey, let's not dampen the festivities. What's your favorite book?"

"My dad's a librarian, and I don't have one. I'm not much of a reader, but give me homework and I'll gladly do it."

We're the only ones at our table now. I look around the room. Several people have gotten out of their seats to dance or talk with other guests.

"Give me a book recommendation," Martha continues.

I turn and hang my arm over the back of my chair. "Have you read *The Collected Tales of Nikolai Gogol*?"

"No."

"You can borrow my copy. I'll bring it to work tomorrow."

"I'll give it a shot."

I gesture to Martha's empty glass. "Need a refill?"

"I can get it."

I stand and take her glass. "No, let me. What do you want?"

"Sprite." She looks up at me. Her eyes are so big, they're almost out of proportion with her face, but they look perfect.

I'm at the bar, waiting for the bartender to fill Martha's glass, when my cousin Hayden joins me.

"Who's the girl?" he asks.

The bartender hands me Martha's drink, and I start back to our table. "Martha. She's a work friend."

"A work friend," he echoes. "You two can't stop yakking. Ask her to dance."

I look over at our table. Martha's gone. "I can't. She doesn't want me to touch her."

Hayden looks toward Martha's empty seat as if it holds a clue that explains why she's so defensive. "I smell abuse. Remember, Aunt Addie hated being touched after she was stalked by that guy in college who tried to rape her."

"I know."

"Or Martha hates you and only came for a free meal and a night out."

"You're a jerk."

Hayden claps my shoulder. "Ian, chill. From what I've seen, I think she's genuinely enjoying your company."

I return to our table. Martha's napkin is in a heap next to her plate, and her bag is gone. She's probably in the bathroom. Before I put her drink down, I spot a blue smudge on the bottom right corner of her cocktail napkin. I bring it closer to my face. In letters that are smeared from condensation is the request I never thought Martha would make tonight.

Ask me to dance.

22

MARTHA

I CAN'T HIDE in this stall forever. This bathroom is freezing, and Ian will think I have really bad stomach problems.

I also can't dance with Ian. Where do I put my hands? We're the same height. I can't put my chin on his shoulder, so I'll leave some space between us, and we can look at each other.

I smack my forehead. Why did I write that note on my napkin?

Because he's not such a bad guy after all, and I can trust him, so he can touch me. I've told him three things I never told anyone else, not even Kaylin.

I grab my clutch off the stall hook and go. I will do this, with confidence. Although, I'm shaking, which makes me look like a nervous wreck.

Ian's standing at our table when I return to the ballroom. He's looking for me, and when he spots me, I lower my face as I snake around the tables.

Ian knots his fingers in front of him. "Do you want to dance, Martha?"

I nod. The deejay is playing Louie Armstrong's "What a

Wonderful World." Good. It's not a romantic song. As we walk to the dance floor shoulder to shoulder, I hold myself and rub my upper arms.

"Are you cold?" Ian asks.

I rest my hands on his shoulders. "No, I'm ..." I run my right hand down his arm and touch the back of his hand. His skin is soft. "I'm ... warm enough," I stammer.

I did not say that.

"Can I put my arm around you?"

I nod.

Ian carefully hugs my waist. My fingers tangle with his and lock together. I let Ian Berkley touch me. The room feels like a desert. What the—?

"Martha, you're really tense. We can sit."

"I'm good." I exhale and try to relax.

"To answer your question about school," Ian says, "I'm staying in retail. I want to run a bookstore."

"Your own?"

"I guess. I'd love to be around books all day and hear people talk about them."

"So, what are you doing at a crafts store?"

"Well." He sighs. "NYC Corner is a holding place until I apply to a bookstore again. I tried a few places this past summer. I had one interview, which only resulted in them keeping my resume on file. Then Liz promoted me, so I'll stay put for a little longer."

Martha nods. "Sounds like you know what you're doing."

"I wish my mom would say that."

My jaw drops a little. "She doesn't support you?"

"She wants me to transfer somewhere in Connecticut. She and my stepdad would cover everything."

Wow. If only I had such an opportunity!

"I don't want to go." Ian moves us to a less crowded area of the dance floor. "Number four: I can't stand being in her house. My stepdad's useless, but my mom is worse."

He's getting personal.

"Number four: I love Russian more than women's studies, but I already got into Montclair."

"You could go somewhere else."

"No. Money's tight. It's probably just an infatuation."

Now *I'm* getting personal.

Ian looks sympathetic. "What if it's not an infatuation?"

"I can't do anything." My tone is getting hard, so in a softer voice I add, "I want to get a master's in public health and open a pregnancy care center. I've had this idea since eleventh grade."

"That's a great goal, Martha."

The song ends. We stop dancing, but we hold on to each other. I study Ian's eyes. They're hazel and specked with green. They're the color of the earth.

"Why'd you ask me to dance with you?" he asks.

I can't tell him how I really feel, so I say, "I wanted you to remember a song from this wedding."

He looks surprised. "Okay. Well, Martha, let's sit. Morgan and Zach are going to cut the cake."

I didn't notice the cake had been wheeled onto the dance floor, and people are returning to their seats.

We let go of each other. My throat feels funny, and my eyes prickle. It's only Ian, my awkward supervisor who tries to act bossy so he doesn't get pushed around. The last guy I'd ever expect to have a good time with at a wedding where I don't know anyone. The last guy I'd ever expect to make me choke up.

When we return to our table, he whispers, "I don't want tonight to end."

I'd better worm out of this possible-friendship compartment. "It has to. Back to work tomorrow being just coworkers," I say with a nervous chuckle. I look across the table where Lara is sitting on her dad's lap so I can avoid the disappointment on Ian's face.

The cake is delicious. It's vanilla with strawberry filling, covered in the creamiest frosting I've ever tasted. When Ian and I finish eating, he gets up and says, "Come meet my dad and grandpa."

We walk to the head table. Mr. Berkley doesn't look much older than Ian with his good complexion and parted bangs, and his eyes are such a dark brown they look black.

Ian taps his father's shoulder. "Hey, Dad."

Mr. Berkley moves his empty wine glass aside and leans closer to Ian's grandpa, who's slightly hunched over in his chair. He explains in a loud voice, "Dad! This is Ian's friend, Martha. They met at work."

His grandpa registers this. He grins, causing an age spot to move up on his cheek. His salt-and-pepper hair and squarish face remind me of my grandpa. "Oh." He takes my hand and grips my fingers. "Hi, sweetheart. Is Ian being good to you?"

"Yes." I withdraw my hand from his. Grandpa used to be charming all those times he came over for dinner after Grandma died. I hope Ian's grandpa really loves his family. I hope he sets Lara and Georgie on his lap and tells them stories about the 1950s or teaches them how to garden or buys them ice cream when their parents say no. I hope he makes them feel safe.

Ian's dad stirs cream into his coffee and looks up at me. "I hope you had a nice time, Martha. This is Ian we're talking about."

"I know," I respond with a dramatic huff. "I could have been home, knitting, studying Russian ..."

Mr. Berkley smacks Ian's arm with the back of his hand. "You went on a Russian lit kick a few summers ago."

"That's cool," I say to Ian, impressed.

"Ian made character charts with all the variants of their names."

I smile at Ian. "You have to keep up with all those Russian diminutives."

His cheeks turn pink, which makes him look kind of cute.

Rose comes up behind her grandpa. She links her arms around his neck and kisses him on the cheek. "Bye, Grandpa. It's time for my little goofballs to go to bed."

He pats Rose's arm. "Good-bye, honey."

"I'm picking you up for Lara and Georgie's birthday party tomorrow, one o'clock."

"I'll be ready to go."

After Rose comes around to hug Ian and Mr. Berkley, I take out my phone. "Ian, it's 9:20. Do you mind if we go too?"

"No, not at all."

I walk around the ballroom with Ian as he says good-bye to his relatives. All of them kiss him and give him big hugs. His aunt Addie asks if she could hug me, which I agree to, and says she hopes it's not too long before she sees me again.

I'm sorry, but it's not in my plans.

It's freezing when Ian and I step outside. I'm about to hug myself, but Ian says, "Here," and drapes his suit jacket over my shoulders. I mindlessly slip my arms into the sleeves. It feels weird wearing a piece of his clothing. Three weeks ago, I would have screamed if he touched me, and a few hours ago I would have chosen to freeze to death before I wore his jacket.

Once we're in his car, he turns on the heat and holds up Jenn Grant's *Orchestra for the Moon*. "My sister left this here. Want to listen?"

"Sure. Never heard of her."

"Gemma watches *Heartland*. Jenn Grant sings its theme song," he says as he pops the disk in the CD player.

We get through four of the songs. Soft melodies. Soothing lyrics. They make you feel as if you're lying on the grass on a sunny day.

"Would Gemma mind if I borrowed this?" I ask him.

"No problem." When we reach my house, he ejects the disk from the CD player and opens the center console to find its case.

"What Russian books have you read?"

Ian hands me the CD and lifts his face toward me in the dark. "*Doctor Zhivago, Lolita, The Brothers Karamazov, Anna Karenina*. A lot."

"*Lolita*? You definitely aren't a choirboy."

"Have you read it?"

"Yeah, when I was fifteen. My dad freaked out when he found it in my room. I love how you have to rely on Humbert Humbert to tell the story, who's, well, not reliable."

"I love ambiguous stories."

"So, why didn't you tell me you read Russian lit?"

"I didn't want you to think I was sucking up to you."

I'm smacked with a pang of guilt. "I would have believed you." We stare at each other, then I break away with "I have to go. Thanks for tonight."

"Can I walk you to the door?"

I slip off his jacket and climb out of his car. "I'll go through the garage."

I enter the code on the pad. Ian doesn't drive away until I reach the door leading into the house and close the garage.

"Marty." Dad's standing in the kitchen, his arms crossed. "Did Ian do anything to you?"

I play with the strap on my clutch. "No. I had a good time. His family's really nice."

Dad's serious expression relaxes. He steps closer to me. "Okay. I'm glad it went well."

THE QUIET EDGE OF MEMORY

I nod. He turns to go upstairs. "Good night, Dad. I love you."

He unfolds his arms and only says, "I'll see you tomorrow."

When I enter my room, Suzanna's sitting cross-legged on my bed, chatting on the phone with her friend Jade.

I restrain a grunt. I want things back to normal—when she wasn't living here, when she was happy with Carl, and Mom and Dad weren't worried about jobs and money. I want privacy so I can listen to Jenn Grant. I only want to think about the songs, not how Ian treated me with so much respect. And tenderness. That word makes me soften. Yuck.

I go into the bathroom to get ready for bed. A whiff of Ian's cologne, that light trace of spiciness, drifts past my face as I change out of my dress. I sniff my arm. I turn to the mirror and see my cheeks redden.

I smell like Ian. Not yuck, but … oddly tolerable.

When I return, Suzanna asks, "Did you have fun tonight?"

"I did," I answer as I pull my laptop out of my backpack. "Ian and I talked a lot, mostly about books, school, family …"

"Mom said he seems nice." She gets under the covers. "I told Dad to stop worrying. Every guy in the world isn't like Aaron."

I sit on the trundle bed and boot up my laptop. "And thank God they're not."

Once Suzanna drifts off to asleep, I grab her headphones off the nightstand and pop Gemma's CD into my laptop's disc drive. Jenn Grant's voice floats into my ears. A tear escapes my left eye, and I rub it off my cheek. Ian has made me cry.

He *is* nice.

What is happening to me?

23

IAN

MARTHA WAS serious when she said we'd be just coworkers after the wedding. It's Tuesday, and we're back to only talking about work at work. Not even small talk.

I told Chris about the wedding. He's happy for me, but his reaction was forced. Whatever. I can't tell him Martha looked like she was tearing up after we danced. Something shifted between us that Chris won't understand. He and Bethany go way back to when they were eleven in their church's kids' choir, so they get each other on so many levels.

I don't get Martha, but I want to.

I vacuum the vestibule and head to the kids' aisle, where Martha's putting away returns.

"Almost done?" I ask.

She slips a coloring book into a rack on the end cap. "Now I am."

We clock out. When we're at our lockers, Martha takes out my book and Gemma's CD.

"Sorry it took me so long," she says and hands them to me. "I couldn't stop listening to Jenn Grant. And I only read three stories: 'How Ivan Ivanovich Quarreled with Ivan Nikiforovich,' 'The Nose,' and 'The Overcoat.' I loved 'The Overcoat.' Akaky Akakievich is so pathetic, it's hilarious. His name means Poop Poopovich."

I laugh. "What song did you like best?"

"'Rainy Day.' The harp melody sounds like rain, but it doesn't. You get me?" Martha closes her locker and turns the combination to secure it.

"Yeah, I get you." I pause before asking, "Can I talk to you about something?"

She glances at her phone before dropping it in her bag. "What is it?"

The heat shoots up my neck and spreads over my face. "I had fun with you on Saturday. Can we hang out sometime?"

She opens her mouth a little and blinks. "Ian, you asked me to do you a favor, and then we were going to revert to—"

"Being coworkers again," I finish. "I know."

Martha heads out of the stockroom. She zips through the store and stops at the exit to open her bag for me to check. "Ian, I don't really want to talk about this ... us."

We step outside. It's drizzling. I try to reach the tenderness I saw in her last Saturday one more time.

"Did I do something wrong?"

"I was playing Be Your Friend for a Night." She pulls her hood over her head. "You needed a guest for the wedding, and I needed a night out of my house. We used each other. We're even. Get it?"

"What I don't get is ... never mind."

"What?"

"You emphasized that you didn't want me to touch you, then you were up for dancing with me." I throw my arms up at my sides. "Why'd you do that?"

She fidgets with the collar of her jacket.

"I remember your face, Martha." Bad move. That sounds romantic.

"Ian, I did it as a nice gesture. I'm sorry if you think it meant something else." She scuffs the toe of her shoe on the sidewalk.

I step back. "Okay. If you ever want to hang out, I'm cool with that."

I catch a glint of surprise on her face.

"Will you be here tomorrow morning to fill in Richard's shift?"

"Yeah," Martha answers, then says, "Good night, Ian."

I give her a wave as I turn to leave.

Disappointment engulfs me. On Saturday, Martha and I got a little close and vulnerable. Now she's defensive again. The wedding and sharing our secrets were a game. Games aren't meant to be taken seriously.

I watch her sprint to her car and get in.

I tuck my book and CD inside my jacket to shield them from the rain. When I get in my car and toss them on the passenger seat, a paper pokes out from the book's inside cover. It's torn from a spiral notepad. In black pen, Martha wrote, *#5: I can't do women's studies. I feel Russian calling.*

I'd send her a secret if this game was still on, but it's over. It's freaky how easy it was to tell Martha the things I can't tell the people I've known the longest.

24

MARTHA

THERE'S a bowl of chicken cacciatore waiting for me on the table when I get in. Meanwhile, Mom and Dad are fighting and don't acknowledge me. The HOA fee has gone up from $125 to $250, and they still have that hefty assessment to pay off.

"We're moving!" Mom insists, jabbing a finger at the door, as if we can leave right now and find a new home. "We'll rent or buy a house that's not tied to a crooked HOA."

Dad starts cleaning the chef's knife. The kitchen is always their battleground. "We are *not* moving."

Mom dries a wooden spoon with a towel that has a hole near one of its corners. "Then find full-time work!"

If you were in our kitchen, you would think I was a ghost, imposing on my parents' post-dinner drama as I calmly consume my chicken. They've been having this fight since Sunday, so I'm not rattled—just tired of hearing the same drama roll out. Every. Single. Day.

"I filled out three applications last week."

"You must be doing something wrong," Mom accuses. "You should have gotten an interview by now."

Dad's holding the saucepan lid that's dripping with suds. "I'm not incompetent. You know how bleak the job market is."

Mom ignores him and stores the leftover chicken in Tupperware. She's getting on his nerves—and mine. First, she turns into an eco-nut. Now she thinks he's playing lazy with job hunting. She's slowly murdering his pride.

I finish dinner and go to my room. Suzanna's in bed facing the wall.

"Hi." I greet her cheerfully to add a happy tone somewhere in this house, but she doesn't respond. I know she's not sleeping because she normally snores a little.

Suzanna's been depressed since Wednesday. She went by the apartment after work to get some kitchen items she forgot. Carl was on the couch with another woman. I didn't ask for details, and Suzanna won't volunteer any.

Mom and Dad's conversation has transitioned to finances.

"I'm still mad at you for asking Marty for cash," I hear Dad say.

"You don't balance the checking account; *I do*."

"Marty needs to save her money too. You're not asking Suzanna for anything."

"She's getting a divorce!" Mom reminds him.

Suzanna groans under the blankets.

"Doesn't matter. Either they both contribute or neither of them does."

Kaylin was right; my house is a time bomb. It's time to take cover.

I sprint to the bathroom and grab my toothbrush. I rummage through the top drawer that's loaded with Suzanna's makeup and find my concealer and face powder.

"If you hate that Marty's helping out, then we need to move!"

Back in my bedroom, I open my bureau that's stuffed with Suzanna's clothes and pull out my pajamas.

"The savings account is not going to dry up," Dad promises. "I put money in there every week."

I yank a work shirt off a hanger in the closet, which is crammed with Suzanna's clothes.

"I'm scared," Mom admits. "I'm scared we're going to need help from food pantries one day or fall behind on our mortgage."

I take my Russian textbook and notebook off my desk—the only spot in my bedroom that's still all mine—and slip them into my backpack. I grab my knitting bag for good measure. Noise-canceling earmuffs sound like a nice project. Then I dig up my phone from my purse to text Kaylin.

There's a message from Ian he sent shortly after we parted ways tonight.

> **Ian**
> I knew you weren't infatuated with Russian.
> Go after what you love.

I clap my hand over my mouth. I forgot to take that stupid note out of his book.

Oh, naïve Ian. You think it's so easy. My parents aren't mild-mannered like your dad.

"I'll look for jobs in Philadelphia and the city," I hear Dad say.

I text Kaylin.

> Can I sleep over? Caught in WWIII.

> **Kay**
> Sure, but same over here. Btw, new garage
> code: 1307.

"I'm going to Kaylin's," I tell Mom and Dad as I cut through the kitchen to the garage. Dad looks at me, then turns his attention back to Mom. They're at the kitchen table with their transaction record between them. They're really duking it out over this financial war.

I get in my car. Before I start the engine, I whip out my phone to respond to Ian.

I'm sorry I led you on.

I stare at my text for an unusually long time. For some reason, I want to hear his voice, and I want him to hear mine. What is wrong with me?

Ian can't get close. Not after Aaron screwed me over. My iron fortress keeps out the risk of getting hurt and the feelings that could turn me into that person I never want to stare back at in the mirror.

Ian just wants us to hang out as work friends.

Before I change my mind, I hit his contact and put the phone against my cheek.

It rings three times before he answers. "Hi, Martha." He sounds tired.

"Ian, I'm sorry about before." My voice trembles. Get a grip!

"It's all right. I'm over it."

"Oh, okay, um ..." I swallow. "Are you free Friday after work?"

"Yeah. You want to do something?"

"Sure." I rub some of my jacket between my thumb and pointer finger. "Ian, I ... I'm tired of being hard."

"You don't have to be hard."

I'm burning with so much embarrassment, I could heat a castle.

"I have to go." I hang up and head to Kaylin's.

When I get to her house, her younger brother and sister are still eating dinner, and her mom is at the sink, washing dishes.

"Hi, Mrs. Hogan. Sorry to drop in so suddenly," I say.

"No apologies. You're family." She shakes water off a cutting board. "Kaylin's in her room studying."

I pass Mr. Hogan on my way upstairs. He's heading out to the garage, carrying a small gift bag.

"What's up with your parents?" I ask Kaylin once I'm in her room.

She closes the door. "My mom's fiftieth birthday was Sunday. My dad got her a ridiculously expensive diamond ring, when she's been hinting for months that she'd love a weekend in Atlantic City."

I sink down on her bed. It's refreshing to be in her room where the art supplies, makeup, books, and clothes are all hers. "How bad was the feud?"

"Not their worst. A few days of swearing and heartfelt apologies. They'll probably make up tomorrow before they leave for work."

I know Kaylin's used to her parents' constant fighting, but I still ask her, "Are you okay?"

Kaylin sits next to me and laughs. "I get worried when they're *not* fighting. Anyway, what's up in your world?"

We lie on her bed with our feet hanging over the side. We used to do this at sleepovers when we were girls and talked way past midnight. I recount how my family is falling apart and everything that's happened between Ian and me since the wedding.

"You're a slab of cement one day and a cotton ball the next." She stares at me, very serious. "Why?"

"He irks me when I least expect it. He senses things in me that I don't want him to see."

Kaylin sits up and crosses her legs. "Then just end things and walk away."

I run my hands over my face. "I can't get rid of him. Yet."

"How come?"

"Kay, he said he wouldn't hurt me."

"Martha Jene, you are approaching dangerous territory." She grabs her pajamas from where they lie on top of her pillow. "Aaron promised you the same thing."

I support myself on my elbows. "Ian's ..."

"Different?" she guesses.

"Yeah, and I believe him."

Kaylin touches my shoulder. "I know you're not looking to fall passionately in love, and sorry for acting like a mom, but be careful."

"You were in his corner when he apologized to me in the bookstore."

"I was trying to calm you down. I wasn't expecting you guys to become BFFs."

Once Kaylin leaves the room to do her night routine, I text Ian.

I'm sorry I hung up on you.

Ian
See? You're not so hard.

I don't reply. If only he knew what I did.

25

IAN

AFTER WORK ON FRIDAY, I take Martha to the new café bookstore that's a five-minute drive from NYC Corner. My neighbors, Kerry and Jim, opened Sunsets, Coffee, and Books last month. They worked in real estate for years before opening their dream business, a rustic place where people can read and hang out.

"This place is so cool!" Martha gushes when we step inside.

I could live here with its floor-to-ceiling west-facing windows, the shelves of books lining the walls, and the smell of coffee—even though I don't drink it.

Martha and I look up at the menu hanging from the ceiling behind Kerry, who's behind the counter.

"I'll have hot chocolate," Martha tells her.

"You got it. And what about you, Ian?"

"I'll have a green tea," I answer as I pay.

Martha already left my side to browse the nonfiction books. I scan the shelves for something I might want. Then I see it. In the gift and stationery section, there's a composition book with a cover that's decorated with book quotes printed in a typewriter font.

"What did you find?" Martha asks from behind me.

"A notebook, and it's mine."

I hurry over to it as if it's the last one on the planet and grab it off the shelf.

Martha sits at a table in the back corner of the shop while I pay at the counter.

"I didn't know you like to write," she says when I join her.

"I sort of do. I keep lists and write random things about the books I read."

Martha sits with her chin in hand and smirks. "Ian, that's writing."

Kerry brings us our drinks. Martha's hot chocolate is topped with frothy milk that's shaped like a leaf.

"I'm taking cre-hate-tive writing," she says once we're alone again. "It's only because my independent study got canceled. My teacher believes you're a writer once you start writing. Okay, great. But every time I write, I feel like I'm pulling words out of my throat."

I sip my tea. "That sounds painful."

"I have an assignment due Tuesday that I haven't started."

"Let me guess: you put off writing to work on Russian instead."

"Correct."

"Are you going to tell your parents you want to change your major?"

Martha shakes her head. "I can't."

We both take a sip of our drinks, eyeing each other over the rims of our mugs.

"My parents are fighting about money, and my sister's soon-to-be-ex-husband is already with another woman." Martha wipes her mouth with a napkin. "So, Suzanna's been really depressed and only goes out for her waitressing job, and when she's home, she hibernates in my room."

"Oof. That's rough."

"She shut down. Hearing my parents yell all the time isn't helping. It's hard to get anything done."

"I know what it's like when your house is a war zone. My parents were never really happy together. My mom walked out on my dad and me fourteen years ago today."

Martha struggles to swallow her drink. "She literally walked out of the house and left you guys? Did she give a warning?"

"No. She called my dad at work and said she had errands to run and couldn't pick me up from the bus, so my aunt watched me. Then my mom called around dinnertime." I squint as the memories slam into my head. Dad's shoulders sagging, the emotion in his voice when he begged her to come back, the hopeless look on his face when she hung up on him. "She wasn't coming home. She wanted to marry Nathan."

Martha's face softens with sympathy. "Ian, I'm so sorry. That must have clobbered you and your dad."

"I never get over it." The day Mom left squeezes me like a python. My brain burns out. *Stay in the present. I'm in a café with Martha.*

"Nathan must be *ah-mazing* if your mom chose him over your dad." She rolls her eyes.

"He's a good dad to Gemma and loves my mom." I shrug. "He's there."

"Understandable." Martha downs the rest of her hot chocolate. "Do you talk to your mom and sister a lot?"

"No. Mom texted me last week to see if I've thought about school. I *really* don't want to go. And I text with Gemma occasionally."

"I can't imagine talking to my mom and Suzanna that rarely."

"You'd get used to it if you had to." I take off my sweater and throw it on the chair next to me. "My spotty communication with my mom's family is probably what holds us together."

"That's how my mom held things together with her parents." Under her breath, Martha adds, "Until my grandma died."

I want to ask her about that, but she gets up and pats the table.

"I want one of those luscious Danishes. You need anything?"

"I'm good."

Martha's in the back of a long line. I dig into my pocket for the piece of register tape I wrote my fifth secret on when there was some downtime at work. I slink over to her chair and slip it inside the breast pocket of her jacket.

A few minutes later, Martha returns with her dessert.

"I don't have anything to do tonight," she says around some Danish. "Let's stay a while."

"Don't you have a creative writing assignment?"

She waves that off. "I'll whip that up the night before. Besides, some of the best writing comes from freewriting. I'll unearth the hidden gems in my subconscious." She holds up her hands and wiggles her fingers. "The page will sparkle."

"I think that's the only time procrastination might help."

"Good. Now, tell me something in one of your notebooks, unless they're top secret."

I finish my tea. "They're not."

The door swings open. A woman who looks our age with her curly brown hair pulled back with a black headband strolls in. Her sports gray shirt reads *The road less traveled isn't just a poem. It's the way to Jesus.* She's holding a bunch of pamphlets and starts placing one on each table, which gets Jim's attention.

"Miss, what are you doing?" Jim asks her.

My tea sloshes around in my stomach. I don't want her near Martha.

She's coming closer. I make eye contact with her and mouth *No.*

"Hi, I'm Rachel. How are you two doing today?"

Martha sags in her seat.

Rachel drops two yellow pamphlets between us. In white letters outlined in black, it reads *Salvation is Never Souled Out.*

"Can you go, please?" Martha asks her anxiously.

Jim darts around, picking up the trail of gospel tracts Rachel left on other tables. Only one customer stuffs his copy into his pocket.

Jim comes up behind Rachel. "You're welcome to come in, and you don't have to buy anything, but no proselytizing."

Martha gives the tract a death stare.

"I'm sorry," Rachel says to Jim. "I won't do it again."

Martha picks up the gospel tract. The sound it makes as she tears it in half cuts through the air like a sword.

Jim and I share stunned looks, but Rachel says, "You seem really hurt, but with Jesus—"

"Don't kill trees for my soul," Martha shoots at her. "And get away from me."

Several customers stare at us. Martha looks from left to right like she's surrounded by wild dogs. She grabs her bag, springs up, and bursts out of the café.

I jog after her. Over my shoulder, I holler at Rachel, "Ever think people have triggers?"

Outside, Martha spins around and says, "Don't even try, Ian!"

"Look, I'm not for that kind of evangelism, but why are you so upset?"

"What did I say?"

"Martha, you need help."

She grabs my arms, which throws me off balance. "Promise me you won't talk about God. Please don't talk about God. I want us to talk about our boring jobs and your nerdy reading habits and my pipe dream to study Russian and our stupid game of secrets."

I cup her elbows in my hands. "I'm not going to upset you. That lady was cringeworthy. Don't think about her."

Martha's eyes look panicked.

A family of four passes us. They all look at Martha.

She hides her face with her hands. "I can't go back in there."

"Let me get our stuff."

I head back inside. Jim's wiping down the table Martha and I were sitting at. I hand him a two-dollar tip before I put on my coat and pick up my notebook.

"Is she all right?" he asks and hands me Martha's jacket. "That girl gives her a religious booklet, and she bolts."

I look at Martha through the large windows. She hugs herself and shifts her weight from one foot to the other.

"I know. It was off-putting."

Jim pushes the napkin holder and container of sugar packets back in their places. "Tell her she's safe here. I don't go anywhere near religion, and neither does my company."

I step outside. I give Martha her jacket, and we walk to my car. We're silent during the ride back to the store.

I park in the spot next to her car and ask, "What happened to you, Martha?"

She rubs the tip of her nose and sniffs. "My grandparents were horrible people, and they called themselves Christians."

She doesn't elaborate, and I don't ask for details, so we sit in more silence. Tension charges between us. It's not hostile. More like holding your breath for too long. There are things we need to say but can't. It will hurt too much.

Without a word, Martha gets out of the passenger side and climbs into her car.

When I get to my apartment, Martha texts me.

Martha
I didn't mean to cause a scene. Maybe I'll
tell you everything someday, when I'm
ready. For now, I just want to hang out.

No problem.

But my curiosity lingers. I hop online and plug *Martha Lane abuse NJ* into some search engines, wondering if she was the victim of some religious abuse case. Nothing.

So I close my laptop, bow my head, and fold my hands in my lap. I pray fervently for Martha. And us.

26

MARTHA

CREATIVE NONFICTION IS AN OXYMORON. Create truth. I'm supposed to write about an experience for Professor Guerra, or, like she always says, everything we write is really for ourselves.

"It's like peering into someone's life through a window," she explained. "You take a piece of time and let it grow." She stretched her arms outward. "You write too long about something that should only take a few moments to explain."

This is due tomorrow. The only thing I've typed in my document is the MLA heading in the top left corner.

There's a light knock on the door. Mom comes in and hands me a folded receipt. "I washed everyone's jackets. I found this in yours."

I unfold it. *#5: After my mom left, my dad was so depressed, it's like he wasn't there. I wrote a story for school about how my birth parents found me and we lived together in Korea. I felt like no one loved me then.*

My chest suddenly feels heavy. Ian must have slipped this in my coat pocket when I ordered my Danish at the café.

"Did Ian write that? Are you two playing some sort of game?"

"No—I mean, kind of." My face burns up as I stash Ian's note in my desk drawer.

"I didn't know if it was garbage or not," she explains. "His mom doesn't sound ideal."

"She's not."

"I wish my parents had put me up for adoption," Mom mutters.

"Your wish is totally valid."

If Mom had been adopted, I would have had different grandparents, maybe nicer ones. Grandparents who wouldn't have dragged me to church and forbidden me from using the bathroom, and—

Tell her tell her tell her. She's your mother.

"Oh, Dad got an interview in Manhattan," Mom says, beaming. How long has it been since I've seen her look so happy and hopeful?

I can't drive a hole through this, so I put on a grin. "That's great, Mom."

"He needs to make it through two interviews. If he gets the job, things can get back to normal." She rests a hand on my dresser. "You think God would listen to us if we prayed?" she jokes.

I drag my finger over my laptop's track pad to turn my face away from Mom. Ian would say yes, God would listen.

"Well, good night, Marty." Mom comes over and gives my ponytail an affectionate tug.

She's really happy. Shut the memories up. Things are okay now, maybe even great if Dad gets the job.

"Good night, Mom."

I hear Mom and Dad converse down the hall. Something about getting batteries for the smoke alarms. Switch out the laundry. I can't comprehend what Dad says next, but it makes Mom laugh.

I put my face in my hands and lean my elbows on my desk. I almost freed the truth.

I'm so tired. I'm tired of being tired. I hold the sides of my chair and scoot closer to my desk. I feel like I'm moving through tar. My computer screen is brighter than high beams. My head is clogged with the memories I can't erase.

I should tell someone what happened. Mom can't handle it. Dad will try, but his stamina is low. Suzanna's dealing with a divorce. Ian would finally realize I'm irredeemable, because I've done something unthinkable ... irreversible. But that might rupture his faith. I can't do that to him. I resent Christianity, but I know it keeps Ian sane because I think his adoption is driving him insane. Kaylin can deal. I can talk to Kaylin.

I take Ian's note out of my drawer and rub my thumb over the sentence *I felt like no one loved me then.*

Holding his words makes me feel close to him. It's comforting. Ian quietly suffered in his childhood and felt so alone, like me.

I pick up my phone and text him.

4 of your 5 secrets are about your mothers.

Mothers. Women. Children. A bond tied with blood and DNA that's broken too often.

I rack my brain for something from my women's studies classes that could help him. If only I'd had the chance to do my independent study!

Mother. Korea. Roots. An idea sparks. Grassroots.

I finish my text with

Have you thought of going to Korea and doing your own search?

I wait for him to reply, but he doesn't. I peer over my phone at my laptop screen. I want to call him, but I can't, because I'm stuck writing this essay.

But the writer's block hasn't worn off, so I dig out my knitting needles and some yellow yarn. I start making a few 3D daffodils. I have the brownest thumb in Jersey, but I like flowers and gardens, so I craft them.

My document is still blank when Suzanna walks in thirty minutes later, carrying the smell of garlic and oregano on her work clothes.

"Hey." She plops on my bed. "Can you keep a secret?"

I put my knitting in my tote and wipe the fatigue from my eyes. "Sure. I love secrets," I deadpan.

A smile stretches across her face. "Carl asked me to come home. He says he's sorry and wants to start over."

"Does he miss your cooking and needs the bed warm at night?"

Suzanna's lips drop into a frown. "No one in this family hopes anymore. He had a change of heart."

Emily Dickinson said hope has feathers and it never stops at all. Hope is not soft, and it does stop. It stops when your childhood is cut short.

"I said yes." Suzanna clutches her hands together on her chest. "I'm going back to my husband. Doesn't that sound nice?"

I cross the room and sit next to her. "Are you insane? Another woman was in your apartment."

Suzanna waves a hand. "Gina was a rebound. She's an ex from high school he tracked down on Facebook because he was lonely. They didn't do anything crazy. Remember, Carl's a terrible liar."

I scrunch up my face. "It's okay to believe that when he couldn't keep his dad's surprise birthday party a secret or admitted he shopped for your anniversary gift the day of."

"You'd want him to believe me if I were the one at fault," she points out.

"Whatever. Make sure Carl gets medieval armor to protect himself from Mom and Dad."

Suzanna's posture falls. "I know."

"If you think he's being honest and won't blast your heart into pieces again, go back and don't worry about what they think."

Suzanna jumps up and plants her hands on her hips. "You're right, and I won't have to hear Mom and Dad bicker about money. And Mom won't be such a penny fanatic with one less mouth to feed."

"Did you hear? Dad got an interview in the city."

"I know." Suzanna leaves for the bathroom. "I hope he gets it. Not just for the money. Mom's crazy, and I'm tired of her making me crazy."

My phone buzzes next to my laptop.

> **Ian**
> I'll think about Korea if you think about
> going after Russian.

I'd better write this paper. It's almost eleven. I'll write an essay about an essay.

I wrote creative nonfiction as fiction, I type, *and it's time to tell the truth.*

Delete. I close my laptop with the screen still on and grab my Russian flash cards from my backpack. I pin my favorite words on the corkboard on the inside of my desk hutch. I whisper each word I hold. Сон is dream. Любовь is love. Дочери is daughters.

If I choose women's studies, the person I could have been will scream inside me, and I'll spend the rest of my life trying to shut her up.

I write *Declared major: Russian* on a flash card and hang it above the one that says, головная боль—headache.

———

THE NEXT DAY, Professor Guerra comes into class and moves her arms in a circular motion as she says, "Groups, groups, get into groups."

Everyone starts talking. Chairs scrape across the floor. Desks sound like out-of-tune trumpets as they're pushed together. I don't move because I don't have anything to workshop. I can't spend my morning letting people I barely know peek through that window of my life anymore. I've made creative writing a free semester-long subscription to my soul. I'm not modifying the preferences. I'm discontinued.

Professor Guerra notices I haven't moved and there's nothing on my desk. She approaches me with her hands behind her back. She always walks around like she's in handcuffs. I thought creative writing was supposed to be liberating.

"Martha, do you have your draft to workshop?"

"No. I closed the shutters so no one can peek through that window."

She frowns. "I wish I could say I'm not hearing you correctly, but it sounds like you're unhappy with this course."

Poetry's next. I'll have a blast writing deep verses that make no sense, but my critique partners will swear they understand me because I was stupid enough to crank out my soul on paper. Then I'll slap it on that purple POE'TREE like I'm in second grade.

"Your creative nonfiction piece is already down a grade because it's late. You're also missing out on getting feedback from your classmates."

I fold my arms and sit back in my chair.

"You can join a group and workshop what they've written and get partial credit." She turns away and adds, "I hope you feel better from whatever's upsetting you."

The wholesome Martha would get up and workshop. She'd appreciate that Professor Guerra cares about her.

But the current Martha is vacant. She stands, grabs her backpack by its top handle, and floats out of class.

27

IAN

WHEN I WAKE up on Saturday, I head into the kitchen to make breakfast. Dad's sitting on the couch, doing his daily Bible reading.

"You don't have to cook," Dad says as I take cheddar cheese, bacon, and sausage out of the fridge. "I can make omelets or some oatmeal."

"I'm in the mood for a casserole."

Mom's hash browns casserole. She used to make hearty breakfasts every morning. Looking back, those mornings hold some of my best memories of when we were a family of three. Dad made his coffee, and Mom teased him, saying he turned the kitchen into a coffee lab. She asked me to do small tasks, like mix batter or get things from the freezer, so I'd feel involved. We ate together, and it was during those breakfasts that I never heard Mom and Dad fight. And when he left for work, they always hugged and said I love you to each other.

Dad closes his Bible and stands. "Here. Let me help." He joins me in the kitchen and starts grating the cheese while I cook the meat. "What's on your agenda today?"

"I'm going to a poetry reading with Martha. It's at school. It counts as extra credit for her creative writing class. She's getting me at ten thirty."

Dad lifts a brow. "Why's it on a weekend?"

"Beats me. This month's an exception. Martha said it's usually on a Thursday."

"You're going to school on a Saturday? Let me know if the building collapses when you step inside."

"Okay, Dad."

He claps my back. "You've been spending a lot of time with her."

My face reddens. I push the sausage and bacon around with the spatula. "Honestly? I'm starting to like her. But there's a chance we might never move past being friends."

"Why?"

"Martha's not a believer. I don't want to be in the same situation I was in with Hana." I lift the pan off the burner and shut the stove off. "She doesn't want to talk about religion."

Dad walks past me and drops the cutting board and grater into the sink. "Do you know why she said that?"

"Look, don't tell anyone." I lean against the counter. "She said her quote-unquote Christian grandparents were horrible people. I'm thinking it was extreme hypocrisy and/or abuse."

"Whatever you say stays here," Dad promises. He plants a hand on his hip. His expression falls. "And, yeah, you're probably right. Religious trauma ... it takes a long time to repair."

"You have any advice?"

"You be your best self for her. Show her Jesus's love and be patient. And if she never comes to faith, you can stay good friends. If she makes the choice to follow Christ, you can decide where to go from there."

I nod in agreement and spray oil onto the casserole dish.

"I was reading Genesis 16 this morning, where God appears before Hagar by the fountain after she runs away from Abram and Sarai."

"Pastor Nick gave a rocking sermon on that," I recall.

"He did. I highlighted the verse 'Thou God seeth me; for she said, Have I also looked after him that seeth me?'" Dad chuckles. "Pastor Nick was so moved when he preached on that verse. How he emphasized the power of the moment when Hagar finally saw the God who was watching her all that time."

I stay still and let this settle inside me.

Dad searches for the hash browns in the freezer. "I'll pray Martha comes to the same realization someday."

"Thanks, Dad."

"You got it. Now, let's get breakfast in the oven. I'm getting hungry."

"Can you make me some coffee? I could use the extra boost. I was up late doing German homework."

Dad grins as he rips open the bag of hash browns. "You're heading to school on a weekend, and now you want coffee? Where'd my son go?"

"Har har. He's still here. He hasn't been abducted by caffeinated academic aliens."

———

WHEN MARTHA and I arrive at school, the almost-empty parking lot makes the atmosphere feel apocalyptic. We stroll to the student center, where several students are trickling into a conference room.

A blond woman stands by a table near the entrance. "If you're doing a reading, please sign in here," she hollers over everyone talking.

To my surprise, Martha scoots over to the back of the line forming at the sign-in table.

"I'm the third person on the list," she says after she puts her name in.

"What are you going to read?" I ask.

Martha pulls a folded sheet of paper out of her purse. "I wrote something last-minute. I'll get three extra points toward my next assignment for attending and three for reading."

"Nice."

We file into the conference room with about fifty other students. Martha leads me to an empty row in the back.

The student who was at the sign-in table stands in the front. "Hey, I'm Lindsay. I head the poetry club." She glances at her paper. "We have eleven people reading. Please"—she takes a breath before continuing—"no erotica, extreme violence, or excessive foul language. And we have refreshments on the table in the back. Okay, let's—"

"Lindsay." I turn my head toward the voice in the back. It's my American lit instructor, Professor Vega. "Poetry club info."

"Oh, if you'd like to join the poetry club, we meet every Thursday during college hours. For those of you who don't know, that's from eleven to one. We meet at noon in the Humanities Building, room 214. It's a chill environment where we write and share poetry." In a singsong voice, she adds, "Sometimes we discuss an assigned reading, but it's fun." Lindsay claps her hands. "Okay, cool. Let's do this. Our first reading is from Kelly Silva."

Kelly approaches the front of the room and takes the mic from Lindsay. She makes dramatic motions with her hands, lifts her arms, and puts her hand on her chest as she recites a poem about love, missed opportunities, and loss.

Martha and I exchange humorous looks.

"A little over the top," she mumbles.

"Poetry is art in many forms," I say with a wink.

When Kelly's done, everyone claps. Someone whistles for her.

Next, a couple reads the death scene from *Romeo and Juliet*. The student playing Juliet gives the guy a big kiss and uses a rubber sword to stab herself before she collapses backward onto the floor next to him.

Laughter floats through the room, followed by applause.

"Martha Lane," Lindsay calls.

"Here I go," Martha whispers to me. "Hopefully, I won't be the next one collapsing up there."

I give her a thumbs-up. "You'll do great."

I watch her walk briskly up the aisle, her dark ponytail swinging from side to side behind her. Lindsay gives her the mic.

"Hi, I'm going to read something I wrote on a whim. I only did this for the sake of that extra credit my instructor was promising."

Some people chuckle at this.

Martha runs her fingers down the side of her hair. "I'm not a very good writer, so bear with me." She inhales. "I wrote a poem called 'I Can Tell You a Story.'"

She begins to read.

> I can tell you a story,
> but it's wrinkled in my brain
> from wild storms of memories
> and clenched fists packed with pain.
>
> I can smooth out the memories,
> but their faces are grotesque,
> and if we were to sort through everything,
> your faith will never rest.

Martha looks up. Our gazes align. My heart jumps a beat. She's writing this to me.

> I could tell you a story,
> and you'll never look at me the same.
> Your face will lock into disgust
> because my soul deserves the flame.

I shift in my seat and wring my hands in my lap.

> So, I won't tell you my story,
> because I want you to always believe in
> the warmth of the sun kissing your skin,
> the fullness of a home-cooked meal,
> and that the God you worship is still very
>   real.

> I won't tell you my story
> because you'll try to save me,
> but I've become irredeemable;
> what I've done is below saintly.

> So, let's hang out in books
> and caffeinated drinks.
> I'll always be your friend
> until the earth eats my flesh
> and my entire being sinks.

Everyone applauds. Martha stands still, looking stunned. She walks with confidence toward me and takes a seat. Her expression stays serious as she slips her poem into her bag.

Martha and I sit through the rest of the poetry reading without exchanging looks or whispers. When it's over, we get up and shuffle to the back of the room to the refreshment table.

"I get it," I finally say. "Your poem ..."

Martha offers a sad smile. "We're still friends, but we'll have to part ways in the afterlife."

Dad told me to show Martha Jesus's love, and sometimes that means telling the truth.

"I know you don't want me talking about religion, but this is no laughing matter."

Martha stares at the floor as we move up in the line.

Slowly, I reach up to touch her shoulder and venture to say, "Think about it. You're talking about eternity after you die."

Martha doesn't wiggle out of my hold or give me a dirty look. She responds with, "Thank you, Ian, for caring."

Professor Vega comes up to me. "Ian, hi. I graded your essay this morning." She hoists her tote bag onto her shoulder. "I love your analysis of 'Paul's Case.' How you linked the destruction of his mind to the end of his fantasies. You got an A. Nice job."

I grab a chocolate chip cookie and respond with, "Oh. Thank you," before taking a bite.

She tips her head. "You look shocked."

"I thought I'd get a B, at most."

Professor Vega holds up an encouraging fist. "Have some confidence in yourself. You're doing so well in the class. I love your posts on Blackboard. Keep it up." She turns to Martha and says, "Great poem, by the way," before heading to the exit.

Martha grins at me once we're alone. "So, you have a knack with words too."

I breathe a sigh of relief. "Truth: my transcript is full of B's."

"Why not hope for an A, then?" Martha suggests. "Sounds like your professor thinks it's possible."

I nod and finish my cookie. "You want to go out for lunch?"

"Sure. Can we go to a drive-thru? I have a lot of reading to do for women's studies."

"Not a problem." I pat my wallet in my pants pocket. "I'll pay."

We leave school, and Martha drives to a fast-food joint. We each order a cheeseburger and fries, then she parks in the back of the lot.

"I know you're not thrilled about your writing class," I say, "but your poetry's really good."

"Thanks. This is a short stint of creativity. After this semester, it's Russian, Russian, and more Russian." Martha chews on some burger. "So, what are you up to the rest of this weekend?"

"I usually spend Saturdays with my dad. It's his only day off. We just chill, sometimes go out for Korean. On Sundays we have church, then my dad heads back to work after dinner."

"What does he do?"

"He's a nurse. He works the night shift at a detox center," I answer before eating a fry.

"Um, is your dad ...?" Martha moves her hand in a circular motion as if she can pull out the right words. "You guys look so alike ..."

I laugh. "It's okay, Martha. He's half Korean like me." I share Halmoni's history. Martha listens intently as I talk about how in 1950 her brothers were forced to enlist in the military, and she fled to the south with her sister and parents from where they lived in Kaesong, North Korea. She witnessed Japan's occupation, then, when she was twenty-two, her parents cut ties with her for falling in love with Grandpa.

"Wow," Martha says when I'm done talking. "Your halmoni could have written a book."

"She was a very private person. She held things in, maybe too much. She tried to build a happy life after she came to the States, but her losses haunted her."

Martha chews some more food and waits for me to go on.

"She and my grandpa had a rough patch when my dad was thirteen. Halmoni lost interest in what she loved doing—piano lessons, cooking, volunteering for the church's food pantry."

"Depression?" Martha guesses.

"Yeah. She and my dad were close, but she lost her temper with him over nothing. She and my grandpa fought a lot. Aunt Addie was away at college, and Aunt Naomi was married, living in South Carolina then; my uncle Martin was studying at Duke. So my dad dealt with this on his own. Aunt Addie said something shut off in him around that time."

Suddenly, my thoughts trail off to how unstable Dad was after Mom left. He slept a lot. Chinese takeout and pizza were all we had for dinner. He barely had enough energy to take care of me. His anger. His girlfriend. The accident.

I bite into my burger and stare through the windshield. I tense up. I don't want to see Mom on Thanksgiving. I don't have to see her.

"Ian." Martha's voice brings me back. "I said I think we all have an experience that shuts us off."

"Oh. Right. Absolutely."

She wipes her hands with a napkin and reaches in front of me to open the glove compartment. "Speaking of family history ..." She pulls out some folded papers.

I set my bag of fries in my cup holder and open the packet. I read the title. "Shattered at Six." I ache inside for her.

"I thought you didn't want to tell me your story."

"That's only part of it."

I scan the first page.

"Don't read it now. Please. I'm too embarrassed."

"Okay." I wish I could touch her arm. "I really enjoy spending time with you."

Martha finishes her burger and balls up her trash before turning her car on. "You're a good guy, Ian."

When I get home, I'll make sure Dad and I put Martha at the top of our prayer lists and cast a storm in heaven for her to realize God sees her.

28

MARTHA

BOYS ARE GOOD AT MATH, *and girls are good at art,* Dr. Sloan writes on the blackboard. The chalk squeaks when she writes the *g* in girls.

"If this is true, then why do the articles I asked you to read for this week argue that women are still trying to find a place in art?"

Because women are associated with creativity, and men get the brainy subjects. Then women want to show off their talents in the subject sexism assigns them, and they're still shoved to the ground. The world is a big trap.

The class responds with silence. The leaves on the trees have changed color. Halloween is in six days. It has taken Dr. Sloan half a semester to assign readings about women and art.

She pinches her red silk scarf. "Anyone?"

Kaylin is fighting to stay awake. She was late to class and whispered in my ear that she binged on a trashy romance novel last night. She claims to have gotten transferitis ever since she received her acceptance letter from Delaware last week.

I spent my night researching Russian programs. I made a chart comparing and contrasting courses and tuition. My top three choices are the University of Maryland, Rutgers, and West Chester University. I like UMD's program the most. A class solely devoted to Dostoevsky will make any Russophile's mouth water. Of course, it's the most expensive college out of the three.

Dr. Sloan's lips are tight. "If no one participates, class is over, and it's five points off everyone's participation grade."

I'm a Russian major, but I still care about women's studies. I'll always be a feminist. My hand shoots up.

She points to me. "Ah, Martha."

"I liked Belinda Walker's essay 'The Battle of Gender and Art.' With the gender wage gap, women are budgeting more to make art. And if they work and take care of kids, they also have less time to be creative."

Dr. Sloan nods approvingly.

Kaylin straightens her back and jumps on my statement. "That explains why only seventeen percent of the art in galleries is made by women."

"I think we bit off more than we can chew." Léa chimes in from the first row. "We can't have it all. Women wanted to vote. We got it. We didn't want to be discriminated against if we're pregnant and working. We got the Pregnancy Discrimination Act. Now, it's like, let's have a pity party because we want to make art."

Everyone looks at Léa. She shrugs. "Feminism just wants."

"But women are doing exactly what men do in the art industry and still aren't as successful. That's a problem," Kaylin argues.

Kudos to me for launching a discussion. I, like so many others, didn't do the readings; I skimmed.

The truth is, besides the poem I drew up for the reading this past Saturday, I've been slacking in school altogether. I didn't study for my Russian quiz I had on Friday; I winged it. And I was supposed to email Professor Guerra my creative nonfiction piece by Thursday before midnight to avoid having my grade for the assignment dropped to a C-plus. I didn't.

I've been feasting on a collection of Marina Tsvetaeva's writings called *Earthly Signs: Moscow Diaries, 1917–1922.* I'm heading to the library after class to renew it for a second helping. It's beautiful. Even the amber-yellow cover is beautiful.

My mind swims to Ian. I'm comfortable talking to him. We have a lot in common. We hang out on a steady basis.

And I'm attracted to him. I feel his eyes linger on me at work. But we will never be more than friends. I don't love his God, and if he read my story by now, he knows why. I'm terrified to know what he thinks.

The class is wrapped in a heated debate about whether women should fight for a place in art. "Feminism had a good start, but it's turned into a global soapbox," Léa remarks.

"We still need feminism," Olivia says. "I'm a muralist. I go to school and take care of two toddlers. My husband works in IT and spends forty hours a week doing what he loves. I'm thankful he supports the kids and me. But I barely have time to paint. My parents and sister joke that I'm playing, but it's *work*. So, shut your mouth, Lèa. Women still need a place in art, and we'll get it."

Olivia deserves a standing ovation.

Lèa slumps in her chair. Defeat is a painful sight on anyone's face.

Dr. Sloan stands in front of her desk with her ankles crossed. She holds back a smile. She got much more than she asked for.

Kaylin's about to nod off to sleep. I elbow her, which makes her gasp. What was so captivating about that novel?

Too bad people aren't addicted to their own love stories. Look at the divorce rate.

Last week I thought Suzanna was insane for taking Carl back. Now I think she might be doing the right thing, trying to mend their marriage. It wasn't all for nothing. She smiled so much on her wedding day, the muscles around her mouth must have hurt, and Carl wouldn't let her go. He was either holding her hand, hugging her waist as they walked beside each other, or they were dancing. His blue eyes said one thing that whole day: I love this woman to death.

"He made a selfish mistake," Suzanna told me. "If I don't accept his apology, I'm scared of losing what could have been."

It's my turn to grab what I want so it doesn't evolve into what could have been. Tonight, I'm telling Mom and Dad I'm dumping women's studies. They won't be thrilled, but I want Russian. Every word and syllable, all the history and literature. My heritage is calling me. I can't silence what's in my blood.

"Martha, what did you think of the song?" Dr. Sloan asks.

"What?"

"Did you listen to Alanis Morrisette's 'Sister Blister'?"

My face flushes. "I ... didn't."

"You're the third person I called on who couldn't answer me." Dr. Sloan smacks her notebook on her desk. "No one cares about what I assigned, so I don't care about class."

She tucks her notebook under her arm and carries her bag without closing the zipper. She trembles as she strides away, leaving us all behind.

We trickle out of the room with defeated looks on our faces.

———

"I'M GOING on to the second interview!" Dad announces before we sit for dinner that night. "It's on Thursday."

"David, that's fantastic!" Mom removes the lid from the slow cooker. She made one of the family favorites: brown sugar chicken with string beans and mashed potatoes.

"You got this, Dad," I say as I sit with my food.

He gives me a confident nod.

"If you get the job, you'll be getting up early to catch the train," Mom points out.

"And I won't be home until sometime after dinner."

"I gave the HOA five hundred toward the assessment," Mom tells him as she loads mashed potatoes onto her dish. "But the president says we can't pay it in increments."

I put my elbow on the table and cradle my chin in my hand. HOAs should be illegal. Not everyone can dish out two thousand dollars at once.

"We'll make the deadline, even if I don't get the job. We'll pay the whole thing at once," Dad assures her.

"I hope you're right because—"

"Stop thinking about money. For God's sake, I can't enjoy my evenings because you act like we're going to end up on the streets tomorrow."

"God forbid you give me credit for doing something that gets this family somewhere."

Dad motions to me. "You have Marty chipping in for groceries for no reason." He jumps out of his chair and grabs his wallet off the counter. He comes back, holding a wad of twenty-dollar bills, and offers them to me. "I went to the ATM today."

Mom watches us with rigid eyes. Her mouth sets in a deep frown.

I take the money from Dad like I'm handling fine china. Mom shouldn't have used my money, but I feel like I'm betraying her, taking Dad's cash.

"We don't have much in savings," Mom says. "This HOA wants everything but our souls. And with you going to Montclair ..."

Mom's sterling-gray eyes are pleading. This is what my family has come to: my parents are making me choose who's right about how they're handling the money I lent them for groceries.

"I don't want to go to Montclair," I venture to say. "I want to major in Russian at the University of Maryland. I either want to teach or do literary translating."

"What?" Mom asks.

"Really?" is Dad's response.

"I can't stop studying it. I'm ahead in my textbook and can understand grammar Alyosha hasn't taught us yet. The literature is the most beautiful writing I've ever read, and I'd love to read it in Russian one day." I fold my hands like I'm praying. "Please say yes."

Mom shakes her head. "No. You are going to Montclair." The frustration rises in her voice. "You got accepted, and you're going to orientation next month."

"No!"

"You didn't apply anywhere else."

"She'll stay home for another semester," Dad suggests. "You'll keep your job, right? Take a few more classes?"

Dad's support is what's keeping my body from clicking into flight mode from Mom's disapproval. "Yeah, Russian 102, and I found this cool Eastern European literature class. I'll ask my advisor to update my graduation form."

"You can't go out of state." To Dad, Mom says, "Will you stop encouraging her to spend our money?"

Dad sets his fork on his plate. "She needs to do what she wants. I don't want her to be miserable, then she goes back to school ten years later. She can take out student loans."

"It'll take her years to pay those off!"

"It's *her* decision."

Mom slides forward in her chair and squeezes my arm. "You

have a beautiful idea setting up that pregnancy care center. Don't ruin it over some fling you're having."

I lean back. "Mom, you're suffocating me."

"Marty, you know what you want. You can contact Montclair and turn down your acceptance."

Whoa. I didn't expect Dad to let me make this final so quickly.

"She's only been taking Russian for two months," Mom argues.

"Ugh!" I put an elbow on the table and splay my hand over my forehead. "Will you two stop bickering?" I turn to Mom. "I'm twenty years old. I found my passion, and I'm going for it, even if it means going to Rutgers or Maryland or Moscow. I'll find a way to pay for it." I lean closer to her and squeeze her wrist. "Can you trust me?"

Mom eats some string beans and keeps her eyes on her plate. She nods as she whispers, "Okay. I trust you know what you're doing."

I lean back and blow out some air.

We stay silent as we finish dinner. I help Mom and Dad clean up, then I go to my room.

There's a text from Ian.

Ian
I did some rotten stuff too. Our neighbor
Mrs. Glazer always called me the little
Chinese boy. When I was 10, I threw an egg
at her house on Mischief Night. Not a
secret. Told my dad about it after she
moved. He tried not to laugh.

I look at my phone, puzzled. Then I remember I texted Ian my sixth secret a few hours ago. I told him that in high school I wrote *I have an STD* on Chloe's locker as revenge for all the bullying she put me through. I made her cry. I feel bad about it now.

We both ruined someone else's property.
Sorry you had such a racist neighbor. Also,
FYI, I told my parents I want to change my
major. My mom's panicking about money,
but my dad's cool with my choice.

Dad knocks on my door. "You have a minute?"

"Yeah."

He opens the door and steps into my room. "Listen, I'm not trying to turn you against Mom. She has a right to be concerned about our finances. UMD is pricey. Maybe you'll get a scholarship. But I'm glad you spoke up for yourself. I'm happy with your decision. You work hard, and I know you won't sit on your butt after you get your degree. You'll make good use of it."

"Thanks, Dad." I turn my phone over in my hands. "Is Mom okay?"

He scratches the side of his head. "Her anxiety probably comes from when her dad lost his job when she was younger. Supposedly that's what fueled his alcoholism. I think she's dealing with some bad memories."

I frown at this sudden discovery. My grandparents really did a number on their family. "Oh, I didn't know about that."

In a whisper, he admits, "I'm trying real hard to be patient. I mean, my dad had a temper, but he wasn't a useless drunk like Gabe." Before he turns around to leave, Dad asks, "You need anything before I go in for the night?"

His question makes my ears perk up. He has stepped on tender ground. Could I tell him I need a quieter home with healthier communication, the old Mom back, and a hug?

"I'm good, Dad. Night-night."

"Good night, sweetie."

I message Kaylin.

> My parents said yes to my major! Well, my
> mom, sort of.

Then I take out my Russian textbook and flip through its pages, gazing over material that I probably won't learn for another year or two. My lips curve into a grin. This. Is. Awesome.

Kailyn gets back to me.

> **Kay**
> Woohoo! Par-tay! So happy for you and
> your new "love." If you go to UMD, you
> won't be far from Delaware.

> YES! And it might be nice to leave Jersey
> for a bit.

> **Kay**
> You're speaking my language. Pun
> intended. I'm not coming back after
> graduation. Too expensive.

Before I head off to bed, Ian calls me. I'm scared he's going to say something about my story, but he asks, "Can you hang out on Friday?"

"I might be lost in definite and indefinite verbs and the history of the Romanovs."

"I'll use mysticism to get Rasputin out of your head," he jokes.

"Ha. Friday works. Want to hit the café?"

"I'm up for that."

"Cool. And come with your seventh secret."

With a laugh, I say, "I'll try."

29

IAN

WHEN I GET HOME from German class on Tuesday, I make a salami sandwich for lunch and read Martha's story.

She was a little girl, anticipating what Santa would leave for her under the tree. But she gets carted off to a church service she doesn't understand with her bladder ready to burst. And when she can't hold it anymore and relieves herself, her grandma beats her and calls her and her parents foul names. Then her grandma finds pleasure in keeping the car locked to terrify Martha some more.

And the terrifying thing is, Martha said this isn't the whole story. What's missing? Why does she think she's going to hell?

I rub my forehead. Will Martha ever trust me enough to tell me everything? Do I *want* to know everything?

I text her.

> I read your story. You didn't deserve any of
> that. I'm here if you want to talk.

Martha's a year older than me, so her story took place when I was five. That was the first Christmas Dad and I spent without

Mom. The pain was fresh, but Dad's family was there for us. We went to church, where I heard the Christmas story and knew who God really is. I was safe. My family hugged and comforted me.

Martha's plea to Jesus echoes in my head. *Do you see her hurting me?*

In her mind, then, she knew Jesus was a savior, and he didn't rescue her from the abuse she was suffering that morning.

I picture a young Martha trying to make sense of this as her grandma beats her in a car. Oh, God ...

I finish eating, straighten up my room, then get dressed for work. And I pray for Martha. That God will soften her heart and heal her pain. That she will know God is not a monster. That she will come to him. And no matter what happens, she and I stay close friends.

When I get to work, Evan meets me at the entrance. "Good. You're early. Clock in. Liz is finishing orientation with the new guy. It's insane in here."

He's right. Who spends $77.42 to make a costume for your poodle? No, miss, the lid to that cake carrier won't pass as a space helmet. And to the couple who's buying black fabric, it's cruel for your son to dress as the Grim Reaper to scare trick-or-treaters off your porch.

Martha's shift starts at three o'clock. When she comes to her register, she says, "Hi, Ian."

"How's it going?" I ask as I pop her cash till open.

"I'm all right. I got your text. I *do* want to tell you everything." She sounds nervous. "When we hang out on Friday."

I stop, holding a wad of singles, and look at her, shocked. "You got it. Oh, and do you want your story back? It's in my locker."

She shakes her head. "You can burn it. Use it as a cleaning cloth."

"I wouldn't do that to your writing." When I'm done counting the money, I give her the variance to sign. "Liz wants you in jewelry. There was a natural disaster."

"From natural beings called shoppers," she jokes over her shoulder.

For the next half hour, I ring up a steady flow of customers. When I have some downtime, I do some cleaning. I tie up the trash that's about to overflow and sort returns.

Behind me, someone says, "Hey, Ian, remember me?"

Sickness fills my stomach. Justin Massey is here, wearing a blue polo shirt. Why, out of all the applicants Liz interviewed, did she choose him?

Justin grins. "You must be behaving yourself if you're a supervisor."

He looks the same with his short, layered brown hair and hooded eyes. His attitude hasn't changed either. The same smirk was glued on his face when he bullied me on the bus.

"I'm doing amazing." I take some bags from the shelf under my register and slip them on the metal rack. "By the way, you're not allowed back here until you're trained."

Justin raises his hands. "I'm touring my new home away from home."

"Look, I don't want Liz or Evan seeing you back here on my watch."

"You wear your supervisor hat with pride. Good thing Alicia's training me on Friday. You and I wouldn't make a good team."

I look at him, hard. "You can't push her around either."

Justin whistles before walking to the exit. "Already accusing me. Nice to see you grown-up."

I put my elbow on the counter and cradle my forehead in my palm. I'm ready to quit.

"Ian."

My head jerks up.

Liz pats the counter. "Don't worry if you and Anthony can't unpack everything today. The shipment's bigger than usual. You know my motto: customers first."

"Okay. Good night, Liz."

I get reeled into the personal shopper trap with a woman whose son procrastinated with a history project. A guy has a return of five hundred dollars of scrapbooking supplies, which keeps me busy for over an hour. Then a woman wants to return two skeins of yarn, but she doesn't have a receipt. I can only give her store credit. As she leaves, she sneers, "I hate you, I hate you, I *hate* you."

Martha walks to her register. "The jewelry aisle is sparkly clean. It's time for your break, right?"

"Yeah. If I don't come back, I took leave without pay to go on vacation," I remark as I head toward the break room.

"I'd miss you."

I turn around and look at her. I grin. "I'd miss you too."

She smiles back.

———

WHEN I RETURN HOME from work, I sit with my Bible on my lap and think about what unfolded today. Martha wants to talk about her past. She trusts me. Dad's advice is working. I'm showing her Christ's love without talking about my faith.

Thank you, God, for sustaining our friendship and for helping Martha to trust me.

I see her in my mind. How defined her low cheekbones are when she smiles. The way she twirls some of her ponytail around her finger when she's deep in thought. The gentle curve of her back against my forearm as we danced at Morgan and Zach's wedding.

I'm falling for Martha. Whoa. Slow down.

But what if she believed in you? I ask God.

I place my elbow on my Bible and lean my forehead on the heel of my palm. Whether or not Martha and I ever date, I hope she knows that God is a loving God, and he did see her grandmother hit her that Christmas morning. He has always seen her.

And the only way to prove that to Martha is through the Word itself. You can't get any more real about God than that.

I open my Bible to the index. *Believe ... comfort ... heart ... heavy.*

Heavy. The burden of Martha's past is heavy.

I'm directed to Matthew 11:28. *Come unto me, all* ye *that labour and are heavy laden, and I will give you rest.*

I fold down the corner of the page. My stomach cramps, and I take a slow, deep breath. I'm going to send this verse to Martha. She might go back to hating me. I could lose her as a friend. And, on a lighter note, I'm not sure if I should use another translation, but Dad is King James only, and that's how he raised me.

I will do this. Martha has to know the God she's feared all these years is the only one who can give her the comfort she deserved fourteen years ago.

30

MARTHA

I GOT HIT with a migraine on Friday, so I called out of work, and I couldn't hang out with Ian. He answered the phone, and when I told him why I couldn't show up, he asked, "Anything I can do?"

His question shocked me. I didn't think he cared about me like that. I told him I'd be fine, and we agreed to make plans for another weekend. I had to spend all of Saturday and the time I had after work on Sunday catching up on schoolwork.

We're getting closer, and I'm terrified. I told him I wanted to talk about something. I can't back out. It wants to come out. It needs to come out because I can't go on carrying this inside me.

I'm pulling an oversized sweater over my head when I hear Suzanna scream from down the hall, "It's my life, and he's *my* husband!"

"Honey, you're moving back into this way too fast!" Mom hollers after her.

I hide in my sweater for a few seconds and groan before popping my head back into reality.

Suzanna runs into the room and rips a suitcase out of the

closet. "I'll move fast! I'll move out today!" She pushes down the lock on the door handle.

"Suzanna Katherine Lane!" Mom exclaims on the other side. "Unlock the door!"

She rips clothes off hangers and throws them into her suitcase. "My last name is Alexander, and I'll die with that name!"

Constant yelling has been the soundtrack in the house since last night. Suzanna broke the news to Mom and Dad about Carl. Dad still wants to strangle him, and Mom's afraid Suzanna will get hurt again.

I'm about to walk over to my dresser to dab some concealer on the blemish over my left eyebrow, but Suzanna beats me there. She gathers her makeup and accessories and crams them into a cosmetic bag.

"You're acting like a teenager!" Mom yells, knocking on the door. "Open up so we can talk to each other like humans."

It's 11:18. Professor Guerra wants to see me at noon. I skipped creative writing last Tuesday but went to school so Mom wouldn't know I cut class. I scoured the library for Russian literature. I'm on page 182 of *The Idiot*.

Suzanna grunts and unlocks the door. Mom's still in her pajamas, and flyaway ends hang around her face. She's always dressed and put together by the time Dad leaves for work. The stress in this house must be wearing her out.

"Suzanna, he dumped you because you can't have kids, and all of a sudden he wants you back? Why don't you stay here while you work things out with him? That way you'll know you're going back to a solid relationship."

Suzanna fakes a laugh. "I thought you'd do the happy dance, having one less person using the water and electricity."

Mom's shoulders fall, and she looks hurt.

I shlep over to my desk and wake up my laptop. I managed to

pound out a creative nonfiction piece over the weekend about the wedding called "A One-Night's Notice." I hit Ctrl + P, and the printer spits out my efforts. My writing's a mess, but so am I. You are what you write.

"If he hurts you again, don't come home," Mom warns, "because it'll be your fault."

Suzanna comes up behind me and squeezes my shoulders. "Hear that, Marty? Mom isn't a money-saving fanatic anymore. She wants me to stay!"

I wrench out of her grip and staple the pages of my story together.

Suzanna grabs her suitcase and starts for the door. "I have faith. Not the religious kind. I'm jumping and know there's a net to catch me called reconciliation." Once she's down the hall, she says. "I'll be back tonight for the rest of my stuff."

"Dad and I will not be helping you move."

She snorts. "Carl has a *very* supportive family."

"We supported *you* when you didn't want to be with him anymore!" Mom retorts. She rubs her eyes and steps into my room. In a calmer tone, she asks, "Are you feeling better?"

"Yeah. I'm meeting with my creative writing teacher."

"I made pancakes."

"Thanks, Mom. I'll be down soon."

She comes behind my chair and leans over to peer at my screen.

I close my laptop. "Don't read it."

"Your teacher reads your stuff, but I can't," she says bitterly. "Both my daughters hate me."

Her accusation feels like a slap on the face. "Mom …"

She shakes her head and shoos my words away. "No. Come and eat, then get lost."

I apologize to Mom after breakfast, but she keeps her back to me and scrubs the griddle in silence.

———

PROFESSOR GUERRA'S office is a mess, as always, and she tries to look happy when I enter. Her workspace is nauseating. Virginia Woolf said writers need a room of their own to concentrate, not to be a slob.

"Thanks for coming." She pulls a black notebook in front of her and opens it to a page tagged with an Ernest Hemingway bookmark. "You missed two classes, and I have a zero for your participation in creative nonfiction."

I sit and place my essay on her desk. "I wrote something."

Professor Guerra picks it up and doesn't even glance at it. "Martha, you missed workshop. I said if you got this in by the twenty-first, I'd give you a C. That was two days past the deadline. You didn't take advantage of that. Then you miss class again." She removes a calculator from the top drawer of her desk. "We've moved on to poetry. There's an assignment due tomorrow."

I slide my hands between my thighs and wait for the verdict. Tick tock, tick tock. I'm a little stumbling block.

Professor Guerra finishes her math. "If you don't miss another class and hand in all your work from now on, you'll get a C-plus, and that's with the extra credit you got from the poetry reading."

I don't react.

She pushes my work toward me. "You need to edit this on your own." She writes something on a sticky note. "I don't know what you're going through, but I'm sorry it's pulling you down. You have a lot of potential, Martha."

Professor Guerra is trying to help me, but those overly used phrases teachers pull out to encourage students are worn down to nothing in my brain. Reach for the stars! You don't know what will happen until you try! You can do anything you put your mind to! Be careful with that one. Some kids put their minds to very dangerous thoughts.

She hands me the note. "I changed the readings for tomorrow. I'll see you then."

I shove the paper in my back pocket and dash out of her office without putting my folder in my backpack.

"Martha, wait!" she hollers after me.

I dump my writing folder inside the first trash can I see in the hall. I fish the poetry book out of my bag and toss that in next. A couple slows and stares at me. "Mind your own business!" I snap, and they hurry away.

I can't decorate my past with creativity; It needs to die.

I have forty minutes before women's studies, so I retreat to my car and text Kaylin that I'm dropping creative writing.

Kay
What??? A W for you is the kiss of death.

> I don't care. I'll go to MSU and take the Russian minor.

Kay
Are you OK? Where are you?

Good question, Kay. I don't know where I went. I disappeared on December 25, 1996. Another Martha inhabited my body, and she did something very bad when she was fourteen.

Before I slip out of my car and walk to women's studies, my text tone chimes.

> **Ian**
>
> I know religion has hurt you deeply, but I feel I should tell you the truth. God is a loving, just, and compassionate God. I've been praying for you since you drove me home. And this verse made me think of you: Come unto me, all ye that labour and are heavy laden, and I will give you rest.

I hold my phone so tightly, my knuckles pale.

Resting is foreign to me. I've been locked in defense mode for fourteen years.

He sends another text.

> **Ian**
>
> Truth is, Martha, I've been thinking about you a lot.

My fingers loosen around my phone. It falls onto my lap. I'm not mad at Ian for being a Christian. I'm mad at myself for letting him get too close to me.

I must push him away. I'll tell him why my soul is past the point of no return. He'll realize I'm a lost cause and leave me alone forever.

I only have time to write:

> I'll tell you everything tomorrow.

I read his response after class.

> **Ian**
>
> I'm in. And here's my #6: My mom cheated on my dad a few months before she left us.

I'm sorry that happened, Ian. And, I'm sorry, but tomorrow the game's over.

31

IAN

IT'S Justin's first day working, and he's already testing my patience. I give him the inventory barcode scanner for his tasks in the framing department. He swings the device at his side and walks away. I tell him to stop because that thing costs a few hundred dollars, and he turns around and smirks at me. When he's at his register, he asks for more quarters and dimes even though he still has some of each in his drawer.

"Don't open those until you need them," I tell him. "It'll save me time when I count you out later."

Justin spills the dimes into their compartment. I cringe as he grabs the quarters.

I ask him to put away returns. He rides on the front of the shopping cart instead of pushing it like a mature adult.

"Cut it out, Justin," I demand, but he ignores me.

At three o'clock, I count his drawer. To his credit, he's only a penny over.

"Not bad for your first day."

He says nothing as he hurries past Martha and roughly brushes shoulders with her.

"Who's the new jerk?" she asks in a loud whisper.

"Justin. He was on my bus from first to fifth grade until he moved to Marlboro. He hasn't changed."

"Where's Evan?"

I pick up the clipboard, which is next to my register. "Jury duty."

"I actually feel sorry for him."

"You won't be up here today unless I'm on break or the line gets long."

"Ooh, goodie." She claps her hands over her chest. In a hushed voice, she adds, "I don't feel like dealing with people today."

"That's me every day. I should take Patience 501 if I want to run a bookstore."

Martha smirks. "Ouch. Graduate level."

"At least my mom would be happy. Maybe she'd finally love me." I glance down at the schedule. "Anyway, there's a ton of new yarn to stock, and Liz wants you to clean the classroom."

"She's stopping the fossilization in there?"

"People are asking for origami classes. Anthony's good at it, so he's teaching it on Friday."

Martha lets out an excited gasp. "Can I teach some knitting classes?"

"I don't see why not." A man places a frame on the counter. I greet him, scan the barcode, and take his credit card. "There's a form to fill out for that. I'll get it for you from the office," I call after her as she walks away.

Business is slow tonight, so Martha and I don't spend any time together at the registers. After we close, she goes to use the bathroom, so I wait for her in the vestibule.

Five minutes pass. Then ten. Is she sick? The only time I'm

allowed in the ladies' room is to clean it. There's no protocol for when you think something's wrong.

I head back inside. As I get closer to the bathroom, I hear Martha shouting.

"I didn't drop creative writing to socialize more! I'm not going to be out that late ... I told you I'd get a C if I finished. I don't want that on my transcript ... I'm sorry you didn't get the job ... You always told Mom we're going to be okay. Is that true anymore? ... I'm dealing with a lot too." There's a pause, then she spits out foul language. Her phone clatters to the floor. Some footsteps.

I back away from the door.

Martha flings it open and stares at me with her mouth agape. "Were you eavesdropping on me?"

My face burns. "You were in there for a long time. I wanted to make sure you're okay."

"Answer my question," she demands.

"I got here when you were talking about your writing class. Martha, we were fine before." I hold out my hands. "Now we're like this?"

"That phone call was *private*." She pushes past me and balls her fists in the air with a grunt.

I follow her to the exit. "I'm not going to blab your personal business to anyone."

She whirls around by the spray paint. "Ian, what you don't understand is ..." She gulps and points to herself. "I'm in so much ... *pain*. I get you have baggage too. We both have crap we hid from our parents ..." Martha falters.

Slowly, I move closer to her.

She looks at me with big eyes, as if she's being chased by a mountain lion.

"Martha, you're safe with me. You're always safe with me."

She grabs on to a shelf and sucks in her breath.

"Are you in physical pain? Do you need—?"

"It's not that," she snaps. "He's dead, but it never goes away."

I reach out and touch her shoulder. "Your grandfather?"

Our faces are so close together. I want to brush back her flyaway pieces of hair.

Martha coils and strolls down the aisle, hugging herself. She plops down on the floor and rests against the shelves. She takes heavy breaths, then says, "If evil has a face, it's my grandfather's. The way he gazed at me that morning ..." She swallows. "And so many other times."

I analyze her words. I squint as the connections begin to form in my mind.

I look at my hands. Anger pools inside me. If Martha's grandfather were alive, I'd need to be locked away so I wouldn't tear him to pieces.

Her grandma led the abuse in "Shattered at Six," but her grandpa did the unthinkable. But there's still something missing from her story.

I sit down next to her and hook my arm around my knee. "Martha, why do you think you're going to hell? What did you do?"

She lifts her head. Her eyes shine with tears as she leans her shoulder against mine. "You want to know why I'm irredeemable?"

I'm completely still.

"Number seven: I killed my grandpa."

32

MARTHA

MY CONFESSION MAKES Ian's face turn a pasty white, and his mouth drops open. "What did you do?"

"I wanted him to die." I wipe my sleeve across my eyes and sniff back tears. "He ..." I make the *m* sound. I breathe in and try the word again. "Mol ... mol ..."

"He molested you?" Ian guesses. "Your grandfather molested you?"

I curl into a tight ball. "That Christmas morning in my story— I didn't wake up when he was carrying me. He was touching me. I begged him to stop, but he wouldn't." I knot my hands into fists and growl, "It's *my* body. He had no right!" I pound my knee. "No. Right!"

The images, noises, and touches caged inside me start to flail. Their edges, quiet and hidden for fourteen years, become hot and knife me. They're breaking out, and it's going to happen in front of Ian.

"My grandparents were banned from our house, but after Grandma died, Mom felt bad for my grandpa and let him back in.

He always found a way to touch me. He said it was our special secret, and if I told anyone, I'd go to hell."

Ian rests against the shelf. "That's twisted."

"The last time, I was fourteen. It was his birthday. We went out to dinner, then had cake at his house. When it was time to go, my parents and Suzanna were helping my aunt and uncle load some hand-me-downs into their car that Grandpa's neighbor, Tori, had given to my cousins. I had to use the bathroom. I didn't lock the door." I spit out, "I was so *stupid*. I was washing my hands, and he came in. He pinned me against the sink. He asked me if I was keeping our secret. I said yes. He said I was a good girl, so he had a surprise. He touched me in new places."

I gripped the sides of the sink as it dug into my stomach. I groaned and stared at my distorted reflection in the chrome faucet. "I felt things I didn't understand, and he smiled at that." Ian's face blurs. "His hand was so ... *cold*." I shudder. "I wanted to break it, to hear his bones crunch."

"Did you really kill him?" Ian asks.

I turn away from him.

"Martha, tell me."

"He walked out of the bathroom. I screamed that I'd tell my parents. I said he'd go to prison, and I hoped the other inmates would kill him. My grandpa slit his wrists the next day. Tori noticed he didn't get his newspaper that morning. She had a key and went in to check on him. She had nightmares about what she saw." I press the heel of my palm to my forehead. "I can't live with this."

Ian balances his arm on his knee. "You're not guilty for wanting to report a crime."

His words just pass through my head. "I wanted him dead, and when it happened, I was happy. Then I really unpacked the whole situation, and I'm, like, oh, my God, I caused it." I sit up straighter.

"That's why I can't figure God out. From the little I know about Christianity, it's supposed to teach grace, love, charity. Not child abuse."

"It does teach good things. People who truly follow Jesus show that."

I rub my eyes. "Don't preach to me."

"Martha, you don't want to talk about religion, but you bring it up, and sometimes you're ..." Ian breathes out. "You're insulting my God."

I look down at the floor. *My God* hits me in an unexpected way. Ian's God. Ian is caring. He respects my boundaries. He prays for me.

"I used to think like you," he goes on. "I didn't go to church for years. My life wasn't easy. It still isn't. But I understand God. Things were perfect in Genesis 1. In chapter 3, Adam and Eve disobeyed God. He gave them the free will to sin, and the world got corrupted. That's why people do wicked things, and wicked things happen."

"Yeah, you were adopted and got a lousy mother, who's a waste of space." Ian's painful expression makes me stop. I cross my legs. "I hope you didn't see anything when she cheated on your dad."

"She said she had an important meeting with someone, so I had to stay in my room." Ian screws up his face. "You don't have meetings in a bedroom and wash the sheets afterward."

Martha's eyes widen. "Your mom cheated on your dad when you were *home*?"

"Yeah, and not caring at all how it would affect me. Do your parents know you were molested?"

"No. My grandpa mellowed out after my grandma died. He cut back on the alcohol, built a decent relationship with my mom. She thought he killed himself because he felt guilty for being such a rotten husband and father. She even cried at his funeral. I didn't know how or when to tell her the truth. It became normal to hide it."

Ian perks up a little. "We talk to our parents all the time but can't say what we need to say."

"I know. It makes you realize how messed up family communication can get." I stand and brush some dust off my pants. "Look, Ian, I'd love to chat more, but it's been"—I wrinkle my face—"a weird night. I should head home."

His expression falls as he fishes his keys out of his pocket. "I understand."

"Can you grab the paperwork for teaching classes?"

"Sure." Ian hurries to the office. He returns with the form, and I slip it into my bag.

We leave the store in silence. When we get to the vestibule, Ian checks my purse.

"All right, Martha. I'll see you Thursday." He starts walking to his car.

"Ian," I call after him. "Don't go."

I feel a sudden pull to be near him, close to him. My arms feel as if they're being controlled by another person as I hold them out. Ian knows seven things I've never told another soul. He's been an honest and true friend in all the sharp turns my life has taken this semester. He has been—and still wants to be—there for me. "Can I hug you?"

Ian turns around, his mouth slightly open from shock, and steps toward me. He says yes by opening his arms.

I wrap him in a hug, closing the divide between us, and whisper, "Thanks for being you."

A wave of relief covers me. Emotion catches in my throat. Relief. I accept that Ian has faith. That it is a part of his identity, and it hasn't made him a monster. A huge chunk of hostility I've carried for fourteen years has been lifted from my shoulders.

My thoughts float to the Bible verse Ian texted me. I will never come to God, but, in a way, it finally feels like I am resting.

It feels so good. And so does Ian's embrace.

Ian rubs the small of my back. "I've wanted to get to know you for a while."

"How come?"

"I figured there was more to you than the hard person you want everyone to see."

My muscles tighten, and heat charges through my body. Get to know you. That's always the beginning of "I like you." Ian and I can never have that; he'll probably date a Christian. That will never be me. Even though I've let go of some grudges toward his faith, no one will ever convert me.

As we pull apart, Ian runs his hands down my arms. I back away to prevent our hands from touching.

"Call me anytime if you want to talk, hang out," he says.

I smile. "Thanks. You too."

We part ways, and when I slip into my car, I fan myself.

What just happened?

I cover my mouth, even though there's no reason to stay quiet, and I burst into giggles.

I have a crush on Ian.

33

IAN

WHEN I GOT BACK from work the night Martha hugged me, I called Chris to catch up, but his phone rang twice and went to voicemail.

He texted me right away.

> **Chris**
> Can't talk. Sorry.

I didn't bother asking why.

On the bright side, Martha and I fall into a steady stream of communication outside of work. We're both bogged down with schoolwork for the rest of the week, so we don't make plans. But we text each other a few times a day about what we're up to, and sometimes we chat around bedtime.

Martha is opening up to me. I asked her how things were going at home. She told me her dad's been working part-time since September, which is putting a strain on her parents' finances and their marriage. Her mom's been looking for work too, with no leads.

"They're not even fighting about money anymore," she confides. "They fight about everything and nothing. My mom gets upset about the kind of groceries my dad buys or which contractor he uses to get the oven fixed. Then he gets angry and verbally abusive."

"I'm so sorry. That's what my parents did before their marriage failed. I don't mean to scare you."

"I'm already assuming the worst," Martha mutters.

We also talk about books. The same common ground that Hana and I stood on that put so many fun memories in our relationship.

Martha texts me on Friday after work.

Martha
Just finished The Idiot. Would love to get into YA. Need recommendations!

> Anything by my favorite authors Marie Myong-Ok Lee and Pete Hautman. Also The Perks of Being a Wallflower, Speak.

Martha
I read Speak. Ever see the movie?

> No.

Martha
Movie night, then?

> We should make a bucket list in a notebook.

Martha
Let's fill one up!

I blink several times to make sure I read her text correctly. Filling up a notebook with things to do with Martha means she wants to stay in my life for a while. I feel a sense of security I didn't know I needed. My friendship with Chris has been questionable lately, and Martha's company is filling that loneliness.

I hope she and I can be more than friends someday. I pray her wounds heal. I can't stop thinking about her younger self being subjected to her grandfather's sick obsession with her body and using his "faith" to manipulate her.

Dad once told me it's a compliment to God to pray for big things, things that seem impossible. So I pray for Martha a few times a day, every day. The verse in Genesis Dad quoted to me the other week is embossed in my mind. *Thou God seeth me.*

I pray it can find a place in Martha's mind too.

———

ON SUNDAY AFTER CHURCH, Dad and I head down to the basement with everyone else for fellowship. We find an empty table and set our Bibles down before going to grab some refreshments.

Before Dad gets in line for his usual cup of black coffee, he asks, "You want anything to drink?"

"I'll have some coffee with cream."

He smacks my shoulder. "You're turning into a coffee connoisseur like me."

"I need the extra oomph," I reply as I head over to the food. "I was up late writing about Anne Bradstreet's poetry."

I get in line and load two plates for Dad and me with salad, cheese, crackers, and fruit. I return to our table and start eating my salad.

Jaylene Leverette stops by. "Hi, Ian." She gestures to my Bible with a laugh. "Every time I see you, your Bible looks bigger."

"You're probably right." I stroke its cover. "Even with the wide margins, I still don't have room for all my notes, and I like to keep everything together. I do what Johnathan Edwards did and add pages."

Jaylene fingers the end of her dark braid, and her cheeks turn scarlet. "That's cool. I'd love for my Bible to look like that someday."

I smile at her. "Just keep studying. You'll find plenty of things to write down."

She nods. "Right, because a believer is never done reading the Bible."

Dad returns with two cups of coffee. "Hi, Jaylene."

"Hi, Mr. B." Her youngest sister, Audrey, dashes up to her and starts pulling her away. Jaylene holds the girl's hand and asks, "What's up, nugget?"

"I want to go potty."

"All right, well, I'd better go. It was nice seeing you, Ian."

"Have a good week," I say.

She gives me a little wave before taking Audrey to the bathroom.

Once Jaylen and Audrey are out of earshot, Dad whispers, "You do realize Jaylene always makes a point of talking to you when we stay for fellowship."

"I know. She's a great woman of God, but I have my eye on someone else."

Dad drinks his coffee. "Martha?"

"Yeah. We're good friends now." I fold my arms on the table. "She's changing, Dad. She doesn't want to rip my head off anymore."

He almost chokes on his salad. "The way I saw your heads huddled together at Morgan's wedding, I didn't think she wanted to get rid of yours."

"She was hot and cold for a while. She's been through a lot."

Dad pats my Bible. "Your prayers are working. Keep at it."

So I do. I pull out this week's bulletin from my Bible and tear off the prayer request slip. I write: *I pray my friend heals from the abuse she went through and comes to faith in Jesus.*

My stomach squirms. I'm inviting the prayer team at church into my hope. First Thessalonians 5:16 says to pray without ceasing. The storm of prayers for Martha is about to spread far and wide.

Before Dad and I leave church, I drop my prayer request into the tithes-and-offerings box in the foyer.

Martha appears in my mind. I still can't believe she wanted to hug me. She demolished the wall she built around herself and let me in. She let me touch her again. As I felt the warmth of Martha's body against mine, I kept hearing the words *Cherish her* in my head. I'm not sure if that was God or my own thoughts telling me that, but I'm diving in. I'm ready.

———

BEFORE MARTHA and I count our registers out later that night, I grab a black Sharpie and a composition notebook from the office supplies section and bring them to her.

"Can you ring me up?"

Martha scans my items. "You need a bag?"

I give her my employee number for my discount and lean against the counter. "Yup. I want each item in a separate bag." I take out my wallet and give her my card. "Oh, and I have a coupon that expired five months ago, but the world orbits around me, so take it."

Martha almost busts her gut laughing as she swipes my card. "Get out! I'm done with your attitude."

"I'm not going anywhere. I want to speak to management."

Martha gives me my card back. "In that case, talk to yourself, Ian."

We can't stop laughing.

After I compose myself, I uncap the Sharpie and write *Read, Eat, Go, Repeat* on the notebook's cover. "There. It's our notebook."

"Two rules." Martha opens it to the first page and takes the Sharpie from me.

#1: Everything stays private.
#2: Don't be shy. Speak!

She turns the notebook toward me. "You can have it first. I want some book recommendations."

"I won't let you down."

I want to dance through the store. What Martha doesn't know is I'm not just talking about the book list. There's so much I hope God has in store for her. And us.

34

MARTHA

DR. SLOAN WANTS us to create a piece of art that reflects one or more of the themes we've covered in class. We could paint, draw, sing, write, and even act. We can work alone or with others, and groups can be as big or small as we'd like.

Kaylin wants to paint a woman who's been vertically split in half by a large fist, and on that fist she's going to write everything that oppresses women. Envisioning this makes my head ache, but art is supposed to make you feel things.

I want to create something that deals with body image. I'll tell everyone I used to weigh three hundred pounds, and after a hard diet I'm still struggling with self-acceptance.

I leaf through the chapter in my textbook on health and body image and come to an essay from Belinda Walker titled "Anyone Have Time for Love? Feminists Do." I'm two paragraphs in when Mom knocks on my door.

"Can I come in?"

"Yeah," I call out.

Mom sits on my bed and strokes my Lone Star quilt. It's made up of blue, seafoam green, pink, and yellow pastels. The colors are faded, but I can't let this go. It belonged to Mom's aunt Martha, my namesake. She and her husband, Roger, were the only ones who loved Mom and Uncle Tim. They were shunned from the family after they told Grandma she'd fry in an extra-hot corner in hell. Mom never heard from them after that.

"Suzanna and Carl are coming over for dinner," she says, crossing her legs. "Dad's not happy, but if Suzanna's happy, we should be happy too. Or at least act like we are."

Suzanna's been gone a week. So far there's been no drama with Carl. I'm still wary, thinking he's going to hurt her, but it's nice having my room to myself again.

"Your father said he'd rather have Ian over for dinner any day."

Carl's earned a permanent spot in the doghouse. Too bad, dude. You dumped Suzanna over something she can't control and fall into another woman's arms—on the couch, no less.

"Which wouldn't be such a bad idea. Invite him over."

I turn sideways and rest my arm over the back of my chair. "I'll ask him when he'll be free. We've been swamped with homework lately."

"All right, well, let me know, and I'll cook something. Does he like anything in particular?"

"I think he eats a lot of Korean. In fact, he likes to cook."

"I don't mind trying my hand at Korean food." Mom tilts her head a little. "Marty, you're turning red. Are you two dating?"

This relaxed and upbeat conversation with Mom is so refreshing.

"No," I quickly answer.

Mom sighs as she stands. "Marty, grab him while you can. The man *cooks*. That's a huge bonus." She gives my ponytail a routine yank before she leaves.

I will never be compatible with Ian. His faith means so much to him, and I can't be that nice Christian girlfriend he's probably been fantasizing about since he got saved.

A sudden throb hits my chest. Whoever that Christian woman is, she's going to be so fortunate to have Ian.

I return to Belinda Walker's essay. A particular paragraph shakes me.

My family's economic struggle consumed us when I was growing up. I learned how to make life work with little money, but I didn't know how to make relationships work with love. I thought it was all about doing. My parents associated feelings with being vulnerable, weak. They didn't have time for that. But I wanted that. I discovered love can make you strong. Its force pushes you to fight for yourself and others. I promised to weave this into my feminist projects so the women after me would know it's not a waste of time. It's in me, in this movement. We must know what it feels like to give it and keep it going.

Belinda Walker is one of the most prominent Black feminist writers. Strong mind, big heart, graceful writing. And lucky Dr. Sloan was taken under her wing when she got her doctorate.

I write *Love is not a waste of time* in my notebook. It sounds like a line from a poem.

———

I HEAR a car come up the driveway and peel myself away from my reading to look out my window.

"My parents don't hate you," I hear Suzanna assure Carl as she hops out of his black SUV. "If they give you the cold shoulder, I've got your back."

Suzanna, I hope you have an army inside you.

I open my door to find *Marina Tsvetaeva: The Double Beat of Heaven and Hell* and *A Cab Called Reliable* on the floor. I asked Dad to get them from the library. Marina Tsvetaeva's eyes are large and bold on the cover. She looks guarded, as if she's shielding the content inside.

I want to know who you are. You have written some of the most beautiful things I've ever read.

I might write a poem for my women's studies project. Now I'm talking to a dead poet. Who am I becoming?

I put the books on my desk and head downstairs. Suzanna and Carl are in the kitchen with Mom and Dad.

"A party of six left me change for a tip," Suzanna tells them.

"Time to find another job." She and Dad start throwing around other jobs she's fit for, like event planning, reception, marketing, and consulting.

"Hi, Marty," Carl says.

"Hey."

"What have you been up to?" He's solid at six feet tall, and his golden-bronze hair is in a military burr cut, but he's so quiet. I used to think he was gentle, but I can't see that in him anymore.

I shrug. "School. Work."

"How's retail?"

"It's there. How's work been?"

He gives me a lopsided grin, a hint of the quiet, awkward Carl. "My dad and I are remodeling a kitchen for a very demanding and indecisive couple."

"Time to eat!" Mom announces as she taps the mixing spoon against the stockpot. It's broccoli cheddar soup tonight.

"I'll set the table," Suzanna volunteers, leaving Carl's side.

I walk up to Dad and hug his arm. "Thanks for getting my books."

"It's no problem."

Another win for tonight. Maybe? Dad seems like he's in a decent mood.

Carl looks lost without Suzanna next to him. He walks over to where Mom's scooping soup into bowls and takes two at a time over to the table.

We eat in an uncomfortable silence. Suzanna's eyes shift from Mom and Dad, then to Carl. Mom looks like the world is suddenly perfect. Dad's watching Carl's every move. Carl looks at Suzanna as if silently asking, "Am I doing okay?" If this were in a TV show, this scene would need a laugh track.

I think of something to talk about to cut the awkwardness. To make Carl feel more included, I tell him, "I changed my major."

I'm so scared this is going to fuel an argument about money, but, to my relief, Mom and Dad stay quiet and Carl says, "That's cool. What do you want to study?"

"Russian."

"Good for you," he says. "Your grandma would be proud of you."

"Marty's hoping to ... go out of state," Dad says carefully. "The University of Maryland is her top choice."

Suzanna cringes. "Isn't that expensive?"

I jump in with "I'll look into financial aid, and I'm only taking two classes next semester, so I can put in more hours at the store."

"And you can get promoted," Dad suggests. "How much is Ian paid?"

His question makes the heat suddenly rise in my body. I shrug. "I think he gets fifty cents more than I do."

"Who's Ian?" Carl asks.

"He's her coworker," Suzanna answers as she dips her bread into her soup. "They went to a wedding together. Now they're like this." She crosses her fingers.

I hold a spoonful of soup up to my mouth and pause. Suzanna's talking as if she can't believe I connected with a guy so quickly, and she's acting as if I'm not even here. It's condescending.

"Ian's not my boyfriend," I insist before eating some more food.

"You're blushing again," Mom adds.

"Yup, Marty has a boyfriend," Suzanna concedes.

I put a hand up. "Can we move on to something else? Please? Yes, I have a new career goal, but I'm not passionately in love with Ian. We're just good friends."

Dad finishes his soup. "We can talk about someone else."

Uh-oh.

He points a finger at Carl and glowers. "I'd rather have Ian sitting across from me now than *you*."

Carl flinches.

Mom drops her spoon into her bowl. "David, *please*."

"Dad, stop," Suzanna begs at the same time.

Dad never confronted Carl for what he did, so he's unleashing his rage now. Suzanna shouldn't have brought him here so soon. Did she expect Mom and Dad to embrace him and shed tears of joy that he's in the family again?

"Dad, this is—"

"I almost—"

"Go ahead, Carl," Suzanna prompts. "Tell my crazy father what's on your mind."

Mom and Dad are still. I bet there's a tornado brewing in Dad.

"I almost ruined our marriage for a selfish reason, and hanging out with Gina was inappropriate."

"*Hanging out*?" Dad sneers. "Suzanna found you on the couch with her!"

The air in the kitchen suddenly feels thin. I still don't know what Carl and Gina were doing when Suzanna walked in on them, but, clearly, it's something he didn't expect her to tell Mom and Dad because his mouth drops open.

Suzanna springs up from her chair and declares, "We're done here." She grabs Carl's hand. "We'll get something to eat on the way home."

"Suzanna, ignore him." Mom pleads. "You have my support."

"You're on their side?" Dad asks incredulously. "When did that happen?"

I set my empty bowl in the sink and slip back up to my room. Writing poetry seems ideal.

"I won't hurt Suzanna again," Carl promises, his voice breaking. "I changed. I know what our marriage is really based on."

Before, I wasn't sure if Carl was being sincere, but I think he's close to tearing up.

"Because your parents told you," Dad assumes.

Carl sighs. "No, David."

"How they work things out isn't our business," Mom interjects.

"It *is* our business! Do you love Suzanna?"

"Of course I do!"

"Then put your guard up, Jenn!"

Suzanna pushes her chair in. "Let me know when you calm down, Dad, then we'll come over."

A few minutes later I hear Suzanna burst out in the driveway, "He always has to hurt someone!" I peek out my window and watch Carl pull her against him. Even though I have issues with Carl's past decisions, I admit he and Suzanna look so solid and permanent. No matter what Dad says, they're staying together.

Downstairs, Mom is slamming bowls and utensils as she cleans up. "Would it kill you to show Suzanna some support and *try* to live through dinner so we could have one night—*one* night —in this house without any fighting?"

I cross my room and stand by the doorframe. My heartbeat thuds in my ears.

"Jenn, I can't sit there while our *cheating* son-in-law tries to sweet-talk us into believing he's a changed man. He wasted no time telling Suzanna their marriage wasn't worth it anymore because she can't have kids. He was in such a hurry to invite Gina over. Do you see the pattern?"

Dad has a point.

"Okay, but I was looking at things from their side," Mom reasons, her voice hard. "Remember how my parents hated how *we* got together? Remember how much I fought with my parents and defended you?"

"Our history is a completely different situation," Dad argues. "I didn't give up on us, nor was I with another woman."

"They still hated you," Mom points out bitterly. "It *is* the same problem at the core."

Complete silence, then I hear shuffling. Mom handles some silverware. She probably has her back to Dad while he stands frozen, looking at her.

"And, honestly, David ..." I hear tears in Mom's voice. "Looking at us now, I shouldn't have fought so much to stay with you."

I rip myself away from the doorway and lunge onto my bed. I hide my face into my pillow. My parents have had some nasty fights, but Mom has never, ever hinted that she regretted everything they went through to make it this far. They always saw their history as a triumph. Something to be proud of that resulted in a lasting marriage.

"You don't mean that, Jenn." Dad's voice is low and raspy.

"We can't agree on anything, David!" Mom explodes.

"That's because you micromanage everything. God, I can't buy food, apply for jobs, or do maintenance around the house without you having an episode."

"An episode? You're making it sound like I have some kind of mental disorder! My father used to talk to my mother the same way."

"The only time he was smart," Dad remarks.

"He was also smart to throw that beer bottle at you when you asked him if you could marry me!" Mom shouts.

A sob slips up my throat. I clench some of my quilt in my fist.

Mom doesn't mean what she's saying. If Grandpa had struck him with that bottle, Dad would have been left with some serious facial injuries and scars. Mom would not have wanted that. Dad was trying for her. For Suzanna, for our future. He's still trying, and he's burnt out. And she's still hurting from the house of horrors her parents called a Christian home.

My eyes are misty. Why does Ian love God when so many gashes will never heal?

"Jenn, I've done so much ..." Dad wavers. "To keep us together. To keep Suzanna. I've always done my best to give everyone in this family what they wanted and needed. Doesn't that mean anything to you?"

"What we wanted?" Mom throws at him. Her voice is sharp and cold like icicles. "Suzanna wants to trust Carl, and you give her no support!"

"We're done talking about them," Dad says. "See, Jenn, our conversations go nowhere, because you're always—"

"No, Suzanna's right; you're always hurting someone!" Mom retorts. "I'm your uneducated wife who can't look after our money, and you think Suzanna's too dumb to make her own decisions. You love only Marty. You give her anything she wants, no matter what it costs."

"I don't give Marty whatever she wants."

It's final. I'm done with Russian. I'll call Montclair to see if I can reclaim my admission if that would make things better.

Besides, isn't the hardest choice usually the right one? Unhappiness is always the answer.

"I don't believe you, David. You got her excited about changing her major when she was all set at Montclair, but you're throwing us into deeper financial troubles."

"Marty didn't *want* women's studies anymore. That's what *you* wanted for her. You were projecting your own desires onto her, and that's not right."

"A lot of things aren't right in this family, David." Mom's voice quivers. "Our marriage has been in survival mode, but it can't go on like this. I think it's time we ..." She shudders. "Call it quits."

"Jenn, no!"

"We'll sell the house, pay off the assessment. You can go with Marty. I'll be okay." She sniffs. "I'll make it."

I punch my pillow and swear. No. My parents cannot get a divorce.

"You need rest," Dad insists. "We can talk again in the morning."

Mom blubbers something I can't make out.

Rest. I remember the verse Ian texted me. *Come unto me, all ye that labor and are heavy laden, and I will give you rest.*

No, God, I cannot rest. There are ugly grandfathers who touch their granddaughters between their legs, and mothers who give up their babies for adoption, and loser husbands who cheat on their wives on couches.

"Jenn, please," Dad begs. "Come upstairs with me. Calm down, and we'll talk about this tomorrow. It will be better that way."

Dad sounds powerless. I roll onto my back and cover my chest with my hands as if that can keep my heart intact. I begin to cry. This hurts so much.

Come unto me, all ye that labor and are heavy laden ...

Why would God want me near him? I wanted Grandpa to die! I deserve nothing.

Mom's sobs become muffled. Is she covering her face, or is Dad hugging her? I don't remember the last time I saw them hold each other or the last time either of them gave me a big, all-encompassing hug.

Come unto me, all ye that labor and are heavy laden, and I will give you rest.

Really, God? You want exhausted and hardened people to come to you, and you make them feel cozy and warm? The people like me who hate you and have hurt Christians like Ian? That's laughable.

I'm not laughing.

An earthquake shakes inside me. The force pushes me upright. I hug myself and bow my head. I'm done with anger lining the walls of this house. Of having a love-hate relationship with my body. Of being afraid of how Ian cares about me.

God, are you there? I'm so confused and angry. Freaked out too. I don't know how I feel about you, and you probably don't care about me, but I really need some rest now, and some peace if you have it. Amen.

Mom and Dad are at the bottom of the stairs.

"Come on, Jenn," Dad says. "Please come with me."

I hear them ascend the stairs together.

For the first time in my life, I breathe out a sincere, wholehearted thank-you to God.

Then I text Ian.

Send me another Bible verse.

35

IAN

I RUB MY EYES. I blink a few times. I'm not hallucinating. Martha wants another Bible verse.

> 1 John 4:19: We love him, because he first loved us.

I tap Send.

God loves you, Martha, and so do I.

I want her to love God so she can have eternity with him, and maybe one day she can love me with his love.

36

MARTHA

IAN RESPONDS IN SECONDS.

God loved me first, and I should love him too.

God, son, perfect, gift, die. The words I clung to from that Christmas are the DNA of the gospel. Jesus died for our sins so we could be with him forever. He was perfect but was nailed to a cross for every sin we commit. He took the blame for things he didn't do and died.

God's son *died*. For me and everyone else in the world.

That is love; therefore, I should love him. Is faith that easy? People spend years trying to understand, defend, or disprove faith. Is it all rooted in a death on the cross?

My throat caves in. I read 1 John 4:19 again. Yes, faith is that simple.

"I need you," I start to pray. "Can you forgive me for wishing Grandpa dead and hating you all these years?"

Yes.

I fall back onto my bed and clasp my hands over my chest. I'm not holding my heart together; God can do that. I'm just wondering if it's going to jump out of my rib cage from the big love I'm feeling.

I laugh and cover my face. Big love. Ian would like that.

I grab my phone off my nightstand and call him. "I believe," I whisper.

Silence.

"Are you there?" I ask.

"I'm here."

"Did you hear me?"

"Martha, what's up? You sound anxious."

"I'm okay," I rush on. "You heard what I said before?"

"I did. You're all his, Martha. God's going to take care of you for the rest of your life. I promise. Give everything to him, and you're going to be okay."

His words feel like one of those all-encompassing hugs I want from my parents. I wish Ian could hold me like that now.

"I love how you put that. It sounds so safe."

"It's what my dad told me after I believed. I wrote it down in my Bible."

I chuckle. "You write everything down."

"Speaking of that, I have our notebook ready for you."

"Record what happened today."

"I'll do that. I'd also like to have you over for dinner. How's Wednesday at six?"

"Okay, but less than forty-eight hours seems like a very long time from now." I'm relieved Ian can't see the huge grin on my face.

"I know. I'm excited to see you."

My heart is doing gymnastics. Ian's excited to see me. That's absolutely thrilling.

37

IAN

I'M PREHEATING the oven when the doorbell rings. It's Martha, and she's holding a pie carrier.

"Hi!" She hands me the dessert. "I made an apple pie."

"It looks awesome."

Martha eyes my sneakers by the door and shuffles off her shoes. "Your apartment's so spacious."

We only have a couch and coffee table in the living room, and all that's on the kitchen counter is the toaster, utensil holder, and mixer.

"My dad's allergic to dust, so we don't have much," I explain as I stick the pie in the fridge.

"I don't own a ton either." Martha crosses her arms over the counter. "I'd rather have experiences, like learn something new or travel."

I show Martha what's for dinner. "Chicken parmesan sound good?"

"Good? That looks amazing."

I shove dinner into the oven. "So, where would you travel?"

"Besides Russia, I'd go to Bulgaria. We have family there from my babka's side. What about you?"

"Nowhere."

Martha wrinkles an eyebrow. "I thought you'd say Korea."

I grab the marinara sauce for the spaghetti. "I'm afraid of what I'd feel once I'm there."

"Oh." Martha looks like she's waiting for me to elaborate, but I don't, so she asks, "Is your dad eating with us?"

"He has a staff meeting. He ate some kimchi fried rice and left at five."

Martha plants her hands on her hips. "I'm sure your chicken parmesan rocks, but why aren't we eating kimchi?"

"I put squid in it. You don't like seafood."

A smile tugs at Martha's lips. "You remember that?"

"Of course."

She steps closer. "One day, I'll try some kimchi, minus the squid."

I lean over the counter. "I didn't think you'd want any. A lot of people I know don't care for it. My mom never tried it. She hated how it smelled up the fridge, and Chris said it smells like farts."

"I hope you guys were really young when he said that."

"We were thirteen."

"Jerk. Speaking of jerks, did Justin behave today?"

"He acted his age because Liz spent her shift on the sales floor."

"I wouldn't give him a 'Terrific' sticker," she remarks. "Yesterday, I was pulling a cart full of boxes out of the stockroom when he was leaving. He said … he said I should beep so people know when I'm backing up." Martha rubs her eye.

"He's lucky I wasn't there. I would have slammed him. Did you tell Liz?"

"It doesn't matter. I'm used to fat jokes."

"You're not fat, and you don't have to take people's abuse."

"Telling Liz won't help."

I go to the stove to place the spaghetti in the boiling water. "Did anyone ever say you look adorable when you're upset?"

She struggles to laugh over a sniffle. "No."

"I want to show you something." I go into my room and open a plastic bin in my closet. I pull out the photo album that has pictures of me from when I was in foster care up until I graduated.

"Can I come in?" Martha asks from the doorway.

"Sure." I sit cross-legged on the floor next to my bookshelves. Martha joins me, and I hand her the album.

She opens it and looks puzzled. "Where's the first picture?"

"It's gone. Fourth grade. It was my week to do that About Me thing where you tell the class all your business from your childhood. I made a poster with some of my baby pictures. Justin and I were on the same bus. He grabbed my poster and threw it out the window. It was raining, and a truck ran it over."

Martha puts her hand over her mouth.

"Then he pulled the sides of his eyes and said, 'You gotta help me! I'm turning into Ian!' Some kids laughed. No one defended me, not even the bus driver."

Martha's so still as she registers this.

"I lunged at Justin and punched him in the stomach. We got suspended from the bus for a week. My aunt Addie used to watch me after school. She drove by the area where he threw my poster, but it wasn't there. I knew it was lost, but I still hoped she'd see it."

"What were the pictures of?"

"The first one was of me at six weeks. I was lying on my back and looked really ticked off. The other one was taken two weeks before I left Korea. My foster mother, Mrs. Shin, and I were at the adoption agency. She was holding me on her hip and talking to me." I smile at the image appearing in my head. "I looked at her intensely, like I understood what she was saying."

Martha stops turning the pages. "Can you find Mrs. Shin? She might have doubles."

"She died in a car accident in 1995. I'm missing the first and last pictures of me in Korea." I rub the side of my head. "I asked my mom if she had extras. Like, maybe she'd asked Dad at some point for copies of my baby pictures. It was stupid to ask her."

"No, Ian ..."

I twist my hands in my lap. "She said she didn't have any pictures of me, and I shouldn't have brought such valuable things to school."

"She should have pictures of you."

"She took all the pictures of Caleb, but she has nothing to remind her of me."

"Who's Caleb?"

I forgot I never told Martha about him. "My parents had a baby before they adopted me. He was stillborn. They tried having another one, but that never happened, so they got me."

She tries the words in her mouth. "They got you."

"Some adoptees feel like a transaction. That's not how my dad sees it, but my mom does. She got another baby, and the experience wasn't accurately described. I came the day before what would have been Caleb's fourth birthday."

"I bet that messed with her emotions."

"It did. She had postpartum depression after Caleb died. My dad turned to religion. My mom thought his faith in God meant he was okay with losing Caleb. He tried to explain himself, but she wouldn't listen. Their marriage took a nasty turn and never got better. I don't think they worked through their grief enough before they adopted me. They rushed into it, hoping a baby would solve their problems."

"I'm sorry, Ian." She stares at the grainy photo of me sitting on Mrs. Shin's lap. I'm looking up at her, and she's holding a teddy bear against her cheek. Her short curly hair frames her face, which is tilted back, and she's laughing. Martha holds the album next to my face. "Mrs. Shin loved you. Every picture says so."

Her words poke a wound. I focus on a tiny stain in the rug. "I don't remember Mrs. Shin, but I miss her so much. I was one of her favorite foster kids."

Martha touches my head full of hair in the photo with her pointer finger. "Why couldn't your birth mother keep you?"

"Being an unwed mother in Korea is taboo. It would have been hard for her to get a job, find a place to live. Some landlords don't want single moms living on their property. Her family probably wouldn't talk to us. Kids in school would have harassed me for not having a dad."

Martha closes the album and frowns.

"I'd have problems too, like with finding someone to marry. I wouldn't have been able to join the military. Ridiculous stuff like that. The crazy thing is, I wouldn't have been a Korean citizen."

"You were *born* there."

"It used to be based on the father's citizenship until 1998. My birth father probably wasn't a citizen, and he isn't Korean. He and my mother were together for a short time, then she didn't hear from him again. Maybe someone was with her when I was born ..." Anger fires up inside me. I snatch the album from Martha, which startles her. "I hate thinking she was alone during all that."

"Was there *any* way she could have kept you?"

"Unless my Korean grandfather or an uncle put me down as his son on our family registry, I had to be an orphan to have rights."

"It's like Korea traps these women so they give their babies away." She reaches down to the floor and grabs the ID bracelet I'd worn to the States. It must have fallen out of the album's back pocket.

"You're right. The adoption agencies profited from their oppression for decades. The media also wanted Korea to look like a barbaric country so adoption advocates could swoop in and save —I mean steal—the children. Some kids were literally ripped out of their mothers' arms."

Martha scrunches up her face. "That's barbaric. So, do you read up on this stuff?"

"Yeah. My dad also dated a Korean adoptee named Lili in college before he met my mom. Her file said her mother was a prostitute, but she remembered a house and her parents' faces. She was a history major and read a ton about the Korean War. My dad later heard she got a PhD to research and expose what really went on in the adoption industry."

"She remembers her parents?" Martha covers her mouth. "Oh, God ..."

I make a disgusted noise. "A lot of Korean adoptees are stuck. We look crazy questioning the truth, wondering about the what-ifs and should-haves because they supposedly weren't possible. We're supposed to be thankful for that."

Martha joins the bracelet's ends together. "Thankful for losing your parents?"

I tilt my head back in relief. "You get it. You *actually* get it."

"I mean, if you never knew your parents—"

"It's like they're dead," I finish. This shocks Martha, but I don't stop. "So I lost them, and I have a right to grieve. It's like my birth parents are these phantom figures; they feel so unreachable. But they're real, because I exist with their DNA."

She gives me the bracelet. "You're always going to be their son, Kang Min Joon."

I squeeze the bracelet before slipping it back into the album.

I'd memorized what's on there. *KANG Min Joon. 9/28/92. Parents: M/M Berkley.* Product name. Shipping date. Buyers.

"My birth mother named me," I say. "A lot of adoptees were named by social workers, but my omma gave me my name."

"Ian, don't rely on the adoption agency and the police. Try a different approach, like DNA. You deserve those what-ifs and should-haves."

This sounds amazing but devastating, because it probably won't yield anything. "I can't bring myself to test yet. I'm afraid of facing more disappointment, and I'm not sure I want to connect with my birth father's side. I'm too angry at him."

Martha gives a sympathetic nod.

"Besides, I don't think my omma wants me to find her. My Korean family might not know I exist, and if they learn about me, they can disown her. Her husband can even divorce her."

"You're her *son*."

"Illegitimate son," I point out. "It's all about the bloodline. She had me outside of marriage with a Caucasian guy. That disrupts everything."

"What's her name?"

"Hye Jin. It was blotted out in the xeroxed copy of my file. I got the original after I searched for her."

"I can't fathom not knowing my mom's name for eighteen years."

"Adoptees learn to live with empty histories. Some of us handle it better than others." I stand and go to my closet.

"What do you mean by that?"

"We're more likely to commit suicide than people raised by their own parents."

She faces my bookshelf and touches one of my notebooks. "Have you ever thought about doing it?"

I put the album away and look at her. "No. Have you?"

"Yeah, junior year." Martha's eyes shift. She rubs some of her shirt between her fingers. "I was hiding what my grandpa did. Chloe and her followers wouldn't leave me alone. Pop-Pop died, then Babka five months later. My grades suffered. We couldn't have another suicide in the family, so I tried to live. I ran on the track after school and ate healthier, got my grades back up."

"Did you get help?"

"I talked to my guidance counselor after school a few times. I only mentioned the bullying." Martha lets go of her shirt. "She called my mom. I thought that would open the communication in my family." She rolls her eyes. "I dream big."

I sit next to her on the floor again.

Martha gets on her hands and knees and scans the titles. "I love your book collection. You have everything from classics to young adult ..." She pulls out Pete Hautman's *Invisible* and falls back on her legs to flip through its pages. "Wow. You *do* write everything down." She holds up the book, displaying a page of underlined text and comments in the margins.

"I like to document how I feel about what I'm reading, favorite quotes, questions I have."

"That's cool." Martha points to something at the beginning of the last chapter. "Your dad took this book away? Why?"

"Oh. That." I burn up with embarrassment. "In twelfth grade, he grounded me for getting a D in gym. I didn't want to get changed. It was stupid rebellion. My childhood baggage was starting to rattle."

"When we can't talk, we hope our actions can do the work, but they're terrible translators."

Martha, where have you been my whole life?

I stand to retrieve our notebook from my desk and hand it to her. "Here. It's your turn to have it."

She opens the cover and scans the list of YA recommendations. "Thanks."

"I also wrote down when you accepted Jesus and made a list of verses that remind us of God's promises."

Martha turns the page and rubs her eye. "I never knew his love was ... so big."

The timer on the stove beeps.

"It's big, deep, endless, wild." Martha and I get up and leave my room. I go to the stove. One more minute before the spaghetti's done. I turn to her. "Do you like your pasta al dente?"

"Go for it."

I dump it into the colander. A cloud of steam hits me in the face. "So, what were your dad's parents like?"

She puts the notebook on the table before joining me in the kitchen. "They didn't have much but were content. They had a cozy house I never wanted to leave. Oh, and they always said yes when my parents said no. And they were so in love. Losing Pop-pop really crippled Babka. I think she died from a broken heart."

"My dad's parents had a good marriage, but my nana and Grandpa John aren't happy. They barely talk to their own kids, even though everyone's in Connecticut. They favored Uncle John. He ruined his life with drugs and alcohol. Mom never got into any trouble and taught kindergarten, but she was second best."

"Do they talk to you and Gemma?"

"Gemma, occasionally. Me, on my birthday, or when they team up with my mom against me." I shrug. "I haven't seen them in years."

Martha opens the jar of marinara sauce that's by the stove. "What are your Thanksgiving plans?"

"I'm going to my mom's. I'd rather not, but I want to see Gemma."

Martha scrunches her face. "Is she that bad?"

"If you heard what sex sounded like at age four because your mom was cheating on your dad several times a month, you'd definitely think she's bad."

Martha's face pales. "She cheated multiple times? And you *heard* them?"

"Nathan used to live in North Jersey. He came over every Saturday to sleep with my mom. She sent me to my room, but I sometimes needed to get a snack or use the bathroom. The more Nathan came over"—I grimace—"the braver he and my mom got. She was supposed to be a mom, but she chose that. This is why I can't let her pay for my college and live with her. She's never apologized for what she did."

"You need to tell your dad."

I shake my head vigorously. "It'll hurt him too much. He was so depressed after she left. If it weren't for his family, I think he would have hurt himself."

"*You're* hurting too much."

"Let's eat. The spaghetti will get cold and sticky."

I'm about to transfer the spaghetti to a bowl, but Martha touches my arm. "Can I be honest with you?"

"You never have to ask that."

"I wanted to dance with you at the wedding because even though you were really annoying, you were so ... nice. I kept hurting you, and you were so *nice*. And you prayed for me."

I coat the spaghetti with sauce and Parmesan cheese. I hand Martha the spaghetti spoon, and she dishes some onto her plate. My patience is thinner than tissue paper. I know she doesn't like being touched, but I want every. Single. Inch. of her.

"You were praying for me, and I was rude to you. I didn't know we had gone through a lot of the same things."

"There's no way you could have known any of that."

Martha waits for me to get my food. She takes my hand and

slowly pulls me to her. "I know I only became a Christian two days ago, but I want more between us than secrets and cash drawers and cafés. I want tenderness."

My hands trail over her shoulders and up her neck. Her rosy-pale skin is warm and satiny. I trace her angular jawline and notice a light birthmark on her left earlobe.

Martha puts her face up to mine and whispers, "Ian, say something."

"You want this?"

"I want this."

I want this too, right here and now. Because what I have with Martha is not what I had with Hana. We're not trying to salvage a mediocre relationship. We're building something strong and authentic. I can be myself with Martha. She sees my faults, my wounds, my goals, my faith ... *our* God.

I close my eyes and press my lips to hers, which are soft. The oven beeps as our kiss deepens. She smells like lavender, and feeling her mouth on mine blows my thoughts in a million directions. I draw her against me, and she hugs my neck. We kiss again.

"We can have tenderness," I promise.

Something bumps into this perfect moment. It wobbles. My mood falls, and I suddenly feel alone even though Martha is so close. I hide my face in her shoulder and exhale.

"You kept trying so hard for us. Why?" she asks.

"You were going to transfer. I was afraid I'd lose a chance with you."

Martha hugs me tighter. We hold each other for as long as we want to feel this new closeness that's making itself at home on our skin. The timer beeps every few seconds, but it's okay if the chicken's a little charred.

38

MARTHA

I DRAW my face close to Ian's for a third kiss, just one more. It's light and quick, but my nerves are doing a wild dance. He sets his hands on my shoulders and runs them down my arms. His fingers begin to wind around my wrists.

I break out of his grip and suck in air through my teeth.

Ian's relaxed expression darkens with concern. "I wanted to hold your hands."

I brush my left wrist as if his touch contaminated my skin. "I woke up that morning to my grandpa pinning me down by the wrists. Then he put his hand up my leg."

"I'm sorry." Ian switches off the stove timer. "Dinner's ready."

"It's okay. You didn't know. Some memories suddenly get activated in my head." I rub the small of his back. "Can I set the table?"

"Forks and napkins are in the drawer by the sink." Ian brings our plates to the table. "No kid should be subjected to what you went through."

"Don't dwell on it."

Ian sits and looks at me, worried.

I grin. "Hey, today's a good day. I just kissed an amazing kisser."

Ian blushes as he starts cutting his chicken. "Have you ever been close with a guy before?"

"Yeah, in eleventh grade." I take a bite of chicken parmesan. This beats anything I've eaten at Lombardi's. Sorry, Suzanna. "My lab partner, Aaron."

"What happened with you guys?"

"We studied together and hung out a few times. He wanted to take me to prom and asked me what flower I'd want for my corsage. Then he ditched me because of ... my weight. It was right after I spent so much time helping him study for the midterm."

"I'm sorry that happened, Martha." He rubs the top of my hand. "I'm with you only because of you."

He said *with you*. Like dating?

"And I promise to buy you your favorite flowers. What do you like?"

Okay, I think we're dating.

"Sunflowers."

"Then I'll get you sunflowers."

I smile at this and look down at Ian's hand over mine. "Next get-to-know-you item: when's your birthday?"

"August eighth. When's yours?"

"April Fool's Day. And, get this: I was born in a car."

He lifts his hand off mine. "You're pulling my leg."

I shake my head. "Nope. My dad didn't get to the hospital in time, so I was born in the passenger seat of a Chevy Malibu. My uncle Tim thought it was an April Fool's joke. Where were you born?"

"A clinic in Seoul. What's your favorite book?"

"I told you I don't have one."

"Come on, Martha. What's that book you couldn't live without?

You flip through it to reread random passages. You'd make bumper stickers and T-shirts with your favorite quotes."

"Okay, okay! *Earthly Signs: Moscow Diaries, 1917–1922*. It's by Marina Tsvetaeva. You can flip to any page and find something you want to rip out and keep in your pocket."

"I'll put that on my reading list."

"Don't look for it in our school library." I point to myself. "I keep checking it out." I pause before saying, "I started reading your favorite book. Ahn Joo sees her mother leave in that cab with her brother. Did you see your mom leave?"

"No." Ian puts his fork down. "Number seven: I knew she was going to leave."

Nausea rolls in my gut.

"Nathan was over. I opened my door to go to the kitchen for a snack." Ian wipes his mouth and crumples his napkin in his hand. "He and my mom were bickering. She blurted out, 'I'll go with you.' He pushed her against the wall and kissed her really hard. I thought I heard my mom say 'sixteen' or 'the sixteenth' over their kissing. She left on October sixteenth. It kills me that I heard that."

"You didn't understand what she meant."

"Still," he says.

I spin some spaghetti onto my fork. "Your mom made you witness some really inappropriate stuff."

Ian looks into my eyes. "Your grandpa did the same to you."

I shift uncomfortably in my chair and look down at my lap.

Do we fall in love to turn someone into a collage of our hidden desires, shame, and scars? Is this what really keeps people together?

"I won't mention your grandpa anymore if—"

"Don't worry about it," I say briskly. "Favorite movie?"

Ian looks taken aback by my knee-jerk reaction. "Um, okay. I like *A Tree Grows in Brooklyn*. I read the book in tenth-grade English. My teacher said the movie is just as good. She was right."

I eat my last piece of chicken. It's an end piece, so it's extra crunchy. Those pieces are the best. "Why's it your favorite?"

"I resonated with Francie. She likes to read, gets kind of lonely. Sometimes I play the DVD while I do homework or get stuff done around here. It's so ordinary, it's good. It's nice to listen to everyday life."

"You're not crazy about school, but you're really insightful. Do you at least participate in class?"

Ian takes our plates. I follow him to the sink. "Enough so the professors don't call on me."

"Ha! I'm the same way."

He looks surprised. "I picture you shooting your hand up, yelling out all the answers."

"No," I say over a laugh. "I like to watch things happen and take it in."

"Favorite song," Ian prompts.

"'Lyushaya Noch' by MakSim. It means best night." I take a bowl off the counter and put it in the dishwasher. "Taylor ham or pork roll?"

"It's Taylor ham on a kaiser roll with egg and cheese."

Ian Berkley, we were destined for each other.

"Biggest desire?" he asks.

"To read Russian literature in the original. Biggest regret?"

"I didn't let my halmoni teach me Korean."

"If you transferred somewhere that offered Korean—"

Ian throws the empty pasta box in the recycling. "Not happening," he cuts in. "I'll finish cleaning later." He opens the fridge and takes out the pie and a bottle of Coke. "Ice cream soda?"

"That's the way to my heart. Extra points if you have chocolate syrup and cherries."

He scoops the ice cream. "I only have syrup. Can you get the cake knife? It's in the drawer to the left of the stove."

I retrieve the knife for him and start cutting the pie.

"Lo liked her ice cream soda the same way in the 1997 adaptation of *Lolita*," Ian recalls as he drizzles chocolate syrup over our ice cream.

"The one with Jeremy Irons? He played Humbert Humbert. I will never watch *The Lion King* the same again."

He brings our drinks to the table. "Have you seen it?"

"No, but I should. I love *Lolita* because another girl had a beast like mine." I finish slicing the pie. "I'm shocked by what you read and watch."

"I'm not for clean Christian stories. I like realistic, flawed characters, tons of details, and a plot that bothers me or leaves me wanting more."

I hand Ian his dessert. "The way you talk about books makes me want to read more."

"If you read anything good, add it to the notebook. I'd love to know what books you like."

"Deal."

We sit, and he eats some pie. "This is good."

"It's the first one I ever made. I wanted this to be special. I never went to a guy's house for dinner. Thanks for having me." A short pause, then I add, "I'm glad we met."

"I am too. I'm glad to see you open up more, chill out ... blush. I'm glad you like me now."

I shield my cheeks with my hands. "You're embarrassing me."

I thought I wouldn't date someone until I shed more pounds, started grad school, had a better grip on where life was taking me, but life (or God?) had other plans.

I finish eating and sip my ice cream soda. My eyes float over to the pie on the counter.

"Want more?" Ian asks, standing up to get seconds.

"No, no. Share the leftovers with your dad."

He places some pie on his dish and comes back to the table. "I don't care if you have seconds."

I stand and push my chair back to get more. Ian is not Aaron.

"You can be yourself with me," Ian says quietly.

I bite the inside of my lip and remain standing at the counter so he can't see me fighting back tears. "It's hard when you're everyone's pin cushion for their fat jokes," I choke out. I return to my chair. "I used to weigh three hundred pounds. In eleventh grade, I got down to a size twelve. It felt wonderful, but people won't let me feel wonderful."

Ian studies me, like he can't picture me twice the size I am now. "Martha, you're fine the way you are."

Ian, stay awhile. I'm not ready to hope for forever, but if that's possible, let's try, because love is not a waste of time.

I rub my eyes and nod. "Okay. I won't hold back. So, can I have some chicken too? The ends are the best part."

"You can have more chicken."

"I'm so weird," I say as I stand to get more food.

"No, you're being yourself. I love it."

39

IAN

I'M SUPPOSED to be with Martha. I wanted to take her to Barnes & Noble. She wanted to browse the literature section and start collecting Russian books. Then we would go back to my place, eat lunch with Dad, and spend the afternoon studying.

But on my day off I'm working a double shift. Alicia's sick, and Evan's back is bothering him. It's almost six. Liz left an hour ago, so Justin and I are holding down the fort. Business has been slow, which is starting to scare Liz. She thought her fifteen-percent off an entire order for anyone with a military ID on Veteran's Day would pull customers in. Only seven people had IDs, and their purchases were under twenty-five bucks.

Justin's stocking the kids' and paint aisles. He was supposed to go on break five minutes ago. He hates me, but he gives me plenty of reasons to talk to him.

"Justin," I call as I walk over to him, "it's time for your break."

He flicks the utility knife open and cuts into a box of stickers. "I don't see a line of people at the break room."

He doesn't challenge Liz or Evan. Alicia has it easy too. He saves his attitude for me. Peel that off, and he's a clean-cut guy with freckles who looks like he would hold the door for the elderly couple at the grocery store or help his younger sisters with their homework.

"You're holding me up. I go after you."

"Right. You're craving your rice and dumplings." He throws a box. I scoot away, and it misses my shoulder by a hair.

"What's your problem? We didn't get along as kids, but let's be civil; we work together."

Justin walks toward me and claps his hands in my face. "All together now!" I jerk back, and he snickers. "You think your position puts you above me, makes you feel validated."

My blood freezes. I am afraid of Justin Massey. Guidance counselors say bullies are insecure. That their words mean nothing. That you're the better person. Somehow this is supposed to make me immune to what Justin has done and is still doing to me. It hasn't. I feel, so I get hurt, because I'm human.

"But people like you aren't valid. You shouldn't be here. You're *Korean*." He sneers his last word.

I hold the sides of my head and wince.

There are thousands of Koreans in New Jersey. Justin has a lot of hating to do.

My heart hammers in my ears.

It feels like I'm behind glass, boxed in by my anxiety.

If I wasn't here, I'd be with Martha. I would have made dinner. We might have shared our favorite TV shows or embarrassing moments. How many times would I have kissed her?

"Gook!" Justin barks, and I jump. He snorts, then goes on his break.

Shut his mouth. Fire him. Help me.

I press myself against a shelf holding fabric bundles. Redbone's "Come and Get Your Love" is on the radio.

A woman taps my shoulder. "Do you have twelve-inch round cake boards?"

"Uh, check the, um ..." My heart jostles in my chest, and it still feels as if there's a pane of glass between me and this customer.

"Baking aisle?" she finishes for me, sounding ticked. "Did that."

Inhale. Exhale. I step away from the shelf. My legs feel like logs. "Then I guess ... I guess we don't have them."

She frowns. "You have problems. This whole store does. I'm going somewhere else for my baking stuff."

I stay in the sewing aisle for another minute before I can hold it together. Then I break into a light jog toward the counter and feel around the shelf under my register. Nothing. I open the shallow drawer underneath that to find a pen without a cap and a stapler. I look under register two, and there it is: INCIDENT REPORT.

I start writing.

Name: Ian
Date: November 13, 2010
Time: 6:19 PM
Please describe in as much detail as possible what you witnessed.

I lean over the counter and press the pen into the paper until the point pierces the page. If Justin keeps harassing me, and Liz doesn't can him, I'm out.

I finish the form before Justin's back from his fifteen and put it on Liz's desk. Someone always needs to be at the registers, but I don't care. If a robber stormed in and demanded all the money, I'd hand it over. Then I'd run out of here and leave Justin behind.

———

DAD'S not home when I get in. He left a note on the fridge. *At Aunt Naomi and Uncle Vinny's. Will bring home bulgogi tomorrow.* Our private joke is you bring an overnight bag to the Cerino house; Uncle Vinny talks forever.

I text Dad:

> My mouth's watering, and you can enter the era of texting.

Dad
Shut up. Love ya.

Martha also texted me.

Martha
I wish today was all ours.

I take my jacket off and call her. When she answers, I say, "Me too."

"You too what?" Martha asks.

"I'm replying to your text."

"I sent that three hours ago."

"I wish I'd gotten out of work three hours ago." I tell her what Justin did earlier.

"He'll get fired."

"Liz will give him too many chances." I go to my room and throw myself onto my bed. "Justin has to shoplift or curse out management to get fired. Alicia calls her St. Liz."

"Liz is weak," Martha concedes.

"She's also best friends with his great-aunt. Alicia heard that's how he got the job."

"I'd love to know how he got his disgusting attitude."

"His parents divorced when we were in third grade. His mom got custody of him and his younger sister and married an Asian guy. I heard he and Justin didn't get along," I explain. "But Justin was close to his dad and eventually went to live with him."

"So, he projects his hate on you, even though you have nothing to do with his stepdad."

I scratch an itch on my shoulder. "Justin's suppressing his pain."

"He had it rough. So did you. But you don't shoot racial slurs everywhere."

"Don't worry. I'm not watching people buy yarn and Mod Podge forever. I'm applying to a bookstore after the holidays. How was your day?"

"Fun fact: you jack up the electric bill if you preheat the oven while you prep a casserole. My mom railed on my dad for that instead of thanking him for cooking dinner. The content in the house contained strong language. I still worked on my poem, somehow."

"You wrote a poem?"

"Yeah, for women's studies. You can read it when I'm done editing. It's kind of embarrassing."

"It's just me, Martha."

"I wrote about my family, what my grandpa did." Her voice dips to a hush. "I also bought a Bible today."

"You're awesome."

"When I got home, I ran to my room so my parents wouldn't see it."

A lot of believers use stories of Christians hiding their faith in places like China or Pakistan to remind us to be thankful for the freedom we have here to love God. I never thought my friend (Girlfriend? Hopefully!) in New Jersey would be an example too.

I pace around my room. "I know you don't have the best impression of church, but will you ever be comfortable going with me?"

"Oh, about that. I was wondering if you could help me with something."

"Okay. Sure."

"I want to go back to my grandparents' church. Just once. But not for a service. Maybe we can stop by during the week. It's open on Monday through Wednesday for office work and Bible studies."

My body tingles. "Are you sure you want to go there?"

"I need to confront what happened to me and go back to where it all started."

"I'd be happy to go with you, whenever you're ready."

"How about this week?"

I'm shocked Martha wants to do this so soon. We throw around our schedules and agree on this Wednesday after I'm done with work at three.

"Thanks, Ian, for everything."

I stand and stride over to my window. "I'll do my best to help you. I know your faith journey hasn't been easy."

"It's hard sometimes, trying to revamp what God means to me."

"I know," I soothe as I finger the slats on the blinds and focus on the raindrops dotting the window.

"I started reading Genesis." She gives a nervous laugh. "Just 'In the beginning.'"

"A lot of Christians recommend new believers start in the Gospel of John," I tell her.

"All right, then. I'll go there first."

I lean against the wall and cup my elbow in my hand. "Martha,

I want to say that I'm really in awe of how far you've gotten. I remember how snarky you were. I remember that car ride home." I'm relieved we're talking on the phone, because if Martha saw me now, she would think I've turned into a tomato, I'm blushing so hard. "Now you know the true God. You bought a Bible …"

I wish I could also tell Martha that she's beautiful. I fan myself with my hand. I'll leave that for another conversation.

"Thanks, Ian. Your prayers really worked."

"I did what I was taught to do." I hear Dad come in, and I look up at my door. "I was trying to show you God's love."

An awkward pause. I hold my breath. Did I say too much?

"Your trying was worth all the fights and constant 'I'm sorrys,'" Martha finally says.

"Thanks." My chest relaxes. "Hey, I have to go. My dad's home from my aunt and uncle's with some bulgogi."

"Sounds delish. Also, I wanted to know if you'd like to come over for dinner, maybe tomorrow after work."

"Sure. I'll pick you up for work, and we'll go back to your place together afterwards."

"Sounds like a plan," Martha says. "Good night."

"Good night."

I join Dad in the kitchen, and when he sees me grinning, he asks, "What's the big news?"

"Martha bought a Bible!"

He hands me a plate of Aunt Naomi's bulgogi. "I'm having seconds, so let's talk."

I tell Dad as much as I can without getting too deep into Martha's personal history and how far we've come since September. When I'm done, he gets up and pours me a cup of ice water.

"You were beet red the whole time we talked," he points out. "Cool down. Then decide when you're going to ask her if you're exclusively dating. It sounds like you've met a strong woman who loves God."

"I'm having dinner at her house tomorrow."

"Hanging out with the in-laws?"

"Don't push it, Dad. Martha needs time." I take a swig of my water. "I value what we have. I'm not messing it up."

40

MARTHA

THE FOLLOWING evening Ian and I are stuck folding T-shirts after we finish closing the store because a mom let her kids mess up the piles so she could shop in peace.

When we finally leave, I tug Ian's arm. "You've been acting weird since you spoke to Liz about Justin."

"She'll make sure we don't work together alone anymore, but that won't shut him up. I told her I can't work with him at all." Ian draws his keys from his pocket and unlocks his car. "She said it's too hard to change the schedule. I get it. But she asked what Justin means to me. I said 'Nothing.' Her response? 'Then what he says shouldn't matter to you.'"

"I thought she had more feeling than that. And sense. She probably values her friendship with his great-aunt over your sanity."

"She also doesn't get how evil Justin is. He thinks he has a right to mess with me because I'm Korean."

I envelop him in a hug, and he folds his arms around me.

"I hate my job."

"Then leave."

"Justin already targeted you. I'm not leaving you here with him."

I press my face into his neck. "Thank you for being my big protector."

"I'm serious, Martha. He's trouble."

As we slip into his car, I say, "Don't think about him. Let's go have dinner with my parents."

When we reach my house, I bring Ian through the garage. I open the door that leads into the kitchen and find Mom is standing by the island, holding a pale-blue paperback book.

My joints lock. I was up late last night reading the gospel of John in my Bible and fell asleep. It probably slipped between my bed and nightstand, and Mom found it when she washed sheets today.

The back of Ian's hand brushes against mine. I can grab it and dash back to his car to escape, but I'd be a coward, and I can't leave Mom here like this.

"Is this yours?" Mom asks, her voice eerily calm.

I step toward her. My legs feel like lead. "Yes."

Mom drops my Bible, and it lands next to her, open facedown. Ian moves forward to retrieve it, but I push him back with my arm.

Mom jabs a finger at my Bible. "Why is this in my house?"

"I'm a Christian." My words come out strong, but I'm trembling.

"Why? After everything I warned you about! Why would you trust *anything* my parents believed?"

"Mom, the God I love is not the God your parents believed in."

Her eyes round with horror as she leans toward me. "*Love?* You love God?"

"Grandma and Grandpa used religion for power and abuse. There are so many good Christians in the world. Can't you look past your feelings and see that? Are you afraid of everyone who follows Jesus, Mom?"

I catch Ian in the corner of my eye looking shocked at my boldness.

"I'm not afraid of them. I don't want you or Suzanna getting close to them or believing anything they preach!" Mom's face reddens with anger. "I didn't raise you to be weak, Marty. I raised you to rely on yourself—"

Ian jumps to my defense. "I told her the gospel, but she chose on her own to believe."

Mom lifts her hands in front of her. Her fingers spread out like claws. She looks at them like she's waiting for them to grant permission to strike.

Her rage makes me stumble backward. Ian holds my arm to steady me.

I squeeze my eyes closed to block out Mom falling apart. Where's Dad? I need him to come home so he can calm her down.

"Martha!" Ian calls.

Mom's hands grab the sides of my head.

"Mom," I gasp, but the word gets lost in my throat.

She pulls me across the kitchen by my hair. I struggle to stay in step with her and almost trip over my feet.

"Do you want to know what my mother did to me when I told her I was pregnant? Do you need a taste of who you could become?"

"No, I don't want to know!" I blubber as tears well in my eyes. "Mom, please!"

Jesus? Do you see her hurting me?

"Mrs. Lane," Ian says from behind her, his voice hard, "get your hands off her."

Mom pushes me up against the wall, still gripping my hair. My eyes flutter as she puts her face close to mine and whispers, "She restrained me like this and slammed my head into the wall until I got sick."

"I won't ever turn into Grandma, but *you* will!" I throw at her.

She strikes my head against the wall. Pain spreads over the back of my head. Ian has to intervene.

Then I hear Dad roar, "What the hell?"

I have never felt so grateful for his presence in my life.

Mom releases me. I let out such a sharp sigh, it sounds like a moan. I put all my weight against the wall and slide to the floor, keeping my hands pressed on my pounding heart.

Ian kneels beside me and touches my shoulder. "Are you okay? Do you need ice?"

"No." I pull my knees to my chest and pant, "I'm fine ... I'm fine."

"You talk some sense into her, or she's out!" Mom shouts at Dad.

"What happened?"

"She has a Bible. She says she's a Christian, thanks to him!" Mom exclaims, pointing at Ian and me.

Dad looks at us, then at Mom again. He puts the bag from the hardware store on the counter, turns to Mom, a hand on his hip. "We promised to never hit our girls. Remember that, Jenn?"

For a brief moment I envision my parents making this promise to each other, sharing some closeness. Where has that gone in their marriage?

Ian offers me his hands and pulls me to my feet.

Mom tries to talk, but Dad holds up his hand. "I don't want to hear it, Jenn. I heard you when I was coming in. I saw you slam Marty's head against the wall, and you wanted to keep doing it. She could have gotten a concussion!" Dad points a finger at her face. "I would have called the cops on you for domestic violence and let them arrest you."

Mom shrinks back. "David ..."

Ian walks me out of the kitchen and asks, "What do you want to do?"

"I want to go to my room and lie down." We make our way upstairs. When we step into my room, we take our jackets off. Ian lays them across my desk chair. I remain standing by the door to catch the rest of my parents' fight.

"I'm so *sick* of your instability," Dad rants. "You're impulsive. You panic all the time. And now you hurt Marty. I can't take this, Jenn."

My heart snaps into pieces. Her parents did so much damage.

"David, wait," Mom pleads.

"I'm not waiting. I'm not waiting for the next outrage."

Ian's next to me. I reach out for his hand. We entwine our fingers and exchange ominous looks.

"Don't do this, David," Mom sobs.

"You wanted this," he recalls, lowering his voice. "You wanted out when we fought about Suzanna. And, you know, I think you're right. It's time to separate."

I clap my free hand to my mouth.

Ian's arm comes around my shoulders. "It's hard. I know."

"I'm ... sorry." Mom struggles with her crying. "Can we talk about some things before ..." She catches her breath. "We make any big decisions?"

"No, Jenn." Dad's voice is still quiet. "My mind's made up. We can't go back. You can't live here anymore."

"You don't mean that." Mom's tearful voice is pleading. She sounds small. Vulnerable.

"I *do* mean it. I'm done. You can go to your brother's. Take what you need from the checking account."

I break away from Ian and stagger over to my bed. As I sit, I hold the sides of my head and moan, "This can't be happening."

He comes toward me. "Can I sit with you?"

I move over and rub my hand over my face. "This is all my fault. If I didn't believe—"

"Martha, no, it's not."

I stay still as Mom and Dad mount the stairs. They briskly walk down the hall to their bedroom. They yell at each other the whole time Mom packs. I don't listen to what they're saying. I just hear noise.

"I'm sorry we didn't get to have dinner together and that you have to hear all this instead."

Ian sits and fiddles with his hands in his lap. "Don't worry about it. My parents used to war like this all the time."

"You get used to it, but it's never easy," I say.

He spaces out, and his posture stiffens. "I know."

"Ian." I pat his arm. "What's bugging you?"

"Your parents yelling is bringing up some memories." I'm about to talk, but Ian rushes on. "I know tonight isn't about me. It's just been a long time since ..." He shakes his head. "This is so selfish."

"No. Tell me."

"My mom's last night home, I spilled my milk. She flipped out." Ian rubs the back of his head. "My dad told me to go to my room. I thought he was punishing me, but I realized he didn't want me to see them crash. Pfft. I still heard a lot of what they said."

"Like what?"

"I have no idea why they started talking about Caleb, but my mom was crying, 'I want my son back.' Whatever my dad said made her furious. That's when things got scary."

Mom comes down the hall. As she passes my open door, she exclaims at Dad, "The only thing my parents got right is I shouldn't have married you!"

"Jenn, you need to go."

I hear Mom descend the stairs with her suitcase. I can't make out her response, but what Dad says next pulls my heart into my gut.

"Because I don't like you anymore." He breathes this out, like he's spent. "You're a completely different person. We can't stay like this. It's killing me."

A long silence. The door opens, then shuts. The garage door rattles the floor.

I get to my feet and creep over to the window. I watch Mom pull out of the driveway and accelerate down the street. She's gone.

I look over my shoulder at Ian. "What made your parents' fight so scary?"

"My dad later said my mom yelled all this crazy stuff, like she wished his mom had stayed in North Korea, then she wouldn't have met Grandpa, and they wouldn't have had my dad."

I step away from my window and rejoin Ian on my bed. "Those are terrible things to wish on someone."

"I know. My mom lost Caleb, but she's not the only one who's suffered. She has no *clue* how much my halmoni went through." Ian sniffs and rubs his nose. "She has no clue how much halmoni loved everyone. After she and my grandpa got over their rough time, she hugged my dad and said, 'My family—everything I have here is the sunshine in my life.'"

"That's really beautiful."

Ian relaxes his shoulders and focuses on the Russian flash cards pegged to the corkboard on my desk. "Then my mom said the worst thing. She called my dad a half-breed."

My mouth drops. "That's sick. How could she ... I can't ... that's so ..."

"That's when I took some books off my shelf and placed them around my bed, like a moat. I thought stories with happy endings would keep me safe."

I look at Ian. His eyes connect with mine, and he brushes my cheek with the back of his finger. We draw our faces closer. I lean in and grab his arm to prevent myself from landing on his lap. My thumb touches his scar.

I want to know what happened. He said he never thought of suicide, so he must have gotten hurt. Or he used to cut himself and isn't ready to tell me. I want to ask him a thousand questions so he has a thousand reasons to stay.

Ian pulls back. I sit up and take my hand off his arm.

I hear Dad's footsteps down the hall. "Marty, Ian!"

I shift on my bed to create some space between us.

Dad opens my door. "Ian, go home."

He nods as he slides off my bed, then walks over to my desk chair for his coat. "Call me if you need anything," he says quietly to me.

I nod.

Ian slips past Dad, who keeps his hand on the doorknob. Once Ian leaves the house, Dad steps inside my room. My Bible is tucked under his arm.

"Marty, listen." He strides over toward me.

I prepare myself for his anger, but he keeps his voice even.

"Besides you and Suzanna, the one thing your mother and I have in common is we hate religion. So"—Dad drops my Bible next to me on my bed—"if you talk about it or try to convert me, we're going to have problems. Got it?"

I pick up my Bible. The cover's bottom corner is bent. I cuddle it against me like a well-loved stuffed animal. "Yes, Dad," I say without looking at him.

"Is your head okay?" Dad's voice is hoarse with emotion.

"Uh-huh."

"Are you hungry?"

"Not really. I want to rest for a little while."

"I'll make you a sandwich when you're ready," Dad says as he leaves my room.

I fold into a fetal position on my bed. Ian had built a moat with children's stories when his parents fought. My fortress was made of my parents' promise to keep this house safe. Both were torn down. That's what happens when you trust earthly securities.

After a short nap, I go downstairs to get something to eat. There's a bag of rice on the counter, and in the fridge I find a container of marinated chicken. A recipe for Korean barbecue chicken is taped to its lid.

Shock and guilt knot up inside me. Oh, Mom.

41

CALAMITY

YOUR WILL to keep going is what keeps you sane. You go for a haircut to get rid of your split ends. You make dinner. You do laundry. You pore over your books past midnight. You move about your life frantically and stop to catch your breath. You joke, saying, "I'm in a hurry; this is Jersey."

You're not alone, but you're lonely. You're trying to look okay, but I see the fatigue in your eyes. When you don't think I'm looking, I see you cup your hands over your mouth and nose and try to control the tears. You wrap your arms around yourself. Do you imagine her holding you? How much has she held you since you were a child?

As I watch you tremble, I tremble inside. Did I make the right choice? I was trying to protect you. But I wonder if there was another way. Plain faith that is not felt in churches and prayer. A faith that materializes in parent-child bonds, solid promises, a wholesome and true love. I question if my efforts were worth it because you're in so much pain.

I want to reach over and touch you, to cradle your cheek in my palm and see your tears glide down the side of my hand. But that would feel foreign to both of us. I'm afraid you will shrink away and look at me with a strained expression. That you will blame me for all that has happened.

But you blame yourself. To keep yourself grounded, you carry your Bible with you everywhere you go. Your eyes take in stories of redemption and the promises of God. You hope and pray that she will come home and love you in the way you want and need. You reason, "If I can change so drastically, then why can't she?"

I get you. I want to hope with you. But my faith in miracles is thinning. So I give you the space to talk. To imagine her with you again with a new kind of love. Because I don't want your mind going to the worst scenario—that you might lose your mother.

Are you ready for that loss? If it happens, you might swarm heaven with prayers and knit Scripture into your memory. But I hope you will also reach into yourself and remember your resilience—the strength you built from all the damage they have done, the power you have gained from surviving.

You close your Bible and sit quietly with it on your lap. You caress the crease on the cover. It's the mark of the last time she was with you. She was angry because you didn't avoid religion, but you needed to avoid her.

I look at my hands. What have I done?

Now I understand why love can hurt.

42

MARTHA

IAN TURNS into the parking lot of Seed of Faith Church and kills the engine.

"Are you ready?" he asks.

There are two other cars here. "I was hoping it'd be closed," I admit.

"You need some time?"

I shake my head and open the passenger door. "I'm going in. If I procrastinate, I'll chicken out, and we will have come for nothing."

Ian and I get out of his car. I take big, confident steps toward the entrance as he trails behind me.

I look up at the building. My stomach turns into a science experiment. I remember how I thought this was a castle with its tall wooden doors, bell tower, and stained-glass windows.

"Grandma, does a princess live here?" I had asked her.

"No. This is God's house."

"Who's God?"

"Marty." Grandma sighed. "You'll find out soon."

I keep walking. I am bigger than my trauma, my grandparents, my fear.

When Ian and I reach the church, I pause in front of the double doors. I squint before I push down on the handle. We step inside.

The last time I stood in this foyer, I had told Grandma, "This isn't a house." I pointed into the sanctuary. "Why are there all those wooden seats?"

She pulled me aside and knelt in front of me. As she leaned in, her eyes narrowed, and her mouth became tense. "Sweetie," she began in a whisper. "If you're a bad girl, bad things will happen to you. Understand?"

Grandpa stood behind her, staring ahead, looking bored with a hand in his pocket.

I frowned, causing my bottom lip to protrude. "My daddy said asking questions is good."

Grandma lifted her chin a little and grinned. "Your daddy doesn't know what good is." She extended her arm in the direction of all the people filing into church. "Everyone here knows what's good, and when you leave here today, you'll know what's good too."

"Martha." Ian's voice transports me back to the present. "Are you all right?"

I press my fingertips to my mouth. "I remember so much."

"If you want to leave—"

I hurry into the sanctuary. I take in the dark-mauve cushioned pews, the huge wooden cross hanging behind the pulpit, the music stands, and the organ.

I turn and face him. "Nothing's moved. It's like a museum of that day."

"Wow," he says from behind me.

I amble toward the left side of the room, to the third row from the back. I caress the arm of the pew as if I appreciate that it's still here after all this time. I scoot into the row and take a seat. Ian settles down next to me.

"This is where we sat," I whisper.

Ian crosses his arms and peers around, taking in how I saw things here that Christmas.

I lean forward and touch a Bible in the rack attached to the pew in front of me. "Except the Bibles were red."

I picture my six-year-old self lying here, curled up as I try to hold in my pee.

I blink.

Grandpa had watched me intensely as I put my fingers between my legs and scrunched up my face. He turned to Grandma and pointed at me.

Sick, foul hypocrite.

I clap a hand to my mouth.

Pedophile. Beast.

The room suddenly feels warm. I grab my knees and dig my fingers into my jeans.

"What is it?" Ian asks, concerned.

I rub the corner of my eye with my pointer finger. "I'm jealous of those who like church. Even a lot of secular people know that you're supposed to feel safe in a church."

Ian leans in close. His eyes fill with empathy. "I'm sorry you didn't get the experience you deserved. And I think you coming back here and sitting in this pew is pretty freaking brave."

"Thanks. You're brave too, for sharing your faith with me when I was so hostile to you."

Ian gives me a wry smile. "You weren't *that* bad ... sometimes."

I nudge him with my elbow. "I was a work in progress." I tuck some hair behind my ear. "Thinking about all the progress I made in here." I touch my chest. "You didn't go through what I did, but, Ian, I'm blown away by your patience …" Emotion seeps into my voice. I turn my face toward the front of the church. "And willingness to walk this walk with me. It's been a really messy and crazy walk, and I'd feel super lonely doing it by myself."

"The morning we went to the poetry reading, I told my dad about you. He told me to show you God's love and be my best self for you."

I let my skin absorb his words, let them swim to my bloodstream, then to my heart. Was Ian loving me before I felt anything for him?

I look down at his hand resting on the pew. I move mine over his and squeeze it. "Just letting you know, the best you is amazing."

He beams at me. "I had a lot of help from God."

We hold each other's gaze for a moment before pulling our hands back.

"We should go," I say. "I need the bathroom."

Ian nods. "Okay."

We stand and head up the aisle. As I step over the seam between the sanctuary and the foyer, a stocky man with a short crew cut of graying brown hair strolls out of an office that's off to the side. "Can I help you?"

I let out a little gasp and stumble backward. I recognize his beard, bushy eyebrows, and the sharp look in his eyes.

"How long have you pastored here?" I ask him, point-blank.

He looks confused at my question. "Eighteen years."

I try to keep my voice steady, but my words sound chilly. "This was my grandparents' church. They took me here on Christmas fourteen years ago. I remember you."

He extends his hand. I give it a light shake.

"Pastor Ron. I always do the Christmas service, so, yes, that probably was me. Who are your grandparents?"

I hold back a disgusted face. "Gabe and Eleanor Fischer."

Recognition flashes on his face. I watch the muscles around his mouth slowly form a smile.

My heart plummets.

Ian's hand brushes against mine. He grabs my fingers and squeezes.

"I remember Eleanor. She was a ball of fire." Pastor Ron holds up a fist. "The women in her prayer group always looked forward to her meetups. They said her zeal for God encouraged them to keep believing, no matter what God's answer to their prayers was."

I twist my mouth. I'm going to hurl. Time to go.

"I don't remember your grandfather as much. He was quiet, kept to himself." Pastor Ron frowns. "Are you all right?"

"It was nice talking—" I force out. "I have to use the bathroom."

Pastor Ron motions to the left. "Restrooms are that way."

I pull my hand out of Ian's and dart to the ladies' room. I push the door open and hurry into a stall. I gather the front of my jacket against my mouth.

Nobody in my grandparents' inner circle even *sensed* who they really were. They never gave a hint, not even to Pastor Ron, about how they treated their family. That's how good they dressed up in holiness.

I clench my teeth and grunt into my jacket. That doesn't clean out all the rage. Not even close.

I give myself the bathroom break I should have taken here fourteen years ago. As I step toward the sink to wash my hands, I hear Ian and Pastor Ron chatting in the foyer. I splash cold water on my face. I don't care that it washed some concealer off a blemish on my cheek.

When I'm done, I swing the door open and say, "Okay, Ian. Let's go," in a chipper voice.

He nods to me. To Pastor Ron, he says, "Thanks for telling me about your church."

"Take care, you two. Sunday service starts at ten if you ever want to call this home."

Sorry, Pastor Ron, but even though this is where I heard the gospel for the first time, it's been one of the settings in my fourteen-year-long nightmare. And he seems like a nice guy, but I cannot fully trust him. What if he's like my grandparents when he's with *his* family? Maybe this is un-Christian judging, but I can never walk through these doors again.

I burst through the exit and gulp in some cold air. As I sprint to Ian's car, I breathe, "I couldn't be in there any longer."

"I figured you didn't want to stay," he says, trying to keep up with me.

When we reach his car and get in, I explode, "Unless Pastor Ron is an abuser like my grandparents with a skewed idea of what good faith is, he didn't know! He had no clue who they really were! Does the man have any gut feelings or intuitions?"

"Some wolves look really good in sheep's clothing," Ian remarks as he starts to drive.

"It makes me wonder how many people they deceived. Their whole church?"

Ian shrugs. "Maybe not everyone, but definitely the pastor and their church friends." He pats my shoulder as we reach a stoplight. "They can't deceive God when he judges them."

My muscles relax as the tension dissolves inside me. "God never changes, right?"

Ian resumes driving. "That's right."

I unzip my purse and pull out my notepad and pen. "Do you have a verse for that?"

"Off the top of my head, yeah. I think it's Hebrews 13:8. 'Jesus Christ is the same yesterday, and to day, and for ever.'"

I jot that down. "The Bible verses you've shared with me—it takes a little while to break down the wording, but I eventually get it." I slip my notepad and pen back into my bag. "What translation do you use?"

"King James. My dad's a big fan. I'm okay with other versions of the Bible, but I always go back to the KJV. I was raised on it."

"I like how flowery and poetic it sounds."

"You know, even after you think you get what Scripture is saying, there are still tons of things in the Bible that you can discuss forever, such as the first two verses of Genesis."

I lean forward in my seat a little. "You mean the very beginning of Genesis isn't to the point?"

Ian laughs. "Martha, have you ever heard of the gap theory?"

"No. What's that?"

"It theorizes there was a chunk of time between the beginning and when God started his six days of creation. Satan was probably at work corrupting the world, so God started over. I have a book on it you can borrow." Ian stops at an intersection. "I don't mean to influence your view on evolution—"

"Hmm." I prop my elbow on the armrest and set my chin on my knuckles. "Sounds interesting. I'll look at it. Honestly, I've never formed a solid view on the age of the earth."

"Well, when I learned about the gap theory, it blew the Bible wide open for me."

"I'll take the wild ride."

"Okay. And will you take a hot chocolate at the café, or do you want to head home?"

"Let's get a drink." I pat my bag. "Besides, I have my poem for you to read."

Ian makes a left, heading toward Sunset, Coffee, and Books.

As I gaze at the sunset oozing into the gray-blue clouds, I think about God's big love, his big creations, his big promises.

My heart is getting bigger too. I need room for all this unfamiliar joy coming in. And maybe it's a good idea to make some room for Ian.

43

IAN

WHEN MARTHA and I get out of my car at Sunsets, Coffee, and Books, she pulls me to her and says, "I want a hug." As she embraces me, she adds, "And I'd like to pay for everything tonight. We each get a drink and a book."

I hook my arms around her waist. The November air doesn't cool down the nervousness running through my body. "And I'd like to talk about where our friendship stands."

Martha's forehead touches mine. "You mean our relationship?"

"You just saved me a ton of I-like-you anxiety."

"Well, we *did* kiss, and you said you'd buy me sunflowers someday. We're either together or you're really skilled at leading me on."

"I wanted to make sure we were on the same page. Now, I'd like to go inside and *read* pages—your poetry—while I drink a latte."

Martha's eyes go round. "You drink coffee?"

"Occasionally, thanks to my dad's perfected pour-over skills."

"So, now that we're dating, I get to learn more about you,

drown in hot chocolate, and get awesome book recommendations. What else?"

A guy walks past us, causing his coat to brush against Martha's. She steps closer to my car, and I follow suit.

"We have to fill up our notebook, and I get to finally tell you I've been attracted to you for a very long time, and I love how you love God, so ..." I catch my breath. "Let's go start something new."

We cross the lot, holding hands. I am officially dating Martha Lane. I curl my fingers into my palm and dig my nails into my skin. Nope, I'm not dreaming.

As we enter the café, I notice a group of students sitting at the round table by the entrance studying for a chemistry test. I follow Martha to the literature section and look up at the wall of titles.

"Close your eyes and pick a book. I'll go too."

Martha shuts her eyes and trails her fingers over the books' spines. She pulls out *Story of a Girl*.

I snag a thick hardcover a few shelves down. It's *The Book Thief* by Markus Zusak.

She taps the cover with her finger. "Let me know if that's worth the read. I've heard so much about it."

"I'll write about it in our notebook." We get in line to order our drinks.

Martha looks down at *Story of a Girl*. "Let's write something about every book we read."

"Deal."

After Martha orders her hot chocolate and I pick the pumpkin spice latte, we take a table in the back.

"I called my mom today," she says as we sit. "She didn't answer. My parents obviously aren't talking. But Suzanna texted me." Martha twists a napkin in her hand several times. It looks like a Twizzler. "She said becoming a Christian was a dumb choice. I asked her if we could talk. She never replied. She and my dad aren't on speaking terms either. She's still mad at him for blowing up at Carl last week."

Suzanna needs to grow up. "I hope your family can reconcile."

"Dad and I are adjusting in case we don't. It's not … hard. I feel so robotic."

Jim comes over with our drinks.

"At first, I'm like, we're adults. We can cook and do laundry." Martha jabs a spoon into the foamy leaf on the surface of her hot chocolate. "But, really, my dad and I don't have a deep bond with Mom. I still miss her, though. I *really* miss her."

After all the fighting my parents did and all the times Mom yelled at me when she shouldn't have, Dad and I were still a wreck after she left. When things were calm, Mom and Dad were happy, and she was a good mom. She'd let me make a mess with spin art or play outside instead of sitting in front of the TV. After dinner, Dad would play the piano while she and I sat on the couch and read books. She came into my room at four a.m. every day until I was almost five to hug me so I knew she wouldn't disappear like Omma and Mrs. Shin did.

Martha digs some folded sheets of paper out of her bag. "My poem."

I take them from her and begin to read.

6 to 20

A girl
with a marshmallow body
and hair the color of the penny
she throws into the fountain at the mall
hopes she'll get a doll for Christmas.
Her babka
makes that doll

from old buttons
and fabric and yarn.

Grandpa gives her
something under the blankets.
Did you know
an alarm clock can be
a cold hand between your legs?

She hugs her doll
because Mommy and Daddy stop
    hugging her
when cuddling with your girl
isn't so special anymore.

Daddy worked himself into a breakdown
to make the marriage work
and keep my sister from becoming a case
    number.
His in-laws wished he had never been born,
so I stop craving hugs,
because I am loved,
even though Mommy and Daddy
never say it.

Mommy was abused in the name of religion,
so I shut my feelings off
to survive
so I can't feel
and realize I'm deprived.

I'm a whole bag of marshmallows.

Let's make homemade Rice Krispies treats!
The kids call me a walrus.
Mom says they don't matter,
but I want her to tell me I'm pretty,
but she doesn't,
so I think she thinks they matter.

The princess cradled in her mansion
who paints her face with too much makeup
and dots her i's with hearts
and decorates her notebooks with stickers,
has bats swooping
out of her rib cage.
People Who Will Never Have Sex,
she wrote.
#1: MARTHA ~~LANE~~ LAME!

I carry
that secret swaddled in bedding
from that Christmas.
How can I tell Mom and Dad?
I want a hug,
but I can't ask for one,
but I can read Shakespeare
and build a college career out of straight A's.

Dad's arms held too many books
and not enough of his girls.
Mom's hands tap-danced over
a calculator to count the pennies
in the checking account
instead of soothing her girls' boo-boos.

Feeling too much
means you don't know
how to survive.
Deflate the pain
to get stronger.
Work to death
to win happiness.
Oh,
and love is
a waste
of time.

But if I kick this
out of my chest
there will be
DANGER AHEAD.
I could have a shiny career
and a big fat paycheck,
but the scars stare at me,
and love is missing.

It might dangle between
those 11 p.m. phone calls
with my BFF
to grab last-minute help
with math and science
and to make sure we're okay
as we swim
through middle school angst.

Maybe it's tucked in unexpected places,
like in that guy's heart

who gave me a one-night's notice
to go to a wedding
so I could sit in the chair
his ex should have filled.
And he worships a God I was raised to hate.

Maybe it comes down from heaven
from God,
but I was too busy hating him
for fourteen years
to see
His love was hung on the cross,
wrapped in bloody flesh
that was impaled with nails
and a crown of thorns.

Keeping those feelings
Mom and Dad told me to throw away
like that worn-out yellow blanket
I kept poking holes in when I was four
is what makes me human.

The pile of aches
bubbles over my edges.
It's okay to have an overstock
of love; it's not dimensional
like dusty boxes packed with just-in-case
        items.
It has no beginning. No end.
Just a face you can't look away from.
I'll hand love out
to Dad when he comes in from work.

I'll give some to Mom
when our family
is together again.

Dad might never put his arms out for a hug.
Mom might never say I'm beautiful.
Not everyone will think
my size twelve waist is small enough,
and the guy who asked me to the wedding
might not be the one at my wedding,
but I can love me
and others
and rest in the truth
that love
is not
a waste
of time.

I look up at her and say, "This is amazing."

"Thanks." Martha takes her poem from me and returns it to her bag. "It's a bunch of sentences chopped up in random places."

I shake my head. "No. I think you translated your experiences in a really special way."

Martha takes a long sip of hot chocolate. "I'm glad you think that. I'm trying to stay in my professor's good graces. She's been annoyed with a lot of students for not taking her class seriously."

I move my almost-empty mug to the side. "What's that about Suzanna being a case number?"

Martha jolts a little. "Oh. My grandparents hated that she was born out of wedlock and wanted my parents to put her up for adoption."

"Back in September, you said you were sorry I was adopted. Is that why?"

"Yeah. My mom was afraid my grandma would show up at the hospital and make a case that she and my dad couldn't raise Suzanna. She was so scared and held on to Suzanna with all her love." Martha frowns. "I don't know where that went."

"It might still be there."

Martha rubs her eye with her thumb. "I hope your birth mother held you like that, even if she knew she couldn't keep you."

"I don't know if she even touched me." The pain's coming too close, so I get off the topic. "I see why you regret dropping creative writing. You're good at it."

Martha puts her coat on, signaling she's ready to go. "It's not because of what I manage to write. It's for the big *W* that's going on my transcript. I gave up on an impulse."

I tuck our books under my arm and slip my other through Martha's as we leave. "Why'd you do it?"

"My past tailed me, so I ran out of my writing class, literally." A gust of wind blows flyaway pieces of Martha's hair around her face. "If pain is the only thing inside you, that's what you get on paper."

"Gemma liked creative writing until her teacher said her main character needed to have a disability."

Martha shakes her head. "That's messed up." We get into my car, and she asks, "Does Gemma have a hard time in school with her disability?"

I close the driver's side and adjust the front of my coat. "Academically, no. Her teachers are accommodating and treat her well, but socially, it's rough sometimes." I tell Martha about the bullying Leo and Walter put Gemma through last year.

Her face twists with disgust when I'm done talking. "That's

dark. What kind of seventh-grader talks about rape and getting hit by a bus?"

"The kind of kid who desperately needs help, or else we'll be reading about his crimes in the news a few years from now."

"Gemma's lucky to have you for a brother," Martha says.

"It's hard balancing having a relationship with her and my mom. Gemma understands that I don't want to transfer anywhere. She gets that my mom's choices hurt me. But I know, deep down, she wishes I could take my mom's offer so we can have some years together." My voice hardens. "But I can't—and don't want to—do it."

"Does she have friends? How's her relationship with your mom and stepdad?" Martha asks.

"A few friends, and, yeah, her family situation's pretty good."

"Then don't base your life choices on her unless she *really* needs you. After what your mother put you through, you need to put yourself first." Martha touches my right arm and looks down. "Speaking of your past, how did you get the scar on your arm?"

I stiffen. "I had a bike accident."

"You said you never thought about suicide, but I thought you might have hurt yourself."

"My mom promised to teach me how to ride a two-wheeler. After she left, my dad was too depressed to do anything. It was spring break and Morgan's birthday. My cousin Hayden and I were in the garage looking for sidewalk chalk. I saw his old bike and wanted to ride it. He took it up the hill in the backyard, put me on the seat, and pushed me forward. I was headed for the porch."

Martha puts her fingers to her lips. "Oh no."

"Hayden told me to pedal backward. I didn't know how, so I steered to the right and went down another hill into a bunch of sticker bushes."

"I hope you were wearing a helmet."

"I was. I'll give Hayden credit there. I knew the bike was going to fall, so I went with it. I had to get stitches on my side; a branch left a gash there worse than the one on my arm."

Martha's mouth gapes. "You could have been killed if that branch impaled you."

"My dad called my mom that night. He gave me the phone. I started crying and begged her to come home. I said I wouldn't spill my milk and I'd clean up my toys." I rest my arm on the door handle and face the window. "I don't remember what she said. I threw the phone and cried so hard I puked. My dad yelled at me and walked away. He was so out of it."

"Your mom leaving messed up a lot of things, huh?"

Mom leaving connects to the bike accident, which connects to Dad's past rages, which connects to the day I saw him at his worst. Anger mounts inside me, making my neck and face tense up.

"Pretty much. My dad forgetting to pick me up from Chris's sixth birthday party or pouring grape juice in my cereal wasn't the biggest deal. But he was cooking once—"

"Ian, you don't have to tell me."

I shake my head vigorously. "No. I want to. He got distracted and left oil heating on the stove to fry some chicken. It caught fire. He grabbed the pan and yelled some obscene things as he threw it out on the porch. I got in a fight with a kid in my class a few days later over a sandbox toy. I repeated my dad's words. My teacher called my dad. When I got home ..." The pain clogs my throat.

Martha strokes my shoulder, but I withdraw from her touch.

"Did your dad hurt you? He seems like such a gentle guy."

"He is, Martha!" I explode, which causes her to recoil. "That's why it was so painful to see him die inside. When I got home, he repeatedly slapped my back." My eyelids battle with the tears that want to spill out. "He thrust me into my room, and I cried until I could barely breathe. He didn't come in to check on me, only to tell me dinner was ready."

Martha shudders. "I'm sorry for asking about your scar."

"Oh, God, no. Don't feel guilty. I need to talk about this. This was the first time I wanted my omma. I wanted her so bad."

"You wanted her because your mother was gone, and you were losing your dad." She leans over and puts her head against my shoulder. "What brought him back?"

I slip an arm around Martha. "His parents and sisters helped out a lot. He went to a therapist, took antidepressants."

"That must have been hard for you too."

I rub her upper arm and bury my face in her hair. It smells like lavender and coconut.

She sits up and looks at me. "You said I was strong for returning to my grandparents' church." Martha kisses my cheek. She stays there and says, "You're strong too."

I turn to her and kiss her lips. She tucks her leg under her and leans into me. She holds my face. The light touch of her fingers and the heat between us split my nerves. Another kiss. One more. My hand finds her hip. My arm feels heavy because it doesn't belong there, but I love feeling the desire for her pulsate through me.

And I can't stand it, so I pull away.

Martha stops kissing me. "What?"

I start the car and flick the heat on, which we probably don't need. "We should be careful."

"I didn't mean to."

"It's both of us," I say.

Martha fixes her jacket collar and buckles her seat belt.

We can't land in the same spot Hana and I lay in on prom night. The thing is, I didn't like being in her dorm for long periods of time, but I've already crossed some boundaries with Martha. It's wrong. It shouldn't feel this comfortable. But it feels right.

44

MARTHA

ON MONDAY I meet Kaylin outside the humanities building. Her painting is propped up against her hip, wrapped in a large trash bag. In a few minutes, I'm going to broadcast my poem to my entire women's studies class.

"Ready?" she asks.

I touch my stomach. "I'm not feeling good. Maybe I'll volunteer to go first in case I have to hightail it to the bathroom."

"Public speaking jitters?"

We approach the stairs to the entrance and pass a garbage can. I'm tempted to toss my folder inside, but I can't repeat the fallout I had with creative writing.

I shake my head. "I think I have a bug, or it's stress. Stomach issues and headaches. I'm trying to get by, but my family is falling apart. But I can't afford to fall apart. I need my job. I have a paper to write for Russian about Tajikistan, which is due Wednesday, and I have a test on Friday."

I've also been trying to pray. I pray for my family to come back together and for Ian to have a peaceful Thanksgiving. In my prayers, I'm begging God for what I want. It feels wrong. Ian had told me earlier this semester that God isn't a genie, but I don't know how else to pray.

Kaylin frowns as she and I enter the stairwell with a bunch of other students and head up to class. "I'm sorry, Marty."

"Thanks. My dad and I are managing."

Dad's been quiet. There's not much going on at the library, so we talk about my classes when our schedules let us have lunch or dinner together. There's no way I'm telling him about the poem I wrote, and I haven't been studying extra Russian. I let Dad return the books he got me from the library because when I'm not at the store, doing housework, or busy with homework, I'm sleeping.

"Have you been able to reach your mom?" she asks.

"I gave up on that. I stopped contacting Suzanna too. She's on Mom's side and doesn't want to hear mine. Even if she can never agree with me ..." We reach the landing on the second floor. I turn onto the next set of stairs. "I want to talk to her. I want her to be a sister."

Kaylin furrows her brows. She's never thought highly of Suzanna; she thinks she doesn't act her age. I can attest to that.

Once we're on the third floor, I push the door open, and we head into the hallway.

"My mom said you and your dad can spend Thanksgiving with us." She moves her painting from under her arm and carries it in front of her with both hands.

"That's really sweet of her. My dad and I will probably whip up a casserole."

That's all he and I are eating these days. They're quick to prep, and we always have leftovers.

At least I'm spending Thanksgiving with someone who loves me. I know Ian's dreading going to his mom's. If my mom committed adultery—and I heard from down the hall—I'd never visit her until she apologized.

Ian and I haven't hung out since I showed him my poem. He has to draw up a business plan for his business class, so he's creating a language school that offers critical language classes for children and adults. Last night, he texted me, wanting to know if he could put me down as the Russian teacher.

Not thinking much of this, I said yes, but Kailyn joked that I shouldn't be surprised if Ian pops a marriage proposal to me soon.

No way. He probably wants to keep his distance for a while. I'm embarrassed about how much I kissed Ian in his car. Kaylin said my excessive kissing means my body is working. I'm surprised I wanted to feel something like that so soon. I'm just glad Ian hasn't said anything about it.

When we reach our classroom, Kaylin stops and sets her painting against the wall. "Wait, I want you to see it." She pulls off the plastic bag to reveal a watercolor painting of a blond-haired woman's face being cut in two by a fist. The fist is covered in words like domestic violence, unequal pay, war, genital mutilation, rape, abortion.

Child abuse.

I feel the blood rush to my face and step back. "Wow, that's gnarly ... bone-chilling ... beautiful."

"Thanks." Kaylin slips the plastic bag over her work. "While I was painting, the word that kept running through my head was *raw*, so I hope I portrayed that."

"You definitely accomplished your goal." I open the door for Kaylin and walk into class behind her. Sita, Léa, and Alyssa are the only ones here.

"Weird," Kaylin mumbles.

"I called Josh to see what's up," Sita says to no one in particular. "He didn't answer."

"If Dr. Sloan isn't here by one-fifteen, we can leave," Léa reminds us as she twists her carrot-red hair into a bun.

I slide my hand inside my folder. My poem sizzles under my palm. I told Kaylin I'd email her a copy after class, but I want to show it to her now. I lift my hand to pat her arm, but she's engrossed in her phone.

"Class is canceled. Dr. Sloan is sick." Alyssa scans her laptop screen. "She put an announcement on Blackboard earlier and sent an email. She wants us to leave our projects in her office by 3:45, no exceptions. Her office mate knows how many to expect."

Léa jumps out of her chair and makes a beeline for the door.

"We're presenting in two weeks because we're still going to the library next week to watch *Maria Full of Grace*," Alyssa finishes explaining.

"How'd your poem turn out?" Kaylin asks as we leave the classroom.

"Too honest. I should stop treating writing like therapy. It gives me anxiety."

Her face clouds with concern. "You wrote your memoirs again?"

"Unfortunately."

We join Alyssa, Léa, and Sita by the elevator. The doors open and we file inside.

Léa blurts, "This class is a joke. Why are we watching *Maria Full of Grace*? It has nothing to do with art."

"Movies *are* art," Sita says to her back.

"If I want to appreciate art, I'll go to a museum, not spend a semester talking about it."

"Then drop the class and go to a museum," I mumble as we step off the elevator.

Humor shines in Alyssa's eyes as she covers her mouth. Léa flings a look at me.

I'm the last one to leave my project on Dr. Sloan's desk. I glance back at it lying on Kaylin's painting. There's no turning back.

Kaylin's waiting for me in the hall. "You're really brave to tell our class what you've been through."

"It's stupid," I counter as I walk past her.

She doesn't move. "Marty, writing can heal you. I've read about these things."

I squeeze my backpack straps. "I don't need a psychology lecture."

Pain flickers in her eyes. "You keep writing about what happened to you."

"The personal is political," I say in a scoff. "That's the slogan for women's studies. I'm following the crowd."

I start toward the elevator, but Kaylin grabs my backpack. "You did more than that." She waits for a professor and a student to pass us. "I painted something that represents women in general. Another group wrote an advice column on eating disorders. You're giving others the privilege of knowing who you really are."

I spread my hands over the cinder block wall. My creative writing classroom had the same prison look. Six years old to twenty. Those years are shackled to my ankles.

In the corner of my eye, Kaylin rests against the wall. She's right; I made something original. It shouts my breakout of the prison Grandpa sentenced me to fourteen years ago.

A tall, dark-haired guy passes us. He waves at Kaylin. "Hey, Kay. How's it going?"

Her expression brightens. "Hi, Andy. It's going all right."

He stops and comes up to her. "You want to work together in lab tomorrow?"

Kaylin stares up at him as if he just handed her a thousand bucks. "I'd love that."

"Cool. See you in class."

After Andy strides off, I glance at her. "He called you Kay."

"I know."

"And he has dreamy blue eyes."

"I know that too." Her face reddens as she puffs out some air. "You have a minute?"

"I have a lot of minutes."

Kaylin takes my arm and pulls me down the hall toward the elevator. "I think we both have things to talk about."

45

IAN

IT'S THANKSGIVING. I'm at Mom's, realizing there are some things I'll never get used to here, like how I'm not in any of the photos hanging in the foyer. She uses Aunt Naomi's cherry pie recipe and says it's her own. And Mom never hugs me. I reached out to give her a side hug, like I always do, and she walked away.

If Mom showed me any sign of love, I'm afraid she'd consider that a bad day.

Nathan slices the turkey, and Mom carries the side dishes to the table. Gemma's by the fridge, pouring her uncle Victor some Pepsi and telling him about the math test she has on Monday. It feels like I'm watching a Thanksgiving special.

I put the silverware on the kitchen table and check the time on my phone. It's 3:57. Two hours until I can leave.

I sit next to Victor. He's cool. He and Sarah live on a ranch in Amherst and work with traumatized horses.

"How early are you opening tomorrow?" Victor asks as he scoops some corn off his plate. Retail probably sounds boring to him compared to healing horses, but he seems genuinely inter-ested in what I do.

"Six, but my shift starts at five."

Sarah almost chokes on her food. "Who's that desperate to buy crochet hooks and yarn?"

I shrug. "Those people exist."

"More money for you, Ian," Mom chimes in across from me.

"Speaking of that, my probation period for my promotion was up earlier this month. I got a ninety-five-cent raise."

Mom gives me a slight nod.

My phone buzzes in my pocket. I pull it out to read the text Martha sent.

Martha
Suzanna's with Mom at my aunt and uncle's. Dad and I are having a micro Thanksgiving. How are you?

"Ian."

I lift my head.

Mom points downward. "Phone away."

She despises mobile technology. Gemma's already had her cell phone confiscated twice in school.

"My girlfriend's in a rough situation."

Gemma's eyes grow large. "You have a new *girlfriend*?"

"You can't do anything for her while you're here. She can wait until you get home," Mom says.

I suppress a disgusted look.

"What's her name?" Gemma wants to know.

I pick up my fork. "Her name's Martha."

"I like that. It's rare ... pretty."

I lean in closer to Gemma. "That makes her even more unique."

"The girl you took to the wedding?" Mom asks. "You don't waste time. I thought you'd pray for a year before you dated someone else."

Racism makes me feel small. So does Mom's bullying.

"You didn't waste any time after you left Dad," I volley back.

"Don't talk to me like that."

Nathan gets up. "I need another glass of wine."

Gemma stays extra focused on cutting her turkey. Victor clears his throat. Sarah dumps more fried apples onto her plate.

"In fact, you used your time very wisely with Nathan while you and Dad were still married." I'm surprised how easily this rolls off my tongue.

Mom holds a spoonful of mashed potatoes up to her mouth. "Everyone here knows we were in touch before I left your father. Get over it."

"Can I be excused?" Gemma asks. Mom ignores her.

I want to speak, but Nathan says, "Ian, move on. That's in the past. Finish eating. Okay?" He stands behind Mom's chair and squeezes her shoulders.

Condescending snake. I stare at Nathan and remember him and Mom running downstairs, laughing as they carried the sheets to the laundry room.

I push my knife so hard into my turkey that the blade screeches against the plate. I drop my silverware. Everyone looks at me.

"It's not in the past," I throw back at Nathan. "It's stuck with me."

Mom spreads her hands out in the air and moves them in rhythm as she says, "I know, I know. It hurt you and your father that I left so abruptly, but you need to move on."

I sink into a laundry day memory. *I wish you could stay. I wish you were my husband,* she cooed at Nathan in the hall. They kissed too hard and made too much noise. I shouldn't have seen or heard any of that.

The words bubble on my tongue. I am a time capsule of Mom and Nathan's secrets. Time to bust me open.

"I can't move on when I heard you and Nathan having 'meetings' in the bedroom when I was home."

"Oh, God." Mom groans, rubbing her eyes.

Sarah covers her mouth. Victor scowls next to her. Gemma stares at Mom and Nathan, bewildered. Nathan's face is as red as the cherries in the pie I probably won't be eating tonight.

"Mom, Dad, is that true?" Gemma asks timidly.

"No," Nathan lies.

Mom's mouth twists.

Gemma wrinkles her nose. "That's gross! I can't believe you guys!"

Sarah beckons Gemma to her. "Come on, hon. Let's go up to your room."

Gemma gives a solemn nod and grabs the dinner roll off her plate before she and Sarah head upstairs.

"Thank you, Ian!" Mom explodes as she stands. "Thank you for ruining Thanksgiving!"

I get up and shove my chair under the table. "You can also thank me for keeping your dirty secret from Dad all these years! He'd worship you if idolatry weren't a sin. He loved you! I loved you!" I'm yelling so loud, my throat is sore. "He loved you no matter what you chose to believe. Then you hurt us. You. Hurt us. So. Bad." I'm shaking so violently with rage. I must look insane.

"So we had sex outside of marriage. Your birth mother couldn't keep her legs closed either, and she left you in the clinic after she had you. I raised you for four years. I did more for you"—Mom points a finger in my face—"than she ever will, but you respect her more than me."

Mom's outburst pulls out a flashback of Martha screaming at me the night she drove me home. *Do you like that he allowed your adoption to happen?* Martha's a different person now, but her words still hurt and twist into my mounting anger.

"Leave my mother out of this!" I roar. "You can't compare yourself to her because you don't know how to love!"

"That's enough!" Victor shouts, shooting up from his chair. "Julie, you've made poor decisions, and, Ian, you're hurting, but let's end Thanksgiving peacefully. Please."

Mom leans toward me. "You think she loves you? Is it love when you use your culture as an excuse to make yourself untraceable? She's a coward, Ian!"

Mom crossed the line. I grip the edge of the table and picture myself swiping everything off its surface. China flies. Drinks collapse. Dinner fails.

This house can't hold all the grief Mom piled on Dad and me for fourteen years, and it can't hold me.

"Good-bye, Mom." It took so much energy to say only that.

Her face relaxes. She suddenly looks younger and kinder. I almost want to take back what I said.

"You're right, Ian. It's time to say good-bye."

For years I hated how Dad forced me to have a relationship with Mom. Now I don't have to anymore, but there's a tug in my chest.

A hand falls onto my shoulder. "Come on." Victor pulls me back and guides me out of the dining room. He gets my jacket from the coat closet.

Mom's crying in the kitchen. I can't make out anything Nathan's saying. I hear the teacher from *Charlie Brown. Wah, wah, wah.*

"Do you feel well enough to drive?" Victor asks.

"Yeah." What would he do if I said no? Funny how people ask this stuff, but there's no way they can help.

He walks me to the door. "You have baggage. Talk to someone about it and get better. You got this."

I give Victor a slight nod, but I don't have a grip on this at all.

"Ian!" Gemma runs down the stairs with Sarah behind her. I open my arms, and she plows into me. "You're always my brother, no matter what."

Sweet Gemma. We don't share a strand of DNA. Yet, she saw me lash out at her parents and reveal their adultery, and she still loves me.

I watch her walk into the kitchen, where everyone has congregated. I hate letting her go.

"Julia, Nathan, did you really do that while Ian was home?" I hear Sarah ask them.

Nathan's talking. *Wah, wah, wah.*

I put on my coat and don't bother to zip it even though it's below freezing. Martha's right; I'm an icy stone.

I remember Gemma's Jenn Grant CD. I grab a pen from the glovebox and write *I'll see you again* on the back of the album booklet and stick the case in the mailbox.

Martha texts me twice to see how things went at Mom's. I don't answer. She calls and leaves a message. I don't listen to it.

I GET HOME from Mom's at eight thirty. I have insomnia, so I read a chunk of *A Thousand Splendid Suns*. After three hours of sleep, I get up at 3:45 for my five o'clock shift so people can haul a bunch of stuff home that will most likely end up in a thrift store or landfill within the next three months.

Alicia and I spend the first twenty minutes at work in a crash course about Black Friday safety and coupons.

"How was your Thanksgiving?" I ask Alicia as we leave Liz's office.

"My mom cooks for thirty people. I keep telling her to downsize her crowd. She always stresses out, but she's happy everyone got together and had a good time. How was yours?"

I shrug. "I went to my mom's."

I'm in the stockroom sweeping up beads that spilled out of a torn bag when Martha walks in.

"I didn't hear from you at all yesterday," she says as she puts her things in her locker.

I lean the broom against the wall and saunter over to her. "We'll talk, but not today."

"Ian, no."

"Martha, I need time."

"You two, it's Black Friday!" Evan hollers at us. He thrusts his arm toward the door. "Get out there!"

"I hope you don't talk to your family like that," Martha throws at him.

Evan cringes, and his posture slumps.

"You grew your thick retail skin," I tell her as we grab our time cards.

The time clock spits out Martha's card, and she returns it to the rack. "He doesn't scare me, and he shouldn't scare you." She walks away and gets swallowed up by the crowd of shoppers.

On my way to my register, I spot a woman fighting with a man over a discounted paint set.

"I got it first," he tells her.

"Give it to me!" she screeches, and the guy pulls his hand away and leaves. She sees me and calls, "Do you have more of these in the back?"

The back—aka the Magical Land of Endless Inventory.

"No," I answer, even though I really don't know.

A bald man waves a list in my face. "Hello? Can you help me find this stuff?"

"I'll get someone to help you."

"Hurry up," he says, annoyed.

I stay planted next to the discount bins. The barcode scanners beeping and people talking and shuffling bags sound extra irritating today. A large man runs down the main aisle and shoves a toddler aside. Her mother catches her in time to keep her from falling on her face.

"What is wrong with you?" she shouts after him.

He snatches a toy race car from the kids' aisle, holds it up like a trophy, and hisses, "Yes!"

Mom's been wrong about a lot of things, but she had a point when she asked me if I want to spend the rest of my life watching people shop.

I don't.

46

MARTHA

I HAVE NEVER BEEN out on Black Friday before. Growing up, this day was for sleeping in and eating leftovers. I never thought I'd be a part of the consumer craze, and I hate it.

I'm waiting on a woman who's deciding if she wants to get her granddaughter a pink or yellow scrapbook for Christmas.

Ian's by the shelves of duct tape talking to a guy about a cookbook. The book in his hand looks so in place, but watching him in the midst of this shopping chaos feels wrong. If he runs a bookstore someday, every Black Friday for the rest of his working years will look like this. Retail screams *stuff*, but Ian doesn't care about that. He cares about eternity.

"What do you think, Martha?" the customer at my register asks.

I think you should have made this decision before checking out. "I like yellow."

"All right, yellow it is." She lays the sixty percent-off coupon on the scrapbook.

"I can't apply that to sale items."

Her eyes go wide. "Why not?"

"Our Black Friday coupon is for regular-priced items."

"Then I don't want it," she snaps and pushes it toward me before leaving.

Ian comes to my register and opens my drawer. "What was that about?"

"She misunderstood our Black Friday deals," I explain as I put the scrapbooks with all the returns.

Justin is coming up here. To steer him away from Ian, I hand him a basket full of kids' merchandise. "Can you take care of these returns? People are going nuts over those race car toys."

"Will do," he says and walks away with the basket.

Wow. His heart pumps some decency into him once a month.

"You're two cents under." Ian closes my drawer. "Nice job for a crazy day."

He's gone before I finish writing my name, and when I get to my locker, he's not there.

"Ian left," Ebony informs me. She's the new seasonal worker Liz hired last week.

"Oh. Thanks." Word zooms around here fast. She already knows Ian and I are tight.

Once I'm outside, I call Suzanna and get her voicemail. I don't leave a message. We're talking, face-to-face.

———

WHEN I GET to Suzanna and Carl's apartment complex, I walk down the sidewalk and ring the bell. I hear footsteps, then Carl swings the door open.

"Hey, Marty."

"Can you get Suzanna?"

"Marty's here!" he calls into the apartment.

Suzanna comes to the door dressed in her work attire: black pants and a royal-blue T-shirt. She cringes.

"Can we talk?"

She shuts the door in my face.

I bang my fists on the door. "Suzanna, grow up!"

"What's going on with you?" Carl asks her on the other side and opens the door again. "Sorry about that, Marty."

I come inside and get straight to the point. "It's not entirely my fault our family's falling apart."

"I can't believe you!" she exclaims. "Ian asks you to a wedding, you go on a few dates, and all of a sudden he's your voice of reason with religion!"

"What Ian believes—"

"I'm talking!" Suzanna gets in my face. "You know Mom suffered from religious abuse. She and Dad protected us from that trash. Then Ian comes along, and you take his religion and forget everything they did for us."

Carl comes over and motions us apart. "Let Marty talk."

Suzanna lets out a huff and glares at me.

"I chose what he believes because it's the truth." I don't sound confident at all; my voice is small and shaky.

"You have your future set up at Montclair and chucked that too." She grabs the laundry basket by the washer and dryer and heads into the bedroom. "Somehow Dad thinks that's okay!"

I venture to follow her with Carl behind me.

"You can't get mad at Marty because your dad—"

"Shut up, Carl!" Suzanna shouts.

He holds up his hands and backs away. "All right. Just calm down."

She resumes her rant. "Mom was trying to save money, and Dad thought it was a big joke. She's been antagonized ever since his hours changed at the library."

"Dad said she didn't have to worry about money."

Suzanna slams a folded pair of jeans onto the bed. "So, it's you and Dad now. Money's tight, but he lets you change your major and go out of state." She jabs a finger at me with each piece of evidence she has against me. "You're with the better guy, even though Ian indoctrinated you. And Dad's in your corner, because Mom goes a little crazy—"

"A little crazy? She tried to bash my head into the wall!" Now I point my finger at her. "Dad isn't happy about my conversion either, so I'm not getting special treatment."

"Good!" Suzanna spits.

"Nobody forced you to drop out of school. You could have transferred somewhere if you dedicated yourself to something other than your social life. The only reason Dad doesn't trust Carl is that he cheated on you. He doesn't want you to get hurt again."

I hear Carl shut the washing machine door and turn it on.

Suzanna presses her lips together. "Ian might hurt you just as bad."

"He wouldn't do that."

"You don't know him." Holding a pile of shirts, she walks into the closet. "A month. You date him for a month and base your worldview on everything he says."

I tightly fold my arms over my chest. "We were friends before that."

She ignores me.

I grit my teeth tighter to hold in my disgust. "You'll never understand."

She didn't see the rocky terrain I crossed to get where I am now. She doesn't understand how finding God freed me from my past and gave me a love and peace that soothed my heart.

Suzanna slips a sweater onto a hanger. "Oh, I understand. Religion is for weak people. You caved, Marty. I'm sad for you."

"Stop it!"

"A guy gives you some attention. That doesn't mean everything he says is true."

She has a point, but giving her a crash course about God's power to change my heart won't convince her I made a wise decision.

I take big strides to the closet and darken its threshold. "I'm not clinging to Ian because he makes me feel good."

Suzanna passes me and leaves the laundry basket by her bedroom door. "I get it. If I were insecure about my body, I'd do the same thing."

"Suzanna, she's your *sister*!" Carl chides her as he comes toward us.

She twists around and shoots back, "My sister, who was so desperate for a guy, she chose religion over our mom."

I stumble backward. It feels as if my heart is getting sucked out of my rib cage. Carl looks from me to her with a shocked expression. I wait for her strained face to melt into remorse. It doesn't.

"You'll never understand," I say as my voice quivers.

"You're right; I won't," Suzanna agrees briskly. "What I do get is you don't care about Mom."

"I *do* care! I know she's hurting, but I need God."

Suzanna enters the kitchen. She plucks the can opener from the dish drying rack and slams it into a drawer. "You think this is all about you! Did you think about the hell Mom grew up in or how Dad hurt her when he kicked her out?"

"Of course I did!"

Carl stays behind me. I glance over my shoulder and catch his pained expression.

Suzanna puts her face close to mine again, so close her breath hits me. I wish she'd stop doing that. Her eyes flare with rage. "Did you ever think any of this hurts *me*?" Her voice becomes thick and wobbly. "We have to choose between Mom and Dad. That really hurts."

"Things can get better. They always had a stormy relationship and worked things out." I try to hug her, but she shoves me away.

"Go hug Ian! We're not a family anymore, Marty! Start your own family with Ian." She throws her hands up. "Be fruitful and multiply! Oh, wait. You're so holy, you don't know how to do that!"

Trigger trigger trigger. Grandpa Grandpa Grandpa.

"Suzanna, listen to yourself!" Carl pleads.

I cover my face. I suddenly want Dad. He pulled me into the world. He got me out of the car that Christmas, put me in the bath, and, later, tucked me in. If our family falls to ruins, he's all I'll have left.

Carl grabs my elbow, but I fight him.

"You were the favorite." She rants on as she dries a vegetable peeler. "Mom and Dad always talked about your perfect grades, your weight, how to stop other kids from bullying you."

I thought our parents' love wasn't deep enough, but Suzanna believed I got more of it than she did.

"I was going through a lot."

"You didn't have to eat so much."

The air stills and thickens. Suzanna steps back. Her face stays hard. She crosses her arms as if to say, *I mean everything I said.*

I'm out of here.

"Tell Mom I love her. Tell her I want her to come home."

"Tell her yourself. She's very happy where she is. She's teaching Erik how to cook and is helping Aunt Felice with her parents. She finally found a place where she's appreciated."

Carl opens the door and motions me forward. "Come on, Marty," he whispers.

"Mom's been talking about separating," Suzanna adds.

I run my hands down the sides of my head and shudder. Our

parents cannot break in this storm. Mom needs to confront her trauma. Dad needs to give her some compassion. They can make it. They *will* make it.

"Dad will be getting divorce papers," she singsongs.

I leave Suzanna and Carl's. Their shouting seeps through the door and floats down the breezeway. I'm numb and dazed when I drive home.

Dad's in the kitchen heating up leftovers. "Come join me for lunch."

My lunch at work was technically a late breakfast, and I'm starving, but I can't face Dad knowing what I know. "I'll eat later." I start mounting the stairs. "I have homework."

"Don't you want to eat?" he asks, walking up behind me.

I wanted Dad, and he's here. Mom cannot beat me. Suzanna cannot scream at me. But I say nothing and go to my room.

I revisit my poem even though I already handed it in. I separate and reattach lines, delete words, replace them, rewrite them. Love is not a waste of time, but when you have a limited supply, you use so much life searching for it.

I finish editing and shut down my laptop. A piece of art exists that is one hundred percent Martha Lane, and it turned out really good.

I sprawl out on my bed. Kaylin's out with Andy, and later she's seeing her friend Sahar. She's probably sick of my past consuming me. On Monday, when I told her about Grandpa's sexual abuse, she said, "Your parents need to know, no matter how much they hate each other. If this new faith Ian helped you find is so good, use it and speak up." Then she slipped out of my car and left.

Ian has made it clear he can't talk, so it's me and God now.

I roll onto my back and stare heavenward. "God, I know my prayers are only requests. I'm trying."

My sister, who was so desperate for a guy, chose religion over our mom.

I smack my hand over my forehead and breathe heavily through clenched teeth. That's not me. I am stronger than that.

The pain is so severe, I can't shape it into words, but I feel them. Is Ian feeling this too?

I cross the room and tear the flash cards and the chart of Russian programs off my corkboard. A few thumbtacks come loose and roll onto my desk. I should abandon God, go to Montclair, and make everyone happy to keep my family together.

But I'd be miserable in school, and faithless.

I tear up the chart and thrust the pieces into the air. They fall around me like feathers. Hope isn't a bird, Emily Dickinson. It's vapor. It can't hold up your dreams.

That peace I was feeling has left. My biggest fear has taken its place: that my family has been right about God, which means Ian is wrong.

I open our notebook and break God's heart on the next page. *IT'S SO HARD TO BELIEVE IN YOU!*

47

PERPLEXITY

YOUR PRESENCE WAS my favorite medicine. I want to watch you move swiftly in the kitchen as you make pizza frittata or homemade bread. I want to zero in on the bones in your hands moving under your skin as you work. I miss seeing you shove your fingers through your hair after you finished cooking, the way you leaned over the counter and told me about your day.

I know. I never said I cherished how much you kept our family intact. Our past is complicated. We fell in love too young and too fast. Then we realized how turbulent life could get, and we got destructive. Now we're fragmented. That's not entirely your fault. I'm sorry your parents didn't give you the love you deserved. I tried to give you that love, but I didn't have the right language and context to help you. Can you forgive me?

You can't. You can't unsee what we've done. Listen to me. There is no hope for our marriage, but we are linked together for life because we share two children. Can we talk about that? You should have been there, no matter how hard things got, but you were always distant.

I'm not alone, but I'm lonely. I didn't fight for you. I should have. My parents hated our relationship; they thought I was after your body and that you wanted someone to take care of you. My heart isn't sewn onto my sleeve, and I'm not fluent in deep feelings, but I loved you. I still do. I ache for you so much. It's as if something is misaligned in my chest, and I can't reach in to snap it back into place.

Maybe you didn't have to leave. We could have fought for our marriage with counseling or in the shadows of late-night conversations and intimacy. We needed to rip ourselves open and touch every hidden wound, even if the truth seared us. Would we have stayed together then?

I assemble a series of what-ifs that are years too late.

The regret widens. You dissolve into a fantasy.

I break inside. What if we shared some faith—just a speck of it? I know you can't tolerate anything that mingles with God.

I'm so sorry.

Maybe religion can help us, or it's a package of lies, but what I have isn't enough. I hope you come back to me, somehow, just for a day, an hour, a few minutes. If that's all I can have, the wait is priceless.

48

IAN

WHEN I GOT BACK from NYC Corner yesterday afternoon, I crashed without eating or changing out of my work clothes. I wake up at two a.m. and go through the fridge to find something to eat. I take out some vegetables, Korean tofu, ground pork, and shrimp to make some stew. It's the best medicine for a Korean adoptee after your mom kicks you out of her life.

When I'm done eating, I'm still hungry—hungry for more of my culture. I open my keepsake box and unearth the Korean flag the adoption agency sent me home with and display it on my desk. I unroll the Hangul chart that Morgan passed down to me and plaster it on the wall by my door.

I understood a lot of the Korean Halmoni spoke to me when I was a toddler. Sometimes she recorded us on my tape player. My cousins and I accidentally recorded over that with a made-up game of *Jeopardy*. *Sagwa* is apple. *Sarang* is love. *Ooyoo* is milk. If I took something that wasn't mine, she'd reach out and say *chuseyo* —please—and I'd give it back. Once she and Grandpa took me to the park, and I ran ahead of them. She asked me where I was going. *"Ian-ah, eodi gayo?"* I turned to her and pointed to the swings.

Halmoni also taught me how to read and write Hangul when I was in kindergarten. I made the sounds correctly with little effort. I love that my brain clung to the Korean I heard as a baby.

But I let go of the chance for Halmoni to teach me more. The next time I saw her, she asked me if I wanted to learn more Korean. There was excitement in her dark eyes. I said no and pulled her over to the contraption I built with my K'NEX.

I had seventeen years with Halmoni, who was my only gateway to Korean. Dad couldn't help me learn it; he and his sisters grew up speaking Konglish with her. So I lost such an easy chance to get my language back.

I trace my finger over the first consonant on the alphabet chart in the correct stroke order. *Giyeok* is the *g* and *k* sound, as well as the first letter of Omma's surname, Kang.

I spread my hands over the poster and press my cheek against its glossy surface. If I were to go to Korea and miraculously find Omma, we'd talk through an interpreter, unless she knows English. I wouldn't know how to get around on my own. I'd understand people's behaviors and some traditions from the stories Halmoni and Grandpa used to tell my cousins and me, but I'd feel like a tourist in my country.

Can I ever be like a Korean Korean?

I shouldn't move there. I'd hate leaving Dad, and I'd look selfish fleeing from a broken relationship with Mom. I also don't want—literally—the whole world between Martha and me.

I am acting like it is, though. I haven't seen her since the night we kissed in my car. I never found out how her Thanksgiving went. It's time to climb out of my own problems and see how she's doing.

I stare at the giant characters under my fingers. I can't build a relationship with Korea. I can't even sustain relationships with people.

That ache boils into anger. I rip the alphabet chart down. I disassemble the flag and place it back inside its box.

I'm proud to be Korean, but I don't know how to be Korean, so I won't remind myself that I should learn how to be Korean.

———

"YOUR MOM LEFT ME A VOICEMAIL," Dad says when I'm prepping breakfast a few hours later.

I pull a German pancake out of the oven. I knew Mom would get her side of the story to Dad before I did.

"What did she say?"

He lifts the grounds and filter out of his coffee dripper and tosses them in the trash. "She said you were ..." He squints. "Inappropriate at dinner." This comes out sounding like a question, as if he doesn't believe her.

That's funny, because Mom's right; telling everyone what she and Nathan did was inappropriate.

"She said you suddenly went off on her about how she left."

"That's a lie." I dig the knife into the pancake. "She called Omma a coward."

A wrinkle appears between Dad's eyes. "Why?"

I tell him everything from Mom banning me from texting Martha to our explosive exchange before I left.

"What happened to her? Why would your mother say that to you?"

I've got the answers, and he's not ready for any of them.

I cut the pancake again and drop the knife. I take a few steps back.

"She's not. My. Mother," I breathe out. The words are heavy and acidic.

Dad swallows some coffee and puts his mug on the counter. "Don't say that."

I storm out of the kitchen and tear into my room. "Don't tell me how to feel!"

Dad follows me. "Ian, calm down!"

The Hangul chart is lying on the floor from when I tore it off the wall this morning. I thrust it against him and yell, "See this? I can't talk to my *real* mom, because you and Julia adopted me! You took my name from me, my country, *everything*! You spent thousands and took me from my mother. Now all we have is pain! Is that the best people can do for unwed mothers and their kids?"

I can't see Dad's face; my eyes are wet. The last time I teared up was when I found out Mrs. Shin had died.

Dad grabs my shoulders. "If you weren't adopted and aged out of the system, you would've been on your own and had no one."

I break out of his grip and cross my arms. A smirk pokes through my anger. "Maybe I would've gotten into male prostitution. Not a far cry from Mom's morals." I hold up a finger. "Wait. Scratch that. No woman would want to do anything with a half-breed."

"Ian, this is uncalled for!"

"Mom's last night home—she apologized, but you ignored her. You went to bed angry. You feel guilty about that."

Dad stares hard at me.

I'm armed with a mound of confidence. Finally, I'll assure Dad that Mom wasn't worth chasing after. "Don't worry. She went to bed with Nathan a bunch of times before she took off."

His anger fizzles and is replaced with shock. "What the—?"

"You thought she only talked with Nathan behind your back. He used to come over."

Dad backs against my desk. He checks out.

"I was in my room while she and Nathan messed around. This happened for months every week on laundry day. I saw him kiss her. I heard her say she'd leave us." I wipe the tears away with my arm. "I wasn't supposed to tell you anything."

He gives me that "lost in a prairie" look. "Your mother made you suffer all that time by yourself?"

"When I finally understood what she and Nathan did, I couldn't tell you. You took meds after she left." I'm seething. "I told you she's not my mother, and you know what? You're not my father."

Dad grabs me again. "Don't go there. Do not go there."

I jerk away from him. I'm so furious, I could tear up the earth. "If you were really my dad, you wouldn't have forced me to visit Mom in her new house with her disgusting new husband. You never went in; you hated seeing her with Nathan, but you made me go. You made me get hurt."

Dad holds out his hands, palms upward. "Ian, I'm sorry," he croaks.

"You were so depressed. It's like I didn't have parents. I always had to take everyone's excuses. Omma wasn't married. My birth father left. Mom left because of your religion. No one's *ever* loved me more than themselves!"

"I did the best I could."

I ball my fists at my sides. "Was your best going out with Nora after work while I was home with Aunt Addie, scared that you'd leave too? You wanted a new wife while I was having attachment issues!"

"I was hurting. I wanted to feel something else. I know. It was selfish."

"You're stronger than that, Dad."

"It didn't go anywhere."

"I'm glad it didn't! She would have left us too. I'd hate her, but you'd be stupid enough to love her after she'd kill your spirit like Mom did."

My anger feels cold and refreshing.

Dad sighs heavily. "We're done talking. You need to cool off." He leaves my room and closes the door.

I'm still. I hear Dad get a plate and walk to the table. When some of the rage leaves my body, I pick up the alphabet chart. There's a fold in its center. I roll it up and put it away.

I shouldn't learn Korean. If I find Omma, I might hurt her too. I might tell her she shouldn't have put me up for adoption, because that didn't teach me what love is. It turned whatever love I have inside me into ice.

49

MARTHA

I SIT on my bed and open *Story of a Girl*.

The main character, Deanna, messed around with her brother's friend Tommy a few years ago in his car, and her dad was the one who found them. He can't look at her the same anymore. I feel the weight of her isolation as I read.

I wish Mom or Dad had walked in on Grandpa molesting me. My childhood would have looked much different if they had.

My phone buzzes.

> **Ian**
> Can you hang out tonight? Sorry it's been so long. I miss you!
>
> It's OK. Making pizza. Dinner at my place?
>
> **Ian**
> Yes! Be there in 20 mins.

I change out of my leggings and CLASS OF '08 sweater and put on jeans and a long-sleeved blackberry shirt. My jeans feel extra comfortable in the waist. With Mom gone and all the emotions I've been swimming through, my appetite has shrunk.

I put on some face powder and head into the kitchen. I pull the damp towel off the pizza dough and divide it in half. This is the only thing Mom makes in bulk. It's her emergency dinner. It freezes well, you let it defrost, slap on some sauce and toppings, and you have a homemade meal on the fly.

I reach into the cabinet next to the oven for the pizza pans and stare at Mom's blue quilted apron hanging on the pantry door. It's her most prized possession from Aunt Martha.

The kitchen feels icy. It took thirteen days for me to feel this. That's when you know your love for your family has gone stale.

I force the dough in all directions until it stretches to the edges of the pan. The doorbell rings. I preheat the oven before I answer it.

"Hey," Ian says, stepping inside. His eyes look tired. He cups his hands around my shoulders and kisses me on the cheek. "How are you?"

"All right," I answer, even though my family's drama is making my head swirl. "Give me your jacket."

"Want some help with dinner?"

"You can finish grating the cheese."

Ian removes his sneakers. "You got it," he says and walks away.

I press his jacket's collar to my nose and take in that clean smell of peppermint and cinnamon before I hang it up. I meet him in the kitchen and ask, "Can you tell me why you've been so quiet lately?" I try to keep my voice neutral, but I sound irritated.

"Thanksgiving was rough." He stays focused on grating the cheese. "My dad and I aren't talking."

I follow Ian to the sink. "What happened?" This must be pretty bad if there's a rift between him and his dad.

He washes his hands and tells me how the conversation during

Thanksgiving dinner went from his job, to me, then to his parents' divorce. "I snapped and told everyone what she did with Nathan when she was still married, and he denied it! I don't get why my mom chose him over my dad." He rubs the towel over his hands too roughly and throws it down by the sink. "My mom told my dad what went down on Thanksgiving. He tried to talk to me about it, and I went off on him."

"Why?"

"I told him about my mom's affair. I said she isn't my mom, and he's not my dad. I meant it. I remember his depression, Martha. I didn't matter to him. He dated a coworker named Nora while I freaked out at home, thinking he'd leave. He hauled me to my mom's house, where Nathan was." Ian's voice breaks. "I used to be afraid of Nathan."

I envision a young Ian retreating into a corner to get away from the man his mother secretly had sex with. I fracture inside.

"You said you wished you weren't adopted," I remind him as I place pepperoni on one of the pies. "It's not only because of your mom."

He shakes his head. "My dad's guilty too. I don't regret what I said to either of them," Ian admits.

"You're numb."

He grabs a pizza and slides it into the oven. "No, Martha. Sometimes I have trouble loving people. I say I'm a Christian, but I can't feel unconditional love."

"No, Ian—"

"It's true. I barely got it, and I can't give it. My mom doesn't love me like she loves Gemma. My dad and his family are great, but ..." Ian lowers his head. "During the cocktail hour at the wedding, I felt so isolated. I was thinking, this is my family, but who *are* these people? I felt so bad for thinking that way, but I couldn't shake it off. Maybe this stems from my adoption."

I consider this. "You think that being separated from your birth mother corrupted some of your relationships."

He shrugs. "I don't remember her leaving me in the clinic, but ... I could be overthinking things."

Ian reaches for the other pizza, but I stop him. "I'll bake that when my dad gets home." I wrap my fingers around his, but he pulls away. Maybe he hurts so much, he doesn't want to be touched. I've been there. I'll let him feel what he needs to feel with no interruptions.

He looks at me. "Do you think there's a certain kind of love that comes only with biology?"

"There could be."

His phone dings. He perches himself on a barstool and reads his phone's screen. "You're alive, Chris?" he remarks.

"What did he say?"

Ian reads Chris's text. "He broke up with his girlfriend and flunked a class. He's home for Thanksgiving and wants to hang out." Ian slams down his phone. "I'll pass."

Chris wants to reconnect, but if he valued his friendship with Ian, he would have contacted him before his life went south.

Ian's face tenses. "In fact, I don't want to see him for a long time. He didn't want me to get involved with you." His voice is raw with anger.

I look at him, concerned. Something's off about Ian's mood. "Chris doesn't know me."

"You weren't a Christian. I'm sorry I told him that. My ex-girlfriend, Hana—we split up before college because we couldn't settle our religious differences."

The timer beeps. I slip on mitts, retrieve the pizza from the oven, and set it on a trivet. "Did you date someone after her? You asked me to the wedding because your girlfriend—"

"That was Hana. We got back together last summer. We broke

up again two days before Morgan's wedding. We couldn't work things out, get past some mistakes we made."

I fold the dish towel Ian was using before. "Do you miss her?"

Ian nods. "Our relationship is the only thing I miss about high school." He turns sideways in his seat. His body relaxes. "I'm sorry I asked you to the wedding like I did. I wanted to hang out with someone who didn't know about my mom, Hana, everything."

"I'm glad I went." I smile. "I'd relive that night so many times if I could."

"I would too." Ian turns his phone right-side up. "When's your dad coming home?"

The clock on the microwave reads 6:06. "In twenty minutes."

I can't see the three of us happily sharing a meal together. Dad knows Ian and I are dating, but every time I mention him, Dad barely says anything. I know he's put off about how Ian's faith influenced me and what my conversion has done to our family.

"Take a load off." He pulls out the barstool next to him.

I sit. "I went to Suzanna's on Friday. It was a disaster." I tell him everything Suzanna and I said to each other. I explain why I wanted to, but couldn't, reach out to my dad and why I didn't talk to anyone else.

"You must have felt really alone. I'm sorry I was in such a funk when you were trying to reach out to me."

"I knew you were going through something, but I would have appreciated some communication."

Ian averts his gaze. "I'm sorry. I'll work on that."

I wring my fingers in my lap. "I have God, but it's hard to believe in him sometimes. I'm losing Suzanna and my mom. I love them—I always will—but they took a really dark turn. I don't have the strength to try with them anymore."

"Sometimes all we can do is pray, even when we're losing faith." Ian reaches for me. "I want to pray for you."

"Now? Right here?"

"If you're okay with that."

I've never had someone pray aloud for me. I extend my hand for him to take. Ian slightly bows his head, and I do the same.

"God, You know how much Martha and her family are hurting. They've had it rough, and there's so much they need to talk about and heal from. Please open the door for her parents to work things out. You value marriage so much, and Martha doesn't want to see her family split. But if they can't reconcile, help her adjust to whatever changes come her way and that no matter how ugly things get, she will always remember you are great and have a purpose for everything."

This is prayer. Be real with God. Care for people's souls. Ask for the best, but acknowledge that the worst can happen. Glorify him.

Ian rubs his thumb over the back of my hand. I want to curl up against him and let him hold me for hours.

"Help Suzanna understand Martha's decision to follow you. And help Martha to be the light in all this darkness that's hanging over her family. Help them realize how important her faith is and welcome you into their lives."

I punctuate his prayer with "Amen." I'm not sure if he's finished, but if he holds onto me for another second, I will explode. I fan myself as I walk around the island to cut the pizza.

"Are you feeling all right?"

"Um, I don't know how to pray." I gesture to myself. "I feel the things I want to tell God, but it comes out like 'I want this' or 'please make this happen.'"

Ian smiles for the first time tonight. "No one's prayer life is perfect."

"It was easy to talk to God when I first believed, but it's hard to feel close to him, maybe because life hurts so much right now." I cut the pizza into slices and ask him, "How many do you want?"

"They're small, so I'll have two." Ian joins me at the counter and takes his plate. "Romans 8:26 says the Holy Spirit helps us pray when our pain is too deep for words."

"Holy Spirit." I muse. "What is that? What's its purpose?"

"The Holy Spirit is the third part of the Trinity, besides God and Jesus. It's described as a person in the Bible. He can think, guide us, and comfort us. He's very active in the world, and now that you're a believer, he's active in your life too."

Ian's last sentence feels like a blanket around my shoulders. "Do you have some verses I can read on that?"

"I can write down a few."

I walk over to the drawer by the pantry and pull out a pad and pen. I hesitate. The last thing Mom wrote on here was a food list. I flip to the second page and tear it off for Ian.

As he's writing, I wash grease off my hands at the sink. "I like how God can understand us through anything."

Ian finishes writing and slides the paper toward me.

"Thanks." I dry my hands and glance at his list. I catch verses from John, Ephesians, and Revelation before tucking the paper in my pocket.

"Give it all to him. He gets what you're feeling." Ian pulls me into his arms. "It's been a while, Martha."

"I thought you wanted us to be careful."

"I do, but I'm not giving up hugging you, unless you want me to."

"No, that would be tragic."

The garage door opens.

"It would also be tragic if your dad found us like this," he whispers.

I hug Ian tighter and don't let go, because I don't care.

Dad opens the door and stops in the threshold.

I move away from Ian, and he squeezes my hands. "Hey, Dad. He's staying for dinner. I'll get the other pizza in the oven."

Dad surveys the scene in front of him. "Hello, Ian."

"Hi, Mr. Lane. How was your Thanksgiving?"

Dad pulls his coat off. "Too quiet."

Half of our family wasn't there. That's a lot of noise missing.

I set the timer and close the oven. Dad's eating with us. At least I can see how he treats Ian, and with my family in pieces, any sense of togetherness is a blessing.

50

IAN

WHEN I GET HOME from Martha's house, Dad is at the kitchen table eating leftover chicken soup. "Did you have a nice visit with Martha?" he asks.

I avoid eye contact with him. I'm embarrassed about all the hurtful things I said earlier this morning. "It was good. Her dad ate with us." I omit how Mr. Lane was standoffish toward me. But he didn't kick me out of the house. That's progress.

"I spoke to your mother."

I head for my room. "I don't want to know about it."

"Ian, we should talk."

"I can't."

I hate seeing his pained expression, but I can't talk to him. My brain is too injured from what Mom did with Nathan and being separated from three mothers.

"I know you're hurting," Dad calls after me, "but don't be hurtful too."

I shut myself in my room. I finish *A Thousand Splendid Suns* and get pulled into *The Book Thief*. I crash at three a.m.

I miss having breakfast and going to church with Dad. When I wake up, he's already asleep for the day, so I eat a toasted bagel with cream cheese and head off to work.

When I walk into NYC Corner, Justin almost hits me with a shopping cart full of returns.

I recoil and scrunch up my face, but he stops in time. "Why are you here?"

"Well, hi, Ian. Nice to see you." He leans his arms on the cart's handle. "Evan's back is out."

"All right. Just don't mess around."

"Noted."

He probably only means the *n* and the *o*.

As I'm clocking in, Liz steps out of her office and says, "No one's been on register one today, so go ahead and sign in. And Justin has discount bin duty. I got a big shipment that will make great stocking stuffers."

"Got it, Liz."

After I sign in to my register, I stroll over to where Justin's helping a customer in framing.

When he's done, I say, "Head over to the stockroom. Liz has a bunch of stuff that needs to go in the discount bins."

"Can we put you in there?"

Another joke about my height, or he's referring to my adoption.

I look back at him and remark, "I'm not for sale."

———

IT'S FOUR THIRTY. We aren't usually swamped with customers at this time on Sundays. People are wrapping up their weekend and getting ready to start up again tomorrow.

Martha returns from her break and passes a couple who look

to be in their twenties. The guy has a service dog with him, a German shepherd.

"Hi," she greets them. "Can I help you with anything?"

The guy holds up a small piece of paper. "Do you take competitors' coupons?"

"Yeah, just not the ones with a discount off an entire purchase."

"Got it," he says.

A few minutes later I walk over to where Justin's opening a box of kids' key chains. "You can go on break now."

The couple with the dog passes by. Before Justin leaves for the break room, he whispers, "Is that your lunch, or did you bring your kimchi?"

His remark paralyzes me. I watch him disappear behind the EMPLOYEES ONLY doors.

He will never stop. It's time to intervene.

Dad told me I shouldn't let my pain hurt others.

Sorry, Dad. What I'm about to do will get me fired. I might even get arrested. But I don't care about my job, my safety, and certainly not Justin.

I take big strides to the break room. I bang the door open so hard against the wall, it scares Justin, who's at the fridge getting his drink.

"Take back what you said!"

He laughs, like I'm a kid blowing this out of proportion. "We go way back, Ian. I've been trying to tell you you're a sub-human, like my stepdad."

I'm shaking as violently as I was at Mom's last week. I try to speak, but I make a sound that's between a gasp and a moan.

"See? You're part animal." Justin opens his water bottle. It cracks, snaps, like me.

I feel like I'm gliding across the room. I stand inches from

Justin, make a fist, and retract. Fear flickers on his face before my knuckles drive into his cheek. Pain fires through my fingers and up my wrist.

It's so satisfying.

Justin's head snaps sideways. He stumbles and drops his drink. Water splatters everywhere. Before he can gain some footing, I slam him into the counter, but he steadies himself. I squint when his fist comes and punches my nose.

Blood squirts over my lips and dribbles down my chin. Justin comes at me again and strikes the side of my mouth. Pain spears through my lips as my back rams the side of the table.

"Your blood doesn't smell like garlic. Have you been laying off the kimchi?" he jokes.

My blood has turned to lava. Time for him to burn.

I charge at him. He starts moving away, but I manage to punch the side of his jaw.

He tackles me to the ground and pins me down by the arms with an unbearable strength. "I'll choke you," he snarls. "It's what I always wanted to do to my stepdad."

I turn my head to avoid his empty eyes.

"What is going on in here?" Liz shrieks from the doorway.

Justin releases my arms and gets up. The left side of his face is bruised.

I sit upright and look down at the crimson stains on my shirt and pants. My wrists are covered with red imprints of Justin's fingers—he squeezed them so hard. With the room quiet, I can hear my heart thudding in my ears.

I open my mouth to answer Liz, but she shouts, "Clean up and follow me to my office!"

Justin picks up the trash can and wipes the water from the floor. I scrub the blood off my face at the sink. The knuckles on my right hand are red and sting with pain.

After we leave the break room and walk through the stock-room, Liz peers out the door. "No customers. Let's go." She beckons us forward, and we cross the framing department.

"Ian," Martha calls. Her eyes bulge, and she covers her mouth when she sees my face.

"Martha, go back to your register," Liz orders as she unlocks her office. "You know someone always has to be up there."

Justin and I shuffle inside and stop in front of Liz's desk. I feel like a defendant standing before a judge.

"This is retail. What could possibly cause a fistfight in *retail*?" Her voice rises with each word.

I look up at Justin. He glares at me.

"I threw the first punch," I admit. My face heats up with shame. "I'm sorry, Liz. I should have gone to you instead of taking things into my own hands." I have no energy to tell her he threatened to choke me to death.

Looking horrified, she snaps her head toward Justin. "What did you do?"

His mouth twists like he's reluctant to purge some of the hate from his insides. "I asked Ian if he was going to eat that guy's dog for lunch."

"You can both be charged with assault if either of you wants to take this further. Do you want to do that?"

"No," Justin croaks.

I'm silent.

"Well, it's not rocket science that you're both fired," she remarks, her words tight. "I want you out of here immediately. You'll get your last pay stub on Friday. Understood?"

Justin nods. I don't move.

"Clock out and get your things." Liz waves a hand like she's taming a room full of rowdy kids. "No, no, Justin, you go first. I don't want you two anywhere near each other."

Justin leaves. Once the door closes, Liz stands and leans over her desk. "Ian, what *happened*? I never ..." She shakes her head. "I expected so much better from you. You're a good kid. I thought you enjoyed being here and wanted to climb the corporate ladder." Her voice cracks. "I wanted to make you assistant manager if you stuck around long enough."

Her failed plan doesn't move me. Retail means nothing to me. It never should have.

"I couldn't take it anymore and snapped."

Liz peers at me over her glasses. "About what?"

"Things I haven't dealt with."

Her face softens. "Ian, I scream revenue, and I don't hang out with my employees, but I'm human. I know things about you from what I overhear on the sales floor. You had a rough start. You were adopted. Your parents div—"

"Justin and I have a history," I blurt out. Then I tell her about the incident on the bus back in fourth grade.

Liz processes this, then walks around her desk and crouches next to me. "Ian, let me give you some advice: reinvent yourself."

I squint at her. Perhaps getting a job with a boss who has a backbone would be more appropriate.

"Don't let your past destroy you. You're better than what I saw tonight. You know that. Now, go clock out. I'll close with Martha."

I stand and unhook my key loop from my lanyard and give her the store key. "Here."

She takes it from me. "I hope you feel better, and I wish you the best."

I don't react to her kindness. "Do you want my name tag?"

Liz waves a dismissive hand. "No."

My legs feel robotic as I leave her office and clock out for the last time.

I'm zipping my jacket and heading to the exit, when Martha rushes toward me. "Ian!"

Without looking at her, I say, "I don't want to talk about it, Martha."

She backs away. "Okay. I'll call you. Feel better."

I nod at her and leave.

I can't face Dad, so I drive to Barnes & Noble and sit on the floor by the windows. I hide behind a copy of Gail Tsukiyama's *The Samurai's Garden*.

When I get home, I slip my jacket off and leave it on the floor. I make a beeline for my room and flop on my bed. I try to read the Bible to put my mind in a better place, but God's Word doesn't reach me tonight. So I drift off in my bloodstained clothes and dream that Liz's store burns down.

51

MARTHA

"WHAT HAPPENED BETWEEN IAN AND JUSTIN?" I ask Liz as we put the registers in the safe.

"Justin made some crass remark to him. Something about having that customer's service dog for lunch."

I hand Liz the cash till from register two. I raise my eyebrows. "Whoa. That's below the belt."

"Yeah, and so was Ian's reaction." She shakes her head and frowns. "He's the last person I thought I'd be terminating."

I clench my jaw in frustration. I want to shout, Gee, Liz, this wouldn't have happened if *you* listened to Ian when he alerted you that Justin is racist.

Liz locks the safe and dusts off her hands. "We're done. Go punch out, and I'll check your bag."

After work I text Dad.

Going to Ian's. Will be home for dinner.

When I get to Ian's apartment, I take the empty spot next to his car. I climb up the stairs to his place and ring the bell. No answer. Several seconds pass, and I try again.

Finally, I hear footsteps. The door opens. I'm not prepared to face what's behind it.

Ian looks horrible. His bottom lip and nose are swollen. There's an angry bruise on his right cheek, and dried splotches of blood cover his work clothes.

"How are you feeling?"

"What do you think?" he responds in a monotone.

"Can I come in?"

Ian opens the door wider. As I take my shoes off, he plops on the couch. "Liz told me to reinvent myself. Motivational speaker garbage. No mention of her failing to can Justin after I reported him for calling me a gook."

I sit next to him. "I know this is frustrating; it could have been prevented." I want to rub the back of his hand with my thumb like he did last night and pull him to me. Last night was sweet. It was the lull before the storm rolled in.

Ian falls back against the couch. "I can't reinvent myself anyway. It's not feasible."

I move closer to him. "You have a plan?"

He runs his hand over his head and heaves a long sigh. "I'd leave everything behind and go to Korea. Tell everyone I'm Min Joon. Spend a ton of time finding my real mom. Learn Korean and eat Korean food that tastes better than what's in New York. I wouldn't come back for a long time."

I grab his arm and give it a little shake. "This is daring and adventurous. It's so you. You jump into the unknown with the highest hopes without a plan."

He wrinkles his nose. "Martha, I don't have a *job* to save up to go. Reinventing yourself is as useless as New Year's resolutions."

"It's a transformation, not a list of goals."

Ian sets his jaw. "Forget it, Martha! I don't want it. I'm only thinking things could be so much better over there because they're really, really bad here."

I let go of his arm. "You can do it. You'll find a way."

He charges out of the living room and disappears into his bedroom. I follow him. He yanks open the bottom drawer of his dresser and leafs through a folder. He pulls out a sheet of paper and comes over to me.

He shoves it into my hands, causing it to wrinkle in several spots. "Read that. It led the detective in Korea nowhere," he says bitterly.

The paper is tissue-thin and covered with typewritten text.

```
Child's Name: 강민준 KANG Min Joon
Hanja: 姜旼俊
Meaning of Name: Min — Gentle, Joon —
Handsome
Name Given By: Mother

Date of Birth: August 8, 1991
Place of Birth: A clinic in Seoul
Weight: 2.4 kg
Length: 46 cm

Mother: KANG Hye Jin
Age: 23
Marital Status: Unmarried
Education: Unknown
Siblings: Unknown
```

The words *All Unknown* sit in the column for his father.

The paragraph underneath says:

THE QUIET EDGE OF MEMORY

The mother, after childbirth, said she
could not raise the child. The only information obtained was her name, age, and
marital status. She kept company with the
bio-father for a short time and has not
heard from him since. The only information
she disclosed about the bio-father is he
is Caucasian.

That's Ian's birth story. He doesn't have a baby book like the ones Mom kept for me and Suzanna that documented her prenatal appointments and all of our firsts. He gets a sheet of paper that holds no emotion and warmth—only the stark information of a single mother whose country would frown at her if she kept her son.

He grabs the paper from me. "What's the point of having a baby if you can't keep it?"

An ominous feeling slinks up my back. "What are you saying?"

"Fun fact of the day: ninety-five percent of unwed pregnancies in Korea result in an abortion." He points to himself, and in a trembling voice says, "I should have been one of them."

I shake my head. "You don't mean that."

This isn't the Ian who likes *A Tree Grows in Brooklyn* and prayed for me and promised me tenderness.

His neck is tight, and his eyes flash with pain. "You said my mom's a waste of space. So am I!"

"Stop it!"

"Nobody cares about adoptees, Martha!"

"I care! You know I do!"

"Not their birth parents, the social workers. Not even God!"

"God cares, Ian! You told me he'd take care of me. Why are you any different?"

"Because it's a lie!"

I let go of him and back up. No. Ian's faith is steadfast. He does not—he cannot—believe this.

"I was a commodity. People want to save adoptees. They use us to make themselves feel like they're doing God's work. Adoption is beautiful. That's all they say in their memoirs and testimonies. But the reality is there's nothing special about loving a kid who's not yours. People who aren't related bond all the time!"

I stare into his bruised face. Fear seizes my chest. He's breaking down. What do I do?

"God's work doesn't traumatize kids. How could ripping a baby from its mother be beautiful?"

"I know, Ian. I know it was probably painful for you and your birth mother." A ball grows in my throat. I gulp. "But you have people in your life who *really* love you."

"I know they love me, but it hurts ..." He falters. "That I don't know if my omma is one of them." He balls his fists in front of his face. "Are you getting what I'm saying?"

I open my mouth to speak.

Ian pants as he begs, "Tell me you get it. Please, Martha."

I'm shaking so hard. "Ian, I'm trying ..." I put my hands over my face.

"Martha!" Between my fingers, I see him step close to me. "Hurting. This much. Isn't. Beautiful!"

I pull my hands off my face and bolt for his room.

"What are you doing?" he asks from behind me.

I burst into his room and spot his phone on his nightstand. I pick it up and scroll through his contacts. There it is: *Dad (work)*.

He comes closer. "Martha, no!"

I shrink away from him and run for the bathroom. I fling myself inside and grab the doorknob to keep my balance. "I'm calling your dad!" I yell as I lock the door.

"You wouldn't like it if I called your parents and told them your grandfather was a pedophile!" he fires back.

The phone rings twice.

"Brighter Future Treatment Center. This is Kendra. How can I help you?"

"Is Mr. Berkley there? I'm a friend of Ian's."

"Please hold."

I cover my mouth to hold back a sob. It leaps out of my throat anyway.

"This is Michael."

"It's Martha. Ian's in trouble."

"What? Why?" His voice carries panic.

I touch my chest. "He's so hurt inside."

"I'm coming. Where are you?"

"Your apartment."

"Martha, stay there if you can."

"I will."

I hang up and leave the bathroom. Ian's door is closed, so I give it a soft knock. I turn the handle, and to my relief it's unlocked. I walk in.

Ian's hunched over on his bed with his back to me.

I place his phone next to him and lean forward with my arms out to hug him.

He draws back. "You had no business calling my dad!"

I lift my hands in surrender. "You were scaring me."

"What did you think? I'm going to kill myself?"

"I did! I called him because I care about you." My voice is coated with tears. "I don't think *you* understand how much that is."

His body jolts a little at my accusation.

I wait for Ian to realize he's hurting me while he's hurting, but he just sits there.

"Please, can I hug you?" I shudder.

"Martha, *get out.*"

"I'm trying to be tender. We promised that for each other."

Ian gets up and backs away, as if I'm dangerous. He looks vulnerable. I collapse inside. "I said go!"

"Ian, what's triggering you?"

"The last time I let Hana touch me in my room, things got way out of hand."

I wonder if he lost his virginity with her, but now's not the time to ask.

He jabs a finger at the door. "Go conduct your suicide watch on me out there."

I turn around to leave. "Good night, Ian." I can't say good-bye; we're not there yet.

Kaylin calls me, but I don't answer.

I sit on the couch and start to pray. I pray that I don't end up on the list of people who have let Ian down. I use the prayer he said for me last night as a template and talk to God.

God, I don't think Ian can put his feelings into words. You promise to understand us if we can't express ourselves in prayer. Help him say the right things to his dad. I really love Ian. I never thought I would, but I do. It's scary and amazing at the same time. I didn't want him to hurt himself, and I'm afraid he'll still do that. God, I can't lose Ian. Protect him and help him walk through this dark time. Help him see that even if he can't find his omma, his family here loves him with a love that's very deep and real, and they would never leave him. Flood every corner of his life with light and peace. Amen.

52

IAN

DAD AND MARTHA are whispering in the living room. Their soft voices feel like feathers brushing against my ears. It's so overstimulating, I grit my teeth and pull my blue-and-green-plaid comforter over my head.

"I never saw Ian like that before," Martha says in a louder voice.

Dad has. The December after Mom left, he and I were at the toy store, buying something for the holiday grab bag my class was having before winter break. I threw a tantrum over a toy rifle Dad wouldn't let me have. He hauled me to my room when we got home, where I screamed and cried for a long time. Once I calmed down, he came to check on me. I threw a Ninja Turtle figurine at his face.

Dad put me in karate so I could blow off my anger. I got kicked out a month later. Neither Dad nor I remembers why.

"You're a sensible woman to call me," Dad assures Martha.

I hear her coat swoosh as she puts it on. "I don't think Ian would agree with that."

"He'll come around." The door opens. "Bye, Martha. Drive home safely," he says as she leaves.

I throw the comforter off and stay lying on my back.

Dad strides into my room and flicks the light on. "Ian." He kneels beside my bed. If the bruises on my face startled him, he's not showing it. "I'm ready to talk when you are."

I keep staring at the ceiling.

"If you're hurting so much that you can't talk, I'm taking you to the hospital."

Should he take me? I want someone else's beginning to life: You're born to a mom and a dad who are married, and they want to hold you until they die. If I don't want my beginning to life, do I want my life at all?

My phone rings. It's Gemma. I can't talk to her now. I'm a terrible brother, spilling Mom's secret on Thanksgiving dinner, and then I got fired because I can't douse the inferno inside me.

I roll onto my side so my back is to Dad. We're silent for several minutes.

Finally I say, "I don't want to hurt you."

"I'd rather you be honest with me than hang yourself in your closet."

I lie on my back again. "Get suicide out of your head. I won't do it."

He stands and hooks a hand on his hip. "Wishing your mother ripped you out of her womb tells me how you value your life—and hers. Think about how an abortion could have scarred her."

"Dad." I slide out of bed and face him. "I wasn't myself. Let it go."

He motions to my shirt. "Get changed. We'll talk in the kitchen."

"I have nothing to say to you. Martha told you everything."

Dad stands in the doorway, his face strained. "Talk to me, or I *will* drag you to the hospital."

I get into my pajamas. I ball up my polo shirt and trash it, name tag still attached, before dropping into a kitchen chair.

Dad curls his finger under my chin and lifts my face toward him. "So, Justin Massey."

"Of course. Martha told you."

"Ian, stop." Dad sighs.

"She had no right to call you."

"Then don't be so impulsive," he retorts and opens the fridge. In a softer voice, he asks, "Did you eat since you got home?"

"No."

"I can make Korean Army stew."

"Maybe something a little lighter. I'll have egg rice."

Dad sets a pot on the stove and heats some water.

"You know, Dad, I'm glad Omma gave me a chance, but sometimes I wish she could have raised me. I wonder if her love would have been enough, even with all the discrimination. Because it's like I don't have a mom now. Mrs. Shin's dead, and Mom hates me."

Dad's getting the rice and seaweed from the pantry. He pauses at my last sentence.

"What?" I ask him.

He shakes his head.

"Is it about Mom? We never talked about the conversation you had."

Dad comes over and squats beside me.

I look at him. Growing up, people never asked him if I was his son. His skin is darker than mine, but we have the same oval face, snub nose, and high cheekbones. Mom got the questions and stares. She ignored them. Maybe she hated being reminded I wasn't really her child.

"You're having a rough day. Do you want to talk about this?"

"I'm ready."

"When I talked to your mom, we had some words. She flew into a rage and said ..." He squeezes his hands together and looks at the floor before finishing. "She said you're not her son anymore."

Maybe everything that happened today numbed me, or I've grown immune to losing mothers. Whatever it is, I could depict my reaction to Mom's choice with a shrug.

But that's shallow, so I nod and lower my eyes. "Did she mention Gemma?"

"She did. She doesn't want you two talking, but she knows if she keeps you apart, you'll still find a way."

"I'd send Gemma snail mail to a friend's house if Mom went that far."

"I know you would." He stands and returns to the kitchen. "I confronted her about her cheating. She said nothing."

I join Dad at the stove. "Mom doesn't know how to love."

"She used to. She used to be perfect."

"I know. I have some nice memories of her."

"Everything she went through damaged her. I tried to get her help. She didn't want it." He rinses the rice and adds it to the boiling water. "I don't recognize her anymore. She said I can't go near Caleb's ashes. You and Gemma might have to spread them if your mother outlives me."

"That's not fair. He's your son too."

"Doesn't matter, Ian. Nothing that's fair matters to her." Dad hands me an egg. "Fry this. I always break the yolk."

I crack the egg. The yolk breaks. "I can't stop reliving those times she had Nathan over. You freaked out when Hayden got me the James Bond books for my fourteenth birthday." I snort. "I could have handled them."

Hayden had gotten me the series because the author's name was Ian. Dad almost choked on his cake when he saw them. He later donated them to the library.

"She signed the adoption papers with me, but I'm sorry she hasn't been much of a mother to you." Dad gets some kimchi for himself and retrieves the squid from the fridge. "You didn't add this to the kimchi."

"Martha wants to try kimchi but hates seafood," I explain as I wash my hands.

"Oh. No problem."

"Dad, I don't understand unconditional love." A load has been lifted off my back. "Christians get this from Jesus because he did such a selfless thing on the cross, right? Then why don't I see more of this kind of love? Why can't I feel it?"

He massages the squid under running water before dicing it with the kimchi. "Ian, you haven't had a lot of people fight for you. Someone might have pressured your birth mother to abort you and she resisted, or maybe Mrs. Shin wished she could have adopted you. But I love you unconditionally. And I love your omma for being so brave. I pray for her and your father every day."

He prays for Omma and my father.

I pull Dad to me and hug him hard. "I'm sorry about all the things I said. You're the only parent I have." I press my face into his uniform. My bruises hurt, but I don't care.

He holds me just as tightly. "I forgive you."

"I'm glad Martha called you," I say against his shirt. I wince as I recall her saying, "I'm trying to be tender."

"I hurt her so badly."

"You did. You should apologize. She was looking out for you."

I draw away from Dad and rub my eye. I want to pull Martha

into a crushing hug and tell her I love her repeatedly against her hair.

"You never mentioned Justin worked at the store," Dad says.

I tell him about the bullying Justin put me through since he was hired. When I'm done talking, Dad says, "Ian, don't job hunt. Focus on school, and graduate in May."

"I need to pay for my books."

"I'll cover that. Take a break. You're going through a lot. And rethink your career path. I know you love books, but you can do so much more than retail."

"I want to go to Korea," I blurt out.

Dad loads my meal into a bowl and slides it toward me. "If that's what you need, tell me when you're going—"

"I'm not talking about a trip. I'm going there indefinitely."

Dad's face collapses, which makes me ache inside.

"I know this is radical, but I want to be a *Korean* Korean, not a tourist. I'll use my savings to rent an apartment, learn Korean. I'll find work and meet other adoptees who moved back there. And I'm searching for Omma on my own."

Dad stands there, unmoving. "You're going to leave," he states, not asks.

"I promise I'll be back."

Whenever that is, I hope I can reconcile with Mom. Find out what I really want to do with myself and do it. Get married.

"When are you going?"

"In August. If things don't work out, I'll come back."

Dad steps closer to me, running his hand along the edge of the counter. "What are you going to do about Martha?"

"Stay with her. Have a long-distance relationship."

Dad looks so lonely. When I'm gone, he'll see his family a few times a week, but he'll be alone for most of the time.

"You have to go."

His words fill me like tteokguk soup, my comfort food.

"Your first night home, you wouldn't stop crying," Dad recalls. "But you took to Halmoni and calmed down when she spoke Korean. I'll never forget what hit me: I have someone else's kid because his mother had no options, and my wife and I want to be parents."

"I didn't think something like that hit you right when you got me."

"This couple at the airport adopted a girl who was around ten," Dad goes on. "She didn't want to go with them. The father picked her up, and she lost it. I was thinking, 'What are we doing to these kids?'"

I use my chopsticks to wrap a piece of seaweed around some egg rice. "You were doing what you thought was best, but a lot of us were hurting."

"And you kept getting hurt. Every time something traumatic happened to you, you closed up. You had a longing in your eyes that killed me. You knew, subconsciously, there were what-ifs with a different mother." He breaks some egg with the side of his spoon. "I never told your mom; I would have scared her, and I thought it was adoptive parent insecurities eating at me."

"You knew your son better than anyone else."

Dad leans down on the counter. "I hope I still do."

53

MARTHA

I KNEW Ian and I would fight about something eventually, like miscommunicated plans or an awkwardly expensive gift. I never thought we'd fight about his childhood hardships pushing him to explode about his adoption.

My mind keeps replaying Ian's outrage as I drive home. Those were the echoes of a boy who needed the people he depended on to mend his wounds before they etched scars all over his brain. The problem is that a lot of those people were the ones who hurt him the most.

When I walk through the door, Dad is—gasp—making chili. My high point of today is that we won't be having a casserole.

"Hey, Marty, want to bake some cornbread?"

I kick my sneakers off and croak, "No."

"What's the problem?"

Inside, I'm screaming, *Daddy, my heart hurts!*

Dad becomes foggy. I bite the inside of my lip to keep from crying, but a high-pitched moan comes out. "I thought ... he wanted ... to die."

"What?" Dad drops the wooden spoon in the stockpot but doesn't come over to me.

"Justin at work said a racist comment about Ian eating dog. Ian beat him up, and they got fired. I went to his place to see if he's okay. We got into a huge fight, and he said he wished he had been aborted."

Dad finally comes closer. "Marty ..."

I want him to hold me. Oh, God, please.

Dad stops and leans against the island. That makes me cry even harder.

"Marty, I knew this relationship wasn't going to work. I got bad vibes when you just *had* to go to the wedding. Then he indoctrinates you, and now this."

"Dad!"

"Listen to me! You're calling him and ending this."

"No!"

Dad returns to the stove and sprinkles seasonings over the chili. "It's nice your heart's bleeding for him, but let it clot, then run. I don't want you staying with him. Someday you'll come home with a black eye and split lip."

"He won't hurt me. Justin harassed him for weeks, and he snapped."

"Marty, he assaulted someone *at work*. Think how he might treat *you* in private."

I come up behind Dad. "You don't know Ian. He was torn from three mothers. His mom committed adultery in front of him when he was five. He confronted her about this on Thanksgiving. She wasn't even sorry. All he wants is a mom who loves him."

"That's just it, Marty," Dad says matter-of-factly. He ladles chili into bowls. "People with a lot of baggage who don't have control over their lives think they have it all together, then they snap."

He's worried about Ian beating me, but he and Mom let Grandpa back in.

My hands become fists at my sides. "You think I don't know Ian? You and Mom didn't know Grandpa."

Dad puts our dinner on the table and stops. "What d'you mean?"

I inhale and drop the truth between heavy breaths. "Grandpa … molested … me."

"He *what*?"

"On that Christmas … and so … many … times!" I burst out. I come at him and grab his arms. "Why did you and Mom trust him? You knew he was sick like Grandma was!"

Dad pries himself out of my grip and guides me over to a chair. "Sit down."

I take a seat. I tell him how Grandpa pinned me down in bed on that Christmas morning. How he used to touch me inappropriately under the table when he was over for dinner or go into my room to "say good-bye" before he left. How he had hours with my body those nights Mom and Dad went on dates and Suzanna hung out with friends. I finish with the last time. "I went to pee, and he came in the bathroom." I can barely speak. "He … he held me against the sink and kept t-t-touch-ing me, and I felt … things."

The color drains from Dad's face. He stares at me, looking devastated, and swears under his breath.

"I threatened to have him prosecuted. I wanted him to die, and he did. I was … happy. I was *happy*!" I inhale deeply. "But Mom cried. She thought he felt guilty for all the other twisted things he did." I grab my napkin to wipe my eyes and blow my nose.

Dad rests his elbow on the table and rubs his forehead. "Marty, why didn't you say something? After all those years?"

"This isn't *my* fault." I clap my fingers to my mouth as if they can hold down the rage growing inside me. "I didn't know how to talk about it."

He slumps in his chair.

"I was only six when it started." The tears come back. "Please say something. Please."

"Marty, I'm trying to wrap my head around this. I ... I'm speechless." He turns his palms upward on the table as if to show me he really has nothing to say.

I thought Dad and I would stick together as this family breaks, but he is not reliable. A family called Unreliable.

I've never felt so alone in my life.

"I figured." I pull my meal toward me. "This family can't communicate. That's why you kicked Mom out. You couldn't talk about what really matters."

Dad rubs the side of his face. "Why would you bring this up now? You just said Grandpa—"

I lift my spoon to dish out some food, but I slam it down on the table. "I'm bringing this up because our lousy communication has made us all suffer."

"And I tried to end some of that suffering for you. I protected you from your mother after she bashed your head into the wall. I put you first." Dad takes a piece of cornbread. "And do me a favor: stay out of our marriage."

"What *marriage*? Mom wants a divorce!"

"I already know that."

I struggle to swallow. "What?"

"I got the divorce papers yesterday."

I'm hit with a wave of panic. "Why didn't you tell me?"

Dad cringes. "I wasn't going to tell you in front of your boyfriend. And I didn't say anything because I wanted to talk your mother out of it. I saw her today while you were at work. I accomplished nothing."

"Keep trying."

"You and Suzanna can stay with whomever you want; your mother and I do what we want. Now, when did you talk to Suzanna?"

"Friday. She tore me apart. We're fluent in anger, Dad. It's killing us."

He sighs and runs his hand over his hair. I've never seen him look so heartbroken.

"You and Mom have been together since you were sixteen. After all you've been through, you can't split up. She needs help. If you tried that with her, things could get better."

"I can't do anything." Dad digs his spoon into his meal. "These past few weeks prove we can live without each other, so we're getting this show on the road."

"You don't want that."

Dad drops his spoon against his bowl. "Marty, she doesn't love me anymore."

I touch my chest. "What about me?" I ask through some chili.

"I don't know. If she abandons you, you can talk to Ian—if he hasn't gone crazy."

I glare at him, my mouth agape. "You did not say that!"

"Marty, this conversation is over."

"Dad, just apologize!"

"Marty—"

"You never say what I really need you to say!" I accuse as I turn toward him in my seat. "You can't talk about Grandpa. You can't even apologize for insulting Ian."

Dad's face is drawn and tired. He opens his mouth and tries to speak, but nothing comes out.

My jaw is tight as I get up from my chair to put my bowl in the dishwasher. "Ian's not crazy. You never gave him any respect even though he's been there for me more these past few months than anyone in this family."

Dad gets up and stands by the dishwasher. "I didn't want him to hurt you after all you've been through."

"You tell me why you don't trust Ian, but you can't talk about Mom or me. This family is done."

Dad shakes his head, his eyes dark with panic. "Don't say that, Marty."

"This family's gone, Dad." Tears slide down my face. "We have no clue—*no* clue—what anyone has gone through or who we really are."

I hold the sides of my head. I can't make out Dad's expression; the tears won't stop.

"Marty, we can talk now. Just stay here—"

The truths, anger, and hurt that I've harbored for fourteen years billow inside me.

I can't hold it in anymore.

"I told Ian everything!" I scream as I scurry out of the kitchen. "He knows about Grandpa. I stole money from you and Mom. I vandalized Chloe's locker. I wanted to die in eleventh grade!"

"Where's all this coming from?" he shouts behind me as he follows me upstairs.

It's coming from the girl my parents never knew. She needed hugs, safety, assurance that she was pretty, and faith. Any kind of faith to tell her life could get better.

I tear into my room. I try to slam the door before Dad is off the stairs, but I'm too late.

"Don't do this, Martha Jene," he protests as he tries to force his way in. "I want to talk to you."

"You had fourteen years to do that!" I scrunch my toes into the carpet to hold myself up as I fight him. "You don't care about Mom or what Grandpa did or who Suzanna and I love! You don't love *me*!"

"That isn't true."

I slam my fist against the door. "Then say it! Say you love me!"

He opens his mouth and exhales. Nothing.

"You know, when Suzanna trashed me, I wanted you, Dad. Just *you*, because ..." I gulp down some pain. "We used to be close. Remember how we were? But you're empty now. This whole family is."

"Marty ..."

I shoot my finger toward the hall. "Get out!"

Dad holds up his hands. "Okay, okay. I'll leave you alone." Then he leaves.

Panting, I drop to the floor. My family let our pain ruin us instead of drawing us closer to one another and growing stronger. That's what happens when everyone's healing balm is silence.

I get ready for bed and check my phone. Kaylin called me twice. I call her back.

"Hey, Marty," she says when she answers.

"Kay, Ian's ..." I slam my fist into my thigh. "He's really hurting." I'm in no mood to talk, but I explain why he got fired and that he lashed out at me when I tried to comfort him. I tell her he wished his birth mother had aborted him. I recount the conversation with Dad and tell her my parents are splitting up.

"Do you need me to come over?"

No, I don't. It hurts that I don't care about her caring, and I'm a lousy friend for using her as my dumping ground for my issues.

"I need space. Please. I'll see you tomorrow in class."

"I'm not going. I already saw *Maria Full*—"

I end the call.

I used to think letting down my fortress would soften me. It hasn't. I'm back to being my angry, bitter self.

54

IAN

THE BRUISE on my face is a dark blueish-purple now. My business professor did a double take when I walked into class yesterday and asked me what happened. I didn't answer her.

In German class today, I get a lot of stares and hide in the back. Brigitte is starting a new chapter, so there's a lot of note-taking, a good excuse to keep my head down.

When class ends, Brigitte approaches me as I'm packing up.

"Ian, what happened to you?" she asks, leaning in and sounding concerned.

"I got in a fight at work," I admit, avoiding eye contact with her.

"Oh. I hope things are okay."

"I worked with this guy I knew back in school. He said some racist stuff to me over the past few weeks, and I snapped." I struggle to zip my backpack. "That's ... that's not me, Brigitte. I ..."

"Ian, I know." Brigitte touches my arm, and I look up at her. Her light-blue eyes are full of understanding. "I've noticed a lot of improvement recently. You're participating more, and your grades are going up. Thank you for putting a lot of effort into this class."

"Danke. I'm trying." I force a smile and hoist my backpack onto my shoulder. *"Auf Wiedersehen."*

"Auf Wiedersehen."

When I get to my car, I turn my phone on. Chris called me an hour ago. We haven't spoken in two months. This is going to be awkward. I've changed a lot, and I'm pretty angry at him.

I call him back.

"Hey, Ian," he says when he picks up.

"I'm sorry I didn't call you sooner and we couldn't hang out." I keep my tone neutral, but I'm boiling inside.

"No big deal. How's life been?"

"Well, I did something really stupid and got fired."

"You got ... fired?"

"Yeah, and you blew me off but text me when your world collapses."

"Ian—"

"So, I have a track record of hanging out with non-Christian girls. I have issues, but so do you. Was taking Martha to the wedding so wrong that you had to ignore me?"

"I didn't want you to get hurt. You almost lost your virginity with Hana. You got back together and broke up. Then Martha comes along, and you're all in. I was sick of you creating your own problems." He pauses to let this register. "Sorry. I wanted a break."

I make a fist in my lap. "I'm glad you took one," I remark, "because I spent a lot of time with Martha, who, by the way, isn't a problem. She loves God as much as you and I do."

I'm just not sure Martha loves me right now after what I did to her.

"That's great." He makes that soft two-syllable chuckle, like he's an adult laughing at a child. "I'm glad things are working out for you."

"Now you're going to tell me about the rough time you're

having? Guess what? Life sucks for me too. My mom cut me off because I confronted her about the affair she was having with Nathan before she left."

"What are you talking about?"

I don't elaborate. "And I'm having a very ..." I catch my breath. "*Very* hard time dealing with my adoption. I needed you to be a friend, not a dad telling me how stupid I was."

"I'm sorry, Ian."

My jaw relaxes. I take my hand off the steering wheel and rest it on my lap. "Bethany broke up with you?"

"She was acting funny for a while and was way too attached to her phone." He stops. I picture Chris rubbing his head. He does that a lot. "She's seeing a guy named Jesse from her Bible studies class."

I sit up, shocked. Bethany, who was so Christlike and devoted to everything she and Chris had, cheated on him? "Oh, man, Chris. I'm sorry."

"I'm guilty too. I snooped on her phone when I was visiting her in her dorm and found all these gushy texts. I suggested we go to our pastor for help. She said no." He blows out some air. "She's a completely different person, Ian. Eight years of love and friendship—gone."

"And you failed a class?"

"Yeah, algebra. I'll retake it next semester. And Gray Ghost died last week."

Gray Ghost was Chris's family dog. I feel nothing. I know—I'm soulless.

"Phoebe's pretty upset," Chris goes on. "My parents will look for a puppy when she's ready. So, why'd you get fired?"

I explain how my job went downhill once Justin was hired. I tell him about Mom's secret I kept buried for years. Then I break the news about Korea. "I'm moving there to get my culture back, and I'm doing a birth family search."

"Really? That's exciting."

I don't bother telling him these plans are terrifying but feel right at the same time. He and I didn't talk about my adoption growing up. It didn't gnaw at me back then, and he doesn't have to know about everything in my life now.

"When are you leaving?" he asks.

"In August. I'm not working, so I'll graduate in May and study Korean like crazy."

"Makes sense."

"I hope you feel better and find someone who wants to minister with you."

"I'm dealing. Sometimes I like being single." Chris chuckles, as if he could laugh off the pain Bethany put on him. "I'll go to Europe alone."

A woman in a blue Mercedes honks at me. "Someone wants my spot. We'll talk soon."

"All right. Cool."

"I'm sorry I was so angry before."

"Ian, we're good, and I'm happy for you and Martha."

I pull my seat belt across my chest and jam it in the buckle. "She's amazing. Let's all hang out before I move."

I'm moving to Korea. This wholesome, content feeling fills me. Besides the Korean words I picked up from Dad's family, my Korean is so limited, and I have so much to learn about life there, but the unfamiliar feels safe. It's where I'm supposed to go.

Chris and I hang up. He had his reasons for ignoring me. It wasn't right, but we needed space. Martha and I opened up to each other, and telling Dad about my adoption pain wasn't so scary after all.

Martha. I love her so much.

We haven't talked since I yelled in her face on Sunday. I don't blame her for not contacting me, but I shouldn't cower. I should have called her sooner.

The student who wanted my spot is gone, so I call Martha.

She doesn't answer. I almost hang up; everything I need to say can't fit into a message. But I hear a beep, and my phone's still against my ear.

"Martha? Hi …"

55

MARTHA

AFTER I SHOWER and get back to my room, I see a missed call and voicemail from Ian. My heart waltzes. Mr. Berkley and I exchanged numbers in case Ian was a suicide risk. I'm so glad his father's contact isn't on my screen.

I select Ian's message and listen.

"Martha? It's me. I'm sorry for what I did the other day. I abused you when you were ..." His voice wavers. "Loving me. The guy last night wasn't me, but if you want to walk away, I understand. I wouldn't have stooped so low if I didn't keep things buried for so long. My mom told me not to tell anyone about Nathan, but I should have spoken up when I got older."

I sit at my desk. Ian grew up thinking he had to conceal his mom's adultery forever. It's scary how much power people hold over you after they exit your life.

Like Grandpa.

"I'm glad you called my dad. I needed him. I told him how I feel about my adoption. Mom told him ..." Ian swallows. "She said

I'm not her son. I can still talk to Gemma but not Mom. I need to find Omma. I'm going to Korea this summer."

I'm so excited for him, I rise out of my chair and start pacing my room.

"I'm moving there."

I freeze in my tracks. A stream of fears rushes into my head. We just started dating. Does he want us to just be friends because he doesn't want to have a long-distance relationship? Does he want to date and marry a Korean woman? Will he want to move there *permanently*?

"I'll apply for an F-4 visa so I can study and work there. I know this sounds nuts, but I have to go. A lot of adoptees return to live there. I want to surround myself with people who've experienced what I have. I'll save up to visit a few times. And I'll come back. I promise."

My stomach tightens. I cover it with my hand and take a breath. *Chill, Marty.* He was deprived of his mother's touch, her voice, her milk. He left his foster mother and lost his language and country. I'll miss him so much, but he needs to go. And he promised to come back.

"I want to see you." His voice wobbles. "Call me when you get a chance."

I do, and he answers after the first ring. "Martha! I'm so sorry."

"I know you are." My voice catches. For the first time as a Christian, I say, "I forgive you." It feels peaceful and freeing and gives me the confidence that Ian and I can work together to restore our relationship.

"I went too far, Martha. And I'm sorry about a lot of things I did, pushing you to have hard conversations you didn't want to have. Then you tried to help me, and I couldn't deal."

"I got a taste of my own medicine." There's a short pause.

"We're both a mess. Maybe we can keep trying together. What do you say?"

"I say yes."

I smile at this. "Me too. So, when can I see you?"

"I can come now. Give me a half-hour."

I touch up my makeup and read some of *Story of a Girl* to help time pass, but I can't sit still. So I prop myself against my windowsill and look out into the driveway like a teenager waiting for her first date to arrive. When Ian's car pulls in, I fly downstairs, tear through the garage, and almost knock him over when I hug him.

"No jacket? Martha, it's thirty degrees!"

I bury my face in his neck and inhale his scent. "Come on." I pull him inside. He closes the door. I back him into the wall to press my lips on his for a firm, long kiss.

He gently pushes me back and breathes out, "Whoa."

I need someone full of trust and love to touch me. I need you to help me forget Grandpa. I'm scared to say this, so I hug him. This is when silence is healing. There's still so much to say, but I just need to be with him to reconnect. I wish my family could do this, but Mom and Dad think divorce will free us from the problems we're too afraid to talk about.

"After I called your dad to come home, I prayed for you. I prayed like you'd prayed for me. It felt like God was so close."

"He was close. You wanted him, and he was there." Ian squeezes me. "You're my best friend, Martha. I love you. You know that?"

"I've known it for a long time. I love you too." I fist some of his shirt. If we keep holding each other, my bones will melt. "We can't stay here like this."

"I know."

IAN SUGGESTS we go to a used bookstore called BookMarks the Spot. It's in a Victorian home. The porch desperately needs a coat of paint, and when Ian opens the door, its hinges sound like a screeching violin.

"It looked nicer online," he remarks.

We approach the dark-haired associate, who looks like he rolled out of bed and schlepped here.

"Do you have any foreign language books?" Ian asks him.

He turns and motions toward the stairs.

"Thanks." Once we're upstairs, Ian walks over to the language section and says, "After you work in retail, bad customer service reeks." I doubt he'll find what he wants; the shelves are bare in so many places.

I scan the room and spot a sign over a shelf in the corner that reads JOURNALISM AND WRITING.

It's time to register for spring classes. I really wanted to take Eastern European lit, but Dad said the withdrawal on my transcript won't look so bad if I retake creative writing. My poem is the best thing I've ever written, so I go to the poetry section and pluck a book off the shelf: *Poemcrazy* by Susan G. Wooldridge.

Okay. I'm not *that* into poetry.

"I found something!" Ian's face lights up as he flips to a random page and holds it up for me to see. Someone had traced over the Korean words with a pencil. "No romanization, which is great. There are sounds in Korean that don't exist in English."

I catch some of the words on the glossy page. 여름 is summer. 나무 is tree. 아빠 is dad.

"That's so cool," I gush. "The elementary level of a language is fun. You learn the alphabet and tons of vocabulary like a child. You can go on forever."

Ian grins. "You look at a Korean book and act like I won the jackpot."

"Because I love languages." I'm still holding *Poemcrazy* as I fling my arms around him. "I love becoming Marfa and speaking words that aren't mine, and they become mine."

He hugs me back. "Just always keep Martha in Marfa."

"And always be Ian under Min Joon."

I jump away from Ian. Behind him, a woman stands at the top of the stairs.

Ian turns around, embarrassed.

"Feeling the love?" she jokes as she heads for the history section.

"Not much for this place," Ian replies.

She browses the shelves, then turns to leave. "I know. It's falsely advertised."

I return *Poemcrazy* to its shelf and sit in an armchair by the window. "You could own this place. Pack the shelves with luscious books and hire nice cashiers."

Ian takes the chair across from me. "I'm not rescuing this store."

"I wish you didn't have to leave."

"Me too, but I need this." He hunches over and props his arms on his legs. "I want to know what my life would have been like if I hadn't been adopted."

That's going to take a long time. Ian could be gone for years. Can we do the long-distance thing for years?

"I'm purging most of my stuff. My dad's keeping my furniture in case Korea doesn't work out. Once I know it is, he's donating everything and moving into a one-bedroom apartment."

"Where are you going to stay?"

"There's a guesthouse for adoptees in Seoul. After I find work, I'll get my own place and study Korean at Sogang University. Eventually I'll settle in Busan and live within walking distance to the beach."

I fold my legs under me. *Settle* throws an ache into my chest.

"When you called me earlier, I thought you were going to say we can't stay together." I chuckle a little and shake my head. "I was afraid you'd say you wanted to stay in Korea forever and marry a Korean woman."

Ian's eyes fill with compassion. "I wouldn't do that to you, Martha. I'm going to Korea to get my culture and language back; I'm not looking for a wife."

I rub my forehead. "Sorry for my ridiculous thinking."

"No, you're fine."

"It's cool that you want to live near the beach. I grew up in Neptune, so we practically lived at the beach in the summer."

"My mom loves the beach, but my dad didn't have time for day trips after she left. It was nice, her and me going places." Ian fiddles with his hands. "My first memory—I was almost three. I woke up in my mom's lap at the beach. She smelled like ocean and sunscreen. She ruffled my hair and asked, 'You want to go back to sleep?' I wish she had stayed maternal ... trustworthy."

The hurt in his eyes. Oh, Ian.

"Does she know you're moving?"

"Not yet. Her dream will come true. She used to threaten to send me back to Korea when I misbehaved."

My eyes bulge. "What?"

"She was being impulsive, but one time I believed her." Ian picks at a hole in the armchair. "I packed some things, and when my dad came home, I told him where I was going."

"So, you were disposable? Why, because she paid money to get you?"

"Probably. My parents fought like usual. My mom said sorry." He shrugs. "Maybe she was."

Ian needs to find his omma. His adoptive mother failed him on so many levels.

"All the decluttering advice I'm reading says to tackle sentimental stuff last. I'll do that first. I don't want most of the things from my childhood."

"You deserve a fresh start." I lace my fingers together between my knees. "I hope when you come back you're full but always want more of Korea, and it doesn't hurt anymore. That's when you know you found home."

Ian looks at me tenderly, and my knees go weak. "I want to write that down." He stands. "And get out of here."

"Good, because I'm afraid we'll find a trap door under there"—I jab a finger at the rug we're standing on—"that's hiding drugs or a dead body."

"Get writing, Martha." Ian wraps an arm around my waist, and I hug his in return. Downstairs, Ian pays for his book. "Have a good day," he tells the cashier.

"Yeah" is all the man says.

When we're back in Ian's car, he asks, "Do you want that poetry book? My treat."

"Oh, no. My dad wants me to retake creative writing to fix the withdrawal on my transcript."

"Are you going to?"

I look at Ian, who's facing me with his arm resting over the steering wheel. "If I can survive my grandpa's abuse and the mess my family is in, I can write again."

"You write great poetry."

"Thanks. I made some changes to my poem, just for me. It was really satisfying. I think I'm onto something."

"Keep me posted on that."

I brush imaginary dust off my lap. "Last night, I told my dad everything. He asked me why I didn't speak up sooner, like it was my fault. Then he had no words, we had some words, and by that time, I was so mad at him, I couldn't talk to him."

"After hiding what your grandpa did for so long, then your dad reacts like that—it must have been really painful." Ian moves his arm off the wheel and leans back. "He's smart. He could have done better."

"I can't ask for better." My throat tingles. "My parents do their best. You know what my mom's parents were like, and my pop-pop was hard on my dad."

"You des—"

I turn in my seat and kiss him. I don't want to hear him say I deserve more. I reach for what I can have now.

Ian pulls away. "Martha, I don't like it when you abruptly kiss me like that."

I face forward. "Okay. I'm sorry."

Ian touches my hand and starts the car. "Hey, we're still getting to know each other."

He doesn't know I want his touch to obliterate the evenings when Grandpa gave me candy and stickers or the biggest piece of cake at dessert and then played with my body and stole my innocence.

But Ian wants us to be careful. There is God's law, and, I suspect, memories he wants to forget that probably remind him of Hana.

56

IAN

DAD'S ASLEEP when I get home. I roll up my sleeves and grab a few garbage bags from under the kitchen sink before going to my room.

I pull a plastic bin stuffed with paper clutter from my closet. Drawings Dad thought would be memorable artwork, a GRE book Mom bought me, and orientation paperwork from NYC Corner. It all goes into recycling. I even throw out the book I wrote in third grade based on the book series *Arthur*. It was one of the few things I enjoyed doing for school, but I don't need to keep it to remember that. I toss my autograph books and yearbooks. The only thing I'm keeping from this bin is my photo album. It's proof that I survived my childhood and made it this far.

I rip my discolored Dalmatian stuffed animal, Kang, off the shelf and toss it. Mom bought him when I was obsessed with *101 Dalmatians* right after my fifth birthday. Not long afterward, Nathan started visiting. Kang kept me company in my room.

I'm putting my baby baptism outfit in a bag for donations when Dad joins me. "What are you doing?"

"Tossing it all to start over."

He opens the garbage bag and looks inside. "None of this can be replaced."

"I know." I throw out my report cards. "Bad times gone forever."

"Come on, Ian." He rescues Kang from the bag. "Don't get rid of Kang."

"I threw him at you when I was mad after Mom left."

Dad glances at Kang, like the memory's in his fur. "I don't remember that."

"You blocked it out. I was hell on legs."

He sits on my bed. "I support you going to Korea, but I hope you're running toward something and not away from anything you should take care of."

"I went back on Facebook and joined a Korean adoptees group. There are nonprofits and volunteers who help adoptees with birth family searches." I lean closer to him. With excitement in my voice, I say, "Some of them found more information in their file that's in Korea."

Dad's face lights up. "Really? Wow. There's always hope."

I find an old pamphlet from the adoption agency advertising the Motherland Tour it hosts every summer for adoptees and their families. I asked the social worker to stop sending these after my birth family search.

"You don't have to deal with your mom. I texted her your plans. She didn't reply."

"Stop giving her updates on my life."

"Ian, she's still your mother."

"No, she's not. I'm not her son anymore." I hold up the pamphlet. "To Mr. and Mrs. Michael Hong Berkley," I read. "If only the adoption agency knew."

"I know you're looking for a better life, but you're going to have problems in Korea too."

"Yeah, if I find Omma, I hope she doesn't cheat on her husband when I'm around."

Dad frowns. "Ian, I'm worried about you. Your emotions are really unstable lately. I think you need some help."

I remember the glass wall that went up when Justin harassed me. I never felt that before. It bugs me, but I push it over.

"Getting rid of this is what's going to help me." I motion to everything on the floor. "And I'm not going just to find Omma. I want to have memories of where I was supposed to grow up."

"Are you going to search for your birth father?"

"Dad, you know the answer."

"He might be easier to find. I bet he has information on your mother. And what if he's not as bad as you think?"

I look at Kang in Dad's hands. "I'll think about it."

"You should. And think about what you'll do in Korea and how much Korean you want in your pocket before you head out of here."

"I'll get any job and learn Korean at Sogang University. You only need a high school diploma for their program."

Dad's about to speak, but I go on.

"I emailed the guy who runs the guesthouse. He's booked in June and July; that's when a lot of adoptees plan trips, so I'm leaving in August. I'm not backing down."

"Ian, this is a huge commitment. Are you sure this is what you want?"

I throw out some graduation cards. "I'm sure. I'll give it my all, Dad. I'm doing better in school. I know I can master Korean if I work hard enough."

Dad nods and glances around my room. "I'll save your books for you."

"I'll declutter them with Martha in case she wants anything."

"How's she doing?"

"Her parents are calling it quits," I tell him as I tie up the trash bag.

Dad's face falls. "Oh, geez. I'll pray for her family."

"Her sister's putting a lot of blame on her." Then I explain Suzanna's logic.

Dad shakes his head. "That's not fair to Martha."

"I hope she gets into Maryland and has her own new start."

Dad tosses Kang at me. "The other night, she asked me to call her if you …" He lowers his voice. "Wanted to hurt yourself."

I rub Kang's worn-out black ear. "I really scared her."

"She loves you, Ian."

"I know. I told her I'm glad she called you, and I'm glad I told you how I feel about my adoption. Thanks for listening."

"Ian, it's unnatural to separate a baby from its mother. I don't expect you to be thrilled about that and preach adoption. You lost a lot, and I think you'll fill that void in Korea."

"I think you're right."

"Okay, then." Dad stands and heads out of my room. "I'm going back to sleep. See you for dinner."

I raid my closet and fill two bags with clothes for the thrift store. I pack Kang, some DVDs, my photo album, notebooks, adoption papers, and the keepsakes from my life in Korea in a box and scrawl *KEEP* on one of its flaps. I display my Korean flag on my desk and tape the Hangul chart on the wall next to my door.

I open my nightstand drawer and dig out a bookstore receipt, some loose change, and my first Bible. I thumb through its dog-eared pages. This Bible was there for me when I became a Christian. It doesn't feel right to pack this away while I'm gone. No Bible should be wasted, and I know who should have it.

57

MARTHA

IT'S FRIDAY, and I don't want to go to Russian, but hiding in a vacant house won't lift my mood. I force myself out of bed and eat some granola and yogurt.

I have Dad, Kaylin, and Ian, but I feel so lonely. Yearning for Mom stabs and slices me open. It's excruciating. How does Ian make it every day, constantly wanting his omma?

In class, Alyosha hands out multiple-choice and short-answer questions about the Soviet children's show *Cheburashka*. We watch the episode "Krokodil Gena." It's done in stop motion, so the characters look like clay and stuffed animals. Cheburashka has the ears of a mouse and the body of a bear. No one knows what he is, and he eventually befriends a lonely crocodile named Gena.

Most of the class saw this when they were kids, so they're doing work for other courses or whispering to one another.

"There needs to be detention in college," Alyosha mutters.

When we're dismissed, Kylie comes to me with a notepad and pen. "Hey, Marfa. Lev and I are starting a study group. We don't have all the details sorted out, but if you'd like to join, we'll put you in the email thread."

This is my new major, so I'd better dive in. I want to breathe, drink, and live Russian.

"I'd love to," I gush as I jot down my school email.

"It'll be great to have you," Kylie says. "You're so good with verbs."

Once everyone's gone, I amble up to Alyosha. "I made up my mind. I'm majoring in Russian."

He pats my shoulder. "You made my week! Where do you want to transfer?"

"UMD in College Park. I'll apply to Rutgers as backup. I either want to teach or translate."

"Great choices." He unplugs the TV and winds up its power cord. "Will I see you next semester in Russian 102?"

"Of course."

He gives me a thumbs up. *"Otleechno."*

Later at work, I find out Jamie got Ian's job, and Ebony is on board for good. Liz still has to find a seasonal worker.

I have to get used to seeing Jamie at register one instead of Ian. I miss having him here with me. He and I might never work together again. That is, unless he actually establishes that language school and recruits me to be the Russian teacher.

Jamie seems cool. She's chatty with customers and is excited to be doing more than cashiering and managing signs. She's a junior at Monmouth University, majoring in psychology, and wants to get a master's in art therapy somewhere in Pennsylvania.

She will change people. Ian changed me. Ian's going to change in Korea. This makes me feel giddy, but the lightness inside me feels foreign, and the devastation from my parents' pending separation caves in. I cup my hand over my forehead. "Hmph."

"Are you feeling okay?" Jamie asks.

"Yeah. Life just stinks right now."

She cocks her head. "If you need to rant, I'm here."

"Thanks. I'm fine."

A lot of people care about me. I feel nothing. It's scary and disgusting.

I wear my happy retail face for the rest of my shift, but my nerves are like jittery sparking wires.

My family is broken, maybe permanently.

It breaks me, and I'm dying to break something.

After I clock out, I enter the bathroom and stand before the mirror. My body tightens as I make a fist and pull my arm back. I imagine a spiderweb of broken glass blooming behind my fist that's splotched with blood, my tired face fragmented by glistening shards. I blink and inhale to suck back some anger. My fist slows its way forward. I could lose my job for this, and I can't afford to pay for the damage. My knuckles kiss the mirror. I hold my fist there before I step away and leave.

I come home, open the garage, and brace myself to spend the next few hours alone. The door runs down the tracks on the ceiling, revealing Mom and Dad's cars.

I clap a hand to my mouth. I touch Mom's Prius. I'm not imagining this; she's home.

I scramble up the stairs leading into the house so fast, I trip over my feet.

"Mom!" I call as I dart through the kitchen.

"Marty?"

I meet her halfway up. Her eyes are puffy and framed with dark circles, and her face is drawn, but she's still my beautiful mom. She opens her arms. I fall against her for that hug I've been waiting so long to feel.

"I'm so sorry, Mom."

She smooths her hand over the back of my head. "*I'm* sorry. I said the worst things to you and ignored you when you tried to reach out. I was becoming my mother, but I won't destroy this family."

I look up at her. "You and Dad aren't getting a divorce?"

"No, we're not," Dad answers from behind me.

His voice startles me.

Dad comes toward us and sits on the bottom step. "You're right, Marty; Mom and I can't quit after all we've been through. Our marriage—this family—is worth everything."

I let go of Mom and grab the banister to sit. Mom and Dad made it through the storm. The skies—our future—is clear. I gaze upward, as if I can really feel the warmth of the sun. My eyes moisten with tears.

Mom sits next to me and folds her arms across her knees. "Dad called me last night. He told me everything. I ran to the bathroom and threw up. I couldn't sleep." She brushes back some of my flyaway hair. "Do you really think you're responsible for my father's suicide?"

I nod.

"No, honeypot. He was a weak man. He wouldn't have survived prison, and he knew it."

"Marty, I feel so bad about yesterday. I was at a loss." Dad squeezes my knee. "And I don't say this enough, and I don't always do it right, but I love you."

"I love you too, Dad. I didn't mean what I said." My throat stings. "We're not empty. I just want us to talk more."

"We will," he promises, "and what Gabe did wasn't your fault."

"Mom got along with Grandpa after Grandma died. We had better memories of him—"

"But *you* didn't," Dad interjects, frowning.

"It doesn't matter how I felt," Mom says. "You matter more. My girls always matter more, so don't ever feel afraid to speak up when you're in trouble."

I lean my head on her shoulder. "We missed you, Mom. Not just for everything you do for us. We love you."

She looks at me, then at Dad, with the same tenderness Ian holds in his eyes. "I love you too. I missed being home." Mom gathers me against her side. Dad holds her hand. We're together again, connecting in a silence that really is a healing balm.

———

AFTER DINNER, I'm reading *Story of a Girl* when Mom comes in my room. "Can we talk?"

I stick my bookmark inside and close the book. "Yeah."

Mom grabs my pillow and sets it on her lap. "Lie down, Marty."

I rest my head on the pillow and curl into a ball. Mom pulls my scrunchie out and runs her fingers through my hair.

"You have beautiful hair," she says. "So thick and such a rich color."

A side of my iron wall collapses, and light reaches a corner of my heart that's been cold and damp for a very long time. Mom finally said that something on my body is beautiful. I press this into my memory like a flower.

"I'm sorry some decisions I made caused so many problems," I say.

"It's all right. Your father and I don't even agree on how we disagree with you, but you're an adult. It's your life." Mom adjusts the pillow under my head. "I know you were trying to be happy."

"I don't feel happy."

Mom holds my hand. "That's because you've spent all these

years trying to cope with what you've been through alone. I think it's time we look into some counseling."

"Okay. I can do that."

"I met with a psychotherapist last week who specializes in family trauma. Her name's Shayna Cohen. You'll like her. She's very understanding and easy to talk to."

"When am I going?"

"Dad and I are going too. We start sessions next Thursday, once a week." Mom rubs her eye and turns her face toward the window. "Tim's helping us. It was hard to take the money. We'll pay him back."

Uncle Tim reminds me of Ian's dad. He's gentle and caring and has a supportive family, but the pain from his past clouds his eyes with sadness.

I sit up and tuck my legs under me. "It's okay, Mom."

"He said anyone who's suffered from Grandma and Grandpa's abuse should get help." Mom pulls me close and kisses my cheek. "Anyway, that's from him and Aunt Felice."

"How's everyone doing?"

"Very good. Erik's in track and field and is suddenly interested in cooking. James is on the debate team. He and Tim duke it out at dinnertime."

"I can't see that."

Mom laughs. "You'll see it at Christmas."

"So, is Suzanna going to counseling with us?"

"She should. Everything we've been through affects her too."

"She's really mad at me."

Mom looks confused, so I tell her how my visit with Suzanna went last Friday.

"Suzanna's like all of us," she says. "She's impulsive and holds things in. We all need to work on our communication."

I get off my bed, and Mom tucks my pillow back under my quilt.

"I wrote this." I take the copy of my poem from my bag and return to my spot next to Mom. "It's for women's studies. I'm presenting it on Monday."

The whole time Mom's reading, her expression stays neutral. She looks up at me when she's done and says, "I didn't know you could write like that."

"Me either."

She frowns. "You don't like how we love you?"

My cheeks burn. "I'll edit some stuff out and ask Dr. Sloan—"

"No, I want you to explain what you wrote."

Mom is making herself vulnerable so she can understand my pain. Love is hard.

"I wanted more. Ian held me more this semester than you and Dad did in a long time."

Pain crosses Mom's face.

"He gave me a lot of what's been missing, and not just hugs. I understand God now." She flinches. "We told each other things we never shared with anyone else. I learned to trust someone new. I know you and Dad love me, but I needed more."

"Marty, do you love Ian?"

"Yes."

"Do you feel comfortable when he touches you?"

I pause before answering. "Sometimes."

"Meet with Shayna in private and learn how to deal with that. Otherwise, you'll project your pain onto whoever you end up with. It will tear you both down. Trust me. I've done this to your father for years."

"I'll talk to Shayna."

"And, Marty ..." Mom rubs her eye. "I'm so sorry about what

Grandpa did. That I never suspected anything. I blame myself for what you went through."

"Mom, don't."

"You must have been scared when he came over."

"I was, but he and Grandma can't hurt us anymore. Now they're the ones who should be afraid."

"Dad told me all the things you said last night. You were suicidal a few years ago?"

I slowly nod. This is probably the deepest conversation I've ever had with Mom, and it feels like I'm cleansing my heart. "I don't want that anymore." I tell her about my faith and my relationship with Ian. I talk about why his parents split and the fallout he and his mom had on Thanksgiving. I explain why he got terminated and that he's moving to Korea. "We're going to try a long-distance relationship."

"Some couples can't even stay together over state lines. Will he come home to visit?"

"He wants to. I could save up to see him too."

Mom stands to go. "You shouldn't have most of your relationship over a webcam. Talking is one thing; being with Ian is another."

I look at my lap. Ian's leaving in the summer, less than a year after we started dating. Can our relationship withstand the distance that's going to separate us?

"I'm not saying it can't work, but you're young. This is your first relationship. I'd hate to see you brokenhearted," Mom says from the doorway.

"Wasn't Dad your only serious boyfriend?"

"He was, and we moved way too fast. Use your head. It's bad enough you think God is worth your time."

I draw back at her remark.

"Why'd you do it, Marty?"

"God isn't a monster. I let go of my old ways and gave him everything. He changed me, Mom."

She's still.

"I have no regrets."

"I don't see how, but, like I said, it's your life."

Mom leaves and closes my door. I fall back on my bed and press my cheek against Great-Aunt Martha's quilt. Mom's never been optimistic about love. Her rooting for Suzanna and Carl a few weeks ago was an exception. I hope, one day, she'll realize my relationships with Ian and God are solid and certain. Then she'd understand why I want to hold on to Ian and my faith and never let go.

58

IAN

AFTER DAD LEAVES FOR WORK, I clean up from dinner and go to my room. Half of my clothes are gone, along with the stack of bins in my closet. The box of keepsakes and a suitcase are all that's left. Three of my dresser drawers are empty. I didn't touch my desk and bookshelves. I still need everything there, but after I graduate I'll part with most of that too.

It's happening. I'm returning to Korea.

I grab my phone off my nightstand and sit on my bed. Gemma and I have only texted since Thanksgiving. She's been working on a DNA model for science and a group history project about 9-11. She said Mom's losing it about everything. I should have called Gemma way before now to catch up.

"Ian!" she exclaims after two rings.

"Gem, how are you holding up?"

"I'm all right." She sounds so down, and it's my fault. "How are you?"

"Doing okay. Look, I'm sorry I ruined Thanksgiving."

"I would have found out everything somehow."

I'm not sure about that. I bet millions of family secrets have been buried and decayed with the dead.

"I thought Mom was only talking with my dad behind your dad's back. That's what Mom told me. I didn't know they were, like ..." She tries to find the words. "*Actually* together."

I twirl a loose thread in my comforter around my finger. "I did, for too long, and I snapped."

"I can't look at Mom and my dad the same. And I feel bad for you and your dad, and it's weird to feel bad for him because I don't know him, really."

"Listen, Gem. Mom and Nathan made some poor decisions, but they love you and take good care of you. Always remember that."

"I want to spend part of the summer on Aunt Sarah and Uncle Victor's ranch," Gemma says. "They do a lot of horseback riding lessons then because kids are out of school. I can help in the stables, and I want to learn how to ride after watching so much *Heartland*."

"Sounds fun."

"Yeah, I think Mom needs some space."

"Gemma? Who are you talking to?" Mom asks in the background.

Anxiety rips through me.

"Ian. You said I can talk to him." She sounds fearful.

"Why are you two talking about me needing space?" Mom shoots into my ear.

Taken aback, I explain, "She was telling me she wants to spend some time at Sarah and Victor's over the summer."

"Okay." Mom lets out a sarcastic chuckle. "I don't need space from my daughter. I need space from *you*. You humiliated me!" she sobs. "You humiliated me in front of everyone last week! I invite you to *my* house for Thanksgiving, and that's how you treat me?"

I slide off my bed and meander over to my bookshelf. "I should have talked to you in private about what happened in the past. I'm sorry, Mom, but you offended me when you said that remark about how quickly I moved on after Hana and I broke up."

"Get over it, Ian. That's nothing."

"You always think religion messed Dad and me up. You say Dad choosing religion is why you left, but you left for Nathan. You made that *very* clear on laundry day."

"I can't believe you spoke to me like that!" Her voice isn't raspy, and she has no trouble screaming into the phone because she wasn't really crying before. "Children should have a certain respect for their mothers, and you give me none of that!"

I glide my finger over my Korean books. *Ten Thousand Sorrows, A Cab Called Reliable, Secondhand World, Necessary Roughness, A Step from Heaven, Native Speaker.* If I were to write my story, what would I call it?

"You told Dad I'm not your son anymore."

"I never said that!"

I pull *Secondhand World* off the shelf and set it next to me. I put *A Cab Called Reliable* next to that at an angle.

"Your father told me you got fired. I'm not surprised. You have no drive whatsoever. I handed you the rest of your education, and you threw it in my face."

"Mom, you can't *force* me to continue school. I thought we would move past this disagreement and try to get along."

"I hoped if I got off your case, you'd wise up." In a lower voice, Mom adds, "I was stupid to hope. You're a terrible influence on my daughter. I was going to let you two stay in touch, but I don't want you near her."

"No, Mom!" Gemma shouts in the background.

"Gemma, get lost!" Mom yells.

I want to snatch Gemma out of that house, but that would be kidnapping. Mom wouldn't mind seeing me get arrested.

I add *Comfort Woman* and *Fox Girl* to my moat of books. It's dumb. That moat I constructed fourteen years ago was useless.

"You know why we're done? You're exactly like your father!"

I grab more books.

"You hide behind your religion. All you do is hurt others. No wonder Hana left you. Martha's going to be next."

It could happen. Martha might get fed up with my baggage and want someone stronger. I don't mean to hurt so much, but the pain keeps coming and never stops. It has to stop.

My moat is done, but her words leak into me, into my lungs. I can't breathe. I cover my chest and push my fingertips into my skin. Once upon a time, Mom was happy she got me. She, Dad, and I used to be a family that was content with hearty breakfasts, piano music, and books.

She continues her rant. "You think you had it hard, but you weren't neglected by your parents. You didn't lose a child."

"I'm sorry your parents hurt you. I'm sorry you lost Caleb." I'm saying the right words, but I don't feel anything. What should I feel? Sympathy while she abuses me?

"Yeah. Okay." She snorts. "You act like me bringing Nathan over made you suffer so much! You would have learned about sex anyway."

"You committed adultery in front of me."

"You didn't see anything! You think I was so bad? I bet you watch porn. Christians do it all the time, then park themselves in a pew on Sundays."

"Mom? I'm done talking to you."

She's silent.

"I'm done trying to have a ..." I can't contain my frustration

382

anymore. "*Normal* conversation with you!" I grit my teeth and squeeze my phone. "I'm done trying to ... to ..."

"What, Ian? What is it?"

"I can't love you. I want to feel more—"

"That's nice," she chirps, "because I'm not your mother anymore. Good-bye."

She hangs up.

The rage uncurls inside me. It slips around my sides and crawls up my back and shoulder blades. I slam my phone repeatedly into the floor. I can't love her. I. Can't. Feel. It. I get on my hands and knees and lean forward on my elbows. I press my forehead against the carpet. Stories can't protect me. They're flimsy, weak, useless, like me. And God.

I stand up and kick some books. I get my jacket and the Bible. I step outside. The crisp night air bites my face.

I'm sick of being ripped apart, but I can't break. I need someone to hold me together.

I drive to Martha's.

If I were to write my story, I'd call it *Available Child, Condition: Unacceptable.*

59

MARTHA

I'M GRABBING my pajamas out of my bureau, when I hear a car come up the driveway. I peer outside my window. The light over the garage turns on, and I see Ian get out of his car.

Why is he here? It's ten o'clock. I put on my sneakers and run downstairs.

"Where are you going?" Dad asks from the living room, where he's watching *The Handmaid's Tale* with Mom.

"Ian's here."

I open the garage door. Ian has a large book with a worn spine tucked under his arm.

Before I can speak, he says, "I should have called. I know you have a lot going on with your family, but I needed to see you. My mom—she and I had the worst conversation."

I beckon him into the garage. "Come inside."

Ian takes his sneakers off at the door. Dad stands by the fridge with his arms crossed. "Ian, what are you doing here?"

Ian backs up a step.

Mom emerges from the living room. "What is it, Ian?" She

sounds wary. Behind her on the screen, Aunt Lydia is guiding the handmaids in shaming Janine for getting gang-raped and having an abortion.

"He needs to talk. He and his mom are having some trouble."

Mom gives the slightest nod. Dad's about to say something, but she smacks his wrist.

Ian draws his book to his stomach. His eyes are dull. His life here is wearing him down. This is why he needs Korea.

I grab Ian's hand. "We'll be in my room."

"He can't sleep over!" Dad hollers after us as we climb the stairs.

I keep my door ajar and plop down on my bed. "You can sit anywhere except here." I offer him a little smile.

Ian throws his coat on my desk chair and sits on the floor next to my bed.

"What did she say to you?"

He sucks in his breath. "Horrible things." He explains how a phone call with Gemma made his mom fly into a rage. She poured acid on his abandonment wounds. She attacked his faith. She's not surprised he got fired. She thinks I'll leave him like Hana did. She feels no remorse for what she did with Nathan while Ian was within earshot. Wow.

I slide off my bed to join him on the floor. "She has no regard for how you feel, what you believe in, *anything*."

"It doesn't matter. She's done with me. And she said I can't talk to Gemma anymore."

"You can talk when your mom's not home, and there's always email."

"Right." Ian's eyes wander. "My mom will brainwash Gemma, and she'll cut me off too."

"Not if she knows who you really are." I touch his knee. "Don't base your self-worth on what your mom thinks."

"I'm working on it. I want to believe this is God's plan, and I'm where I'm supposed to be, but I hate how I got here."

"Then you need to love how you get to the next chapter. You have to break the world open to find your omma."

"I'm writing that down, and I love how you call her that." He turns to the large black book lying on the floor and gives it to me. "This is for you."

I carefully open it and leaf through its pages. It's a Bible Ian's highlighted and filled with his own reflections and prayers. "You're giving this to me?"

"Read the inside cover."

This Bible belongs to Yeong Soon & Jacob. Ian's name is written underneath that. Then, *Martha. December 3, 2010.*

I look up at him in awe. "Don't you want to keep this? Your grandparents—"

He touches the Bible. "It's okay. It was in like-new condition when my grandpa found it after my halmoni died. I'm done filling it up, so it's yours."

Ian is letting me into such a private part of his faith. He trusts me. He wants us to draw closer to each other and God.

I put the Bible down. I lean over to kiss the yellowish-green bruise on Ian's cheek. He comes closer, so I move my lips toward his mouth.

I yearn to smell his scent in the sheets, to be so close to him, and I lose track of time and myself. Would I crackle under his hands, or would my pores release Grandpa's abuse and absorb new memories?

Ian's lips graze mine, then he withdraws. "I can't. I made some mistakes with Hana. It's not worth the regret."

I rest my back against my bed. "Do you want to talk about it?"

Ian rubs the side of his neck. "Not tonight."

"Sometimes I don't want to be careful. I want you to help me forget my grandpa."

Ian's eyes flash with recognition. He folds his leg and sets his arm on his knee. "Is that why you've been kissing me so much?"

I nod. "You know, your mom left the same year my grandpa started abusing me."

"Oh. Right, 1996."

"We got messed up around the same time and met fourteen years later." I throw my head back. "It never goes away. I'll always remember his hands wandering over me like a newt, the smell of tobacco, being trapped under his body."

"I'll always remember the sounds. I want to burn them off my brain." He pauses. "Let me know if I do anything that brings back those memories. I want you to feel safe with me."

"I want you to feel safe too." *Always* makes me test out *forever*. "My parents don't think we'll last. My dad's afraid you'll turn violent on me, and my mom has no faith in long-distance relationships."

"You know how much I want to have forever with you, so we can serve God together and be free from everything we dealt with?"

I tingle inside. He wants forever. We can be so close and vulnerable and conquer our triggers. I'll wait through college and Korea. I'll hope and stretch my faith as wide as the sea. Hope does have feathers, and it can sit on my soul for as long as it wants.

"They don't know what we talk about, how much we support each other," I tell him.

"They should know."

"We're starting counseling next Thursday."

Ian cracks a smile. "I'm glad you're taking that step. Tell them whatever you want. They'll listen, Martha."

I open my nightstand drawer and take out a pen and our notebook. "It's your turn to have this."

He flips through my latest entries. His face darkens with worry. "Frustrated with God?"

I flush. "I was. I'm feeling better now."

Ian nods. "We all get like that, and we all need a place for our messes." He turns the page. "I like what you wrote about *Story of a Girl*. 'It was like a quiet heartbreak.'" He lowers the notebook to look at me. "You do have a gift with words. You're going to be fine retaking creative writing."

"Thanks. I think so too."

I registered for it yesterday. I chose a morning class with Professor Guerra. I was so disrespectful to her when I was falling apart. I owe her an apology as well as my best writing.

I scoot over on the floor closer to Ian. "I'd like more book recommendations. Have any Christian ones?"

He clicks the pen open. "This could take all night."

I shrug. "So?"

Ian winks at me.

I hope, one day, Ian and I could have all night in an apartment in Busan that overlooks the beach.

———

I WAKE up the next morning to the sound of Mom clattering pans in the kitchen. It's a melody to my ears. Things are getting back to how they used to be. They might be even better.

I change out of my pajamas, and before heading downstairs, I call Kaylin.

"Hi," she answers, deadpan.

"Kay, I'm sorry for ignoring you. I've been so consumed—"

"How are you treating Ian? He blew up at you after he got

canned, but I didn't hurt you." She sounds somewhere between disappointed and defensive. "I know you're going through a lot with your parents separating—"

"They're not."

"That's … great." The irritation fades from her voice. "I hope you're not accepting abuse and thinking Ian's the best you can do."

"It's not like that." I sit at my desk and start pinning some Russian flash cards onto my corkboard. I tell her everything Ian's been through with his adoption and his parents' divorce. I tell her about his plans for Korea and that we hope to stay together through it all.

Kaylin's quiet.

"Ian knows he was abusive. He doesn't remember being adopted, but it scarred him."

"Okay. I'll try to understand." Kaylin falters. "I thought you got sucked in. Like, you were clinging to him because you're finally dating someone and thought he could do no wrong."

"All the fat I carried around will always be with me in spirit," I say, getting defensive. "You're not the only one who thinks I'm stupidly in love with Ian."

"Marty—"

"I should have called you sooner, but Ian needed me. I'm his only close friend now. And I know this is crazy, but I love him. He and I connected in this wholesome way. He makes me want to do big things, take risks. I can be so open with him and know I'm always safe."

"It's not crazy. Not if it's real." She pauses. "Can *I* be open about something?"

"Yeah."

"I know you're having a rough time, but you threw me in the backseat when I was trying to help you."

I'm stung with guilt. "My head wasn't in the right place, but you didn't deserve that. I'm sorry, Kay."

"I know you are. I appreciate it, Marty."

"Things will be different. Let's start now. Want to grab lunch at the mall? I'll pay."

"I can go for a gyro. How's noon?"

"Works for me. How are you and Andy?"

"Pretty good. I told him about Phil. He opened up to me too. He had a rough childhood. His parents care more about money than their kids. He lives with a friend now and works at a burger joint. We're staying in the friend zone for a while. It's nice to connect, hang out. I mean, if he and I can't be friends, we can't be a couple."

"That's true." I hang up the flash card for *window*: окно. "Ian and I had a disorganized beginning."

"You still found the way," Kaylin says. "Maybe you're where you should be."

After we're done talking, I rush downstairs. Suzanna's at the stove with a carton of eggs and some Taylor ham. We stare at each other before she says, "Hi."

I slowly step into the kitchen. "I didn't expect to see you."

"I want to talk."

"Where's Mom?"

"Food shopping." Suzanna takes two oranges from the fridge and peels them.

"After the way you treated me, I can't eat breakfast with you."

Her face falls. "I don't blame you. For the past few weeks, I actually hated you. That's why I said what I did." She tosses the orange peels in the trash. "Carl had a long talk with me. I was scaring him."

"Look, I know you've suffered too. Mom and Dad's fights are vicious and leave a mark. But you trashed my relationship with

Ian, which isn't your business." I jab my chest with my thumb. "You think everything I went through is *my* fault. You never let me give my side of the story while Mom was gone."

"Marty, I'm sorry."

I place a hand on my hip. "You need to grow up. You act like you're in high school, and I'm sick of it."

She flinches. "Mom told me about counseling. I want to go."

I park on a barstool. "You should, because someone else was inhabiting your body."

"I'll take a step back and listen before yelling at everyone." She leans over the counter. "Mom told me about Grandpa. If I'd known, I would have run into the bathroom and smashed his face. Why didn't you say anything?"

Her question throws me back to what Dad said when I told him. I stay composed. "Do you know anything about sexual abuse? I couldn't speak up. He said I'd go to hell if I told anyone. He groomed me. I believed him. It became normal."

"Is that why you had ... weight problems?"

I don't answer. I don't have to.

Suzanna turns to the stove and assembles our Taylor ham sandwiches. "I'm so sorry. I don't know what came over me. You're my sister. We'll always be sisters."

She's trying. Forgive her. I slide off my seat and hug her. "Apology accepted."

She closes her arms around me. "You're strong, Marty. I hope Ian knows that."

"So are you."

Suzanna steps back and takes our breakfast to the counter and sighs. "Right."

"You're dealing with infertility. You forgave Carl and didn't care what anyone thought."

Suzanna sits next to me and bites her sandwich. "Mom and

Dad give us a hundred reasons not to do something, but we do it anyway. Must be the Lane daughters' trademark."

"Stubbornness: the best family emblem," I joke around a slice of orange.

"Tell me about Ian. Mom heard him leave around one this morning."

Ian and I were up late, writing a list of things to do before he goes to Korea. Go to the Strand Bookstore—why Ian hasn't been there yet is a mystery—double date with Kaylin and Andy; graduate; go to the beach; use recipes from novels to make breakfast, lunch, and dinner; take a day-long road trip with no destination and see where we end up. I played Elena Frolova's music on my laptop, and we talked about books. I want to have thousands of nights like this with him.

The muscles around my mouth ache as I talk because I'm smiling over my words. I recount the fights and tender moments Ian and I had. I talk about the wedding, the café, and his cooking. I tell her about Korea and our plans. She doesn't give me weird looks or discourage me from having a long-distance relationship.

"Wow. You made it through a lot together."

I made it because that's what my family always did. Mom broke free from her parents' abuse. Dad worked hard to keep Suzanna. Suzanna forgave Carl. I survived molestation. I might not have always loved how my parents loved me, but they taught me how to be strong so I'd be alive when things get better.

I love someone who's strong too, and I feel proud to love him.

"Mom and Dad taught us resilience," I say. "One day I'll thank them for that."

Suzanna rubs my arm. "Thank them today."

I smile. "I will."

60

IAN

I ACT as if nothing is wrong. I haven't told Dad about my fallout with Mom. I don't want to hear him call her my mom and talk about forgiveness. I go to school. Martha and I talk on the phone. I'm not feeling much, but I push out some normalcy so everyone thinks I'm okay.

I take Martha out to a seafood restaurant. She has chicken Française with linguine, and I order a lobster roll. A live band is singing a song about being a wallflower. Martha talks about the knitting class she's teaching next week and fills me in on the job her mom got in the deli at a health-food market. Our waitress takes our empty plates and hands us dessert menus.

"You want something?" I ask Martha.

She pats her stomach. "Too bad I didn't get my second piece of chicken wrapped. That Black Forest cake has my soul."

"Did our appetizer steal your heart?"

Martha pushes her menu away. "Nope. Your name's on that."

"In that case, let's dance off dinner."

We walk to the dance floor holding hands. Martha cups my

shoulder, and I wrap my arm around her waist. We can touch and look at each other without feeling awkward. Time has done a lot of awesome things for us.

"The wedding was cooler," Martha whispers with a grin.

"Why?"

"We kind of sort of liked each other. The unknown felt exciting and scary. Now the thrill is gone. It's kind of like saying good-bye to the beginning of us."

"Martha, you don't need to say good-bye to any part of us." I squeeze her waist. "We're writing a story, and I'm keeping all the pages."

The song ends. The band's lead singer is small and dark-haired with pink highlights tucked behind her ear. She plays some notes on her keyboard. "Hi, I'm Sadie. The next song we'll be playing is 'Satisfied' by Jewel."

Martha nuzzles her face against my shoulder. "I love this song."

I listen to Sadie singing about saying I love you and not being afraid of getting hurt. You just let yourself feel satisfied.

Martha and I sway to the music. She looks at me lovingly. I take in the familiar feeling of her body against mine. We stop dancing. I let go of her hand and lock my arms around her. She draws me closer, and we kiss, slowly.

I used to think people were being poetically stupid when they said you feel like there's no one else in the world when you kiss someone this way. I take that back, because that's how I feel right now.

It's so satisfying.

Martha and I were both abused and bullied. We're young. Maybe we don't get what true love is. We might not get married. But we made something real, and I pray we keep it alive for as long as we can.

My phone buzzes in my pocket. I ignore it. It goes off again.

"You can answer," Martha says, releasing me.

I pull my phone out. It was Nana. Not good. She only calls on my birthday.

"I'll be back," I tell Martha, and I leave her on the dance floor.

I move around other dancing couples and head to the men's room. I call Nana and get a torrent of Mom's latest grievances.

I give Nana my side of the story, and she says, "*You* said you don't love your mom. How could you say that?"

"I said—"

"Why are you going to Korea?"

Someone flushes a toilet and leaves without washing their hands.

"I want to find my omma and learn Korean."

"That won't solve anything." She clicks her tongue. "My *daughter* is your mother."

"She said I'm not her son."

"You're going over there to find a woman you have nothing to do with instead of putting your real mother first. That tells me a lot about you."

"Nana, please listen to me."

"Ian, no."

She hangs up. Her words cut deep. They shouldn't. We barely have a relationship. But when the people who are supposed to love me fail to love me, the pain is unbearable.

I leave the bathroom and spot Martha putting a few bucks in the tip jar by the stage, where Sadie and her band members are packing up. Martha sees me and smiles, then her mouth drops into a frown.

We meet at our table, and she asks, "Who was it?"

"My nana. She's on my mom's side." I'm about to call our waitress over for the check, but it's on the table, already filled out. "You paid for dinner?" I ask incredulously. "I said it was on me."

"I wanted to treat you."

The heaviest sadness I ever felt drives into me. I press my palm to my forehead.

"Ian, are you upset about the check or your nana?"

"I'm not mad at you. Thanks for paying."

We don't talk in the car. I play Christmas music to throw some feelings in the air.

"Can you come in for a few?" Martha asks when I drop her off.

"No. Sorry." I don't wait for her to get inside before I peel out of the driveway.

I want to max out my credit card, underage drink, and feel alive.

A swarm of flashbacks comes in. I see Mom pull Nathan into the bedroom.

I'm at a red light. *Sail across the intersection.*

I'm five again. Dad repeatedly strikes my back. Try to breathe. Try to live.

Mrs. Lane bashes Martha's head against the wall. If I hadn't told her about God, she wouldn't have suffered like that.

I need Uncle Vinny's gun.

Justin pins me down. *I'll choke you.*

If he killed me, we'd both be where we belong.

That's nice, because I'm not your mother anymore. Good-bye.

I do not have a mother. I *could* have a mother, but, inside, she's gone.

I don't care that Chris's dog died. Mom wouldn't care if I died either.

My anger grabs on to Chris for ignoring me this semester. Let go let go let go. Bethany *cheated* on him.

I can't. I … can't. I. CAN'T!

I go home and rip open my keepsake box. I throw Kang and my photo album in the trash. Kang reminds me of Mom. My photos remind me of the ones Justin threw out that were on my poster. I mix his name with every dirty word in English.

I start tearing up my notebooks, when Dad peels me away from the wreck I'm creating.

"What's going on? Did you and Martha break up?"

A sob comes out. "Get ... away ... from me."

I feel no love, no life. I'm shaking from the anguish and rage roaring in my nerves. I need prairies. I need the world.

"Ian, talk to me."

I double over and grip my knees. I stay focused on the carpet. That familiar pain grabs me. It squeezes my heart before traveling over my upper back. Breathe in. Out.

"Dad, get out of here." I seethe. My voice is low. Dangerous. "I want to be alone."

"Ian, why are you so *angry*? I'm here. We can talk about whatever you want."

"I don't want to talk, and I don't want you here." I scrunch up my face and growl, "I said I want to be alone!"

"I'll leave. But get some rest. If you don't want to talk to me, talk to God about it." Dad backs off and shuts the door behind him.

God. Right. Okay.

I stagger over to my bed and sit, staring ahead for a long time.

I ball my hands into tight fists and press them against the sides of my head.

I want the pain out. Why won't it come out?

I cover my face with my hands. Tears gather in my throat. One escapes my eye and trickles between my middle and ring finger.

I imagine myself at the edge. It hides in trying to live, look happy, be thankful, then the ground stops under me. My gut springs into my throat. I fall, forget, rip the past and future. There is no better tomorrow, better life, better me.

Dad's in his room. His phone rings.

I wipe my sleeve across my eyes and creep into the kitchen. I open the cupboard over the mixer. I find the painkillers for Dad's back. No blood. No noose. My answer.

I grab the pills and my water bottle. I lock my door. I return to my bed and pour the pills into my hand. I squeeze them so hard my knuckles whiten.

Dad's talking to someone from work. They need coverage. Can he come in for a few hours?

My body remembers Omma leaving me. Every single cell.

Why did God let adoption rip so many children away from their mothers? Why didn't you keep me, Omma? If Korea rejected us, we'd have each other. Why wasn't I enough, God? *Why*?

No love. No faith. He let the adoption happen. He let the grief and rage crawl all over me.

I hold myself and rock back and forth. The pills grow warm in my fist. I peer at my open closet and spot my suit hanging between some shirts. I will never get married.

I open my hand. My lips move. Dad, I'm sorry. Help me. Dad? Dad!

His phlegmy cough cuts through the walls. His allergies are the worst in winter and summer. I will die at winter's border.

My brain remembers me leaving Mrs. Shin.

Dad, find me. Please. I can't speak.

I hear Mom and Nathan having sex.

Get out of me! *Get out!*

My phone buzzes. Nice sound effect. Flies love dead bodies.

61

MORTALITY

Your
memory
has a
very
quiet
but
A N G R Y
edge,
and
it's
here
to
kill
y
o
u.

62

ADVERSITY

YOUR TOUCH IS my favorite medicine. I want to feel your shoulder against mine as we sit close together and talk about poetry, life, and God. I want you to tell me how you're doing as I wait here. I know. This hurts. We fell in love slowly but deeply. The quiet edge of memory stalked us as we shared too much too quickly. It became bigger, sharper, louder. We are an open cut. It's hot, swollen. It stings. We close it, then explicit images and sounds keep ripping it open. I can't deal anymore. Can you?

You can't. We'll change that someday. For now, we run to fantasies. Our bodies move fluidly and melt together. You hide your face in my chest. I cup my hand over the back of your head and slip my arm around your waist. We exchange I love yous and promises. That's what we deserve to remember.

I want to hold you forever because there is only one of you. Can we talk about that? It's such a primal and stark truth, but our depression made us think it would be okay to dispose of ourselves.

No one leaves me alone after what happened, but I'm lonely. I'm here and you're there. I ache for you. I never thought I'd ache for you. I spit out the hopelessness people have in young love. *You're naïve. Date other people so you know what you really want.* The chances we took and the trust we built show me exactly what I want. I want you forever. Do you still hope for that? There's so much we left unsaid.

I open my notebook and write, *I've been defeated more times than you know.*

I'll tell you everything. You'll listen. And you won't look at me the same anymore.

I'm so sorry.

Whatever happens to us, I just hope I'm gazing into your eyes when I can finally say I'm free.

63

IAN

TIME PASSES ON PAPER. Day 1, 2, 3. My pen records the sounds of slamming doors, footsteps of different rhythms, and patients shouting, crying, and talking. I eat matter. The nurses take my vitals and give me my meds. I don't want to take antidepressants because I can't believe I've sunk this low, but doctor's orders. The pills mess up my sleep and make me nauseated. I don't want to talk to a psychiatrist, but I do it. If I don't talk, no one will know what's in my head, and if I don't let it out, I won't get out.

Dr. Singh says I suffer from depression and have trauma I haven't processed. I feed that trauma through my head, throat, and mouth. Paper orphan. Absent mommy. Wrecked daddy. Patient 1391473.

Dad visits me. I was in such bad shape the first two days I was here, I don't remember him sitting at my bedside. He promises to come in the afternoons before he has work. That makes it sound like a routine. How long will I be here?

Day 5. Dr. Singh and I talk about my adoption. That gets me talking about my parents and Caleb and Nathan and laundry day.

I'm back in my bedroom in our old house. I'm holding Kang. I want Mom, I need her, but she slips away with Nathan.

"Ian, stay with me," Dr. Singh says.

The memory squeezes my chest. I arch my back, look up at the ceiling.

Dr. Singh claps twice. "Ian, can you look at me?"

I look at my hands. I want to rip Kang. I need to rip me, so I do. Someone touches my shoulder. Arms and limbs tangle together. My chest hits the floor.

I'm back at work, in the break room. Justin pins me down. His hands lock around my throat. He squeezes my neck. My scream bleeds out of my dream and oozes into the day. I try to roll over but can't. My wrists are strapped down.

Korean War. Mixed-race babies. Unwed mothers. Stillbirth. Infertility. Adoption. Affair. Divorce. Secrets. Here. An animal.

Day 7. Pills. Wander. Sleep. Group therapy.

We're walking shipwrecks and dock at a table, where we pass around stories of self-harm and dysfunctional lives.

I hang out with a guy named Kyle. He was supposed to get his associate's this month but quit three weeks ago. He tried to kill himself after his dad beat him up and disowned him for coming out. He'll be discharged in two days. His aunt can help him for a month, then he's on his own. I hope he makes it.

Day 8. Dad brings me some novels. He hangs a smile on his face and asks how I'm doing. I lie and say okay. I'm afraid I'll stare at a bottle of pills and it will lure me into this crisis all over again, and then I'll be here for months.

Day 10. I make a breakthrough with Dr. Singh. We talk about my adoption and some of those laundry days. This shakes me, chokes me, makes me cry. Dr. Singh is soothing and patient. I tell her I don't understand unconditional love, thanks to my adoption and Mom's abuse.

Dr. Singh says the relinquishments I went through and the lack of emotional validation I experienced shape how I feel love and attachment. Things are starting to make sense. Dr. Singh will help me regulate my feelings and strengthen my self-worth. She says solid relationships are essential to healing. I smiled at her for the first time when I told her about Dad, his family, and Martha.

They want to keep me here longer. I'll miss Christmas. That doesn't matter; I don't feel God anymore. I know he's real and believe the gospel is true, but where was he when I needed him the most? I helped Martha find faith and lost mine.

I'm sorry, Martha.

Day 13. Pills. Read. Therapy. Dad visits. I'm allowed to have my laptop. I force myself to email my professors. My school inbox is stuffed with messages from them, asking where I am and warning me that I'll fail unless I have a medical excuse. My instructors reply in time before grades are due. I'll get an incomplete in all my classes and take my German final in the testing center in January.

Martha wants to visit me, but I told Dad no. I don't want her to see me like this, and she'll probably break up with me. I promised she'd always be safe with me. I can't even keep myself alive. I play the good boyfriend and order her a Christmas gift anyway.

Day 14. Dad skips Christmas Eve service. He visits me before work. We have an open, raw conversation. I scrape out every wound inside me.

I'm still angry about some of the choices Dad made after Mom left. Spending time with Nora after work. I have flashbacks of Dad smacking my back after I said those obscene things in school. I hate how he yelled at me and left me in the kitchen with my vomit after the bike accident. I tell him about my last conversations with Mom and Nana.

Dad apologizes and hugs me. "Walk away from that family and

don't look back unless they're willing to change. Then forgive everyone when you're ready."

I press my face against his chest. I'm free. I don't have to call Mom anymore. Go to her house. Give her side hugs she never returns. Hear Nana abuse me on the phone. But I won't let go of Gemma. I am the worst brother because I haven't spoken to her since Mom's last outrage. I'll call or email her when I get home. I'll say I got sick and was bogged down with finals. I'll tell her everything, someday.

Day 15. Christmas Day. Dad gives me a Christmas gift from Martha. She bought me a men's study Bible. Inside, she wrote *Thank you for showing me peace, giving me love, and guiding me to God.*

Martha feels so far away. She's a believer now, but I'm backsliding, not sure if I'll return to God. There's no way to tell her this without breaking her heart. Even if we stay together, I feel like I'm abandoning her in her faith. The guilt weighs a ton.

I start my final essay for American lit to distract myself. I'm writing about how Esther Edwards Burr and Sarah Prince used journaling to express themselves in a patriarchal world. The pen is loaded with power. It talks for us when we can't.

Day 16. I email Chris, telling him where I am and why. He gets back to me within an hour. He's shocked that my adoption and Mom's affair pushed me this far. He told me he and his family are praying for me. He closed his message saying he wants to hang out sometime after I get home.

I reply with *That works. Not sure when I'll be out. Thanks for the prayers.*

I make a watercolor painting of the beach in art class. I study German. I read nine chapters in *Harry Potter and the Order of the Phoenix.*

Dad says the life is back in my eyes. I hug him. He has suffered hard but quietly. Life wrecked him, and he got up and fought. I will fight too. I'm so grateful he is my father.

I tell Dr. Singh I'm feeling better about my adoption. I mean it.

Day 17. I'm getting used to my meds. I participate in group therapy. I can't stop writing. It feels good, and then I remember the notebooks I ripped up and get angry. I almost email Martha to get my mind somewhere else. I can't do it.

Day 18. I'll be discharged tomorrow. Twice a week I'll have sessions with Dr. Singh, and if I keep improving, we'll switch to weekly appointments.

There's a new girl in group. Her dad just died in a hit-and-run, and her boyfriend got with her best friend. She's gaunt, empty. She is at START. May she get to the finish line that I found.

———

WEDNESDAY, December 29. I pack up my things and stare at the bare room that's kept me safe and alive for nineteen days. Dad puts an arm around me, and we leave. A heavy door clicks into place behind us. I suck in the crisp air and lift my face to the cloudy sky. I made it.

We get in the car, and I say, "I want to go grocery shopping."

Dad looks at me. "You're up for that?"

"Let's get Korean for lunch, then go to H Mart."

"Ian ..."

"Come on, Dad. Let's celebrate my escape from hell on Earth. I mean, if you're okay with going to Edison."

He starts the car. "If you're in, I'm in."

Dad and I head up to Edison. For lunch, we split an appetizer of Korean pancakes. I order bulgogi, and Dad has beef seaweed soup. I savor every bite of my meal. Anything beats hospital food.

In H Mart, I'm like a kid in a toy store. I fill up our cart with ingredients to make fish cakes, soups, vegetable pancakes, kimchi, and dumplings.

"Slow down," Dad says, pushing our cart and trying to keep up as I dart to the registers.

He has no clue how much I want to get back to cooking.

When we're home, Dad hands me an envelope. "Merry Christmas." Inside is a check for two hundred dollars. In the memo field, he wrote *Korea*.

I smile at the conversation I had with Martha in this exact spot about having experiences instead of things.

"Thanks, Dad."

"You bet."

"Your gift's on its way." I ordered him a coffee gift box a few days ago.

"Looking forward to it." Dad starts chopping a head of Napa cabbage into bite-sized pieces. "Yay or nay on the squid?"

I fold the check and slip it into my pocket. "Yay."

"Is Martha ever going to try your kimchi?"

"I don't know."

Dad looks confused. "She got you a Christmas gift. You haven't spoken to her since—"

"I know. I'm screwed up and exhausted. I can't help you with the kimchi."

"That's fine."

I tear out of the kitchen. Before I crash, I text Martha.

> I'm home. Super tired. We'll talk soon.
> xoxo.

Forced words. A holding place until the end.

64

MARTHA

THE MESSAGE IS CLIPPED, but I hear Ian softly speak the words.

Ian
I'm home. Super tired. We'll talk soon.
xoxo.

He loves me. We're not breaking. We cracked and will fuse together. I will pray for a thousand tomorrows.

Tears prickle my eyes and glide down my cheeks. We were dancing and felt so in love, then a half hour later, Ian wanted to die. I cover my face. The tug in my chest bursts into agony. He made it, but his hurt will never disappear. I'm scared he'll try again. Is he immune to self-harm, or did he wake up death?

I claw at my mind for remedies: mother tongue, the vow of till death do us part, his own flesh and blood. God?

Finding her. Only her.

One day, I'll ask Ian everything. He can answer me, unfiltered. I will listen and love him unconditionally.

Finally, he calls. A lifeline to more time, more life, more of him. "Martha, it's me."

"It's so good to hear your voice." I try to sound cheerful, but I'm shaking; I don't know what to expect.

He clears his throat. "It's no music to your ears. I just got up from a nap. I don't know where to start, but I want to say I'm sorry. I hurt you with everything I did."

I splay my hand over my face as if it can hold my emotions in.

"Martha, do you want to stay with me?"

"Of course. Why would you think—?"

"I was an animal in there. I still feel like one. That's why I didn't want you to visit."

WARNING! Disconnecting a mother and child may result in permanent damage.

"I'll wait for you to get better. You know I will."

"I should have never asked us to share secrets," Ian says bitterly. "Look what that did."

"We did it because we trust each other." I rub the hem of my sweater between my fingers. "What we keep hidden can show the world who we really are. Thank you for letting me know you."

"You're smart to think that, Martha. You're the sunshine in my life."

A smile breaks out on my face. "Your halmoni's words."

"She meant it every time she said it, and so do I."

"Ian, thanks for being my first." I let go of my shirt. May he be my only. "Can I see you tomorrow?"

"It's my uncle Martin's birthday. How about New Year's Eve?"

"Come on over," I say.

"Okay. We can talk about books and life and people."

"And have ice cream sodas with cherries and watch a movie," I add. "What should we watch?"

"You pick."

"*The Irony of Fate*," I suggest. "It's a Soviet romance comedy that takes place on New Year's."

"I'm down for that. I'll hug you while you drink your ice cream soda and watch *The Irony of Fate*." I hear the humor in Ian's voice.

"I love you. Those words can never hold it all," I tell him.

"I know, but we can."

I cup my elbow in my hand and tense up to mimic the tightness of a hug. I'm dying to tuck myself against him.

"Hey, Martha, I'm kind of fading. I'll have more energy Friday. I promise."

"I understand. See you then."

"I love you," he says before we hang up.

We stand at the edge of 2011. I hope we fill several notebooks with our story that will swell with big love. I sit at my desk and let some of it fall into our notebook.

> I pray for a thousand tomorrows
> to build something eternal.
> If it hurts, I'm here.
> If I lose hope, you're here.
> If it falls, we start again
> and wait to feel that flutter
> in our chests
> that was promised years ago
> from the master of poetry.

I close the notebook and hold it against my heart so nothing can come between these nine lines and the seven letters of forever.

65

INSANITY

YOU DON'T RECALL her leaving, but it rumbles inside you like the earth's plates during an earthquake. They rub together and rattle, arousing logic that doesn't make sense. She gave you up because she loves you. She left you, so everyone will leave you. The neurons in your body didn't collect her voice, the scent of milk and blossoms, the closeness known as skinship in Korea. You got secondhand motherhood. Ouch.

She could go too. This fear wormed out of your anguish, which stands on plush ground. Move. Get off. Go back to God. He will tell you it's okay.

You can't. I get it. Life betrayed you.

She gazes at you tenderly. Her lips part. She's ready to fill the air with everything you've missed for nineteen days. You lean forward. Is she saying, "Have me"? You wanted that for a long time.

Her face contorts. Her words become clear. "Half-breed."

You spring back. What did you think? You're a beast. You're a threat to yourself, to everyone you love. She's better off without you. Don't burden her. Once upon a time death tried to snag her, but she dodged it. She has strength. Once upon a time God made you gentle. You don't believe. You have nothing.

What's that? Stop? No. No one listens to you.

You try to move. Look down. Remember the straps? Yes? You slept most of the time. The nurse asked if you'd calm down. You nodded.

You're out. For now. People get readmitted.

Count the days. One, two. Two days until New Year's. Can I see you? I don't have any plans. Let's welcome 2011 together.

I know. You're tired. I'll wait for you. To try again. Rest now. In peace.

66

IAN

"GET THEM OFF," I grumble. "Get them off."

"Ian, wake up. You're having a nightmare."

Dad's face materializes. I jolt. He takes his hand off my chest. I grab his wrist to stay grounded in reality. The swoosh of the heat fills my ears, and my ceiling fan comes into view behind Dad.

I let go of him and sit up. I hurt so bad, I can't talk, so I pull up my sleeves and show him the souvenir from the hospital.

Dad takes my wrists and rubs his thumbs over the traces of my scratches. "My God," he breathes.

"A nurse tried to stop me. I went berserk. They strapped me down. I know my brain's been a really dark place, but I felt dehumanized. I still feel ..." I deeply inhale. "Feral."

"Ian, you overdosed. No one expects you to come out of this a miracle."

I tell Dad about the nightmare I just had. "I'm sick of feeling defective and crazy and hurting others." I get off my bed and leave my room. "Is that going to be the rest of my life?"

Dad follows me into the kitchen. "No, it's not. You're hurt, very deeply. It'll take a while to get to a solid place."

The Napa cabbage is draining in a colander. Dad chopped all the vegetables. He mixed the sweet rice flour porridge with the garlic and fish sauce. The kimchi just needs to be assembled. I get the bag of red pepper flakes from the freezer. I grope for that solid place.

It's here. Apologize. Forgive. Walk forward. God? Is that you?

"Dad?"

"Hang on." He emerges from his room with his phone. "My boss said I can take the sick days I have left before New Year's, so I have off until the second."

"Dad, I'm sorry for being so rotten to you since Mom left."

He shoves his phone in his pocket. "You couldn't deal and did reckless things. I did too." He goes to the sink and transfers the cabbage to the huge stainless-steel bowl we use only for kimchi. "But we're always a family, no matter how ugly life gets. I'm not going anywhere."

"I always knew that. Hearing you say it makes it real."

"I'm sorry for the memories you're stuck with. I failed you. You said your mom killed my spirit. She did, and she pushed you too far and killed yours." He takes the pot he used for the kimchi porridge and fills it with soapy water. "Don't let her win. You have a lot to go after, and you need to be alive to get it."

"You didn't fail. You had it rough. Halmoni's depression, losing Caleb, Mom leaving."

His eye twitches at the memories.

"I made it because of you. You stuck by me when you were suffering. I constantly hurt you, and you still put me first." I lean against the counter and let out a shaky breath. "You're my lifeline. Literally."

When I hadn't responded to Dad saying he was leaving for

work, he kicked my door open and found me unresponsive. I was loosely gripping the empty pill bottle on my chest.

"I bombed out when I was with Nora."

"You're only human, Dad."

"I wasn't supposed to fuel your attachment issues. I should have been fixing them."

"They can't be fixed." I dig out a cup of pepper flakes and level it off with my finger.

"With the right therapy, you can learn to have secure relationships. Look at you and Martha. That's something."

The solid place quakes beneath me. "We won't last."

"Why not?" Dad challenges, his voice hard. "Don't base anything off a nightmare. Martha wouldn't hurt you like that."

"Everyone falls off my life like dead flies." I swirl the pepper flakes into the porridge, which goes from a light brown color to a dark red. I drop the wooden spoon against the bowl and count my failed relationships on my fingers. "Omma, my birth father, Mom, Hana. Chris thought I had to grow up before he could be a friend again. And you know what's going to happen with Martha? She'll get sick of my dark moods, or I'm going to walk away, because this thing comes alive"—I touch my chest—"and I can't feel anything for the people I'm supposed to love."

"You need to tell Dr. Singh everything you just told me."

I clamp my mouth shut, grit my teeth. I'm packed with anger.

"Write it down to get it out of you."

I take the measuring cup that held the garlic and hurl it toward the sink. It hits the faucet before tumbling inside. I grab the sides of my head and burst out, "Stop talking!"

Dad returns the pepper flakes to the freezer and stares at me. "Ian, what ...?"

"Is this healing?" My eyes burn. "I rip my guts out in front of a therapist and relive hell in my journal?"

"It's more than that. So many people are here for you." Dad's voice catches, and his eyes are pleading. "Martha told me she'll stay with you. She'll wait for you while you do your birth family search and study Korean."

The tension loosens inside me.

"She wants Korea to be your home for as long as you need. That's where a lot of the healing's going to happen. She wants to join you after she finishes school."

Martha wants to live with me where it all began. I tremble with emotion. Oh, God. Martha. My Martha.

"That's love, Ian. Let her give it to you."

Love I'm trying to feel so I can give it. Adoption is not love if it skews love.

I wipe my eyes with my arm. "I shouldn't have pushed her away."

"When we're done, take it easy, then call Martha. You have a lot to talk about. And be kind to yourself so you can be kind to others."

I can trust her. Our love survived my worst nineteen days. It can survive Korea. I hope it lives forever.

I add the vegetables and porridge to the cabbage and plunge my hands into the bowl. The kimchi makes a satisfying crinkling sound as I toss and fold it. Its bright colors blend with the paste and turn an orangey-red. I pop a piece of cabbage into my mouth and chew. Today, I will not swallow sorrow. I swallow the sour, salty, and slightly sweet taste of home.

67

INFINITY

FOR NINETEEN DAYS, I watched you fade. Your eyes swirled with confusion and fear. For nineteen days, I wanted to hate him for doing this to you, but a wall in my brain barred me from going there. I wanted to bulldoze it down. You barely ate. You were quiet. You didn't cry. You struggled to get to work and school. You didn't want to study for your Russian final. I told you to move forward, but you stayed on the side of the road with him. It was either the trappings of young love or compassion that made you do that.

I hoped it was the former, but I remembered how meek he looked when he picked you up for the wedding. How he looked out for you when you were persecuted. He has this vulnerability that gets to you. Not in a bad way. There's a lot packed inside him: baggage, good intentions, and his constant desperation to keep going. That desperation is there because he's been trying to live since the day he was born.

We're here, but you were lonely. We sat with you, urging you to talk, but you couldn't. For too long, this family didn't know how to communicate. Then we needed to and couldn't. I know. Suicide is heavy. The reality that he almost died kept you company. That's the only part of him you had because he didn't want you to visit. His dad told you not to take it personally. You tried not to, but it hurt.

For nineteen days, you hoped. You prayed to this God he worked so hard to help you find. You wrote in your notebook. You waited for him to come home.

He did. Now he's here for New Year's Eve. You give him your notebook. You huddle your heads together. He hands you a book of poetry by Marina Tsvetaeva in Russian and says, "One day, you'll be able to read that." You hug him. He knows what you love. My good vibes set in.

We make a prime rib with mashed potatoes, string beans and bacon, and fried apples because he didn't have a Christmas dinner. He's careful, closed off but courteous around us. Carl makes small talk with him, and slowly he opens up. He talks about his dad and their Korean background. He describes the rough time he's having with his mom. He's trying to keep in touch with Gemma under his mom's toxic radar. He doesn't want to tell Gemma about his crisis. He just wants to be a brother.

He's postponing his move to Korea. He needs more therapy and wants to feel better before he goes. His neighbors will hire him at their bookstore café. They're not thrilled about why he got fired from NYC Corner but are willing to give him a chance.

He looks animated when he talks about Korea. He wants to be fluent in Korean and is thinking about opening a language school when he comes back to Jersey. You smile at this. You know he's supposed to leave, but I see the hurt pass over your face. You'll miss him when he goes. I will too. You'll join him there. I'll hate seeing you leave, but you have to go. You do and believe some crazy stuff, but I won't fight you anymore.

Everyone talks until the food residue is crusty on our plates.

Suzanna shares her plans to open a catering business. I talk about selling the house and renting. You mention visiting UMD and Rutgers. He wants to accompany you and says you'll make a day trip out of it. I picture you two traveling for hours. You could write a novel from your conversations.

After dinner, you go to your room. "You don't have to talk about the hospital," you say.

"I want to tell you. You loved me through everything, and I ignored you." You close the door, but I can hear him. "I was in a dark place, mentally and spiritually. And I was so scared our relationship was toast."

The person he was for those nineteen days is disappearing. You'll work through that time and figure out how you'll get through the next nineteen days and so on. You'll ring in 2011 with a load of pain but some healing inside you. You hold stories that a lot of people can't carry, but you're helping each other do it. I hope you have each other for as long as you want.

I clean up from dinner, go upstairs, and collapse into bed. I hear you two go downstairs into the kitchen. You make ice cream sodas and talk about Russian movies. You head back to your room, and he says, "I'm going to take you out on a stress-free date. No last-minute wedding invites or crises. Just us, like we are here and now."

"I believe you." Your voice is muffled. I picture you moving against him, where you belong.

I believe him too.

68

MARTHA

I GLUE your letters into my notebook, which is packed with plane tickets, recipes, and scraps of ephemera that deserve to stay out of the landfill.

I wanted to handwrite letters, and you love doing it. Sometimes we add doodles, a few lines of a poem, or a watercolor painting. Mistakes and messes make art realistic, not perfection, you said. I collect your words like seashells.

I'm at the beach, holding a time capsule. Inside, there are coins, a typewriter sticker, an enamel pin that says *reckless artist,* a gospel tract, a pen, and the latest letter I wrote you.

That letter holds a secret I locked up for too long. After high school graduation, I went to an open house party a few blocks from home. There was a bonfire. The flames washed everyone in a warm orange. Then I saw Aaron. I danced in his arms. We got drunk. The next morning I woke up in an unfamiliar bedroom. The pillow next to me was dented. In a panic, I sprang up and zigzagged through a living room of sleeping bodies and left.

Anger and shame flood my body. I mouth the truths, the

things only my father and I know. He was the only one home when I came in with unkempt hair and a button missing from my dress. It's time for you to know everything too.

I step into the water. Sea-foam snakes around my legs. I grip the time capsule and go in up to my waist. The waves swell, push against me, and pull back. I remember my younger self on the beach. My mind was innocent, my skin blank.

I stand sideways to counter the rolling waves. They suck the time capsule out of my hand. I catch a glint of its metal surface against the water. I feel naked. I wasn't ready to lose those pieces of me.

I want the ocean to hold me. I'd swim back before it pulled me out too far.

What if I didn't?

I curse death and ditch the horizon. I walk to the shore, closer to you.

I envision you without my secrets, waiting for my next letter, surrounded by your schoolwork and books.

I step out of the ocean. The breeze whips around me, causing my saturated clothes to cling to my goose-bumped skin. Those items could make someone a writer, a believer, or just bitter. I'm shivering. Whoever opens the capsule will know me. If I wait too long to tell you what I did, they will know me better than you do.

I run off the beach.

LONGEVITY

Un
con
di
tion
al
love has always held you,
and
you're
still
here
to
f
e
e
l
it.

PATERNITY

YOUR VOICE IS my favorite sound. I used to love hearing you talk about the cabbage sprouting in the garden, your new jjigae recipe, and your latest trip to the beach. You recounted stories about the Land of the Morning Calm. You squinted, and your voice was raw as you talked about your search for her. Your search in Korea went nowhere. Your distant DNA relatives either couldn't help you or never replied to your messages.

Then your face softened at the mention of friendships with adoptees like you who've scoured Korea for clues, leads, and hope, only to face a dead end. I know. Adoption is complicated. You were hurt too young and too many times. The years of waiting stretched into double digits. You paced between acceptance and anger for what happened to you. I'm sorry you suffered such a deep wound before I knew you. I'd do anything to give you an alternate first chapter.

You crammed that space with years spent tirelessly studying Korean and inserting yourself back into a country that cradled you for thirteen months, then cut you out once it could profit from your status as a paper orphan.

When you returned, you spoke fluent Korean. You cooked and ate only Korean food. But you didn't find your omma. That broke you, slowly. I've seen every emotion glide over your face when you think no one's looking. Those quiet escapes amplified into outbursts that spread pain through your chest and over your back. I thought the powdery scent of baby skin and a lush branch on your family tree was your healing balm. But you swaggered between a dark, chilly place and here. And them.

She comes through the door and looks at you, taking in the tiredness around your eyes and the life you've lived without her. Your books, the framed photos on the wall, and the blue floral Korean dinnerware sitting on the open kitchen shelves.

Before you can speak, she hooks her arm around you and nestles her face in the hollow of your neck. She returns to the safe place you promised her on day one and closes the gap that's been blown into your family. You bite the inside of your lip, shaken by her forgiveness and grace. You whisper apologies and promises into her hair like you used to when everyone lived together, happily, as in a child's storybook.

This time, she believes you. She knows the better you always existed underneath the rages. You taught her to love God and believe in the gospel, even though you blamed him for this life you struggle to love. You stood by her when there was alcohol in the fridge and her medical appointments and stays at treatment centers were littering your calendar.

She believes you because you tell her you accepted your broken family tree. You hushed the innate desire to touch your mother to know she's real and hear her voice and capture the tones of missed lullabies. It grieves you to do this. It feels like you're saying good-bye to your omma, but her name will always beat in your heart.

You transfer everything true and good to the family you know, the people you can touch and hear and hold. The quiet edge of memory wants to break this peace in your pain, but you close your yellowed adoption file and move on.

You cradle her face between your hands. "You. I should have put all my hope in you and lived for you."

She struggles to smile over the tears pooling in her eyes. "I've waited so long for you to say that."

You wrap your thumb in your sleeve and dry her cheeks. "Don't cry," you soothe. "The tteokguk soup has enough salt."

She manages a laugh and sniffs. "You made my favorite?"

You turn to the stove and remove the lid from the pot to reveal the rice cake soup. You ladle a generous portion into a bowl and offer it to her. You both stare down at it with adoration. Your tteokguk soup overflows with many Lunar New Years and talks about books and life and people.

"The last time I made this was the night before I ... kicked you out."

She pauses, calculating the time in her head, and takes the bowl from you. She doesn't just look at you; she looks into you and sees the remorse and you trying. You will open yourselves like journals with smudged, wrinkled pages, the markings of weathered lives with ample blank space to fill with better days.

You will call them. You will reunite at a table covered with steaming dishes and freshly baked bread. The familiar sounds of making chrysanthemum tea and conversations about essays and math will fill your mornings. You will decorate your calendar with piano lessons and language school. You will restore your garden and plant sunflowers. You will put on your wedding band and know intimacy again.

The immense pain still makes you imagine the end. You despise the wounds your mothers inflicted on you but passed that suffering down to your children, something you will have to face. You might never forgive yourself for the damage. But they waited for you in the past and hope. Anguish and faith. Freedom and fate. They waited for you to walk away from the edge and realize everything you have built and mended with them is what makes you complete and real.

You know you can't curl up with despair, so you wipe the dust off your Bible and crack it open. You fold your hands in prayer and talk to God. You ask him for the strength that's been so hard to find in yourself. You grab on to his power and love—something unchanging and reliable.

May you keep your life and always hold it next to theirs.

ACKNOWLEDGMENTS

A big thank-you to my family for dealing with the huge chunks of time I've put into writing this novel. A shout-out to my husband, Ben, for being my first reader and giving me the unwavering support I needed.

Much love and—I promise—tons of ice cream for my daughters. I appreciate the quiet time you gave me to do my "homework."

Hugs to my parents and siblings for always calling me a writer and encouraging me to never give up on seeing my name in print.

This book would not be what it is today if it weren't for the editors who put in the time to read and critique my work. I'm so grateful for Tiffany Schmidt and Jo Whittemore's invaluable guidance that strengthened the plot and made my novel shine. Thank you to Susanne Lakin for such a thorough copyedit and giving my story the balance it needed as I neared the finish line. And many thanks to my proofreader, Ronni Davis, for her input, heartfelt reactions, and careful attention to detail.

It was an amazing experience working with Kara Starcher on designing the book cover. Her talent and expertise helped to create the design I've been envisioning for my book.

I will always cherish my friends in the Ozarks and the Northeast who cheered me on in this writing journey.

I couldn't have finished my drafts without Samantha Becker's excessive—and much-needed—reminders to finish by the deadlines I set. Thanks for reading so many drafts and kicking my butt when I needed it so I could get my story out there. Your friendship is a gift.

A thank you to David Levin for reading my story. I'm sorry it wasn't about superhumans.

And, God, thank you for giving me the talent to write. Your love helps me realize I am here for a reason, I have a purpose, and I am enough.

ABOUT THE AUTHOR

Therese Vercellone was born in South Korea and grew up in New Jersey. She graduated from Montclair State University, where she studied English and Russian, and holds an MA in women's studies from Southern Connecticut State University. After living in Missouri for several years, she knew she was a Jersey girl at heart and returned to the Garden State. When she's not writing, she's making a mess art journaling, tackling her to-be-read pile, or spending time with her husband and two daughters. *The Quiet Edge of Memory* is her first novel.

You can visit her at theresevercellone.com.

www.ingramcontent.com/pod-product-compliance
Lightning Source LLC
Chambersburg PA
CBHW020520110726
47899CB00004B/1188